The Peach Blueprint

SWEET ROMANCE & WOMEN'S FRIENDSHIP FICTION

HILTON HEAD ISLAND
BOOK FOUR

ELANA JOHNSON

feel good fiction

ELANA JOHNSON

ISBN-13: 978-1-63876-246-1

Chapter One

J oy Bartlett disembarked from the plane, her heartbeat one giant bass drum. She couldn't believe what she was doing. Still, her step landed smoothly as she navigated the airport in Charleston, as she'd flown in here several times now.

She knew where the rental car counters were, and she knew how to get from there to the cars without even looking at the signs. She could drive from Charleston to Hilton Head easily now, and she couldn't wait to spend Christmas with her besties. Well, some of them, at least.

Bessie had gone to Peachtree to spend the holidays with her daughter. Joy knew they had plans to talk about opening a franchise here in Hilton Head of a bakery. It wasn't franchised anywhere else yet, and when they'd gone to lunch last week, Joy had told her to simply open her own bakery.

Why should she put money in the hands of her boss?

She was an excellent baker, and with all the tourists here on the island, there was definitely room for another bakery—especially one that only delivered the best Texas sourdough... in South Carolina.

Bessie had started sketching out new plans, and she called Joy almost every day to talk about it.

Joy herself had not started talking to anyone about making a move from Sweet Water Falls, Texas, where she currently lived and worked full-time, to Hilton Head, South Carolina. Half of her Supper Club had made the move now, and the pull for Joy to do so felt like the weight of gravity on her soul.

At the same time, Joy was forty-seven years old, and she couldn't go jump off a cliff—or move halfway across the country—just because all of her friends were doing it.

No, Joy had to have a blueprint first. She needed to be able to see her life here before she could commit to embracing anything that required her packing up almost fifty years of Texas lineage and moving it.

She hadn't mentioned a possible relocation to either of her sons, and she had no husband she had to check off with. Her single grandchild pulled at her just as strongly, and she lived in Texas.

"Thank you," she said to the rental car attendant as he lifted her bag into the back of the SUV she'd drive for the next two weeks. She'd packed a big bag and a backpack, but the latter would ride shotgun next to her.

The drive passed quickly, and before Joy knew it, she was turning into the parking lot of a restaurant called Mead's.

She'd not eaten here before, but she'd been told it was amazing, and at three-thirty in the afternoon on a Thursday before Christmas, likely to not be busy.

There weren't very many cars in the lot, and Joy pulled into a spot in the first row next to the building. She had no idea what kind of car Scott drove, as they'd been texting back and forth a lot over the last few months, but their vehicles had not come up once.

"You're insane," she whispered to herself. She met her own gray-blue eyes in the rearview mirror and reached to fix the errant strands of her hair. Her ex-husband had once told her he loved her eyes, because he couldn't quite identify the color of them. Not quite blue, but not quite gray, he'd landed on "slate."

Joy had been describing herself with that adjective ever since. Her hair was blonde, starting to pull in some gray she didn't bother to cover with anything synthetic. She wasn't trying to pretend to be an age she wasn't, and she rather liked her shoulder-length hairdo that waved down even on the worst of hair days.

She wasn't Lauren by any stretch of the imagination. The woman always looked like a million bucks, without a single strand of hair out of place. But Joy had learned not to compare herself to Lauren a long, long time ago.

Joy swallowed and checked the clock on her phone. She'd made good time from the airport, and she'd arrived a bit early. She leaned her head back, a hint of exhaustion pulling through the tight muscles in her shoulders.

She'd have to eventually tell her friends that she'd lied to them. It wasn't really a lie, as she'd had a couple of months to rationalize away this extra day on the island. One, Scott had asked her to come in a day early.

She'd agreed.

No crime in that.

Two, she hadn't wanted anyone to know. Not Bessie. Not Lauren. Not Bea or Cass. If they knew, she'd end up going out with Scott and then staying up all night detailing everything to someone. She didn't want to do that. She wanted a quiet evening to herself after the date so she could determine how she felt about the man.

Right now, as they'd only been texting for the past three months, every cell in her body vibrated in anticipation of seeing him in person. They video chatted often, but there was something different about being in the presence of another human being—especially a man like Scott Anderson.

He'd tickled her interest the very first time they'd met, though she'd tried to put a barrier between them. It helped that he'd barely looked at her, and then the second time they'd "met," he'd come right out and said he couldn't remember her. Constructing that wall had been easier then. Keeping him out of her thoughts had proven nearly impossible, and Joy really only achieved it when she slept.

"He canceled his date to stay home and talk to you," she reminded herself. Every time she thought about that evening back in September, she grew warm. Then immediately cold, for now she had to live up to the reputation of a woman who could make a man cancel his date to stay home and talk to someone who lived over a thousand miles away.

Someone knocked on the window, and Joy jumped a Texas mile in her seat. A strangled yelp came from her throat, and she threw up both hands as if she'd ward off the unwanted evil trying to get to her through the glass.

Scott stood there, and he laughed right out loud. The rental car window didn't mute it so much that she couldn't hear it, and while her adrenaline poured through her, she also calmed. She grinned at him, all that nervous energy joining the hum already in her veins until it became a roaring buzz.

She reached for the door handle and popped the seal there. "Hey," he said, grabbing onto the door and opening it the rest of the way. "Sorry. I realize how creepy that was."

Joy slid from the SUV and had to look up at Scott as he stood about eight inches taller than her. His golden hair shone with that red she'd been dreaming about, and she had the strangest urge to run her fingers through it.

"Hello." Awkwardly, she reached for him and sort of stutter stepped into him while she grabbed onto him to hug. "It's good to see you."

"In person," he said. "In the flesh." He held her easily, effortlessly, and Joy told herself to calm down.

She moved out of the way and closed the door. Only then did she remember her purse. "Oh, I need my purse." She retrieved it and smiled at him again.

"Can I hold your hand?" He grinned at her and looked at her out of the side of his eye. "I mean, I feel like we've been together for months, but I've never actually held your hand."

Joy stepped with him, and on the next forward movement, her fingers slid into his. She smiled and said, "Yeah, this is nice."

"Mm." Scott took her into the restaurant. "You've never been here?"

"No, sir," she said.

"Chester didn't bring you to Mead's?" He acted scandalized, his grin playful and full of teasing. She'd talked to him via video where he did this too, and she found him so adorable. "I'm shocked by that."

"Really?" She flirted right back, the action easier in person than she'd anticipated. "Why's that? Do they serve... questionable meats here?" She glanced around like she'd see a horse or a dog on its way to the kitchen.

Scott laughed, the sound as delicious in person as Joy had heard through her phone. "No," he said. "But it's definitely some of the best food in all of Carolina." He spoke like a lifelong Southern boy, and Joy had to admit she sure did like that.

"When you come to Texas," she said. "I'll take you to my favorite place."

Scott's lighter blue eyes lit up. "You want me to come to Texas?"

Joy grinned at him. "I just invited you, so yes." She turned toward him as they approached the hostess station. "What do you think? Can you ever take time off?" He owned a huge landscaping company, and he worked outside seemingly day and night.

"Yeah," he said slowly. "For you, Joy, I think I can take some time off." He spoke in his slow, sexy, Southern drawl, and Joy swore the ground vanished beneath her feet for a few seconds.

The earth swooped and trembled, and then Scott was right there to hold her steady. "All right," she said simply. "We'll work that out later."

"Two," Scott said to the hostess. "And we want a booth away from all the noise, if possible." He knocked on the top of the podium. "Thanks, Sam."

"You got it, Scott." She plucked two menus from the side of her stand and smiled at the pair of them. "This way."

Joy's phone rang, which sent her heart into another somersault. She plucked it from her purse, pausing as Scott started after Sam. The number was unfamiliar, but something inside Joy's mind recognized the number, and she needed to answer it.

"I need to grab this," she said.

"Sure." He looked to Sam and back to her. "I'll get the table and come back for you."

She nodded and swiped on her phone, turning her back on the rest of the restaurant at the same time. "Hello?"

"Miss Bartlett?" a cool female voice asked.

"Yes, ma'am."

"This is Sophie from The Island Sand Bar."

"Oh, sure," Joy said. She'd booked a room at the seaside

hotel for tonight. Tomorrow, she'd be staying with Lauren in her cute cottage house.

"I'm so sorry, but we won't be able to have you stay with us tonight."

Joy's stomach dropped to her feet, where it wobbled and hung there for a moment. "I'm sorry?"

"Our kitchen flooded, and that sparked a fire. We have no electricity." She sounded truly sorry. "I've already called our sister site, but unfortunately, they're full."

"Okay," Joy said, really drawing out the word. "So...I just have nowhere to stay tonight?"

"I can provide a list of hotels in the area, and you can make some phone calls." Something banged and then zapped. Sophie shrieked, and Joy pulled the phone away from her ear. The screen darkened, and alarm stitched through her.

She turned in a full circle, her mind doing the same thing.

"Joy?" Scott asked. "You okay?"

She faced him and shook her head. "Uh, maybe? That was my hotel, and they had a flood that killed their electricity. I don't have a room tonight." She looked up at him like he'd know what to do.

Call Bea, she thought. *Or Cass. She has a huge house.*

But that would require her to tell them she'd come into town early—just to see Scott. She'd have to tell more than Lauren that she'd been texting him for the past three months. She wasn't sure she wanted to do that quite yet, and the longer she searched Scott's face, the more she thought she didn't want to call one of her friends.

"Let's go sit down," he said, taking her arm in his. "We'll figure something out, okay?"

She nodded and let him lead her to a table in the far corner of the restaurant, with big windows that looked out over a pond. She had no idea what possessed her, but the moment she slid into the booth, she looked at Scott doing the same and blurted out, "Maybe I could stay with you?"

Chapter Two

Scott Anderson had a big laugh, and he used it a lot. His first instinct after Joy—the gorgeous blonde he'd been crushing on for a solid six months—asked if she could stay with him was to laugh.

Hard.

He managed to pull back on that before anything escaped his mouth. Thankfully. He did need a few moments to stare and blink while he tried to come up with what he should say or do instead.

Joy Bartlett waved her hand like she was swatting away errant flies. "Never mind. That was so stupid. There are like, fifteen thousand hotels here. I'll find another one."

Scott's face did relax into a smile then. The woman had just asked to stay with him. He hadn't known where they'd be when he saw her. Flirting and texting and even calling a woman was something Scott excelled at. He could talk to anyone—literally anyone—but he didn't tell Joy that. He wanted her to feel special, and she was.

He enjoyed talking to her more than anyone else in his life right now, that was for dang sure. He couldn't wait to finish with his lawns, bushes, shrubs, trees, and pools to get home, shower, and then talk to Joy. She evened out all the odd things inside him, and Scott liked her far more than any other woman he'd dated in oh, at least five years.

"I totally want you to stay with me," he said, leaning forward and ignoring the waitress as she approached. In the end, he decided he better not be so open and flirtatious and...scandalous in front of a stranger.

He looked up at the woman—not a stranger—and his face split into a grin. "Kate," he said. He slid out of the booth and hugged the woman. "This is a secret," he murmured in her ear, and then he faced Joy.

She also stood and Scott put his arm around Kate, who he hoped looked enough like him to assure Joy they were related. Kate stared at the side of his face too, but Scott ignored her. "Joy, this is my cousin, Kate Arnold. Kate, this is Joy Bartlett."

No qualifier, though Scott knew which one he wanted to use. He'd been talking to Joy for three months. They hadn't seen each other in person once, until today. He shouldn't have brought her to Mead's. Instead, he should've insisted on meeting her in Charleston and taking her somewhere there so they could be alone.

Everywhere Scott looked, he saw people he knew. It wouldn't be long before Grant, Harrison, Blake, Oliver, and

Ty knew about this date. And that meant Joy's Supper Club friends would know too.

His pulse blipped in his chest as Joy put that stunning smile on her face and leaned forward to shake Kate's hand. "So great to meet you," she said in that sexy drawl that was so much like his, but so different too.

"Oh, where are you from, honey?" Kate asked.

"Texas," Joy said. She smiled and met Scott's eye.

"Let's sit," he said. "We don't need to stand." He slid back into the booth. "I want the smothered potato skins, Katie. And the strawberry lemonade sweet tea." He picked up his menu and looked over it to Joy. "It's incredible. It's why I wanted to bring you here." She'd talked about her sweet tea, which was her grandmother's recipe, as well as several other varieties around her small town in Texas.

Her face lit up. "That's this place?"

"Yes, ma'am." He grinned at her and didn't look at the menu again. He didn't need it.

She looked up at Kate. "Do you have peach?"

"Absolutely. Peach it is." She didn't write anything down. "Any other apps?"

"I haven't even looked," Joy said.

"I know what you want, baby," he said, and he swore he didn't mean to sound all sultry. His voice just came out that way with Joy. He looked up at Kate, his face heating when his cousin smiled so wide, those drawn-on eyebrows so dang high. "She'll like the artichoke dip, please. And bring us an order of the bar pretzels—double the hot mustard sauce."

"You got it, Scotty." Kate turned and walked away before

Scott could growl at her for using his childhood nickname. He hadn't been *Scotty* for decades, and blast her for embarrassing him on his first real date with Joy.

He cleared his throat and turned his attention back to the woman across from him. "Everyone on the island is going to know about us by nightfall." He shifted in his seat. "I sort of forgot she works here."

Joy's surprise hit him straight in the throat. "So my friends..."

"They live on the island, "he said. "And they all have husbands or boyfriends who are well-connected locals." Scott shook his head, his chin dipping down in regret. "Sorry, Joy. I know you wanted to keep this a secret."

She picked up her phone calmly, and Scott loved this aloof side of her. She'd shown it to him plenty of times this past summer, when he'd been blatant in his feelings and asked her out to her face. Twice. Maybe three times, even when she had a boyfriend.

"Not exactly a secret," she said quietly. "I'm just...I don't want the pressure of talking about us yet." She looked at him. "You get that, right?"

"Yes," he said, but he wasn't sure if he did or not. Kate would razz him about Joy, and that didn't bother Scott. He could admit he liked her—he wasn't trying to keep that a secret. It almost felt like Joy wasn't sure of her feelings for him, and that thought rang so true, he knew it was.

Take the flirting down a notch, he told himself. He could. For her, he would.

"One problem at a time," she said. "I need a hotel tonight."

"You could tell your friends and then stay with Lauren," he suggested, but Joy shook her head before he even finished the sentence. "I was going to say...before Kate came over." He swallowed and wished he had his strawberry lemonade sweet tea. "I totally want you to stay over, but I'm not in my place right now, remember? I've got a studio apartment on the edge of the ocean, and that might be a little...intimate for our first date."

Joy's face turned a delicious shade of pink, and that satisfied Scott greatly. "You're right," she said. "I forgot."

"That said." He leaned back in the booth and folded his arms. "I want you to, for the official record and all that. But, I also have someone you can call about a hotel room. In fact, I'll text him now."

He took his phone from his pocket and started tapping. "I stayed there for a few nights before I got into this studio. Ty's great, and if he has anything, he'll give it to you, I'm sure."

"I know Ty," she said. Scott looked at her, surprised. "I mean, sort of. He's the real estate agent who helped Lauren buy her house."

"Oh, of course." Scott had forgotten about that too. He couldn't hold things in his head the way he used to, and he let extraneous details flow through his mind without holding onto them. This skill normally served him without a problem, but his ability to forget anything and everything sometimes got him into trouble—like when he hadn't remembered meeting Joy the first time.

He hadn't had a day go by where he hadn't thought about her since seeing her sunbathing on Harrison Tate's deck, months and months ago. Even after she'd turned him down. Even after she'd been sassy with him, and he figured he had no chance with her. She'd burrowed into his skull, and his brain wasn't letting her go.

Of course, then she'd texted him out of nowhere in September. He could scroll all the way to the top of their messaging thread and re-read the message, but he didn't need to. He had it memorized.

Hey, it's Joy Bartlett, and I just heard you're going out with someone tonight. I don't want you to. That's bold, I know, but as I thought about you going out with anyone but me...I didn't like it. Call me. Or text back. Or don't and enjoy your date.

He'd never gotten a bigger shock in his life than that text, and he could still see himself coming to a complete standing halt as he read it. The mowers and edgers had continued around him, and he'd laughed and laughed and laughed.

Then, he'd promptly messaged her back, saying he was finishing up one last lawn for the day, and then he'd call her that night. He'd canceled his date with a woman whose name he'd already forgotten, and he'd been talking to Joy every day since.

Ty's message popped up, and Scott smiled. "He says he's got a room at Beach Beauty, and that's a nice property."

"Can I afford it?" Joy wore a worried look, and Scott had

learned over the months that her default was worry. She worried about everything, from how her sons were doing—a legitimate concern—to her students, to if her cat was lonely at home during the day while she worked. She worried over him too, and Scott sure did like that, because he knew Joy only worried about things she really cared about.

He reached across the table and took her hands in his. Touching her...there was nothing like it. Phone calls, video chats, and texting were one thing. Being with her, holding her, touching her, seeing her only a few feet away...that was magic.

"Yeah," he said. "You can afford it, because he said it's free."

She shook her head, her expression turning hard. "I don't need his charity. I can pay something."

Scott grinned and shook his head. "This isn't a contest, Joy. Are you going to insist on paying for dinner tonight?"

"No," she said, the set of her jaw a tad on the stubborn side.

He cocked his head and pulled his hands back to his side of the table. "Why not?"

"We're on a date."

"He's doing you a favor."

"I don't need a favor."

"Then the hotel is part of the date," Scott said. "Dinner and a place to stay." He smiled at her, and Joy finally cracked.

"You're impossible," she said.

"You like impossible," he threw back at her.

She laughed then, and that sound while they were in

close proximity could never be replicated over the phone. He joined her, and then as they quieted, he said, "I'm so glad you're here."

"Strawberry lemonade sweet tea," Katie practically yelled. "Peach sweet tea." She set both glass mugs down with loud clunks. "Do y'all know what you want to eat?" She looked back and forth between Scott and Joy, her auburn ponytail swinging as she did, as if she hadn't just interrupted something sweet and tender and intimate.

Scott gestured for Joy to go first, because he needed another moment inside the feeling streaming through him and he didn't want to speak and ruin it. He wanted to keep Joy in his life for a while, and that meant he had to figure out how to hide all of his flaws until she was madly in love with him.

However long that took. However much time she needed to figure out that he was the one for her. Only then would he allow some of the...less great things about himself be known.

"This place is too nice," Joy complained as she entered the room Ty had gotten for her at Beach Beauty, a gorgeous beachfront property that boasted a restaurant and their "famous" key lime pie on the first floor.

"Oh, my word, Scott, look at that view!" She hurried over to the bank of windows across the room while he towed one of her suitcases across the threshold of the room.

She sighed; the door closed; Scott left her large suitcase by her small one and went to join her at the windows. "I told you this was a beautiful property."

"I can't believe it's available."

"You're a few days before the Christmas crowds." He lifted his arm around her, and Joy sank into his side. The sun outside had started to set, as it was December, and that meant they got less daylight hours. They stood there and watched it sink lower and lower, the reflection on the water almost gone before Joy said, "This was the perfect day."

"Was it?" he asked. "Flying for most of it, then driving here, and then me scaring you in the parking lot?" He chuckled and adjusted his hand lower on her arm to keep her close.

"Everything after three-thirty," she amended.

"Hmm." He pressed his lips to her temple. "That sounds like everything with me, sweetheart."

She didn't deny it, and instead said, "Yeah."

Scott needed to leave right now, or he wasn't sure he'd be able to bring himself to do it. He dropped his arm and turned away from the view, from Joy. His eyes landed on the big, puffy, king-sized bed, and everything inside him tightened. "Well, I better get going." He swallowed and walked on wooden legs toward the exit.

"You're not working tomorrow, are you?" she asked, following him.

"No, sweetheart. We're going on that alligator thing in the morning, aren't we?"

"Yeah, I was just checking."

He turned back to her at the door, and she came within inches of him. Too close, but not close enough at the same time. "I'll bring breakfast, unless you want to eat downstairs." He gave her a smile punctuated with raised eyebrows.

"No." She returned his grin. "You promised me a chocolate croissant. That's what I want."

"And coffee with caramel," he said, sliding his hand along her hip. "And we have reservations at Lighthouse Point for lunch. Then, I guess I'll have to let you go see Lauren."

Joy returned his smile and put one palm against his chest, branding him. Sealing him as hers. "Thank you, Scott." She tipped up onto her toes, and Scott easily took her into his arms. Did she want him to kiss her? Could he do that and then walk away? He honestly wasn't sure.

She smelled like peaches and vanilla, and he couldn't wait to taste it on her lips. He leaned down, giving her plenty of time to stop him. She didn't.

Scott touched his lips to hers, expecting heat, and getting burned instantly. He held for a moment, took a breath, and then stroked a better kiss across her lips. She responded eagerly, and Scott couldn't help but wonder if she'd thought about him every day since last summer, despite going out with another man.

She sure kissed him, and kissed him, and kissed him like she had, and that was just fine with him.

Chapter Three

Kissing Scott tonight hadn't been anywhere on Joy's blueprint. She'd suspected she'd kiss him on this trip to Hilton Head, but the first night?

It had just felt right, and she now found herself unable to *stop* kissing him. In her head, she heard Lauren and Bessie telling her to just "go with the flow" and "enjoy her Christmas break, whatever it brings."

The problem was, Joy didn't enjoy spontaneity as much as her friends. As anyone, really, because she disliked being spontaneous at all. The man sweeping her off her feet with a single kiss that would not stop hated making too many plans. On paper, she and Scott shouldn't be together at all.

But in person, whenever she saw him, something fizzed in her blood that had gone dormant a decade ago. Longer.

"All right," Scott finally whispered as he ducked his head and broke their kiss. "I should go." He cleared his throat. "I *have* to go."

She stumbled back a step, glad it seemed normal though her feet felt too thick at the end of her legs. "All right," she said. Her head buzzed, a throb starting at the back base of her skull. It had been a long travel day even though she'd lost an hour by traveling to the East Coast from Texas.

Her smile wouldn't leave her face as Scott fumbled with the doorknob and then backed out of her room. "See you tomorrow, my Joy."

"Mm." She gripped the door and moved into the space where he'd been, watching him as he turned and walked down the hall. He didn't look back at her until the corner, and then he glanced over his shoulder, waved, and disappeared toward the elevator.

She sighed with pure happiness prancing through her and went into the room, letting the door fall closed noisily behind her. The loud banging of it made her cringe, but the view in front of her made her procrastinate opening her purse and fishing for a couple of painkillers.

The last of the sun disappeared somewhere behind the inn, turning the sky a beautiful shade of navy blue, slate gray, and peach. The water still held a little bit of light, but the tips of it didn't dance with bright white the way they did with the sun shining overhead.

Joy turned and faced the room, the bed looking fluffy and inviting dressed in a beautiful white duvet with six pillows piled at the head of it. Since she'd only be here for one night, she didn't bother unzipping her suitcase and unpacking. When she got to Lauren's tomorrow, she'd get set up in the guest bedroom by hanging up her dresses and putting her shoes in the closet and her swimming suits in the dresser.

She'd just sank onto the bed to discover the fluffiness of it when her phone rang from the recesses of her purse. Joy ignored it for now, knowing it could be Lauren. She didn't want to have to lie to her and say how stressed she was about packing for the next two weeks. And of course, Lauren knew Joy hated packing and always left it to the last minute, so if she answered the call from Lauren, she'd have to lie.

If she didn't answer, Lauren would text, and Joy could simply say she'd gotten it done—not a lie—and she was tired. Also not a lie.

She'd told Lauren she wanted a car for the duration of the trip, so no one was planning to pick her up at the airport. In fact, no one was expecting to see her until evening tomorrow, and Joy laid back and gazed up at the ceiling, the next twenty-four hours in front of her utterly wild and free.

Joy had no dishes to do. No garden to weed. No alarm to set. She could do whatever she wanted, whenever she wanted, and while she considered herself a responsible woman, she also liked the wide-open possibilities in front of her.

She rolled onto her side and then back to a sitting position. She did have a "swamp tour" tomorrow morning with Scott, and they had to be at the dock to board the boat by nine-thirty. So she did have to set an alarm.

Not that she'd sleep so late that she'd miss anything. Joy had usually worked for a couple of hours by the time nine-thirty arrived in the morning. As she'd gotten older, she hadn't needed as much sleep—or rather, she hadn't been able to sleep as well as she had in her younger years. Unfortunately, along with that, she didn't have to eat three meals each day either.

So while her "dinner" with Scott had been in the middle of the afternoon, she wouldn't need dinner. She just wanted a little sweet treat.

Being the touristy place it was, Hilton Head Island offered a range of dessert shops and restaurants, and all of it could be delivered to wherever she was. She looked up the address for Beach Beauty from her texts with Ty, put in her room number, and ordered a pint of Cookie Monster ice cream from Hellman's Homemade Ice Cream shop, and then added on a blondie and a pecan butter bar from a place called Squared. They, apparently, made bars and other items in four-inch squares, and they were right on the way for her dessert delivery driver.

Joy did unpack her toiletries and pajamas while she waited for her solo dessert course, and she turned from the wide windows as dusk took over completely when someone knocked on her door.

She found a young man standing in the hall with a bright yellow box in one hand and a plastic sack hanging from the other. "Joy?" he asked.

"Yes, sir," she said, taking her treats. "Thank you."

He nodded, tapped something on his phone, and headed down the hall. A door slam, a wince, and several steps later, and Joy settled at the built-in desk in front of the windows to savor every last bite of her post-dinner treats.

But there was no spoon in the bag with the ice cream. Frustration licked through Joy, and she muttered, "Who doesn't send a plastic spoon out with a delivery order? Do they think we bring them with us?"

Joy overpacked, to be sure, but she hadn't thought to bring cutlery with her. She picked up the phone and called down to the front desk. "Yes, hello," she said. "I just had an order delivered, and I need a spoon. Do you happen to have any I could come get?"

"I'll transfer you to Cove," the woman said.

"What? No, I just need—" Flowery music came through the line, and Joy sighed. She opened the yellow box to find two neat treat squares inside, so all would not be lost. She simply enjoyed ice cream over all other treats, and in her eyes, cookies and cream ice cream over a blondie couldn't be beat.

The minutes ticked by, and Joy finally got up and put the ice cream in the tiny compartment that probably wouldn't keep the treat frozen. When someone finally answered the phone, she'd been listening to wordless music for at least ten minutes.

"Cove," a man bark.

"Yes, hello," Joy said. "I'm wondering if there's a spoon I can come get, just for tonight."

"A spoon?"

"Yes," she said. Something banged on the other end of the line, and Joy blinked rapidly. "I had ice cream delivered, but there was no spoon."

Her cellphone rang, this time without the tell-tale ring that indicated Lauren. No, this was Scott. She spun toward windowsill where she'd left her cell, already reaching for it as the man at Cove said, "Lady, we don't just hand out silverware. You'll have to go to the store for that."

"I'm staying in the hotel," she said, realizing she'd never said that. "Don't you have room service?"

"No," he said. "And we don't deliver."

"I can come downstairs," she said. "It'll be—"

"No," he said again. "Good-bye." He hung up, and Joy blinked again. Blink, blink. Meanwhile, her cell went to voicemail, and she cursed softly under her breath as she hung up one phone and lifted the other one to see better.

Definitely Scott. Definitely missed his call. She tapped to call him back, and while her phone struggled to connect, another call came in.

From Scott.

She tapped to end the call going to him and swiped to answer the one coming in. "Hey," she said. "Sorry, I was on the phone with this rude man who wouldn't give me a spoon."

"I...okay," Scott said. He sounded like he might start laughing at any moment, but he sighed instead. "I have good news and bad news."

Joy turned away from the windows and started pacing toward the door. "All right," she said. "Start with the good news." Then she'd have something to cling to when he canceled their plans for tomorrow. Or told her the entire island already knew she was here, that the two of them had gone to Mead's that afternoon.

"I can bring you a spoon," he said.

She frowned as she reached the door and turned back the way she'd come. "Okay?"

"Bad news is, this studio I'm using because my place is being painted? The waves were extra splashy tonight, and there's water streaming down one of the walls."

Joy pulled in a breath. "It's not our day, is it?"

Scott sighed again, a long, drawn-out sound that told Joy the bad news hadn't finished yet. "I called Ty, but he said he doesn't have anything that will allow pets, and I've got Ghost. I've tried two or three pet-friendly hotels, and they're full. I called Jeff, but he didn't answer..."

Joy turned around, that beautiful bed staring her in the face. A slight indent still remained in the fluffy covers where she'd laid and sat. She drew in a big breath. "Okay," she said, because she was a mother in her mid-to-late-forties, and she could solve this problem. "So you'll bring me the spoon and stay with me. I'm pretty sure I saw a pet-friendly notice when I checked-in."

"I just saw the one bed, sweetheart," he said, the words grinding through his throat.

"There are six pillows," she said. "More than enough to keep us..." She cleared her throat. "Apart."

"That's what you want?"

Joy didn't know what she wanted, but she knew Scott couldn't come here. "I..."

"My brother's calling." He sounded beyond relieved. "I'll text you in a minute, okay?" The call ended before Joy could confirm.

"What is happening?" she asked the empty room, the

sunlight almost all faded now. First she'd lost her room, and it hadn't been too terribly hard to get this one. And now Scott's place was leaking too. Was this Christmas destined to be full of saltwater and broken hearts?

Joy pushed against the negative thoughts, because she tended to see things as glass-half-full. She'd worked hard in her therapy sessions after Wendell's departure from her life to overcome the lies he'd put in her head.

That she was weak. That she always saw the good in things—and that made her naïve and not to be trusted. That she didn't have the experience he did, so how could she possibly know what it was like to live outside small town Sweet Water Falls?

He'd always made their life there seem so quaint, so simple, and so utterly boring. Well, Joy happened to love her small Texas town, with farmers and ranchers and cowboys who blocked the two-lane road, their windows down as they caught up. She liked the way the thunder rolled through the sky, and she adored working with her first graders.

"You'll find things to love about Hilton Head too," she murmured, again not sure where the words had come from. The truth was, Joy missed Lauren, Cass, and Bea. They all lived here now, and the sky was as blue here as it was in Texas.

Hilton Head had way more tourists and visitors than Sweet Water Falls could ever dream of, but in the off-season, it didn't feel rushed or hurried. It still possessed that small-town charm that appealed to Joy's heart and warmed her soul.

She didn't have to make any long-term decisions right now. She and Scott had been dating for a few months now, and while Joy could admit that seeing him, holding his hand, kissing him, was better than video calls and text chats, she still didn't have to declare she'd be moving here by the New Year.

She wouldn't be. But come summer...

Joy sank onto the bed again, exhaustion pulling her shoulders down as she looked at her phone. She tapped to open the Internet browser, and right there, in a tab she never closed, sat the South Carolina requirements for teachers.

She had almost all of them. A few more credits, and Joy would have her teaching license—and it would work in Texas or South Carolina. She'd have to take a test here was all, and with the courses and training she'd been taking for over a year now, Joy had all the confidence in the world that she'd pass.

So what was she waiting for? A divine sign from heaven? To give herself permission?

Her phone chimed, and again, Lauren's name popped up on the screen. Joy rolled her neck and tapped to dial her friend.

"Hey, there," Lauren said cheerfully after she'd connected the call. "No, that goes outside, honey." She drew in a breath. "I just got a new patio set, and Blake and Tommy are helping me get it in before the holidays."

Joy should've said, "That's so great. Tell me about it." Or "Will we have Supper Club outside on your new deck?" Or something to keep Lauren talking.

Instead, she said, "I'm on the island. I came early to see Scott Anderson. We're dating."

Lauren said nothing, but Joy heard evidence that the call remained connected. Finally, she said, "Why do you sound like you've swallowed poison?"

"I don't know. I—" Joy released a terribly long sigh, wishing she had words to explain the things in her head. In that moment, she realized something.

Nothing needed to be worked out in her *head*. It had to all align in her *heart*.

"I'll tell everyone all about it tomorrow," she said, a smile touching her face. "Okay?"

"Who else knows you're here already?"

"You and Scott," Joy said. "It was a secret."

"Mm hm," Lauren said with a touch of knowing in her tone. "You've always loved a good secret relationship." She laughed, and that made Joy do the same. Oh, how she missed Lauren. She missed their lunches, planned or spontaneous. She missed hugging her and listening to her talk about her job.

In short, Joy felt like she missed so much by living in Sweet Water Falls when so many people she loved lived here in Hilton Head.

You don't love Scott, her rational voice said as she and Lauren finished laughing. "I'll call you tomorrow," she said. "I have ice cream right now, and a swamp tour in the morning with Scott, and well...I can't wait to see you."

"Tomorrow," Lauren said. "Enjoy your scandalous day, Joy." She was obviously grinning as she spoke, and she ended the call as she issued more instructions to someone about where to put the umbrella for her new patio set.

Joy lowered her phone to the bed, stood, and retrieved her ice cream. She still needed that spoon, but a phrase running through her head drowned out all her other concerns.

You don't love Scott...

...but you could if you'd give a real relationship with him a real chance.

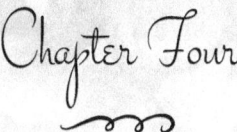

Chapter Four

Scott pulled open the door to his brother's truck and climbed in. "Thanks, man. I really owe you one." He hauled his overnight bag with him, running through a mental checklist of everything he'd shoved in the bag. If things hadn't happened so fast, Scott would feel better.

He reminded himself that he wasn't leaving the country. He wasn't even leaving town. If he forgot a toothbrush or a pair of underwear, he could go get it. Or go to the store.

"No problem," Jeff said. He wore a beard where Scott kept his face clean-shaven, but they had the same blue eyes that crinkled extra-well along the outer edges when they smiled or laughed. Jeff's hair held more dark brown while Scott's tended to shine red-gold in the summer sun, but it was wintertime, and the sun had already set.

"Where's Ghost?"

"Harry's gonna come get him," he said, looking past the restoration trucks that had come and toward the studio apartment. He couldn't see it, which meant he didn't have to see Ghost's sad, doggy eyes, begging him not to leave him there in the rising water. "He left as soon as I called him."

"You could've brought him," Jeff said. "Sandy has pills."

"It's fine," Scott said, because he'd already be displacing one niece tonight. He didn't need to make the other break out in hives.

"You didn't want to call Mom and Daddy, huh?" Jeff asked as he pulled away from the curb.

"I just need to make a stop at Beach Beauty," Scott said as he fastened his seatbelt. "And no. Mom's house smells like the inside of a refrigerator that's been unplugged for a decade." He shook his head, able to smell the slightly off, decaying, moth-bally scent right now. "And Daddy keeps asking me when I'm going to get back together with Melanie. I'm tired of telling him...about that."

Jeff glanced over to him, but mercifully, he didn't say anything. He knew all about Melanie and the five-plus years Scott had invested in her. She'd left town after some wild accusations about his inability to commit, and Scott had somehow been the one left questioning everything in his life.

Six years. He'd been reeling for six years, and no, he didn't want to re-explain himself to his father. Yes, he'd been set up by his daddy, who had a very close business associate —who happened to be Melanie's father. Apparently the break-up had caused an unintended rift for Scott's daddy, and while Scott had apologized a hundred times and tried to explain twice that many, the message never seemed to get across.

He shook away the thoughts from his past, and said, "You have to turn right here." Then he braced himself as Jeff swung the truck in a wide arc to make the left-hand turn.

"Why are we going to Beach Beauty?" he asked. "I thought they didn't have any rooms."

"They don't." Scott slid his hand up his leg to his pocket. "My, uh, a friend called me and said she needed a spoon."

"She?" Leave it to Jeff to pick up on the things Scott wished he'd leave on the table.

"Yeah, she." Scott looked out the window, hating himself for calling Joy a mere friend. She was his friend—his girlfriend. "If you must know, I'm seeing her."

"You're seeing someone?" Jeff didn't have to sound so surprised. "Like, seeing her-seeing her? Or you've been out once or twice?"

Scott leaned his head against the glass, glad it radiated coolness from where the air conditioning blew on it. "Both, actually."

"You're all the way to dating her after the first date?"

Scott pressed his lips together so he wouldn't sigh. Then he lifted his head and looked at his brother. Jeff glanced over to him, then back to the road. When he looked again only a moment later, his eyebrows shot up. "Well?"

"Why do you care?"

"*We* care," Jeff corrected. "Row was just talking about setting you up with a new secretary at her office."

"No," Scott said automatically. "I told your wife to stop trying to blind-date me back into the dating pool."

"You had fun with Carla."

"Carla? Who's Carla?"

"The woman she set you up with a few months ago?" Jeff looked at him like he'd gone crazy. "You don't remember a woman you went out with?"

"I didn't go out with Carla," Scott said.

"You didn't—what?" Jeff looked at him for so long, Scott started to worry about what they might hit on the road in front of them.

"I canceled on Carla," Scott said. "Even if you thought I went out with her, it would've been one time. Months ago." He couldn't help muttering the last couple of words. "No, I'm going out with that gorgeous blonde who stayed at Harry's over the summer. Joy?" He'd spoken of her several times, especially with the person he trusted the most—his brother.

"Joy?" Jeff was apparently going to phrase everything as a question tonight.

"She texted the night I was supposed to go out with Carla," Scott said, looking out his window again. "She said she didn't like the idea of me going out with anyone but her." He smiled just thinking about that text. It had changed the trajectory of his whole life since September.

"The one who you've asked out a couple of times, and she turned you down? This is the same woman?"

"Yep." Scott's smile only grew as the lights from Beach Beauty appeared on the horizon. "That's her. She's in town from Texas for the holidays, and she flew in a day early to see me. We ate at Mead's this afternoon, and I—well, we kissed

—and now she needs a spoon for her ice cream." He produced the utensil from his pocket, still grinning like a fool.

"Oh, so we like this woman." At least Jeff didn't make it a question this time.

"We've been texting and calling for three months," Scott said. "Yeah, I like her."

"A long-distance thing," Jeff mused, but he didn't expound on the thought as he pulled into the parking lot and then the drive-through drop-off zone.

"Be right back." Scott hurried to unbuckle and get out, then he dashed inside the seaside hotel, the scent of salt-water hanging in the air. It mixed with pine needles, the source of which burned on a waist-high counter at the check-in desk.

He continued through the lobby and up to the fourth floor, where he'd dropped off Joy earlier. He knocked on the door, then leaned close to the crease. "Joy, sweetheart, it's Scott. I have your spoon."

When she didn't answer the door in the next several seconds, he pulled out his phone to text her. *Your spoon is here*, he said. *Should I leave it in the hall? Did you get in the shower or something?*

Only five seconds later, the loud unlocking of the dead-bolt filled the air. The door still only opened a couple of inches, and Joy's beautiful gray eyes blinked at him. "You brought me a spoon?"

"I said I would," he said, holding it up. "Do you think I'm going to attack you with it?" He started to laugh, but

Joy rolled her eyes, closed the door, and took off the safety latch.

This time, she opened the door all the way. "You said you'd text me in a couple of minutes about your housing situation." She looked down to his feet and back to his face. "No bag. You found somewhere?"

"Jeff came to get me," he said.

"Your car isn't working?"

"I got boxed in by the emergency crew my buddy called," he said. "So yeah, my brother came to get me, and we stopped here, and here's your spoon." He extended it toward her, and the lines on Joy's face softened and the tension in her shoulders relaxed.

She took the utensil and met his eyes again. "Thank you, Scott."

"Anytime." He tucked his hands into his pockets and rocked back onto his heels. He wanted to blurt out everything about his past dating mishaps. That, or kiss Joy again until his lungs begged him to breathe.

Instead of doing either, he said, "He's waiting for me downstairs, and he has an early shift at the country club tomorrow, so..."

"Go on, yeah," Joy said. She smiled and saluted him with the spoon. "You've saved me, Scott. Thank you."

"See you tomorrow."

She faded back into the room, her voice reaching right into his soul when she said, "Can't wait," and then let the door click softly closed. She latched it all up on her side, and Scott realized he stood inches from a hotel room door, sighing longingly.

He pulled himself together and hurried back downstairs to Jeff. The moment he got in, his brother asked, "You're still doing the evening rock work at The Strand, aren't you?"

"Yep," Scott said. "Joy's going to her friend's house after our lunch tomorrow."

Jeff nodded and put the truck in gear, but he clearly had more to say. Scott wasn't going to probe, because he never volunteered more information than necessary. Jeff asked him annoying questions too, and they could talk about Melanie in vague, general terms. It wasn't like Scott couldn't say her name or anything.

A soft scoff escaped his mouth when he thought about telling Joy about that particular part of his past. "Mishap" didn't even come close to describing what a nightmare that relationship had been. Nor how close he'd come to losing himself completely.

He leaned his head against the rest behind him and closed his eyes. *It's over,* he told himself, because his connection to Melanie was over. Six years of over. *It's done. You're still here, and you're better than you were before anyway.*

Scott just needed a guest bedroom, and then he could queue up the next episode in his current comedy series. He'd been dealing with his grief, his feelings of betrayal, and his self-loathing since Melanie left with two things—laughter and lawn-mowing.

If he didn't work himself to death, he could spend evenings laughing. No one he'd met in the past six years would ever guess that Scott wasn't the happiest, easiest-going man on the planet. If he didn't think too hard about anything, then he didn't get too worked up. And he'd rather be alone and happy than with someone and miserable.

For the first time since everything in his life had imploded, Scott wondered if he could be with someone *and* happy at the same time. It was such a novel concept to him, and while he'd seen it in the lives of his friends and family, it had never really been an option for him.

Until now.

Until Joy Bartlett.

"Maybe," he muttered as his brother pulled into his perfectly suburban driveway. *She's just a maybe for now.*

Still, his mouth tingled for another taste of her, and even Scott could admit he'd experienced a life-changing, electrifying, incredibly hot first kiss with Joy. So hot, he needed a cooling-off period before he'd dare kiss her for a second time.

But there would be a second time. A second date. A second everything—and that was something Scott hadn't done in a while. He'd always told Jeff he was just waiting for the right woman to snag his attention, and boy, had Joy done that.

Oh, yes, she had, and Scott didn't mind one bit when he walked into his brother's house with Jeff and he immediately said to his wife, "Scott's dating a woman named Joy."

Rowena choked and immediately paused the movie. Silence fell over all of them, and Scott rolled his eyes. "Who's Joy?" she demanded at the same time he said, "No questions."

"I'm going to bed," he continued. "Thank you so much for letting me crash here."

Rowena launched herself off the couch. "The girls are sharing tonight," she said, following him upstairs where his two nieces usually slept in separate rooms. "I had Chelsea put some towels in her room for you, and Jeff's got his early morning, so there will be coffee."

"Thank you, Row," Scott said, and when he reached the doorway of his guest bedroom for the night, he turned back to her. "I'm going to get a hotel for tomorrow if I have to, okay? It's just one night."

"You can stay as long as you want." Rowena tucked her dark hair behind her ear. "I promise I won't hound you about Joy." She smiled, and while blondes were one-hundred percent Scott's type, Jeff had always liked brunettes more. Just another difference between them. "Though I did have the perfect woman for you..."

Scott laughed, his default. "No, your firm just hired a new secretary." He lifted his eyebrows as if to add, *Right?*

Rowena sighed and rolled her shoulders. "I'm gonna talk to Jeff about *not* telling you every stinking thing." She turned and headed for the top of the stairs. "It's my movie night, and the girls don't have school tomorrow, so don't be surprised if you don't see us."

"All right," Scott called after her, and then he went into his fourteen-year-old niece's room. Everything was purple and teal or a shade of it, but Scott wasn't going to complain. Water didn't cascade down the walls, soaking his shoes and his bedding, so he'd definitely taken a step up tonight.

Now, he just needed to check in with his buddy about the status of the studio, then make sure Harrison had gone by to get Ghost, and finally, he needed to find a hotel—at Christmastime—that would take him and his dog until he could work out a more permanent solution to his housing issues.

Chapter Five

J oy swiped on several more brush loads of mascara, really liking the way it added drama to her face. She felt washed out from head to toe, as she had skin that barely held a tan, her eyes couldn't decide if they were blue or gray, and her hair had started to take on more silver than blonde.

"Faded," she murmured to herself.

But the mascara made her feel younger. Sexier. Seen.

She'd just capped the makeup when someone knocked on her door. Scott's sexy bass said, "It's me, Joy. I have your breakfast."

She practically skipped out of the bathroom and unlatched the protection locks and the deadbolt without double-checking this time. There was just something about daylight that made everything seem less scary.

The sunshine pouring into the room also illuminated Scott's handsomeness as it hit his face. He smiled and held up the light blue pastry bag. "Chocolate croissants, as promised."

"You're a lifesaver," she said.

"Twice now," he said as he entered her room. He didn't lean to kiss her, and Joy's pulse hammered against the back of her tongue. "There's got to be some sort of reward for saving a woman's life *twice* in less than twenty-four hours."

He put their breakfast on the TV cabinet and faced her. In khaki shorts and a polo the color of Georgia peaches, his skin looked tanner than usual, and his hair shone with that auburn tint she liked. He brought the scent of sugar and spice with him, and Joy let the door fall closed as she stepped into his arms.

"Mm, you smell good," he said. "What is this? Honey? Milk? Cucumbers?" He laughed as she stepped out of his arms, and Joy put a smile on her face too.

"I think all three," she said. "The bottle was attached to the wall. I just used it." She went over to the bed, where her packed suitcase still sat open. "Did you get your car? You can help me carry these down to mine, right?"

"Yes, and yes," he said. "The studio is drying out. I found a hotel for tonight and tomorrow that will take me and Ghost, *and* I've been caffeinated already this morning."

"After yesterday," Joy said. "We both deserve a day where everything goes right." She lifted her windbreaker and indicated it. "Do you think I'll need this?"

Scott switched his gaze to the dark gray jacket. "Yeah, sure, bring it. It can be chilly in the shade."

"You're wearing shorts."

He looked down like he had to check to make sure. "Yeah, well, I don't get cold." He took the windbreaker from her, and Joy went into the bathroom to get the last of her cosmetics. With everything packed and ready, she zipped her suitcase closed, and they each towed one out into the hallway.

He loaded them into the back of her rented SUV, then they went to his truck. He opened the back door to toss in her windbreaker, and the back seat held a couple of backpacks and had empty water bottles littering the floorboards.

Joy reached past him to put down her purse. "Do you live out of this thing?"

"Sometimes," he joked, his sunny smile hitched in place.

Joy had no reason to complain, so she said nothing as she got in the passenger seat. She'd leave her car here, and Scott would drop her off after their lunch at Lighthouse Point. Then she'd head over to Lauren's house. Already, her hands trembled with nerves from all the anticipated questions.

She reminded herself that while her friends could be a little overbearing sometimes, their interest in her life stemmed from a place of love and respect. They wanted nothing for her but happiness, and after everything that had happened with Wendell...

Well, they'd be happy about this dating development with Scott. At least Joy thought they would be.

"So," she said as Scott left Beach Beauty in his rearview mirror. "Tell me why a man like you has never been married before."

Scott yelped, and the truck slowed to a near stop as he

applied the brake. He looked over to her, shock coursing through his expression. "I'm sorry?"

"Oh, come on." She glanced in the rear-view mirror, but they weren't holding up traffic. "You're a successful business owner. A beach runner. A guy who loves people and dogs. By all accounts, you should be married with a wife and kids, blissfully in love with your life."

She opened the blue pastry bag and extracted a raspberry fritter. "And you like the same doughnuts as me." She gave him a smile, replaced his doughnut in the bag, and swapped it out for her croissant. "See? There's even coffee waiting for me right here." She indicated the to-go cup, which she knew would have her caramel coffee in it.

"Who says I'm not blissfully in love with my life?" he asked. "Do you have to be married and have kids to be blissfully in love with your life?"

"No," Joy said simply. "I was married and have kids, and my life was a nightmare." She kept the smile on her face out of sheer will, as she hadn't been anticipating saying anything of the sort.

She took an overly large bite of her croissant and looked out the passenger window so she wouldn't have to look at Scott.

"Joy," he said.

She just shook her head, so she wouldn't spray flakes of buttery pastry all over his truck. He wouldn't care, because he obviously didn't keep his vehicle clean, but Joy didn't need the further humiliation.

He gave her several seconds to chew and swallow, and then he asked, "Was?"

"You're not going to let this go, are you?" she asked.

"You led with a question that's impossible to answer," he shot back.

"I thought we liked impossible." Joy turned her head to look at him then. "I mean, isn't that what we are? Impossible?"

"Why would we be impossible?" he asked.

"Because I don't live here," Joy said. "You and me..." She didn't want to say they didn't make sense. They did exist on opposite ends of the spectrum, but that didn't mean they didn't make sense.

"I like you and me." Scott reached over and threaded his fingers through hers. He lifted her hand to his lips and placed a kiss on the inside of her wrist. "Okay?"

Joy settled back into her seat and nodded. "Sorry I led with an impossible question."

"I'm sorry your life before you met me was a nightmare."

She caught the implication, and it made her smile. "You think things have been so rosy since you nearly scared me out of my swimming suit? Is that what you're saying?"

He laughed, of course, because Scott laughed about a lot of things. "That suit had a malfunction," he said. "The only thing I did was help."

"Mm." Joy let the silence take over then, and she enjoyed the easiness of being with Scott. He didn't try to stuff the truck with conversation either, and several minutes later, they rolled up to the dock.

He helped her out of the truck, and Joy tucked her windbreaker over the strap of her cross-body bag. Scott checked them in with the tour guide while Joy examined the nearby boats. When Scott came up beside her, his fingers trailing lightly along her waist, she looked at him.

"These can't be the boats we'll be on," she said. "Can they?"

"Why not?" he asked.

Joy eyed them again, sure either her or Scott—not both of them—would sink the one closest to her. It drifted lazily on the murky, greenish-brown water, and none of this reminded Joy of the brilliant blue water and white sand beaches she'd visited right here on the island this past summer.

Trees grew right up to the water's edge, and plenty of moss and other living things—animal or plant, Joy wasn't sure—covered the pillars supporting the dock.

"They don't look safe," she finally came up with. "How many people go on these tours?"

"There were eight spots when I registered us," Scott said.

There was absolutely no way eight people, plus a guide, could fit in any of these boats. Joy quickly counted seats in the one furthest out, and she made it to ten chairs. Fine. There was the room, but that boat didn't look any safer or able to float than the one now bumping the edge of the dock as the waves intensified.

Four more people showed up in the next several minutes, two of them children. They ran out onto the dock, and Joy smiled at them from behind her sunglass lenses. "Turtle!

Turtle!" one of the boys yelled, waving frantically for his parents to come see.

Neither of them moved, and Joy was reminded of her and Wendell. Except in her marriage, she'd eventually make her way out to see what had her boys so excited, and then Wendell would belittle her for caving to their demands.

"I'm their mother," she'd always told him. "I want them to be excited to show me and tell me anything and everything."

Joy hadn't realized how toxic her marriage and her relationship with Wendell had become until it was too late to fix either. He hadn't wanted to anyway, and he'd been the one to file for divorce, push the mediation meetings, and separate their lives.

Her sons had been nothing but supportive of her, and since they were both adults, she'd made no effort to ask them about their relationship with their father. Her brain fired, and she made a mental note to do that. They might be suffering right now too, and the way Joy's resolve hardened told her at least one of them was. Mother's intuition.

Scott had told her previously that he didn't have kids. *Never married. No kids.* When she'd gotten that text, she'd messaged Cass just to find out if it was really true. She was married to Harrison Tate, and Harry had sold the landscaping business to Scott a few years back. They were good friends, and Cass had confirmed that Scott had indeed never been married and had no children.

Those facts—especially the never been married one—still dumbfounded Joy a little bit. Scott was so gorgeous, so funny, so put together. There had to be something keeping him from getting down the aisle, and Joy had an excellent nose for sniffing out such things.

In her head, she heard her friends from the Supper Club warning her not to go looking for trouble. Bea would tell her she was trying to sabotage the relationship from the beginning, and Lauren would say that Joy was projecting things onto Scott that didn't exactly exist. Bessie would simply smile and tell Joy to "follow her gut," and "try to have fun," and Cass would watch them all, hold her tongue, and then finally...

Finally, Cass would ask Joy the true, burning question about her resistance to letting go and allowing herself to dive headfirst into a real relationship with Scott.

Why can't you do it? she thought.

"We're getting on, sweetheart." The pressure from Scott's hand intensified along her lower back, and Joy blinked her way back to the present. The family had moved ahead of them down the dock, corralling their kids onto the biggest boat at the end. Thankfully.

She and Scott stepped onboard, and Joy's whole world wobbled with the undulation of the water. Her hand tightened in Scott's, and he steadied her until she took a seat on a bench that ran the length of the boat. He sat next to her, grinned, and stretched his arms out like bird's wings along the edge of the boat.

"There's a breeze today," he commented, and Joy turned her face into it.

"I love boats," she said. "The ocean. All of it."

"Is that right?" he asked.

"Yes, sir." She turned toward him, the interest in his voice prompting her to do so. "You don't think I do?"

"I think we should go sailing this Christmas." His smile filled his whole face. "I've got a boat I'd be willing to take you out on. Maybe for a Christmas Eve sunset." He leaned closer and closer until he'd moved near enough to whisper and she could still hear him.

She smiled and tucked herself against his chest. He lowered his arm around her shoulders, and Joy felt absolutely claimed. She liked that, and warmth filled her from head to toe. "I need to see what the ladies are doing," she said.

"I thought you guys had a shared calendar," he said.

"We do." Joy closed her eyes as the boat backed away from the dock and the top of it no longer blocked the sun. "But I don't have it memorized. I'm not on friend duty until tonight."

Scott laughed, the sound of it practically under his breath, and his lips swept across the tender skin just in front of and below her ear. A thrill ran down her arm and her spine simultaneously, and Joy turned toward Scott, intending to kiss him, just as the tour guide said, "We've gotten a report of a mama alligator out here this morning, so I hope you folks are ready for a good time."

The kids gasped and started chattering to their parents about the possibility of seeing an alligator, and Joy could admit the idea enthused her as well. The tour guide took them around a small jut of land and then back along the river, and the trees grew more densely, crowding out the sunshine completely and creating a serene environment for birds, frogs, alligators, and plenty of other wildlife.

Joy listened to the guide talk about the habitat, the climate, and the life that lived there in South Carolina's Lowcountry. It didn't take long for her to slide her arms into her windbreaker, and Scott tucked her back into his side once she'd done so.

The boat puttered along, and the guide stopped a couple of times for them to see tiny alligators. "These here are the second-years," he said. "They like to hang out in this pond, where the bigger gators don't bother them. See them there? On the logs?"

Joy could not, but Scott pointed and whispered, "The one is sunning at the top left."

She saw it then, and she marveled at how still they could stand. Or sun themselves. One finally slithered into the water, much to the delight of the boys on board. Joy grinned and looked at Scott like they'd seen a great treasure that day too.

"All right," the guide said. "We're just gonna go 'round to this other pond, where I think our mama is. It's best if we're calm and quiet, okay? She won't like us near her nest at all, and she'll hiss at us to warn us back. If you hear hissing out here in the water, it's not a snake, usually. But an alligator, and you best be gettin' out of there."

Yet he drove them down another narrow channel of water and into another pond area, all the while taking them toward the danger as he talked about the foliage around them. Several minutes later, he said, "Yeah, I think she's right...over...here."

He turned the boat so the side where Joy sat faced the land, and she saw what was clearly a footpath between trees that led to a parking lot. A black car stood there, and when the guide cut the engine on the boat, hissing met Joy's ears.

"That guy needs to back out of there," the guide said very quietly. "Hear that, folks? She's already upset."

They drifted with the whims of the water in the pond, which pushed them ever closer toward the riverbank. Where the angry alligator was.

"Oh, I see her," the guide whispered. His hand came up in a point, and Joy adjusted her eyes a few degrees to the left. "See her right there? She is not happy we're here."

The family talked in hushed voices to one another, and Joy found her heart pounding out of fear or excitement or both.

"Normally, I'd let us get a good, long look," the guide said. "But whoever rolled up in that car already aggravated— oh." The car started to move, and as it backed up slowly, the guide restarted the boat.

He backed them away from the mama alligator and her nest, and from a safer distance, they watched her as she stared directly at them. She didn't hiss again, and eventually, the guide said, "There you have it, folks. Mothers protect their young across a wide range of species." He turned them around and got them going back into the smaller waterway channels.

"Oh, we've got a family of ducks here," he said pleasantly, and that got him talking about the water fowl that lived on the island. Bea and Cass had taken a trip to the Everglades—a National Park in Florida—a few years ago, and as Joy listened to the guide talk about the birds, she thought she'd have liked to have gone.

They all made it back to the dock without sinking, and once Joy had put her feet back on steadier ground, she turned to Scott. "That was great. Very educational, and I actually started to relax after the hissing stopped."

He chuckled and took her hand in his. "I'm glad you liked it."

"We have a lot of birds in the Coastal Bend of Texas too," she said. "You'll have to come see them sometime."

He looked at her, some of his usual joviality sliding off his face. "Do you mean that?"

Joy let him open her door for her, and she climbed up into his truck before facing him again. "Of course I mean it. I just invited you to Sweet Water Falls yesterday."

"Yeah, but that was...yesterday." He moved into the bench seat, his hand sliding up to cradle her face. "I wasn't sure—I mean, I don't think either of us knew if this would be a real thing once we got to be together in person."

"Is it?" Joy asked. "A real thing now that we're in person?"

"More real than ever," Scott said as his face filled with a grin. His stomach growled, and that stopped his forward movement. He laughed and dropped his head as he backed out of the doorway and closed her door.

As he settled behind the wheel, Joy found a flush in his

face that she found sweet and sexy, but she said nothing. "All right," he said, clearly not going to talk about what he'd said or the fact that his bodily functions had interrupted what was sure to be their second kiss. "Lighthouse Point for lunch. You ready?"

"So ready," she agreed, and this time, she reached across the distance between them and took his hand in hers. She'd enjoyed being claimed by him, and she figured he might like it if she did the same. "I told Lauren I came in early to see you."

"Whoa, ho, ho," he said, half combining laughter with words. "You did?" He looked over to her once he reached the stop sign. "And?"

"And nothing." Joy smiled. "She seemed happy for me."

"Was she surprised?"

Joy thought for a moment. "She didn't seem to be, no."

Scott let the conversation die there, but it chewed slowly in Joy's mind. Lauren hadn't seemed surprised about the relationship, though Joy hadn't really told her about it. She hadn't kept it a secret—at least from Lauren—that she liked Scott, but no one knew just how much they'd been communicating in the past few months.

"I'll tell everyone at dinner tonight," she said as the arrived in the more thriving part of the island where a shopping center, lots of restaurants, the official yacht club, and the historical lighthouse stood. "Is that okay?"

"Perfectly fine with me, sweetheart," he said. "You're the one who wanted to keep us a secret."

"I didn't—"

Scott grinned and shook his head. "I'm not upset about it, Joy. I kinda liked sneaking around with you." He opened his door. "Stay right there. I'll come get you down."

After he'd slammed his door, Joy whispered, "I like sneaking around with you too, Scott."

But she had to tell her friends tonight. She valued their opinions, and maybe they'd be able to help her unknot her confusing feelings, the constant questions about where she should live, and whether or not she had the guts to leave Texas.

Chapter Six

Lauren Keller flipped a page in her cookbook, wishing she had half the skills necessary to make the desserts in this volume. She'd stuck her famous lemon bar recipe in the front of it, and once those had gone into the oven, the shiny, beautiful pictures of pies, brownies, and soufflés had lured her into the pages of this book.

A timer went off, and Lauren left the book open to a double chocolate cheesecake brownie while she turned to get her offering for tonight's dinner out of the oven. She should be down the hall in her office, getting some work done for a client who needed to see specs for their marketing materials once the New Year began.

But she and Blake had decided to both take a full two weeks off for the Christmas holidays. That was what Tommy, Blake's son, had off from school, and in fact, she expected the pair of them to walk into her house at any moment.

Since she slept less than normal humans, she'd work on the marketing docs in the middle of the night. No one would be the wiser, and she'd meet her deadline.

She slid the lemon bars onto the stovetop and touched the button to turn off the oven. "That's done," she said, turning to face the book. "You're going away." She closed the book over the brownies and put it in the small cupboard above her microwave, which hung over the stove.

Her phone chimed, and she focused there, desperately wanting the message to be from Joy. It was, and she reached for her device with slightly shaking fingers and a pulse that raced around her throat. "Calm down," she muttered to herself. She just hadn't seen Joy in person in over four months now, and Lauren missed her terribly.

Not only that, but showing a girlfriend a diamond ring via a picture just wasn't the same as having her there to see it in person. Joy would wear the diamonds in her eyes as she exclaimed over Lauren's engagement ring, peppered her with questions about the wedding, and gushed over how amazing everything in Lauren's life would now be.

She didn't expect that marriage could fix everything—and she didn't even think her life needed to be "fixed" all that much anyway. But Blake had promised that he and Tommy would be her family, and Lauren was really looking forward to having something and someone to be able to always rely on.

On my way! Joy had texted. *If it's still okay for me to come hang out there, I should be to your house in about fifteen minutes. If I don't get lost.* She'd followed her words with a

GIF of a man looking into the distance as if he had no idea where he was.

You're not Bea, Lauren tapped out with a giant smile. *You'll be fine, and yes! Get here now!*

She quickly navigated over to her text string with Blake and sent him a quick message. *I know I said you guys should come here before dinner, but Joy's on her way, and I want some girl time with her. Is that okay?*

Terrible. Blake responded lightning fast, the way he usually did. *But doable. I haven't been able to get Tommy off SquareSpaces yet anyway, so we're still at home.*

Thank you! Dinner is at whatever time you can stop and pick up the food...

If they were in person, Blake would've laughed. Lauren closed her eyes, her smile already on her face as she listened to the man's laughter in her mind. He'd have grabbed her around the waist and brought her flush against his body as he said he'd get dinner whenever *she* wanted it, from wherever she wanted it.

Tonight, she'd ordered from an Italian restaurant, because the build your own pasta bar fed a crowd quickly and easily. Bessie and Sage weren't on the island yet, and Scott wouldn't be joining Joy, but Tommy was a growing teenage boy, and he could eat double his body weight in breadsticks and marinara sauce.

Bea and Grant were returning to the island tonight from picking up his daughter, Shelby, and they'd be at tomorrow night's dinner, along with Bea's daughter and son-in-law, her single son, and her son with the very serious girlfriend. So serious that Bea had informed them all that they might get engaged this Christmas.

Any other year, the thought of a couple in their twenties getting engaged would've sent Lauren into a depressive tailspin. But this year, she couldn't wait to see Bea's adult children, as she hadn't been around them since their mother had moved to Hilton Head, four and a half years ago now.

Cass and Harrison were hosting the big meal at their beachside mansion, but only Cass's son would be there. Her twin daughters were off on their own adventures this Christmas. Lauren, Blake, and Tommy would be there, and Joy had told Lauren that yes, she'd invited Scott.

Bessie was coming to Hilton Head with her daughter Wynona, and Sage was bringing what she called her new beau—her Newfoundland rescue dog. She hadn't been able to get him on the airplane with her, so she was making the twelve-hundred-mile drive with Gypsy, and they'd left Texas two days ago and planned to arrive tomorrow as well.

I'll grab dinner at six and head your way, Blake said. *Does that give you enough time?*

Lauren honestly had no idea what time it was right now, and she twisted to look at the stove. Just after three. *Perfect*, she told her fiancé, and then she caught herself admiring her own diamond ring.

She blinked and actually snapped her fingers, as if trying to get her own attention. "Go get the wedding binder." Lauren hurried out of the kitchen and down the hall to her office, where she got hit with much cooler air. She'd moved near the end of the summer, but September in South

Carolina was no joke, so she'd learned that her office sat on the cooler side of the house, and it could always be counted on to be several degrees colder than everywhere else.

The binder sat right on the edge of her desk, because she'd literally just finished putting in all the dividers today. She'd only been engaged for three days, so she'd made good time in gathering all the pieces she needed, then thinking through what needed to be done and when, and the next step was starting on the plans.

Joy loved weddings and planning, and Lauren had told her several times to perhaps think about doing wedding planning as an occupation. Joy claimed that she'd miss the kids too much, and that she loved working in a more service-oriented profession. Lauren hadn't pushed the issue, because Joy had always seemed happy with her work at the elementary school.

"I'm here," she called. "I'm coming in."

Lauren ducked out of the office, the white wedding binder under her arm. "Hey." Tears rushed at her at the sight of Joy's blonde bob and that happy, symmetrical smile. "Oh, it's so good to see you."

She dropped the binder onto a chair as she passed, and she and Joy collided in the foyer hallway. They clung to one another, neither of them saying anything, for several long seconds. Lauren finally sniffed, and that somehow gave Joy permission to step back and wipe her eyes. "Wow." She let out her breath, upon which rode a light laugh. "I wasn't expecting to cry."

Lauren wiped her own eyes, her smile shining through

despite her emotion. "I miss you, Joy." She linked her arm through her best friend's and turned to face her house. "So, this is the house with all my stuff in it."

"It's amazing." Joy commented on the new window treatments, as well as the pale yellow cupboards. "They're just not the same in pictures," she said as she ran her fingertips along the top of a drawer.

"You know what else isn't the same in a picture?" Lauren held out her left hand while Joy faced her.

Joy's eyes grew big, and she grabbed Lauren's hand. "I haven't seen this in person." She looked up at Lauren, shock in her expression. "It has its own zip code, I suppose, being that size." They laughed together, and Lauren pulled Joy into another hug.

This time, when they parted, Lauren said, "Details, Joy. I need details about you and Scott."

"I, uh, texted him back in September when you told me he had a date that night."

"You did?"

Joy nodded and barely touched one fingertip to the top of the lemon bars. "These are perfection, Lauren. I don't know how you do it."

"They're the one thing I can make."

"Not true." Joy gave her a smile as she took in the rest of the house. "This is such a great place. Will you and Blake live here after you're married?"

"Don't think I don't know that you're changing the subject." Lauren tilted her head and gave Joy a pointed look. "But no. His place is bigger, so I'll move over there."

"And when is the blessed day?" Joy spoke without any frustration or sarcasm at all. Lauren didn't even think she had it in her.

"March thirty-first," she said.

Joy's surprise widened her eyes one more time. "Three months. Huh."

"Huh? What does that mean?"

"It means you have a lot to do in three months. This is your first wedding, Lauren. It has to be everything you've ever wanted." She took Lauren's hands in hers. "Tell me I can help you plan something while I'm here."

"Oh, I'm putting you to work right now." Lauren squeezed her hands and then went to retrieve the binder. "I finished getting this ready this morning. I have a couple of calls out to my preferred events centers, but people are already on vacation for the holidays."

A thread of worry pulled through her, but Lauren tried to dismiss it. If nothing could be booked for a wedding in three months, she and Blake would find a park or a public stretch of beach. It wouldn't be cold, and Lauren's dream wedding had always taken place outside anyway.

Joy flipped from the venue section to the catering divider, then the dresses, then flowers, then photography. With her eyes still down on the empty sleeves and pages, she asked, "Have you told your mom? Jess?"

Lauren's heart deflated like a balloon that had a very slow leak "Not yet," she said.

Joy looked up then, the lecture already in her eyes. She didn't have to say it out loud, and the best part about Joy was that she didn't. She simply said, "I passed a really huge nursery on the way in yesterday. Do they do wedding flowers?"

"If it's Jorgen's, then yes," Lauren said. "They're on my list." She flipped to the front page of the flower section. Every divider that marked a new section had a list taped to the back of it—Lauren's preferences, based on what she knew about Hilton Head after living there for several months. She tapped the taped list of florists. "Right there."

"Is Blake helping with anything wedding-related?" Joy asked.

"He's going to be in charge of the food," Lauren said. "He knows what I like, and he's from the island, so we thought it was a good fit."

Joy turned the pages back to catering, which did not have a list taped to it yet. "Ah, that's why this section doesn't have a list." She giggled afterward, and Lauren hipped her away from the binder.

"He'll do it," she said, but she couldn't help laughing too. "I know I'm a little crazy when it comes to planning."

"It's amazing," Joy said, her smile so genuine and so lovely. "Don't apologize for it."

"Tell me about Scott," Lauren said, lifting her chin like she'd just issued a challenge.

Joy's smile changed in an ever-so-subtle way. "He's great, Lauren, really." She ducked her head, but her hair wasn't long enough to hide behind. Everything about her had softened in a breath of time, and Lauren could see how much she liked him.

So it wasn't a surprise when Joy lifted her head and said, "I like him too much already."

"Why too much?" Lauren asked. "You've been talking to him for months."

"I kissed him last night. First date."

Lauren grinned and shook her head. "Let's sit down." She led Joy over to the couch, where they collapsed side-by-side, nearly identical sighs coming from their mouths. "I'm assuming he kissed you back." Lauren leafed through her binder mindlessly, hoping that would encourage Joy to keep talking.

"Mm, yeah," Joy said.

"And I can tell just from those two tiny words that it was a *good* kiss." She dared to throw Joy a peek from the corner of her eye.

Joy's smile had returned, and she nodded. After a few seconds of them both looking at nothing, Joy said, "I just worry that we're doing something stupid."

"And what would that be?"

"Why does everyone think I live here?" Joy sounded genuinely upset, and Lauren abandoned her fake quest to study her empty wedding binder.

"Sweetie, you can move here tomorrow," she said.

Joy rolled her eyes. "And if they don't think I live here, they act like moving here is so dang easy."

"Tell me why it isn't, then," Lauren said.

"For one, I can't go weeks and weeks without working," Joy said pointedly. "I get a good settlement from Wendell, yes, but even with my job, it's barely enough. Moving takes money. Buying a house or renting takes money. Feeding yourself while you find a new job takes *money*."

Lauren didn't want to fire questions at Joy. She tended to get deep into her own thoughts, so there was no question that she'd already examined everything from every angle. "You own the house outright, don't you?"

"Yes." Joy sighed and pulled half of the binder onto her lap. "It reduced my settlement, but I own the house. You know, the one *in Texas*."

Lauren smiled and flipped all the way back to the front of the binder. "Okay, so one of the venues I really like has a ballroom with a retractable roof. You know, like they have on baseball stadiums."

Joy leaned a little closer to the binder, as Lauren had put in a couple of pictures for the venues. She figured she needed to get that nailed down first, and she turned fully toward Joy. "Let's go tour it tomorrow."

"Sure," Joy said. "Can we just show up?"

"No, you need tickets." Lauren closed the binder and slid it onto the table. "I didn't see you bring in your bags." She got to her feet, but when Joy didn't, Lauren turned back to her. She didn't like the apprehension on her friend's face. "Joy."

"I'm worried I'm going to be in your way," she said. "Bea's house is full, but Cass and Harry have plenty of room."

"Bessie, Wynona, and Sage are all staying there." Lauren frowned and sank back to the couch. "I want you to stay here."

"It won't cramp your newly engaged style?"

Lauren studied her for a moment. "Blake doesn't stay over here. I don't sleep over there."

Joy's cheeks pinked up and her gaze dropped to her lap. "You said the office was small."

"Come see." Lauren got back to her feet. "I know you like to unpack when you first arrive, so let's just do it, and then I can show you where I'm going to plant all my peas this year." She grinned at Joy, offered her a hand up, and the two of them went into the office.

Lauren had pushed her desk against the wall and set up a queen-sized air mattress on a portable and collapsible frame. "See how amazing?" She'd pushed it against the wall, so a narrow aisle still existed between the bed and the desk.

"It's higher, so you don't have to roll off the bed, *and* I got a luggage rack." She yanked open the closet doors, which accordioned out to show a rack just dying for a suitcase to hold.

Joy sniffled and leaned her head against Lauren's bicep. "It's perfect, Lauren. Thank you."

Lauren smiled, because she felt so...different than she had when she'd first moved here. She wanted nothing but the best for Joy in the next two weeks, and while she wasn't going to needle her about moving here, she was going to keep talking about the possibility of it.

And Scott could have a very big role in that.

"All right," she said. "Knowing you, you'll have two suit-cases, so let's go get them and get unpacking. You can tell me all about your secret twenty-four hours with Mister Hotterson."

Joy burst out laughing then, and that only added more fuel to the happiness fire burning in Lauren's life. Now, she just had to figure out a way to get the rest of the Supper Club in Hilton Head...for good.

Chapter Seven

Cassandra Tate reached to push the button to open her garage, then eased her SUV to a near-stall as the door lifted. Her husband for the past six months didn't use the double-garage closest to the house, but the third stall way down on the end, and as Cass glanced to her left, she didn't see Harrison's truck.

She hadn't really expected to, but disappointment still cut through her. She came to a stop and put her vehicle in park, and before she'd gotten out, the back of the SUV started to raise. She went that way to find her son there, grinning in the carefree way he had. "Oh, hello, sweetheart." She brushed her lips along his cheek as the lift gate finally arrived in the all-the-way-up position.

"I heard the garage from the hammock," he said as he reached in to start collecting the food Cass had gone to pick up.

"It's a bit chilly for the hammock, isn't it?" she asked.

Why, she had no idea. Conrad didn't seem to feel cold—he was very much like his father in that regard.

"Only when the wind kicks up." Conrad smiled as he headed for the front door, and Cass looked at the mass of Mexican food she'd ordered. They'd had the street tacos from Bernardo's for Supper Club before, but Cass reasoned this wasn't Supper Club.

Besides, who didn't love a good taco? Bernardo's didn't skimp on the steak either, and Cass had ordered ground beef, steak, chicken, and fish for tonight's family dinner party. That was what she'd been calling it in her head anyway.

It wasn't Supper Club, because that was the six of them only. Well, Cherry Forrester too, but she hadn't come to Hilton Head for the holidays. Tonight's meal included spouses and significant others, as well as children.

Tommy, Blake's son, at fourteen, would be the youngest person there, and Lauren had offered to pay something toward the food because she claimed Tommy could eat like no one she'd ever seen.

Cass had already raised one son, and yes, they could eat and eat and eat. She picked up the few bags of tortilla chips and toppings, leaving the long foil trays of rice, beans, and meats for her son.

Conrad met her on the way out as she went in, and she set about getting everything set up on the long island counter in the kitchen. Bea and Grant would be bringing his daughter, all of Bea's kids, two significant others for her children, his parents, their dog, and all the drinks for the group.

Cass left them room at the end of the counter and then arranged the chips, the lettuce, and the soft flour tortillas at the head of the buffet line. Her dining room table could seat twelve, and Harry had put the double leaves in it that morning before he'd left for work, but that would barely accommodate Cass and Bea and all of their loved ones.

Her party of three felt very small, but Cass reminded herself that Sage was coming alone, as was Joy, and Bessie just had her daughter with her. Lauren would be there with Blake and Tommy, and that brought their total to twenty-one.

Conrad had set up two folding tables and Cass had covered them with dark green cloths to emulate the pine tree standing in her living room. Her son returned with the rest of the food and Cass arranged it along the countertop, and then she and Conrad started setting places.

She found such joy in hosting people in her home, and sudden emotion overcame her at the last time she'd hosted more than a dozen people for a meal.

West's funeral.

Her husband had been gone for over almost three years now, but Cass missed him every single day. Her face felt distorted as she tried to hold back her tears, and she sniffed to contain the leakiness that had approached out of nowhere.

She felt Conrad looking at her, and Cass lifted her head. "I'm okay," she said. "I just miss your dad at times like this."

Conrad said nothing, but he laid down the fist full of knives in his hand and walked the length of the table to take her into a hug. "I miss him too," he whispered. Then he just held her tightly, and Cass gripped him back.

The moment passed, and she pulled away. She gave her son a watery smile and shook her head. "Grief is so sneaky." She resumed putting out spoons, and then she went around the table with a cluster of napkins in her hand.

White, as Cass loved the more muted colors of Christmas. She had some low, rectangular centerpieces that boasted the red, pink, and white poinsettias, but that was the only crimson she was allowing at tonight's dinner party. Well, if someone wore a festive sweater, she wouldn't send them home to change, but she abhorred red tablecloths on principle.

"How's school?" she asked her son. He'd been in town for a couple of days now, but Conrad didn't volunteer information. Cass had to pull every sentence out of him, and it was worse than extracting wisdom teeth.

"Fine," Conrad said.

"You've got to be getting close now," she said. He'd be finishing up his third year at Baylor this spring, and Cass cut a glance over to him as he set out glasses they'd fill with ice right before the party started.

"I'm thinking of doing law school," he said.

Cass nearly dropped the last of the spoons in her hand, barely managing to catch them before the clattered all over the dishware she'd laid out already. "Law school?" She'd never once envisioned her son becoming a lawyer.

"I've enjoyed my ethics class." He set down the last glass. "My professor said I might consider it. I'm considering it."

"Well..." Cass didn't know what to say. "I—how will you know if you want to do that?"

"Doctor Gerry said to take some pre-law classes. I registered for one next semester. Then I guess I'll know." He gave her a smile that was so quintessentially her son. "Mama, you're worried about this."

"I'm not," Cass said. "I just didn't know you wanted to be a lawyer."

"Yeah, well, I don't think I'm going to be a professional rugby player, so I've got to do something."

"Sure," she said. "You're a really great rugby player, Conrad."

"Yeah, but there's no money in it." He grinned at her. "I might stay in Texas and do summer semester if I like the pre-law class. I might not be able to work as much."

"Your daddy can help you with law school," Cass promised him.

A moment later, the garage door opened, and Harrison called, "I'm home." The sound of his boots hitting the floor followed his statement, and Cass faced him as he entered the kitchen. "It smells good in here," he said.

"Bernardo's," she said as he arrived at the island and lifted the lid on the nearest tray.

"Mm, yes." He grinned at her from across the kitchen. "Steak." He pinched a strip between his fingers and popped it into his mouth. "How'd things go with Theresa?"

"She's going to talk to her board about the colors." Cass very nearly rolled her eyes but refrained. "I didn't know I'd need board approval for literally everything, or I wouldn't have taken her on."

"Hopefully once they're through this part, it'll be smooth sailing." Harrison came around the island and took Cass into his arms. He smelled like the wind and sweat and metal, and Cass absolutely loved it. "I'm gonna go shower, baby. I'll be out in a jiff to help with the rest of the set-up."

"Mm-kay," she said, releasing him.

He grinned at Conrad, fist-bumped him, and asked, "Did you tell her?"

"Just now," Conrad said.

"Good man." Harrison headed into the master suite while Cass stared at her son.

"What?" Conrad finally asked.

"Harry knew about the law school thing before me?"

Her son shrugged. "Your Supper Club knew you were dating him before I did."

Cass's mouth dropped open. "So this is payback for something that happened over a year ago."

Conrad's laughter bubbled out of his mouth. "No, Mama, come on." He drew her into a side-hug and passed her a stack of salad plates to put down. "He happened to wander by my computer as I was looking at my schedule for next semester. It wasn't planned."

Cass got busy again, because when life got confusing, she needed to stay active to hold onto her sanity. Her therapist helped with that too, and by the time she had the plates out, her shock had worn off. "I hope you get the answers you're looking for," she said, trying not to sway him one way or the other.

"Me too," he murmured, her first hint that her ultra-confident, smart, handsome son might not have the world figured out. He always acted like he did, and he got along with everyone, so sometimes, it was hard for Cass to know how he was really feeling.

Harrison had just returned to the kitchen and was laying out serving utensils when the doorbell rang. "They're early," he said. "I'll grab it."

"It's unlocked," Cass said. "We came in that way, because the trays were so big."

She still needed to light the candles to simulate the scent of pine, and the tree needed to be plugged in. She'd debated playing something from her record player tonight, but with the number of people who'd be in the house, she'd decided against it.

Harry jogged toward the front door anyway, because whoever it was hadn't just walked right in. Cass flicked the button to get the lighter to ignite, and she held it to a burnt wick as voices filtered back to her.

She straightened once the first candle had been lit, her eyes landing on Joy. "Oh." She tossed the lighter, not really caring where it landed, and hurried toward her friend. She wrapped Joy in a tight hug, her eyes pressed closed as she breathed in the familiar scent of coconut and sunshine and salty spray.

"You're here," she murmured. "How was everything yesterday?" She stepped back as quickly as she'd invaded

Joy's personal space but kept her hands on Joy's shoulders. "The flight was okay?" She blinked at Joy, because Cass understood the back and forth of flying from Sweet Water Falls to Hilton Head.

"Great," Joy said. "I actually came in a couple of days ago." She backed further out of Cass's embrace, falling to the side of a tall, brown-haired man. She threaded her fingers through his, looked at him, and then returned her attention to Cass. "To see Scott. Have you met Scott Anderson?"

Cass painted a smile on her face, though she wanted to punch the air and tell Joy that she'd known something was up. And of course she'd met Scott. He'd only asked Joy on a couple of dates last summer that she'd refused. The last interaction that Cass knew about between the two of them had happened at Harry's old place, with Scott trying to mow the lawn during Supper Club and Joy putting him in his place.

"Yes, of course I've met Scott. How are you?" She took his offered hand and leaned into him for a semi-hug the way good Southerners did.

"Great," he said. "I hope it's okay that I'm crashing." He shot a look at Joy. "Joy said it would be okay."

"It's absolutely fine," Cass said without missing a beat. "When did—you two are—?" She looked between Scott and Joy and back again.

Joy grinned and then started giggling. "Don't hurt yourself, Cass." She removed her hand from his and curled her arm around his bicep. "We're dating."

Harrison chuckled too, and Conrad silently slid another

place setting onto the table. Cass heard and saw it all, but she still managed to ask, "Did I miss a text?"

"Nope," Joy said. "I figured I'd tell everyone tonight."

Cass cocked her head, all the dots lining up. "Dirty trick," she said. "You knew it wasn't Supper Club and you wouldn't have to explain."

Joy's smile only got bigger, and somehow that tickled Cass as funny. She laughed, and that prompted Joy to do the same. Cass drew her into another hug, sighing out the last of her giggles. "I've really missed you."

"Same," Joy whispered, something extra-tight in her grip telling Cass that she definitely had a lot to say—and she would, when they had some time alone together.

Chapter Eight

B eatrice Turner made it to the top of Cass's steps, glad the porch on this million-dollar beach home was so big. She turned to face her crew, and she held up both hands to get their attention. There were ten of them descending on her friends, and they'd taken two cars to get to this tip of the island.

"Everyone," she called, waving her hands. "Listen up."

Her daughter Meredith joined her on the porch, along with her husband. Stewart put his arm around Meredith almost protectively, and they exchanged a glance that only a married couple can. An entire conversation lived in that moment, but Bea didn't understand it as well as she used to.

"Ted," she said as her middle child laughed loudly with his girlfriend. Bea had cried when her children had all arrived at the beach house where she lived with her husband, Grant. They had Fresco, the mutt Bea had gotten in Texas and then brought here to South Carolina, and she smiled at the dog as it leapt up the steps to her side.

He loved coming here to play with Beryl, and Bea lowered her arms and reached down to pat her pup. She looked at her people again and said, "There are twenty-one of us here tonight. Ten right here. Ten of us. Be...pleasant."

"Mama, are we ever not pleasant?" Curtis asked, a hint of disgust in his voice. That might've been from the way Ted hung all over Courtney, because Bea noticed the daggered glare Curtis sent toward his brother. Ted didn't notice at all, his grin as wide and as sunny as ever.

He'd finished college a couple of years ago, but he wasn't super happy with his job in Dallas. Bea wondered where he'd go next, what he'd do. Ted had always had a good head on his shoulders, and he'd always known exactly what he wanted to do.

Even now, he worked in cybersecurity and would hardly tell her a thing about his job. *Too many classified documents*, he'd say, and Bea never could tell if he was joking or not.

He was far happier on this trip than she'd seen him in a while, and she suspected the beautiful brunette curled into his side had a lot to do with that. Curtis acted like he'd never had a girlfriend before, as the jealousy radiated off him.

"These are my friends," she said. "My Supper Club ladies and their husbands and partners and friends. We can't be animals."

"Thanks a lot," Curtis said. "I promise to be pleasant." He stepped past her and opened the door.

"Starting now," Bea called after him. She looked over to Grant. "He's acting like someone spit in his lemonade."

"It wasn't me," Ted said as he came up the steps and went into the house. Meredith met Bea's eyes while Grant took his daughter and the dog inside.

"Mama." Meredith crossed her arms and looked at Stewart. Bea wasn't sure if she should call for help or just wait for her daughter to keep talking. Then a smile came to her face as she swung her attention back to Bea. "Stewart and I are going to have a baby."

Bea sucked in a breath as her hands flew to cover her mouth. "You are?" She flew into her daughter's arms, her tears ruining her dinner party makeup. She didn't care at all, because this was a big moment.

"That's so exciting." She pulled away and hugged Stewart. "You two are going to be the best parents ever." She beamed at them, noting the soft smiles they exchanged with one another, almost like they were shyly dating and just now telling people about their relationship.

"Hon?" Grant came back out onto the porch as Bea wiped under her eyes. He glanced over to Meredith, who did the same. "What's happening out here?"

"Meredith—" Bea cut off and looked at her daughter. "She—they have some news."

"We're ready to tell people," Stewart said. "Meredith is pregnant, Grant."

Grant's face burst into a smile too, and he let loose one of his hearty laughs. "Wow, that's fantastic." He hugged the happy couple too, and then gestured for them to go inside the house. "Cass is going to start yelling about the air conditioning at any moment," he said. "And Joy has a surprise for you I think you're really going to like."

Bea's eyebrows lifted, dislodging another puddle of tears. She quickly swiped those away and then entered Cass's house alongside Grant. He started to close the door when he said, "Oh, there's Bessie and Sage."

He still let the door settle closed before he accompanied Bea further into the house. She swept the area, almost expecting something to pop out at her. Instead, she found Joy standing beside a handsome man and accepting a drink from him with a starry smile on her face.

Bea's feet came to a complete standstill as she drank in the scene in front of her. If Joy and Scott Anderson were alone, she felt certain they'd take a sip of their bubbly champagne and then lean over to taste the fizz on each other's lips.

As it was, Cass and Harry stared at them, as did Bea and Grant, and all of the teenagers and twenty-somethings in the room.

"Joy," Meredith said, breaking into the snow globe of giggly privacy she and Scott had somehow created. "It is you." She grinned as she advanced toward the woman. "I haven't seen you in so long."

Joy grinned at Meredith, her gaze skating past her to Bea, who cocked her head and lifted her eyebrows as her daughter and her friend hugged.

"Someone's been keeping secrets," Grant murmured in her ear. "I'm gonna go find out what I can from Scott."

Bea said nothing as he eased past her and went into the

kitchen. Meredith turned toward her and brought Joy back into the living room. "I'm due in May," she said. "The very end of May." She beamed at Joy and then Bea. "We find out what the baby is after the New Year."

"That's wonderful," Joy said, sounding very sincere. She stepped in front of Bea, her smile only clicking down one notch. "Why do you look like I've poisoned you?"

"You're dating Scott? I thought you didn't like him."

"Really?" Joy asked, grinning widely again. "That's what you thought?" She laughed as she hugged Bea, who melted upon contact. Joy gave the best hugs in the world, and Bea couldn't stay mad at her over anything.

"How long has this been going on?" she asked, her voice right at Joy's ear.

"Three months," Joy said.

"You're telling her?" Cass sidled up to them. "I couldn't get a word out of her."

"Meredith snuck me away from Scott." Joy reached up and tucked her hair. "I really don't want to repeat myself a bunch of times." She volleyed her gaze between Cass and Bea, all of them looking toward the front door as it opened again.

Sage and Bessie walked in, with Bessie's daughter, Wynona. They all looked like they'd been traveling all day, because they had been. Sage held the leash leading to an enormous, pitch-black dog, who had the happiest face of any canine Bea had ever seen.

"Oh, look at him," Bea gushed as she rushed toward the newcomers. "How was the last leg of the drive?"

"Great," Sage said with a smile. She never got too ruffled over anything, and Bea always loved spending time with her, because she felt more grounded afterward. "He's a real trooper."

"A world traveler," Bea said as she crouched down in front of the Newfoundland. "Just like your name, Gypsy. Yes." The dog's smile rivaled that of any golden retriever, and he barely moved as Beryl—who was a golden retriever—and Fresco—who wasn't—arrived and started up a sniff-fest.

Ghost came trotting after them, and Scott's dog was as sweet as pie. He joined in all the sniffing, and Bea looked up at him as the canines greeted one another.

"Cass will want them to go outside," Grant said. He put his hand on Bea's lower back as she stood, and when their eyes met, he added, "We are *not* getting another dog."

Bea pretended to pout, though she had been about to ask him if they could get a big, black gentle giant like Gypsy. Or maybe just a medium-sized pooch that loved to hang out with them like Ghost. She opened her mouth to argue, and then said, "Fine," instead.

Grant smiled at her, greeted her friends, and took Gypsy for Sage. The other dogs followed along, like the big Newfie was their new king.

Cass and Bea went back outside with Bessie, Sage, and Wynona to get their luggage, and Bea carted a backpack upstairs for Bessie.

"This feels like it has bricks in it," she complained as she hefted it up onto the guest bed on the second floor.

"It's Christmas, Bea," was all Bessie said, and then she

hugged Bea in a proper hello. "Mm, it's so good to see you. I miss you in Sweet Water Falls."

Memories of a past life flashed through Bea's mind. She could see all forty-five of her years in Texas, so many good ones with this woman in it. Her Supper Club. Raising her kids. Beach days, hiking days, graduation days.

So much good existed in that life, and Bea had brought a lot of it to this one—including her friendship with Bessie Clifton. She wanted to hold her forever, committing each moment to memory, but she stepped back, a fresh round of tears pricking her eyes.

"Bea," Bessie said, and she shook her head. "Don't cry."

"It's just—I'm emotional, because Meredith just told me she's pregnant, and it's Christmas, and you're here." She wiped at her face again, glad she hadn't let too much liquid ruin her makeup.

"Meredith is pregnant?" Bessie asked, her face lighting up. "That's great news, Bea."

"I know." She hugged Bessie again, only stepping back when Wynona came into the room. Bessie only had the one daughter, and they looked so much alike with their hazel eyes and blonde-with-a-hint-of-red hair. Wynona let hers grow long and wild, and it started to curl about halfway down her back. Bessie kept hers near her shoulders, and it hung straight and shiny, no waves in sight.

"Are you guys going to be looking at commercial rentals while you're here?" Bea asked.

"You leave no room to just breathe, do you?" Bessie

smiled through the sentence, and she looked over to her daughter.

Wynona said, "Yeah, we're going to be doing some drive-by's tomorrow, and then we'll take the holidays off. We have that realtor friend of Grant's showing us some places next week."

"Ty?" Bea asked. "Isn't he so great?" She drew Wynona and Bessie into a three-way huddle. "And you wouldn't know it from first looking at him, but he's over fifty. I think he and Sage would be amazing together."

Bessie laughed and shook her head again. "There you go, Bea. Setting people up who don't want to be set up."

"Who doesn't want to be set up?" Bea demanded as their trio broke up.

"Sage," Bessie said with plenty of emphasis. "She's perfectly happy with her dog." She looped her arm through Wynona's, and they left the bedroom together. The two of them, along with Sage, were staying here. Joy was staying with Lauren, and Grant had pulled as many of his rentals as he could for her children. The two boys were staying together, and Meredith and Stewart had the first rental house Bea had stayed when she'd originally come to Hilton Head for her cleansing beach vacation.

Then she'd met Grant and fallen in love, and she'd uprooted and relocated her entire life. She didn't regret a moment of it—except for some of the moments she missed with the Supper Club when they met in Texas, and she and Cass had to video-chat in. Lauren lived here now too, and the three of them got together with food while the other three did the same twelve hundred miles away.

It wasn't the same, but it was something, and Bea wanted to cling to the thread of it for as long as she could. Supper Club had been life-saving for her when it had first formed, and then all over again when she'd been going through her divorce. Without her friends...Bea didn't even want to think about where she'd be.

"Mama," Curtis called, and Bea realized she was still standing in one of the guest bedrooms on the second floor. She exited it and looked down the hall just as her youngest gained the top of the stairs.

"What's going on?" she asked. She'd seen her son wear this dark look before. Many times, in fact, when he wasn't getting along with his siblings.

"I can't stay with Ted and Courtney," he growled. "I just can't. They make me sick."

"Honey, they're just in love. It's—"

"Mom, I can't. Harry said they had space here if I want to stay here." Curtis looked at her with his dark blue eyes crackling with thunder and lightning. It rolled through his expression the way storms did through the thick, Texas sky, and Bea sighed.

Her shoulders slumped. "It's fine with me. We'll have to go get your things."

"I can sneak out early tonight," he said. "Take the SUV and go get my stuff. Bring it back."

"You won't have a car here."

"I don't care," Curtis said. "I want to run on the beach with the dogs, and I'll keep Fresco if you want."

Bea reached up and cradled his face in her hand. "Why do they upset you so?" Curtis tried to look away, but Bea held him in place. "Ted hasn't had half as many girlfriends as you, Curtis. What's this really about?"

Curtis dropped his chin, his entire demeanor changing. "I've been dating this girl for a while, and she broke up with me last week," he muttered. "Didn't want to take me home for the holidays to meet her family."

Bea's heart wobbled in her chest. "I'm so sorry, son. Was it Bianca?"

"Yeah."

She drew Curtis into a hug. He'd dated a girl named Gracie a couple of years ago too, and they'd gotten serious before she'd called things off too. Curtis had been out with a string of young women then, with nothing much sticking until Bianca. "I'm so sorry, son."

"I just need a break from how perfect they are together," Curtis said. "Plus, I think Teddy's gonna ask her to marry him on this trip, and I just don't want to stay with them."

Bea stepped back and nodded. Ted had asked her about a proposal a few weeks ago, and Bea had told him she'd be delighted if he asked Courtney to be his wife. It hadn't happened yet, and she wasn't sure what Ted was waiting for. He'd seemed sure when he'd called, but he updated her the least about his life.

"Don't make a big deal out of it," she said.

"I was hopin' you would tell them." Curtis raised his gaze to her, and he had the good sense to look sheepish.

Bea sighed an oversized sigh and turned him toward the steps. "Fine," she said. "I'll talk to him. Now, come on. If Lauren and Blake are here, Joy will be talking about her new boyfriend, and I don't want to miss anything."

"Oh, yeah, they got here a few minutes ago," Curtis said.

Bea's pulse leapt against the back of her tongue. "Great," she said, practically flying down the stairs. "I'm missing it right now then."

Chapter Nine

J oy looked past Lauren to the whirlwind that was Bea as she scurried down the steps. She scanned the room in a single second and then strode toward where the group of Supper Club ladies had congregated.

As Bea moved toward her, Joy flicked a look into the kitchen, where Scott had been cornered by Harry, Grant, and surprisingly, Conrad.

Bea arrived out of breath and asked, "What did I miss?"

"Nothing," Bessie said. "Joy won't say a word."

Joy needed another drink, but she'd already consumed one, and she wasn't a big drinker to begin with. She lifted her empty flute to her mouth anyway, disappointed when she only got a drop against her tongue.

"Why is it so hot in here?" she asked.

"That's just you," Cass said.

"Maybe it's the fires of hell licking against your feet for

keeping your boyfriend a secret," Sage said in the most matter-of-fact tone on the planet.

Joy blinked in surprise. Nothing really ever ruffled Sage, so to hear her speak with that level of...mocking. Disdain. Something...stabbed right into Joy's heart.

"You said you were going to look for something to rent here," she said. "That none of your kids wanted the hobby farm."

"Yes, well, I obviously didn't, did I?" Sage gave her a smile, but the flint remained in her eyes. "It's fine, Joy. Tell us about Scott."

Her breath shuddered on the way in. "I—I didn't know how things would go at first," she said. "I texted him at the end of September. We've been chatting and calling and such since. I flew in a day early to see him."

Her throat threatened to close up on her. "I honestly thought that might be the death knell for us. It's easy to call at night, right? He doesn't disrupt my day. I live my life, and then have some fun conversations at night."

Joy could admit she liked having a long-distance boyfriend. It was almost the best of both worlds—she didn't have to make a lot of sacrifices to have Scott in her life, and she wasn't lonely in her downtime either. She hated thinking that way, but it was true.

"Anyway, it wasn't like that at all when I got here. It was like...explosions. I kissed him on the first date, and—"

"Before or after dinner?" Lauren asked.

Joy gave her a glare that felt dark as night as it left her eyes. "After," she said. "We didn't rehearse this."

"You have something to rehearse with her?" Cass asked.

Joy surveyed her friends. They were all taking this news well, she'd give them that. Maybe not Sage, surprising as that was, and she hadn't anticipated Cass to care if Lauren knew about Scott before she did.

But she sure seemed like she did. "I maybe should've texted all of you at once," she said. "But Lauren is relentless, and she kept calling and texting the day I got here—and I couldn't lie to her."

"Oh, so I have to be relentless." Bea folded her arms, the frown between her pretty blue eyes almost comical.

Joy gave her attitude right back to her. "As if you aren't already."

"*I* didn't know about you and Scott," Bea said.

"I was staying with Lauren," Joy said, wishing she'd done things differently when it came to her friends. "I felt guilty lying right to her face. None of y'all asked if I was seeing someone or not, let alone if that man was Scott."

"Why would we—?"

"Ladies," Bessie said over Cass, her voice much quieter and yet powerful enough to get Cass to go mute. She smiled at Joy. "I think it's wonderful that Joy is dating again." She stood next to Joy, so her view into the kitchen rivaled Joy's. "He's hot, isn't he? Didn't we want her to go out with him last summer?"

Bessie looked around the congregated women. "Why are we upset about this? Because we couldn't pepper Joy with questions for the last three months? Don't we want our friend to be happy?"

Joy wanted to throw in a, "Yeah, don't you?" but she kept her mouth shut.

Instead, she snaked one arm around Bessie and said, "Thank you, Bess. You're the best."

Bea softened, and she nodded. "Of course I want you to be happy, Joy." She glanced over her shoulder to the men in the kitchen. "You like him?"

"Yes," Joy whispered, because maybe if she didn't say it too loudly, it wouldn't be too true.

"He's like the night," Cass commented, a thoughtful note in her voice. "To your day."

"What do you mean?" Joy asked. "He definitely laughs more than I do. He loves everyone, and they love him." Just watching him grin and chat and laugh with his friends told her that. "I'm optimistic, but serious. He's..."

"Just a little different than that," Cass said. "That's all I meant."

"Opposites attract," Lauren said with a smile. She lifted her hand and covered her heart. "I didn't mean to tag-team you. I just wanted you to tell the girls about the kiss *after* the date." She smiled, and the natural beauty Lauren was shone through. "So they'd know you weren't rushing things."

Joy's seriousness cracked. "You don't think kissing on the first date is rushing things?"

"Not after three months of talking," Lauren said.

"Concur," Sage said. "I *am* happy for you, Joy." She hugged her and turned to face the rest of the house. "Now, are we eating or what? It feels like a junior high gymnasium in here. Boys on one side. Girls on the other." She went into the kitchen to mix things up while Joy laughed with Bessie.

"Gymnasium?" Bessie asked. "Do people still use that word?"

"Mom," Wynona said. "What's a gymnasium?"

That got all of them to laugh, and Joy felt the tension lighten from her shoulders. Cass turned to Lauren and said, "I heard you got engaged in the grocery store."

"I have held nothing back," Lauren said. "I told you all that he announced it over the PA system." She looked down at her diamond ring as she spoke, something so pure and radiant shining from her.

"I thought it was happening at the Country Club," Cass said. "I didn't realize he'd called an audible."

"Sweetheart," Harrison said as he joined the group. "Should we eat?"

"Yes." Cass gave him a quick kiss and moved into the kitchen. Thankfully, that eased the burden on Joy even further, and she found herself holding out her glass for Harry to pour her a refill.

"He seems to like you, Joy," Harry said almost under his breath. He took a sip of his own drink as his wife started to detail the food that she'd bought for that evening. Harry cut a look at her out of the corner of his eye, and Joy's curiosity piqued.

"Harry?" she asked.

"He'll act like he's okay when he's not," Harry said. "Just...keep an eye on him, would you?" With that, he moved away before Joy could answer.

She blinked, trying to figure out what he'd said. She took another sip of champagne, thinking maybe the alcohol had made her mind slower than normal. Bea's children had joined her on the island this year, but Cass's daughters were absent, just like Joy's sons. She had video calls with them both on Christmas Day, and her heart ached to see her boys, their wives, and her grandbabies.

Just when she thought she might be able to erase the physical distance between her and Scott, something—in this case, someone—always drew her back to Texas.

"He'll act like he's okay when he's not," she mumbled to herself. Scott always seemed to be looking for the next person to talk to, the next cluster of people to bond with. She hovered on the outskirts of a party, content to stand with people she knew and was extremely comfortable with.

She wouldn't sit down first tonight, because then people would have to choose to sit by her. No, she'd rather choose who she sat beside, and she waited for Bea to get situated with her children before she approached the table.

Scott met her as he came out of the kitchen, and he asked, "Well?" as he took her champagne glass and set it on the counter.

"Well, they all know now," she said with a smile. "And we're still alive, so I think it went well."

He pulled out the chair beside Bessie for her, and after she'd sat down, Scott took the seat next to her. Grant sat on his other side, and Joy decided that was perfect. Grant was as outgoing as Scott, and they'd been friends for a while now.

Across from her, Wynona sat beside Curtis, the two of them laughing and talking already. Tommy and Shelby were the lone children there that evening, and they too sat down on the end of the table with Bessie and Joy.

"So," Joy said, determined to have a good time tonight and talk to someone, even if some of her friends felt a little betrayed. She'd known they'd react this way—in fact, every single reaction she'd gotten that evening had been precisely in character with who her friends were.

Cass and Bea demanding to know more. Bessie standing up for Joy. Lauren wanting to make sure that Joy was heard and understood. Sage, well, Sage had acted a little out of character. Joy had expected her to be the happy-go-lucky woman she was, but she'd even seemed a little miffed to be left in the dark about Joy's relationship.

She looked over to Sage, who sat on the other side of the table beside Wynona. "Is it because you think I might leave Sweet Water Falls?"

Sage looked at her, everything about her reminding Joy of the earth she loved to work in. Her eyes, her hair, even her olive skin seemed like she'd covered it in mud, let it dry, and then come out stained.

Sage's eyes blazed for a moment, and then she said, "Partially, yes. And not that long ago, if this was me or Bessie or even Lauren, you'd have been upset."

"I know." Joy reached across the table and covered Sage's hand with hers. "I know, Sage. I'm sorry."

"I'm not really upset," Sage said with a sigh. "I'm just...

Lauren was right. Last year, when she said things were changing. They are. They have. They did." She looked down the table to Cass and Harrison, then Bea's children and over to Bea and Grant. "They still are."

"Ow," a woman said from down the table, and Joy's attention got diverted that way. The brunette that Ted had brought with him took something out of her mouth. "What in the world is this?" She held it up, then shrieked. "Teddy!"

The clattering of silverware and the scraping of chairs happened in a flurry, and more than Joy exclaimed over the ruckus as Courtney threw herself into Ted's arms. He laughed like something hilarious had just happened, and then he said, "Where'd you toss that ring, baby?"

The dots got connected for Joy at that point, and she drew in a sharp breath. "Was that a diamond ring?"

"Seems like it," Scott said as more people at the main table got to their feet. A hunt for the diamond ensued, with Courtney apologizing over and over while every one of them looked for the ring. Joy sat down at the other end of the folding tables, but she got up along with everyone else, suddenly praying that the ring would be found.

What a terrible thing to lose, and she kept looking at Ted, who was obviously trying to find the ring without looking like it mattered if the ring was found. Finally, Sage said, "There it is! It's on Gypsy's back!" She pointed to her fluffy black dog, and every eye zeroed in on him. "It's stuck in his fur."

Harrison stood closest to Gypsy, who waited at the back sliding door, and he reached out and plucked the ring from the mass of black fur. Pinching it between his fingers, he grinned at Ted as he handed him the diamond.

Ted took it, wiped it clean with his napkin, and then fell to both knees, right there in the dining room with everyone watching. He held up the ring and said, "Courtney, I'm madly in love with you. We've met your family and survived, and mine and survived, and now I want to build our own family together. Will you be my wife?"

"Yes," she said amidst simultaneous laughter and tears. "Yes, of course I will." Joy applauded, one of the first to do so, and everyone else joined in as Ted slid the diamond onto Courtney's finger and then pulled her down to kiss her.

As they all retook their seats and started straightening plates and forks and glasses, Scott glanced over to Joy. "There's never a dull moment around here, is there?"

Joy snorted and then laughed. "No, sir," she said. "There sure isn't."

He leaned closer, his happiness residing in his eyes. "Christmas Eve with just the two of us will sure be boring then."

"Oh, I don't know," Joy said. "We might be able to have a conversation that doesn't look like we're planning to elope by New Year's." She grinned at him and straightened, feeling the weight of all of her Supper Club friends. Sure enough, they all watched her and Scott—even Wynona was staring— and Joy very nearly rolled her eyes.

In the next breath, the party resumed as normal, and Joy turned to Bessie. "Are you still working on that bread book?"

"Here and there," Bessie said, ducking her head. In

Bessie-speak, that meant "Not really," and Joy didn't push the issue. Bessie could argue back if she had to, but she often didn't feel the need.

Joy wasn't the type to press anyway, and she smiled as she said, "I think I'm going to finish up my teaching degree in the next couple of months."

"Joy," Bessie said with pure delight in her voice. "That's fantastic. Good for you."

Joy swelled under the compliment, and she said, "Thanks, Bess."

"What does that look like?" Scott asked, and Joy turned to him again.

"I'm doing my classes online," she said. "Then I just have to apply to waive my student teaching, because I literally work in a school, with students, and then if that gets approved, I graduate. Finally."

"That's great, baby." He sounded genuine too, and he didn't ask what she planned to do with her new degree. He never asked her if she planned to stay in Texas or move here, and Joy swore it was all she thought about.

She didn't want to ask him right now, in front of everyone, because there were too many women here with excellent hearing. *So tomorrow*, she told herself. She and Scott had planned a romantic Christmas Eve dinner for just the two of them, mostly so Blake and Lauren could have their romantic Christmas Eve dinner too.

Tommy was going to his mother's just for the night, and then he'd be back in the afternoon on Christmas Day, and

Joy didn't want to be a burden to Lauren's first and only engaged holiday.

"What did you hear about your place?" she asked.

"What's wrong with your place?" Grant asked as he lifted a fish taco to his mouth.

"It flooded," Scott said. "It's still drying out. I'm at the Liberty Lodge through the holidays. They take dogs, and I've got Ghost."

"Where is he tonight?" Bea asked.

"He's with the other dogs outside," Scott said. "I'll take him with me after this." He dunked a chip in the chunky guacamole and stuck the whole thing in his mouth.

"What are your plans tomorrow?" Bea asked. "Are you two coming to the Beach Benefit?" She dripped sour cream over her taco and picked it up.

"I don't know what the Beach Benefit is," Joy said, cutting a look toward Scott. He was still crunching through his chip, but he shook his head.

"I donated a bunch of money," Scott said. "Or Jeff did. I've never actually been."

"Well, they buy presents with all the donations," Bea said, her voice a tad on the condescending side. As if giving money wasn't enough. "Then those have to be wrapped and sorted and delivered. That's happening tomorrow, if you two are free."

"I doubt they're free, hon," Grant said softly. "We'll be at the beach about lunchtime too," he said louder. "If anyone wants to join us there." He looked down the table to Shelby, who nodded with a smile.

"It's not exactly beach weather," Scott said. "But I always love a good stroll in the sand." He looked at Joy, who absolutely wouldn't say no to holding his hand while they walked on the beach.

"Seems like that would fit my blueprint," she said without giving away anything, and Scott laughed.

He took her hand in his, kissed the back of it, and looked right into her eyes. "I'll bring breakfast in the morning, okay?"

"Not before eight-thirty," she said. "Okay?"

"Your wish is my command," he said, bowing his head slightly. He went back to eating and chatting, and Joy did too, but she couldn't help wondering what else her blueprint needed to have before she could start building.

She didn't even know what she was building. A new life here on Hilton Head? Having her degree would help that. Living here would bring her closer to Scott. So many things that seemed so crinkled would be ironed flat if she could only decide what she was trying to build.

She loved the energy in Cass's house. The magic of love, family, and laughter. She wanted to be with her friends all the time, and Bessie was already thinking about moving here too.

Why couldn't Joy admit that she was too? What was she holding onto in Texas, exactly? In moments like this, with the soft white lights on the Christmas tree, and so much cheer in the air, Joy couldn't remember.

She wanted the Hilton Head beach life, and as she finished dinner and exclaimed over a Santa Claus that a baker in North Dakota had made out of sourdough rolls, Joy finally conceded to herself that her beach blueprint was for a new life here on Hilton Head Island.

And possibly a brand-new life with the gorgeous Scott Anderson...if the blueprint called for him.

Chapter Ten

S cott woke the next morning when his phone rang. He
groaned and rolled over at the familiar ring tone. He
answered the call from his brother with, "If you're not in the
hospital, I'm going to put you there."

He normally didn't mind an early-morning wake-up
call. He and Jeff got up brutally early in the summer to beat
the Carolina heat, and he enjoyed getting done with his work
in the early afternoon. Their winter hours, however, allowed
more time for sleeping in, and it was the holidays. They
weren't even working today, tomorrow, or the next day.

With Joy in town, Scott had also arranged to be gone
from the landscaping business he owned and operated for an
additional two days beyond that. Then he'd be back in the
truck, out in the community, mowing lawns, and clearing
beds of pine needles, and countless other tasks that his
clients paid him to do.

"Bad news," Jeff said, and that made Scott sit up and

take notice. The words and the grave tone of his brother's voice.

"You really are in the hospital," Scott said, a wave of guilt nearly sucking the breath from his lungs.

"No," Jeff said. "Mark's coming tomorrow."

The air did vanish completely from Scott's body then. He couldn't speak. Couldn't think.

"You have to still come," Jeff said, and he started talking faster. "Momma wants us all there, and it'll be okay. I'll be there with my family, and Lily is bringing her family and her husband's parents. Mark is one person, and Momma and Daddy will seat you way down on the other end."

Scott let his brother continue to outline why it would be okay for him and Mark to be in the same room together for a meal on Christmas Day. Finally, he blurted out, "Stop talking," and Jeff cut off mid-sentence.

They sat on the line in silence, though Scott's heartbeat reverberated through his chest, his organs, his ears. He couldn't...do this. Couldn't be in the same room as Mark.

"He's not with Melanie anymore?" he asked, though he wasn't sure why that was the single thought that had emerged in the tangle of ideas in his head.

"He said they broke up six months ago," Jeff said.

Part of Scott rejoiced, and he had a distinct feeling of vindication. A scoff fell from his mouth, but he wasn't sure why. No other words came forth, because a very dangerous and very terrifying idea had just occurred to him.

"I can't bring Joy then," he said. "I was going to bring her. Introduce her to everyone." Well, obviously not everyone, as his younger brother hadn't been home for Christmas in a decade now. Mark had a problem with everyone in the family, and he'd been marching to the beat of his own drum for his entire life.

He'd left the South and gone north and west, and if Scott heard him start another sentence with, "In Seattle, we..." he might sock him in the mouth.

And now Jeff wanted him to endure Christmas dinner with him?

"I can't," Scott said.

"You can't be alone on Christmas."

"I won't be alone," Scott said. "I'm sure Joy's friends will have something going on."

Jeff sighed, the noise almost like he was trying to blow out the fifty candles on his birthday cake—a party Scott had attended and Mark had not.

"Maybe he wants to apologize," Jeff suggested.

That made Scott laugh, and the sound of it was full of bitterness and pain. Anger, even. "I doubt it, Jeff. Come on."

"Fine," Jeff said, his tone in the resignation department now. "He won't apologize. But he didn't win, Scott. Row says *she* ended things with him."

Scott shook his head. "I don't care." His statement was only partially true. He didn't care what Mark did with his life. He didn't care to see him again. He didn't care if Mark was well or not well.

At the same time, he really did care about his brother. They'd grown up together. They'd been friends once. They were family. Of course Scott cared about Mark, but he knew it was for all the wrong reasons.

He only cared to know if something bad happened to him. Then, Scott could feel like he was getting what he deserved for all the terrible things he'd done and tried to do to him and Jeff.

"I don't know how you're as civil to him as you are," Scott said. He stood and groaned as his muscles and bones found where they were supposed to be. He wasn't exactly a neat freak, and most of his clothes that weren't covered in grass clippings, mud, and sand ended up draped over the recliner in the corner of his bedroom. His dirty things got stripped in the laundry room and put straight into the washing machine, so he did have some sense of cleanliness.

But he never made his bed, and he kicked off his shoes and left them wherever they landed. Since he lived alone, he could usually find what he needed with little fuss. Besides, he was in a hotel right now, and it didn't matter if he'd dropped his clothes over the back of the desk chair last night and left his shoes by the bathroom door.

He didn't spend much time at home anyway, because Scott was the type who liked to be going, going, going. Surprise actually coursed through him when he moved over to the coffee maker in the tiny slip of a kitchen in the room and saw that it was almost seven o'clock.

Jeff hadn't said anything about how he could still talk to Mark and be nice, and Scott didn't need to sit on an open call where nothing was being said. "I have to go," he said. "I'm meeting Joy in a little bit for breakfast."

It was Christmas Eve, and Scott didn't want anything to ruin the next five days. He wouldn't allow it, because he'd lose Joy back to her job and life in Texas before long, and he wanted to carve out a big enough presence in her life to court her back to Hilton Head.

He'd seen Grant do it with his wife, and Scott couldn't help dreaming of a similar result for himself. The first time he'd seen Joy—really seen her—he'd been enamored with the woman. She'd refused him, which only made her more attractive to him, and he'd enjoyed the game of getting her name and number and asking her out.

She'd said no, but Scott had been told no before. He simply hadn't given up. He may have moved on and gone out with other women, but the moment Joy had texted...

"I'm nice to him, because he's our brother," Jeff said. "And he didn't try to steal *my* business and *my* girlfriend."

Scott's hands stumbled over the can of wet dog food he'd just opened to feed to Ghost, and some of the gravy spilled onto his fingers. "I have to go," he said again, and he put the phone on the tiny counter in the hotel room where he and Ghost were staying and stabbed at the red button to end the call.

He fed his dog with angry motions and washed his hair in the shower with aggressive scrubbing. By the time he was shaved and dressed and had leashed Ghost for their morning run, Scott mostly felt like himself again.

Except he wasn't. Mark had changed him when he'd gone behind his back to try to buy the landscaping business and he'd lured Jeff's girlfriend to his side too. Apparently, blood wasn't thicker than water in those cases, and Mark had disappeared from Scott's life the same way his girlfriend had.

He'd had time to get over it. He'd worked with a therapist for nine months to talk everything through. He'd gotten the landscaping company, and he'd turned to working long hours to avoid going home alone at night, and he only dated women superficially.

"Until Joy," he murmured to himself as he waited for Ghost to find the perfect place to take care of his business.

The sun had been up for about thirty minutes, and Scott realized his morning routine was all off. He normally ran first and showered second, and he told himself he could shower again, and he'd be the only one to know.

He and Ghost reached the harder packed sand, and Scott picked up his walk to a jog. Ghost trotted alongside him, the way he always did. He didn't know what he thought about. He just let the music pound in his ears as he put one foot in front of the other.

He hadn't set his odometer either, and this wasn't his normal running beach. Still, his body knew when to turn around and go back, and he returned to the Liberty Lodge and re-showered and re-dressed for the day.

While he and Joy had planned to spend Christmas Eve together, they hadn't made set-in-stone plans, so he texted her as he looked at Ghost. *Am I bringing my dog? Do you want to go to the Beach Benefit? The beach with friends? What are we thinking today?*

Joy called, and Scott grinned, finally relaxing since the

last time his phone had rung. "Hey, sweetheart. Merry Christmas Eve."

"Merry Christmas Eve," she said, her voice like sweet music. "I think bring Ghost. Let's just have a relaxing day. Lauren says we can eat breakfast in her garden, and then we can maybe go do a little shopping. Just walk around. Then yeah, we can go to the beach with everyone for a bit."

"That all sounds good," he said.

"I just got an email from Bordeaux's," she said. "They confirmed our reservation for four-thirty. I know that's early for dinner, but they're closing early tonight."

"I can eat any time," he said. "Especially at Bordeaux's."

Joy wore a smile in her voice as she said, "So you've bragged before." She laughed lightly and added, "Are you on your way?"

"Almost," he said. "I'll pack a quick bag for Ghost, and then yeah, we'll be on the way. I have to stop and get break-fast, and then I'll be there."

"See you soon," she said, and Scott ended the call and got the things he needed for his dog. He took Ghost to work with him every day too, so he had bowls and water bottles in the truck, along with extra leashes and waste bags. He still put everything, including his sunglasses and a ball cap, into a backpack before he left his room and hit the highway.

He stopped at McCall's to grab some fresh fruit, and then he drove through Gourmet Goods for the pastries and coffee. Finally, he pulled into the parking lot at Omelettos, and dashed inside to pick up the order he'd put in last night.

With everything in his possession, he drove to Lauren's

house, where Joy was staying. Two SUVs sat in the driveway, so Scott pulled up and parked along the curb in front of the house. He looped the bag of fruit over his arm, then picked up the blue pastry box and balanced the to-go containers with their omelets on top of that.

He couldn't get both coffees, and he dang near dropped everything when Joy said, "I can help."

He spun toward her, not having heard her footsteps in the grass. She wore a gorgeous dress in a deep pine green that made her eyes and hair look brighter than ever. "Wow," he said. "Someone looks amazing in green."

Joy's smile filled her face, and she said, "Thank you."

He backed out of the doorway and let her lean in to get the coffee. "Around the back?"

"If you don't think it'll be too cold."

He reached back in to finally motion at Ghost that he could get down. "It'll be fine," he said. "Is Lauren still here?"

"She just got in the shower." Joy followed him toward the garage, and they went through a gate that led into the backyard.

Scott, ever the landscaper, scoped out everything as Ghost started doing the same thing, only with his nose. Scott usually found lots of things that needed tending to or that he'd do differently, but he whistled in appreciation at the yard. "This place is incredible."

Lauren had perfectly trimmed bushes along the back fence, with two tall magnolia trees that would bloom beautifully in the springtime. The grass was clipped and dormant for the cooler months, and she had a cleared patch for a vegetable garden that had clearly been attended to. Nothing sat out of place, not a single tool or glove or stone, and Scott could appreciate that.

A patio had been bricked off in front of a sliding glass door, and it held an elegant black wrought iron table and chairs. He slid the pastry box and omelets onto that, and then got the bag of fruit off his arm.

Joy set down their coffee, and together, they faced the yard. "Lauren likes working out here."

Scott slid his arm around her and said, "You like working in the yard too, if I remember right." She'd sent him pictures of her roses and flower beds.

"Yeah," she said. "I do." She looked up to him. "I suppose I can still do that here, right?"

"Of course," he said, tiptoeing ever nearer to the conversation they needed to have about their relationship. The long-distance thing was okay for now, but Scott definitely wanted her to be closer. He wanted to see her every day, not once every quarter. He wanted this relationship to be the one that lasted forever.

He gazed down at her, so many things teeming on the tip of his tongue. Instead of saying any of them, he leaned down and she tipped up, and he kissed her. He had to believe that she could feel the same zipping energy flowing in her veins that he did in his. This couldn't be one-sided.

He didn't trust himself with women, but as he continued to kiss Joy, he amended the thought. He hadn't trusted himself before her, but Joy Bartlett was changing everything about him, and he just had to be brave enough to let her.

"So," he murmured after she broke the kiss but didn't step away. "We might not be able to go to my parents' tomorrow for Christmas dinner."

Joy pulled away completely then, shock in her face. "Why not?"

Scott sighed and looked out at the immaculate lawn and garden again, his eyes following his pup as Ghost continued to explore. *Why not?*

What a great question—and it happened to be one he didn't know how to answer.

Chapter Eleven

⁓

I nstead of answering the question she'd asked him, Scott said, "I brought breakfast for everyone," and turned back to the table. "I thought Lauren and Blake were eating with us."

"They are," Joy said, watching him. Scott kept his face ducked away from her, and Joy didn't know what to make of it. "Scott."

"Blake will be here in about fifteen minutes," Lauren said, interrupting them. Joy turned toward her as she came outside from her bedroom door, her hair falling over her shoulders in dry waves. She obviously hadn't washed it, though she wore a dark purple robe. "I'll get dressed and be out in a few minutes." She smiled at Joy and Scott. "Hey, Scott."

"Lauren, your backyard is spectacular." His voice went back to its regular, upbeat tone, and Joy knew then that something had definitely turned him into a quieter version of himself.

"That patio is new," she said, beaming across the space between them. "And the sliding door off the dining room and the whole patio set."

"It's all amazing," Scott said. "It really fits with the space." He glanced at Ghost as he jumped up onto the patio. "I hope he's okay here. I can put him on a leash."

"Thank you, and Ghost is fine here. My cats don't come outside much anyway." She waved and turned back to the house. "Okay, I'll be right out."

Joy opened the blue pastry box while she waited for the door to slide closed down by Lauren. "Are you going to tell me why we can't go see your family tomorrow?"

"It's..." Scott let out his breath measure by measure, the sound one, long leak. "It's my brother."

"I thought you owned your landscaping company with Jeff." Joy spread out a napkin, one for each person, tipped the lid of the box back, and reached for the plastic bag. She had no idea what she'd find inside, and the strawberries, oranges, and tangerines were a surprise. "You got fresh fruit?"

"There's a cute little stand on the highway up here from the lodge. She said the oranges are from here, but everything else is from Georgia and Florida."

Joy looked up at him, feeling very open. Their eyes met, and Joy reached over and cupped his face in her palm. "What's going on for Christmas?"

"My younger brother is named Mark. I haven't spoken to him in, uh, six years now."

Joy's eyebrows flew up before she could control her reaction. "You have a younger brother," she said. Scott had not mentioned his younger brother at all. Only Jeff, who was a couple years older than Scott, and a sister named Lily that was almost Scott's Irish twin. She was only thirteen months younger than Scott, and according to him, they got along well.

He'd never mentioned a younger brother.

"I'll give you the five-minute version," Scott said almost under his breath as he set out the fruit in the top of the pastry box. "And we can talk more about it on the beach." He finally allowed himself to meet her gaze. "Okay?"

"Okay," Joy said. "And if you don't want to say anything right now, I understand." She certainly had things she hadn't aired for him yet, including some of her past relationship issues with her ex-husband. She'd read once that people took their first-marriage problems into their second one, and Joy wanted to be very, very careful about not doing that.

It was why she really wanted to see a blueprint of how her life here would be lived *before* she actually started living it. She called herself cautious; last night, after Scott had dropped her off, Lauren had called her "unreasonable."

"Maybe you can be thinking about it, and we can decide what to do." His phone chimed once, then twice, then several more times. *Bring, bring, bring-bring!* "That's my mother." He pulled his phone from his pocket and silenced it. "She'll lecture me the same way Jeff did when he called this morning."

Joy pulled out a seat and took it, then reached for the coffees. She removed the four of them from the holder and took hers and then handed Scott his. He didn't sit down and start sipping but wandered to the edge of the patio.

"The last woman I dated seriously was Melanie Baker. This was before the landscaping company. Before...well, pretty much before I became the man you know and have been talking to."

Joy took a sip of her coffee, noting the caramel notes that usually relaxed the tension in her neck and shoulders. She tried to breathe out slowly, the taste of mocha caramel still on her tongue. Some of the tightness dissipated, but then Scott took a breath, and she tensed right up again.

"I used to date with the intent to find someone to marry, but after everything happened...I stopped." He stroked Ghost absently, almost like he didn't know he was doing it.

Questions flew to Joy's mind, but she held her tongue. She only got a few minutes for this explanation, and she didn't want to derail Scott.

"My brother, Mark, decided he liked Melanie too. She cheated on me with him, and they've been together since. Until recently, I guess. I don't know. I haven't spoken to him for a while." He turned to face her. "When Harry listed the landscaping part of his company for sale, Mark tried to buy it out from under me. Jeff found out about it, and we were able to get it before Harry could sell to a mysterious, out-of-town buyer."

"So Mark doesn't live here on the island."

"No." Scott shook his head and took the few steps to the table. He sat next to her and wrapped his long fingers around his cup of coffee. "He hasn't been back for any holidays or anything in years. He's been in the Pacific Northwest for ten years."

"Then how did he and Melanie meet?"

"I used to talk to him," Scott said. "I took her to Seattle one year for her birthday so she could meet him. We were serious, you know? Anyway, I guess it started then. I don't know. I didn't ask for details." He wore a look of absolute misery on his face, and Joy wanted nothing more than to cheer him up.

"And we can't go to Christmas dinner because Mark and Melanie are going to be there?"

"Rowena—that's Jeff's wife—said they broke up. It's just Mark coming." Scott looked away, such a look of sadness on his face. Or regret. Something. No matter what, Joy enjoyed seeing him without his laughter guard in place. She liked the happy-go-lucky side of him, but she wanted a real life partner too.

She curled her fingers into his, and a soft smile touched his lips. "I'll do what you want, Scott," she said. "No pressure from me, okay?"

"I know you want to meet my family."

"I want you to have a good holiday," she said, employing her motherly tone. The one she used to use on her sons to get them to fall into line. "I want *us* to have a happy Christmas together. If that's just us tomorrow, then that's fine. We'll find something to eat, and we'll exchange our presents, and it will be good. Okay?"

His eyes met hers, and they shone with that blue electricity just like they had the first time she'd met him. "Joy, you're my favorite person in the world."

She grinned at him and leaned toward him. "I kinda like you too." She touched her forehead to his and whispered, "I know I'm usually the one that's a mess, trying to make decisions about what to do. What we should do, or not do, or when I should fly to the island or whatever."

"You're not a mess," he whispered.

"It's kinda nice to know you have some real things you're dealing with in your life too," she said anyway.

"I maybe work too much," he said.

"What do you mean?" she asked.

"I'm coming outside," Blake said loudly. "I have orange juice and milk." He stepped out onto the patio from the dining room part of the house, carrying a half-gallon of milk and a pitcher of juice. Lauren followed him, now wearing a sundress in green and white and a big sunhat with a wide brim, carrying a plate with butter on it.

They piled everything onto the table, claimed their coffee, and took their seats as greetings and hellos were said. Once the silence fell again, Lauren said, "It feels like we interrupted something."

"No," Joy said at the same time as Scott. He actually looked relieved to stop talking about the real things in his life. "Nope. We're good." Scott grinned and looked at Blake. "You got Tommy to his mom?"

"Yeah, bright and early." He yawned, which made Joy smile. "We were on the first ferry over to Carter's Cove. He'll come home tomorrow afternoon."

"Lauren said he got settled into school okay," Joy said, and Blake and Lauren looked at her.

"He seems to be adjusting well," Blake confirmed.

Joy smiled and then reached for Lauren's diamonded hand. "Did you get us tickets to tour Island Aisle?"

Lauren had just taken a bite of a buttered croissant, and she lurched forward as she pulled it from her mouth. Her eyes got big, and she nodded. "Soon," she managed to say around her mouthful of food, and Joy giggled as she reached into the box for one of the chocolate croissants she loved.

She couldn't see one. "They were out already, sweetheart," Scott said. "I got you the blackberry lime tart. Give it a try." He took out the pastry for her and passed her a plastic spoon. The crust looked positively scrumptious with its golden brown color and the dark blackberries glistening in the Christmas Eve sunshine.

Joy took a bite, the tart lime custard divine on her tongue. Sweet and creamy, with that tang that made her look at Scott with delight running through her veins instead of blood.

"I got tickets for early next week," Lauren said. "Scott will be back at work, and I won't be stealing you from him."

Joy didn't know what to say to that, so she just took another bite of her tart and smiled with her lips closed. As breakfast continued in a slow, carefree way with her and her friends, Joy thought she could really get used to mornings like this on Hilton Head.

She reminded herself that this was Christmas, and none of them were working that day. She picked up napkins, the images from that peaceful breakfast in her head. They made a very good addition to her beach blueprint, even if they only happened on holidays and weekends.

While Lauren lingered outside with Scott and Blake, Joy took the trash into the kitchen. She tugged her phone out of her purse and tapped to open her Internet browser. She'd never allowed herself to see how many elementary schools there were here in Hilton Head. She assumed at least one, and she had checked to see if her teaching degree would work here or not.

"Three," she said aloud. Her job possibilities shrank, but Joy didn't have many more choices in Texas. In fact, Sweet Water Falls only had three elementary schools too. So the floor plan for her blueprint was exactly the same, whether she moved here or stayed there.

Move here or stay there?

The question seemed to be on repeat in her mind, and Joy had no idea how to answer it.

"Sweetheart," Scott said. "Blake just said he has some tickets to a movie premier if we want to go with them to see *The Grump Before Christmas*." All of his more solemn characteristics had melted away, and he grinned at her as he came into the house. "It's in an hour, and we can still meet up with everyone at the beach later."

"Can we?" she asked.

Lauren entered the house with the juice pitcher. "I texted Bea, and she said they won't even get there until twelve-thirty."

"Grant loves the beach," Blake added. "They'll be there all afternoon. It's easy entertainment for everyone."

Joy included herself in that category, and she saw no reason not to take in a movie before they went to the beach —other than she wanted to hear more of Scott's tale about his unmentioned younger brother, and she'd have to wait to do that.

"All right," she said. "But I want a lot of buttery popcorn." She grinned at Scott. "Movie theater popcorn is my love language."

He laughed and wrapped her in a hug. "Good to know, my Joy," he said through his chuckles. "Good to know."

Joy sure liked it when he called her his, and she could definitely see that becoming part of her permanent blueprint too. Now, if she could figure out what kind of house she wanted her life to emulate, she could actually start putting the pieces of her blueprint in place.

Chapter Twelve

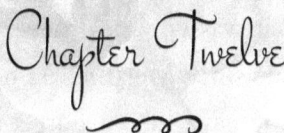

S cott dug down deep in the sand with the umbrella shovel, finally reaching a depth he knew would hold the apparatus down in the unrelenting beach breeze. He normally loved the wind at the beach, but it was pretty whippy today.

Grant had already set up a shade for his big party, and they'd clearly been at the beach long enough to pass out sodas and sandwiches. Shelby even had a Bluetooth speaker playing some holiday music, and that made Scott smile.

As he worked to get the umbrella Joy had found in the back of her rental SUV up and secure, he thought about something she'd said yesterday.

By all accounts, you should be married with a wife and kids, blissfully in love with your life.

He did love his life, even if he lived some of it from behind a film of waxed paper. He loved the business he'd been able to buy, though some days felt like a trial of his patience. All entrepreneurs experienced anxiety over the ups and downs in their market—at least according to the business training he'd taken a few years ago.

He was no different. He did harbor some extra nerves over dating, and that was why he'd never let himself be too serious about anyone since Melanie. As he got the umbrella up and in place, Joy gave him a gorgeous smile and said, "Thank you," in her cute Texas accent. She dropped her beach bag into the shade and unfolded her beach chair, leant to her by Lauren.

She arrived in the next moment, a carrier of sodas in her hands while Blake carried everything else they'd need at the beach that day. "This is a perfect spot," she said, smiling at the umbrella in the sand and Bea's chair only a few feet away, in the cooler puddle of shade from their covering.

"Diet Coke with raspberry," Lauren said as she handed Joy a drink. "Scott, yours is the blue raspberry Mountain Dew." She really drew out the words as she extracted the cup from the holder. "Where do you want it?"

"I'll take it," Joy said. "He's got to go back to the car and get his chair and his backpack and his dog."

"There's room for Ghost, right?" Lauren asked. "If I put my chair here?" She took it from Blake and put it next to Joy.

"Yeah, course," he said. "I'll hang out on the other side of Joy." He gave the two women a smile and turned to head back to the parking lot. He ran on the beach most mornings, so he knew the familiar squish of sand under his feet. The sun did shine warmly today, and plenty of people had come to the beach for the afternoon.

Not as many as he'd seen packed onto the white sand strips in the summer, and Scott turned his face to the warmth and light, a smile filtering way down into his soul. He loved Hilton Head with his whole heart. He and Jeff both lived here, while they'd grown up in nearby Beaufort. Their sister lived in Savannah, and everyone would congregate at his parents' house tomorrow about two for a dinner at four.

"If you go," he muttered to himself as he reached the asphalt of the parking lot. He hadn't answered his mother's texts from that morning, and he reasoned it was because he couldn't very well pull his phone out during a movie. It was dark in there, and the bright screen would've distracted those around him.

Blake had gotten the tickets from a client, and he'd hosted the private movie premier for friends and family. Scott couldn't be "that guy" who sat on his phone the whole time, even if the movie had been a ridiculous romantic comedy.

Joy had enjoyed herself, and while romcom wasn't his thing, it didn't have to be. He enjoyed being with Joy, and nothing else really mattered.

As he opened the back of the SUV and pulled out the chair Lauren had said he could use, he realized he had his answer. If he was with Joy, it wouldn't matter if Mark was there. He went to the back door and opened it to Ghost's happy face.

"Hey, buddy. You melting in here?" They'd literally left him there for five minutes, and the interior wasn't too hot. Ghost panted while Scott clipped the leash to his collar and shouldered his backpack.

Then, armed with everything he needed for the next few hours, Scott faced the beach again. When his feet met sand, he took out his phone and dialed his mother.

"There you are," she said in an exasperated voice that told him she could still get him to do exactly what she wanted though he was forty-four years old. "I texted you all morning."

"I was on a date, Momma," he said. "And we went to a movie. We just got to the beach. It's the first chance I've had to talk." None of that was exactly a lie. He hadn't wanted to interrupt his breakfast with friends to argue with his mom about Mark.

"I know Jeff already spoke with you," she started.

"Yeah," Scott said, cutting her off. If he let her get going, she wouldn't quit until she ran out of steam. "Don't worry, Momma. We're going to be there still."

Her sigh of relief punched Scott in the chest. She'd likely been worrying all morning, and he hated causing more grief for his parents. They knew exactly what had happened, and while they'd tried not to take sides, he knew they were on his. They didn't talk to Mark much either.

"He just called late last night," Momma said, a trace of regret in her voice. "We can't say no to him. He says he won't even touch down in Charleston until two, and then he has to drive here, and the flight could be delayed..."

Scott smiled, because it sounded like Mark would do what he always did: Sail in late, make false apologies, drop rude comments, and exit their lives a couple of hours later. At least until the next time he decided to grace everyone in South Carolina with his presence.

"When's his flight back to Seattle?" Scott asked.

"Nine-thirty," she said. "So with the drive and the two-hour check-in time...he says he has to leave by six."

"So he might be there for two hours."

"Might be, yes," Momma said.

"I'm bringing Joy," Scott said. "I think you know how big of a deal this is for me." He practically threw the last sentence into the wind, hoping the breeze would whisk the words away.

"We do, yes," she said in her Southern drawl. "We can't wait to meet her. Jeff says she's just the nicest thing ever."

"She's amazing," Scott said as his friends—and Joy—came into view. "I'll be on my best behavior for Mark, Momma, okay? It's Christmas, after all."

"And you want that pretty woman to fall in love with you."

Scott laughed, because his mother had always been able to cut right to the chase. "Yeah," he admitted. "That too."

"I love you, Scotty. See you tomorrow."

"Yep." He let her hang up, and he set up his chair next to Joy, who had turned her seat slightly to face Lauren and Bea more. He didn't mind, because she wore the once-malfunctioning swimming suit without anything over it, and the skirt went almost to her hip. She held Ghost's leash loosely, and the dog watched the activity on the beach. He picked up his Styrofoam cup from where she'd half-buried it in the sand, and he took a long, delicious drink of the cold soda.

"Ah." He smacked his lips and stretched his long legs out in front of him while Ghost circled and lay down in the sand in front of Joy and Bea. He'd changed into his board shorts before returning to Lauren's to pick up Joy, and he could peel off his shirt, spray on some sunscreen, and be ready for the day. He slipped his feet out of his flip flops and closed his eyes, feeling more relaxed and more comfortable with himself than he had in a long time.

He hadn't anticipated telling Joy about Mark on this trip. Mark never crossed his mind much anymore, though he'd been such a driving force in shaping who Scott was today. As he took a fun-sized bag of chips from Blake and tore into them, he realized he didn't have to be embarrassed of who he was.

Scott ran a reputable business here on the island. He employed seventeen people and treated them with respect and professionalism. He showed up on time for his own jobs, he paid well enough, and he had good friends who cared about him.

"Here's where the party is," Harry said as he dropped a backpack next to Scott. He grinned down at him. "Help me set up the umbrella for us?"

"I'm in the shade, brother," Scott said.

"When Cass takes your spot, you won't be." Harry grinned at him and pulled out his own sand-digger. Scott got to his feet and moved his chair out of the way so Cass could set up camp with her girlfriends.

Harry got his umbrella up right behind the one Scott had pounded into the ground, and he, Blake, and Harry made a row in the shade behind the women.

"Tommy's not here?" Conrad asked.

Blake looked up and over his shoulder to the young man. "He went to his mother's. Sorry, bud."

Conrad seemed disappointed, and Scott couldn't sit still with his bro-friends for much longer. "You want to throw a Frisbee or something?" He got to his feet and pulled his shirt up and over his head. "I just need to spray down, and I'll go out with you if you can handle playing with an old man."

He grinned as Conrad did. The younger man shook his head. "You're not that old, Scott. But yeah, I'd love to throw around." He dropped his bag in the sand, no need for chairs or umbrellas for someone in their early twenties, and pulled a bright red disc from the front pocket.

Scott took a couple of minutes to spray himself with sunscreen and take another big drink of his soda pop, and then he bent down and whispered in Joy's ear, "I'm gonna go play Frisbee with Conrad."

It could've been his imagination, but he swore she shivered. "Okay," she said, barely turning her head to look at him.

"Ghost is okay here?"

"He's just fine," she said. "I'll come grab you in a few for our walk?"

"Absolutely." He then went with Conrad, almost

looking forward to the hard conversation with Joy. This morning, he hadn't wanted to say a word. But now, he figured he could tell her anything, and she'd wear that understanding, kind look in her eyes. She'd tell him it didn't matter, and they could still be together.

Maybe his mind played tricks on him sometimes, but he sure did like Joy, and he didn't want Mark to ruin that because he decided last-minute to pop in on the family for Christmas.

So he wouldn't let him.

He laughed and threw the Frisbee with Conrad, both of them going into the water a couple of times to either catch it or retrieve it. He wasn't sure how long they stayed away from the others, but when Joy came walking toward him in her sexy, swinging dress of a cover-up and his leashed dog, Scott jogged toward Conrad. "I have to be done for a bit, bud."

Conrad followed his gaze up the beach, and said, "Yeah, I see how it is."

"Yeah? How is it?" Scott couldn't look away from Joy, so that was probably what Conrad saw.

"Well, I've seen Harry look at my mom like that, so my guess is you like Miss Joy a lot." Conrad ducked away from Scott as he said the last of the words and then added, "Thanks, man. It was fun."

"Yeah," Scott called after him as he jogged up the beach. "It was." Conrad saluted with the Frisbee as he went past Joy, who grinned at him the way Scott imagined she would her own sons. She had two of them, and she said she'd be doing video calls with them in the morning before their personal gift exchange. Then they'd make the drive to Beaufort, where he'd introduce her around to his folks and his family.

Scott's heartbeat suddenly thrummed harder in his veins. "Hey, beautiful," he said as Joy came within earshot. "You ready for this?"

"Which way should we go?" she asked, handing him Ghost's leash. "Left or right?"

"They're the same." He grinned at her. "It's just beach and more beach, my Joy." He took her hand and lifted it to his lips. "Mm, you taste like sunscreen." Not a great tang on his tongue, but he didn't mind too much.

She smiled at him, adjusted her sunglasses, and pointed them down the beach to the north. "This way feels good."

"Does it?" He chuckled. "How do you know?"

"You just do." They set off together, both of them barefoot and walking in the darker, wet sand closer to the water while Ghost didn't care if his paws got wet or not. "I don't walk on the beach much," she said. "This is nice."

"I love the beach," he said. "The taste of the air. The sand in my hair. All of it."

"It's messy," she said. "I swear, my boys used to bring home more sand than they left on the beach." She spoke in a dry tone that made him smile.

"I do too," he said. "But it's still great."

"Ghost is going to be a sand ball when he leaves here."

Scott laughed. "They have that foot shower up by the parking lot. I'll rinse him off before I take him back to the hotel."

Their feet ate up several paces of sand before she said, "What have you decided about tomorrow?"

"I think we'll go," he said. "I called my momma on the way back from the car, and she'll be really upset if we don't."

"Can't upset your momma."

"I try not to," he agreed.

Joy didn't say anything, and if Scott had to guess and if he looked at her, he'd find her lips pressed together while she contemplated saying what was on her mind. "Just say what's on your mind," he said. "I want us to be open and honest with each other."

She paused, her steps slowing to a stop. She turned into him. "Do you?"

"Yes," he said simply. He studied her for a moment, not sure he liked the doubtful look in her eye. "Have I given you a reason to think I don't want us to be honest with each other?"

The wind streamed into his face, pushing Joy's hair forward over her shoulders as it did. She said nothing, and Scott didn't like that.

"Joy, really?"

"It's just—you said something at breakfast this morning that bothered me."

"Okay, what?"

"The part about how you don't date with the intention to marry."

Scott blinked at her, sure he hadn't said that. Had he?

Chapter Thirteen

J oy was not comforted by the way Scott stared at her open-mouthed. "I want to know if that's still your intention, or if that's changed. And if it's changed, why? What's different?"

"I—" He didn't finish the sentence, instead blowing his breath out and focusing out at sea.

"Because if we're not dating with some sort of long-term intention, I—"

"You changed it," he practically yelled over her, his gaze snapping right back to hers. He reached up and ran his hand through his hair, which was half wet and half dry. Joy had sat in her beach chair, only inches off the ground, her appetite for this man growing with every toss of that Frisbee.

He had a runner's body, which meant not an ounce of fat and plenty of muscles, and he clearly ran on the beach without a shirt most days, because his skin glowed with the kiss of the sun. Scott stood several inches taller than her, giving her a bird's eye view of his impressive pecs when she looked straight ahead, as she did when she couldn't hold his powerful gaze any longer.

"The moment you texted me, it changed," he said. "No, when I saw you fumbling with your strap."

"You didn't even see me the first time we met."

"To my great dismay," he said. "Because then I wouldn't have been tortured all summer by you going out with someone else." His eyebrows came together, making him seem stormy and upset, though Joy didn't think Scott could ever truly be upset.

"And you're still holding onto that?" he asked roughly. "What do I have to do to apologize completely? The twenty times I've said it isn't enough?" He turned away and started walking down the beach again, leaving Joy to scramble after him.

She hadn't meant for their romantic Christmas Eve stroll on the beach to take such a sudden turn, but she also wouldn't hide behind her fears and worries anymore. "My ex-husband turned everything on me," she said behind him, trying to get her shorter legs to eat up as much beach as his longer ones. A futile attempt, because he walked in the sand every day, and Joy hadn't for months. "Scott."

He slowed and waited for her, something her ex-husband would've never done. "I—" Joy panted, trying to catch her breath and organize her thoughts. She hadn't planned to talk about Wendell at all right now.

They walked side-by-side again, their paces matched and even, and after several steps, Scott slid his hand into hers again. "I'm sorry I didn't see you at that party, Joy," he said. "It's the biggest regret of my life, because you seem to think it's so important."

She sighed, wishing she hadn't projected her feelings of invisibility onto him. "Some of that has to do with Wendell," she said. "He never saw me. He never listened to me. If something happened that I dared to bring up, it was always my fault. I always ended up apologizing, even for things *he* did." Her own voice tasted bitter against her tongue. "I need to figure out how to stop blaming you, but —" She exhaled, knowing exactly what she was doing.

He gave her space to think, to reason, to find a way to organize her thoughts before she gave them voice. "My friends think I'm standing in my own way. Blaming you for that party, so I won't let you get too close. So I won't start building my life here—with you."

"Are you?" he asked quietly.

Joy looked up into the sky, wishing the truth was anything but what it was. "Yeah," she finally said. "I think I am."

He only nodded, his eyes trained on the sand at his feet. Joy wanted him to look at her the same way he had when he'd seen her sauntering down the beach toward him and Conrad. That devilish grin. The chemistry that had arced from him to her, even across yards and yards of sand. The way he'd laughed with Conrad, never taking his eyes from her.

He made her feel so young, so beautiful, so desirable. Joy hadn't felt any of those things in such a long time, and her heart and soul yearned for the male attention she'd been deprived of for so long.

"Before I met you, Joy, I wasn't looking to date anyone seriously," he said. "But since you...it's all I can think about. So you asked me why someone like me hadn't settled down into a life with a wife and kids—and the answer is simple: I hadn't met you yet."

Tears flooded Joy's eyes. "Well, that's just the perfect thing to say." She didn't even care that her voice came out nasally and that the first track of tears spilled down her face before she could wipe them away. She turned into Scott to hide the rest of them, and he drew her into his chest for an intimate hug.

"Great, now I've made you cry," he whispered.

Joy's throat had completely closed, and she couldn't speak.

"I didn't know your ex made you feel so worthless," he said after several long moments.

She took a deep breath and stepped out of his arms. Her hair wasn't long enough to conceal her face, but she kept her chin pressed toward her chest anyway as she wiped her tears away. "I don't want to talk more about it today." She lifted her face to his. "Is that okay? Can we talk more about it another time?"

"Any other time," Scott said with a kind smile. He too wiped under her eyes with the pad of his thumb, a gesture so sweet and so beautiful that Joy almost burst into tears again. "Joy, I am so sorry I overlooked you at that barbecue. I honestly don't remember much of that night, and maybe I had a lot going on with work or something. It wasn't you, I promise you that. It was all me, and how...checked out of living my own life I've been."

She nodded, though she didn't need him to apologize. He was right—he'd done so plenty of previous times. "Forgive me for standing in our way."

"Done," he said as they started strolling again. "As long as you forgive me for what's going to happen at Christmas dinner tomorrow."

Her eyebrows lifted. "What's going to happen at Christmas dinner?"

"Well, it's my whole family. Siblings, parents, nieces, nephews, so really, anything is possible." He grinned. "We're loud and a little bit Southern and a lot rowdy when we all get together."

"Even with Mark there?"

"Maybe *because* he'll be there," he said, some emotion clouding over in his eyes. "Jeff will be in ultra-protection mode. My momma won't stand for a bit of horseplay or teasing or fun at all. Daddy will be growling about everything, just you wait and see." He chuckled, but it wasn't up to his usual carefree caliber. "My sister will try to minimize everything."

"And what's your role?" she asked.

"Isn't it obvious?" he asked. "I'm the comic relief."

Joy grinned and then tilted her head back and laughed. "Yeah, I can totally see that."

Scott didn't laugh with her, and as she quieted, he said, "You have a beautiful laugh, Joy." He looked at her and

ELANA JOHNSON

slowed his step again, reaching over and cradling her face in his strong, capable, somewhat rough hand. "It goes with the beauty in your face, and the gorgeous person you are inside." He leaned toward her and touched his lips to hers, only for a moment. "We're okay, aren't we?"

"Yes," she whispered, stretching to reunite her mouth with his. "We're okay."

He kissed her properly then, never taking things too far as they stood down at the water's edge for all beach-goers to see. "All right," he said, breaking their kiss. "Let's get back to the shade."

They turned around, and Scott groaned. "I didn't realize how far we'd come."

It all looked like sand and people and umbrellas to Joy, and a blip of uncertainty beat through her veins. "I don't even know where we are."

He chuckled and drew her close against his side as they matched their strides together again. "It's a ways," he said. "And I'm starving."

"If you pass out, I'll alert the lifeguards," she said dryly. He laughed, and Joy loved making him do that. He felt full of life, and Joy needed more of it—of him—in hers.

LAUREN'S DOORBELL RANG THE NEXT MORNING, causing Joy to nearly topple off her air mattress in the office. "I got it!" she called, but Lauren's footsteps were already coming toward the doorway. Joy had kept it cracked a couple of inches, and her friend said, "I'll let him in, Joy," as she went by.

Joy rolled out of the squishy bed and onto her knees on the hard floor. "Oof," she grunted, and then she pushed both palms against the mattress and got to her feet. She hurried to close the door, because she'd been reading in bed, completely negligent of keeping track of the time.

She'd been up for hours, and she and Lauren had shared their first cup of coffee together before Joy had come into the office to call her sons for their Christmas morning check-in. Since she hadn't gotten dressed to sip caffeine with her best friend, Joy had then climbed back into bed and opened a book.

The time when she should've gotten up to get dressed and make sure her hair wasn't a nest had been forty-five minutes ago, and Scott's deep voice and booming laughter came through the closed door as Joy whipped off her pajamas and yanked open the closet door to find her Christmas Day outfit.

She'd only told Lauren about the specific choices in her wardrobe after she'd arrived and they'd been unpacking together. Joy had anticipated meeting Scott's family today, and she'd wanted to be comfortable. She pulled down the pair of black slacks that had a four-inch slimming band in the waist and quickly stepped into them.

Her blouse screamed Christmas, because Joy loved dressing up in festive blouses and sweaters, matching them with the perfect pair of earrings, and really looking like a walking rendition of the holiday she was celebrating.

And Christmas had no shortage of such things. She had ugly Christmas sweaters from years past, but she'd wanted to appear sophisticated and put-together. She couldn't afford to dress as well as Lauren or Cass, but she'd found a navy blue blouse that had multi-colored holiday lights stitched across the bottom hem, which was irregular as it followed the shapes of those bulbs instead of being straight. With the pops of color, Joy felt enthusiastic and sufficiently bright enough to meet her boyfriend's family.

She had dangly Christmas light earrings too—one red and one bright blue—and she hurried to thread those through the holes in her earlobes. That done, she grabbed the gift she'd found, bought, and wrapped in Texas, and left the bedroom.

Scott lounged on Lauren's couch, a coffee mug in his hand. As Joy entered the room, he dang near threw the mug as he jolted to his feet. "Good Christmas Day," he said. "You're the most beautiful woman in the world." He drank her in from head to toe and back to her head, and Joy flushed along every inch of her skin.

"Good Christmas Day?" she asked. "Are we British now?" She cut a look to the kitchen, where Lauren leaned against the stovetop behind her, watching and listening without shame.

"I just—didn't want to swear," Scott said with a grin. "Just wow." He reached her and took her into his arms. "I love this blouse. I love these pants. Those earrings. Everything about you is simply—flawless." He whispered the last couple of words right in her ear, probably trying to keep Lauren from overhearing everything.

Joy enjoyed the safety of his arms, but she cleared her throat and stepped back. "I have your gift. Looks like you got coffee. Do you want to...go somewhere?"

"I'm headed to Blake's," Lauren said. She pushed away from the stove and opened the drawer where she kept her keys. "Don't go anywhere. Open your gifts by the tree." With that, she opened the garage door and left her own house.

Joy didn't know what to say to that, so she indicated the couch, and she and Scott sat down together. "I just have the one gift." She hadn't seen any presents from him, though he'd told her he'd gotten her something.

She passed him the candy-striped-wrapped package and sat back, sudden nerves firing against all their endings. "It's just something silly."

Scott gave her a kind, sexy smile and then tore into the package. He'd barely gotten the paper off and the lid lifted on the box when she said, "They're gloves. You know, because you work outside a lot, and I thought, you must need a lot of gloves, and these are supposed to be indestructible, but lightweight. Breathable."

He looked up as he lifted the pair of taupe-colored gloves from the box.

"I thought you'd like them." She shrugged. "I love the pair I use in my garden. I've had them for years and never had to replace them. I mean, you do way more yard work than I do, but I thought—"

ELANA JOHNSON

"Joy," he said, effectively silencing her.

She swallowed, the motion so thick and so hard.

"I love them." He smiled at her and pulled apart the two gloves to break the plastic piece holding them together. He then proceeded to put them on, and she'd guessed right at buying an extra-large pair. "These are incredibly light." He sounded a little surprised, and that made Joy loosen up a bit.

"There's something else in here," he said, his eyebrows up. He lifted the envelope with his gloved hand, and Joy liked that he hadn't just tossed them aside. Or even tried them on and then immediately removed them.

"That's for—"

"Can I just open it?" He chuckled, and Joy realized he wasn't really upset.

"Yeah." She swallowed again. "Go on and open it."

He did, still wearing the gloves, and pulled out the gift certificate to Hand, Foot, and Stone. His expression brightened, and he said, "You got me a massage."

"With the ability to upgrade to their monthly club if you like it," she said. "You kept saying your shoulder was bothering you on those big jobs, and I thought it might help."

"Thank you." He took her face in both of his gloved hands and kissed her. "What an amazing gift." He kept his eyes right on hers as he said it, and Joy hadn't felt so seen and so appreciated in all her life.

Scott then cleared his throat and said, "Okay, my gift is going to pale in comparison to this one, but I suppose I shouldn't have let you give me yours first." He grinned as he got to his feet and went over to the kitchen island.

A laundry basket sat there, and he picked up the whole thing.

"Scott," she said with plenty of disbelief when she realized it was full of presents. They'd all been wrapped in the same paper—a pretty white and green holly print—and none of them very well.

He put the basket at her feet and said, "Merry Christmas, my Joy," in that throaty voice that made her muscles soft.

She picked up the top present, which was clearly something soft that should've been put in a box before being wrapped. She looked from it to him. "You're not great with paper and tape, are you?"

"It's not my specialty," he admitted as he retook his spot on the couch. He grinned, unconcerned that she was mocking his wrapping job.

"I worked as a gift-wrapper one Christmas in college," she said. "I'm a little offended you didn't comment on my impeccable wrapping." She held up the gift. "And this." Joy laughed, and he joined her.

She ripped off the bad wrap job to reveal a fluffy pair of socks with silver-stitched snowflakes on them.

"So your feet don't get cold," he said.

She had no idea what he was talking about, and she searched his face for an answer. "Have I said I get cold feet?"

"No, it's more about how you've acted," he said, grinning.

Joy caught up to the pun, and she whapped the socks against his chest. "I'm going to keep these, Mister, because I happen to like wearing big puffy socks like these when I read."

"Noted," he said, still chuckling.

"But I'm not going to need them when it comes to us." She let her eyebrows rise, hoping he got the message.

"Doubly-noted."

"Cold feet," Joy muttered as she put the socks back in the laundry basket and pulled out the next gift. "You realize I have to take all of this back to Texas with me, right?"

"It's all small stuff," he said. "Nothing really." He still hadn't taken off his gloves, and for some reason, Joy found that so sweet.

She opened a ring light to Scott saying, "So you'll be well-lit for our evening calls," and "It folds flat, look." He showed her that, and Joy marveled at him.

"You got help with these gifts, didn't you?" she asked.

Scott blinked at her. "No," he said. "Why?"

"I maybe mentioned the idea of a ring light once," she said. "*One* time, Scott."

He leaned closer to her, those eyes pulsing with pure male energy. "I listen to you when you talk, Joy."

She wasn't sure what came over her, but she closed the distance between them and kissed him. And kissed him. And kissed him.

Eventually, he stopped kissing her back and said, "You better keep opening, sweetheart. We have to leave for my folks' soon."

Joy realized they lay on the couch together, and she'd been wrapped up in his arms. She didn't move, though the laundry basket of presents begged her to get back to them. Instead, she closed her eyes and breathed in and out with Scott, thinking this had already been the best Christmas Joy had experienced in at least at decade. She didn't dare move, just so she could hold onto this magic for another moment, and then another.

So she didn't move, and instead just lay in her boyfriend's arms, almost desperate to freeze time as he lovingly stroked her hair off her face over and over again—all while still wearing the gloves she'd bought him.

Chapter Fourteen

cott turned the corner and saw too many cars parked in front of his parents' home near the middle of the block. He'd tried to drive Joy's SUV, but she said she didn't mind his messy truck. She hadn't used the word *messy*—that all came from Scott's mind. He knew he wasn't clean, especially in his work truck.

He tossed empty water and soda bottles over the seat back to drop onto the floor until he decided to clean them all out. He ate lunch in the truck as he drove from job site to job site. He sometimes got wet and muddy and shed his clothes in the backseat, put on fresh ones—which he kept behind the seat—and moved on with his day.

"Seems like we're late," Joy said.

"Nah," Scott said. "Dinner won't be ready until four, and it's barely two." A quick check of the clock above the radio confirmed that. "My sister got here early this morning to help with the cooking." He saw her deep purple SUV.

"And it looks like Lily drove separately from the rest of the family. Both of their cars are here."

He turned into the driveway and up only a couple of feet to park behind a luxury SUV he didn't recognize. His heartbeat thumped in a strange, twisted way he didn't understand, but he turned off the ignition in his older truck and sat in the silence with Joy.

"That's not a rental," Joy said quietly.

"So it's probably not Mark's car," Scott said. He looked over to her. "There are going to be a lot of people here. Fifteen, with us and Mark and everyone."

Joy smiled at him. "We had more than that the other night at Cass's house."

"Yeah, but we both knew all of them." He took her hand in his and looked at how their fingers fit together. She didn't spend nearly as much time outside working as he did, and his skin was rougher and tanner. She gardened, but she wore gloves, and she kept her nails trim and neat and painted with a barely-there gray polish.

"There's someone at the window," Joy whispered, and Scott turned his attention to the house. It was a single-level, sprawling, near-mansion that had five bedrooms in two wings of the home. He'd loved it growing up, because he got to sleep on the opposite side of the house from his parents, and no one in Beaufort had locked their doors or had security systems back then.

"I used to sneak out all the time from that far-right window there." He nodded to it, and it wasn't the one with the curtains fluttering, as if someone had just dropped them. Which they had.

"Oh, so you're one of those." Joy laughed lightly and added, "One of my sons is like you. Couldn't tie him down if I wanted to, and I just gave up. I figured if the police didn't bring him home in the middle of the night, he was probably all right."

"Which son?" he asked, grinning, because that so sounded like him.

"My youngest," she said. "Hank."

Scott smiled and released her hand so he could unbuckle and get out of the truck before his momma, Rowena, or Lily came to get them. "I'd like to meet your boys," he said. "One day."

Joy didn't answer as they got out of the truck, but when she met his eyes as he waited for her near the hood, she wore anxiety and concern in her expression that told him she'd heard him. Her kids were both already adults. Both married. Her oldest had a little girl. Both lived in the Dallas-Fort Worth area, and while Joy didn't live too terribly close to them, she did see them often.

She hadn't said as much, but by how much she talked about her kids and grandkids, Scott suspected they were a major reason Joy didn't want to relocate to South Carolina. As they walked up the bricked front sidewalk to the porch and double-wide doors, Scott wondered how hard it would be to start a landscaping company in the Coastal Bend of Texas.

Getting Anderson Landscaping off the ground here had

nearly killed him, and they had more clients than they could clip for now. Scott thanked the heavens above for that every day, but he still lived with some fear that it would all vanish out from under him at any given moment.

He didn't bother ringing the doorbell or knocking as he opened the front door. "Momma," he called, because this house opened into a formal living room with a hallway running along the wall to his left. No one ever walked on the carpet there, but it bore vacuum lines in it. He wouldn't find a speck of dust anywhere, and the faint scent of his momma's favored lemon floor polish still hung in the air, despite the blast of roasted meat he inhaled over it.

"Mm, smells good," Joy said as his mother came around the corner up ahead. The huge family room, kitchen, and dining room sat in the middle of the house, with hallways branching left and right into the wings.

"Lily said you were here." Momma smiled as she bustled forward, her apron snapped around her neck and bearing something that looked suspiciously like cranberry sauce. "I just checked on the brisket, and it is going to be delicious." She beamed at Scott and drew him into a hug. "Oh, it's so good to see you, Scotty."

"You too, Momma." He hugged her hard, squeezing her and holding on for a few extra seconds before he stepped back to Joy's side. "This is Joy Bartlett." He beamed at her too, and she could probably see where he got that inclination from.

Momma practically glowed as she moved into Joy for a hug. Thankfully, Joy was from the South too, and she knew the greeting procedures for mommas. In fact, she seemed to melt into the hug, and she smiled as her eyes drifted closed.

It was such a perfect picture that Scott felt the cold part of his heart warm right up. He'd been trying not to let Joy all the way in, but with the way she hugged his mother, she kicked down his defenses and walked right into his heart.

"It's so great to be here," Joy gushed at Momma. "Your home is lovely, and Scott's told me all about your meat buffet for Christmas, and I can't wait to try all of them." She flicked him a look, her eyes burning brightly—almost blue instead of gray now.

"My momma, Franny," he said. "Daddy's—"

"He's out on the spit," Momma said. "Come on. I'll take you. He's doing the smoked turkey for today, and the wind has been causing him some trouble."

"I'll bet it has," Joy said as she moved behind Momma in the hallway. "Wind is not good when you want to keep smoke in one place."

Scott followed them both into the back of the house, where he found Jeff and Rowena standing at the sink, peeling potatoes. Lily had just gone outside, and she walked across the patio to only one of the three barbecue grills along the edge of it.

"What else are y'all making?" Scott asked, slipping into his Southern boy accent.

"The barbecue chicken just went on," Momma said. "It keeps, you know."

"Mm, I know," Scott said with a smile. Joy slipped her

hand back into his, her fingers so tight that he knew how she felt here with all these strangers.

"Daddy's got the turkey in the spit smoker," Momma said. "The brisket is slow-roasting on one of the grills out there. We'll put the ham steaks down in about an hour." She turned to Joy, her smile filling her whole face. "They don't take long, and the ham gets a little dry if you let it go too long."

"I can imagine," Joy said, and Scott stifled a laugh.

"Row and Jeff are doing the potatoes. We'll get them seasoned and wrapped and in the smokehouse too. They take a while; then we mash 'em up with lots of artery-clogging things, because it's Christmas."

"It's Christmas!" Jeff and Rowena said in tandem, and Scott burst out laughing. He wondered how many times Momma had used that saying today, and he knew it wouldn't be the last time he heard it.

"Oh, come meet Lily's folks," Momma said. "All the girls are out on the wheelers, too, so you'll have to meet them later."

"What about us?" Rowena asked. "She doesn't get to meet us?"

Scott took Joy around the already-set Christmas table and the peninsula that separated the kitchen from the dining area. "Joy, this is my brother, Jeff, and his wife, Rowena. Guys, this is Joy Bartlett."

"I can see the brotherly resemblance," Joy said as she looked from Scott to Jeff, who hurriedly wiped his hands on a tea towel that had a brown hen stitched into it—one of Momma's creations.

"Joy Bartlett," Jeff said as if trying out her name in his mouth. "It's so great to meet the woman who makes Scott grin like an idiot."

They both looked at Scott, who was, well, grinning like an idiot. "Stop it," he said to Jeff, but he didn't really mind. No woman had made Scott feel the way Joy did, not even Melanie, and he'd dated her for five years.

"Jeff and Row have two girls, Chelsea and Sandy."

"And Sandy is the one who's allergic to dogs," Joy said as she shook Jeff's hand and gave Rowena a hug.

"Yeah, but she seems to forget when we come here," Rowena said dryly. "Fran and John have a couple of dogs, and I guarantee they haven't left her side since we arrived." She smiled and turned back to the sink. "Come on, baby. Your momma wants these in the smokehouse real soon."

Jeff ripped off a piece of aluminum foil, reached into the sink, and plopped the peeled potato into his hand. He wrapped the foil around it, squished in the ends, and placed the now-wrapped and ready-to-be-smoked potato on a waiting tray.

"Come on," Scott murmured. "If we stand here much longer, we'll be put to work."

"I can help," Joy said. She seemed to follow him slowly, and Scott assumed she'd escape from him soon enough, and that later, he'd find her in the kitchen working away.

"Bill, Willow, you remember Scott." Momma indicated

ELANA JOHNSON

him like he'd be coronated later, and he kept his smile wide and friendly for Lily's mother- and father-in-law.

"So good to see you again," he said, shaking both of their hands. "This is my girlfriend, Joy."

"Lovely to meet you," she said. "Where do y'all live?"

"Oh, she sounds like she's from our neck of the woods," Bill said, his face brightening considerably, though he'd been plenty happy before. "We're from Texas. Hondo, out in the Hill Country."

Joy also laughed in a bright, vibrant way. "Fellow Texans." She beamed at Scott and leaned into his chest. "What do you know?" She focused on them again as they settled back into the horrible wicker chairs Momma loved. "I'm from Sweet Water Falls. It's a tiny blip of a town along the Coastal Bend."

"We've been there," Willow said in a shaky voice. She looked much older than Scott remembered her being, but Lily had gotten married five years ago, and he hadn't seen Willow White since. "It's by Beesville."

"Yes," Joy said. "Right near there. Beautiful country."

"That it is," Bill said with a wistful sigh. "It's humid here, ain't it?"

"Momma!" Daddy bellowed from the smokehouse. Scott turned in that direction along with everyone else. Daddy lumbered toward them, as tall as he was, and he indicated the billowing smoke coming from the barbecues. "That's not supposed to be on fire!"

"Daddy, I'm right here," Lily said from somewhere in the middle of all the smoke. "It's under control."

"Under control?"

"My dad sort of bellows everything he says," Scott whispered in Joy's ear. "Did I forget to tell you that?"

"Mm, yes, you did." She edged even closer to him, which he didn't mind one bit. So maybe he'd forget to tell her other things, and then he'd whisper them to her so she had to lean closer to hear him.

"Daddy," Scott said, forging forward when he wanted to go back inside the house. At least the air conditioning was running there, and then he wouldn't be here when Daddy started yelling about not being able to eat barbecued chicken that had been on fire. He literally smoked meat for this feast, but Scott knew from experience that this was the wrong kind of smoke.

"John, come meet Scott's girlfriend," Momma said.

That got Daddy to tear his eyes from the line of grills, and he did step around them, his eyes crinkling with the first hint of his smile. "Yes, yes," he said, and he'd taken the decibels down to a tolerable level. "Joy."

"Yes," Scott said. "This is Joy Bartlett. Joy, my daddy, John."

"So great to meet you," she said, stepping into him and hugging him, black meat apron and all. "Thank you so much for having me this year. I've heard so many amazing things about the meat you cook."

"Is that right?" Daddy asked, and he suddenly only had eyes for Joy.

"Yes, sir," she said, the perfect picture of a Southern lady. "In fact, I was hoping you'd give me a tour of your

smokehouse. I'd love to see what's going on back there."
She linked her arm through his as if he'd take her
right now.

Scott's eyebrows lifted as Daddy turned on a dime and
headed right back off the patio, Joy at his side. She chatted
with him, and about the time they reached the smokehouse
—which sat several paces away from the house—she tipped
her head back and let loose a round of laughter. The sky
caught it and whisked it away, but not before the carefree,
happy sound of it embedded in Scott's heart and made it
grow three sizes.

"Oh, so it's serious with her," Lily said at his side.

Scott hadn't even realized he'd migrated to the edge of
the patio and now stood even with the barbecue grills. Or
that Lily had tamed the barbecue chicken, put out the fire,
and closed the lid. Only a trail of smoke lifted from it now,
and his sister waited right next to him with her tongs still in
her hand.

"I guess," Scott said, trying to play it off as casual.

"Yeah." Lily hipped him and grinned bigger. "That look
on your face doesn't say 'I'm in love with her already' or
anything."

"Lily, don't," he said, but he lacked the proper warning
strength in his voice.

"You didn't even introduce me to her," she said.

"We're not leaving for hours," he said. "There will be
plenty of time."

"She's wonderful," Momma said, the way Scott
suspected she would. "I mean, of course she is. I knew she

would be." She laid her head against Scott's bicep on his right while Lily did the same on his left.

"I'm so glad you came," Lily whispered. "I promise you I will sic Chaz on Mark if he even looks at you wrong."

"It's fine, Lily," Scott said.

"I will too," Momma said. "In fact, I lectured him good and long when he called to say he was coming."

"He didn't even ask," Lily said.

"You did?" Scott tilted his head down to try to see his mother's face, but she watched the smokehouse like Daddy and Joy might not make it out alive.

"Absolutely," Momma said. "And Lily, all you kids are welcome here, no questions asked. So don't be blamin' him for that."

"I'm just saying," Lily said, clacking her tongs together. "If it's the day before Christmas, you call and *ask* if you can show up for the meal. You don't just say you'll be there and want to make sure dinner is still at four o'clock."

"Well, dinner *is* at four o'clock, isn't it?" Momma bickered back.

"Oh, brother." Lily rolled her eyes and turned around. "I'm not doing this today, I'm going to see how the sauerkraut is coming."

Scott groaned, because there was nothing worse than the smell of hot sauerkraut. "We're doing that again?"

"Chaz loves it," Lily said over her shoulder. "Oh, and Scott?"

He twisted to see her pause at the sliding glass door. "Yeah?"

"Merry Christmas. I'm sure glad you're here with Joy."

Scott said, "Merry Christmas, Lil," and she went inside. He resumed watching the smokehouse, wondering what look he wore on his face and why Lily had thought he was in love with Joy. Would she be able to see it too? Worse, would Mark?

"So," he said, blowing out a long breath. "What lecture did you give Mark. Holiday Lecture Four? Or Holiday Lecture Seven?" Both were about minding one's manners during the meal, thinking of others before oneself, and holding one's tongue.

"Well," Momma said. "It was kind of a combination of a lot of them, and I'll tell you, if he even puts one hair of one eyebrow out of line, I will escort him out of the house myself." With that, she turned and marched back into the house too.

Scott wasn't sure if he should follow her lead or wait for Joy. In the end, he wanted to be in the same space as Joy, so he crossed the lawn and opened the door to the smokehouse just in time to hear her say, "...to be a surprise."

"What's a surprise?" he asked, and Joy jumped back from the huge metal barrel where Daddy had lit the wood chips to smoke the turkey. It smelled like hickory to Scott, who'd grown up with enough meat buffet Christmas dinners to know.

Daddy also wore a look of surprise, and he shoved something in his back pocket. "Maple and hickory this year," he bellowed. "Should be a sweet treat."

Chapter Fifteen

J oy couldn't help giggling as she left the smokehouse
behind.

"As if he didn't just have the door open," Scott
grumbled. "My word. Maybe Momma should give *him* a
lecture for today."

She turned back to him, really enjoying seeing him with
his family. His father had plenty of the same thick hair as
Scott, but his had started losing its color several years ago.
Scott got all of his height from his daddy too, and Joy
reached up and brushed an errant piece of ash from his face.
"We were just talking."

"You said something about a surprise," Scott said. "I'm
not deaf." He threw Joy a dark look and started across the
lawn. She hurried to catch him, because she didn't want to
be the cause of any ill feelings on Christmas Day. Not when
he already had so much on his mind.

"Scott," she said when it became clear she wouldn't

catch him before he reached the patio and then the house. She didn't want to have a heated conversation with him—or even a serious one—in front of near-strangers. And everyone here was a near-stranger. "Baby, wait."

She'd never used a pet name for him before, and perhaps that got him to slow, stall, and turn toward her. Joy wasn't sure, but with him stopped, she caught him in only a few more steps.

"Look." She ran her hands up the front of his shirt, bumping over his muscles under the fabric. "It's almost Chaz and Lily's anniversary, right?"

"Yes, it—how did you know that?" He peered down at her, his attention on her singular. "You didn't even meet Lily yet, as she pointed out to me once you'd gone into the smokehouse."

"Her momma slipped me something to give to your daddy for a gift your parents and Chaz's are putting together. I guess Lily doesn't leave them alone very often, and they've found it hard to get it to him."

Scott blinked a couple of times. "So you were passing notes for my sister."

"Yeah." She smiled up at him. "Nothing secret or surprising between us, okay?" She sure liked Scott, and while he'd mentioned the protein buffet and she was from Texas, even Joy was impressed with what she'd seen so far.

"Okay," he whispered.

"Now." Joy put her hand in his and looked past him to the house. "I want to see the bedroom where you grew up. Do you think your momma will let us go inside?"

"I'm forty-four years old," he said in a deadpan. He looked toward the corner of the house. "But we better go in through the garage." He took her that way while Joy laughed again. He chuckled with her and told her that he'd tried to get Jeff to sneak out with him when they were kids.

"He wouldn't, huh?"

"Never," Scott said. "He worried too much that he'd get in trouble. That's why I bought the landscaping company too. Jeff likes the stability of a nine-to-five job."

"He runs the company, though, doesn't he?"

"A large part of the administrative stuff, yeah," Scott said. "But he's still just the CFO. I'm the owner and CEO. I'm the boss. I have to make all the decisions, and I'm the last one to get paid."

Joy waited while he opened the garage door, and then she stepped inside the murky space after him. "So this door leads to a small mudroom," he said as he took her up four cement steps. "There's two hallways that lead out of it. One into the boy's wing, and one into the kitchen. So...shh."

He lowered his voice as he opened the door and slipped inside, as if he really was arriving at three a.m. and didn't want anyone to hear him. His mom and siblings chatted in the kitchen, and a hissing sound accompanied their voices. Joy didn't think they'd hear them even if they tried.

Scott closed the door silently behind her and indicated the open doorway to his left instead of the one directly in front of them. She went that way, and the hallway here wasn't as wide as the one that led into the kitchen.

"Can you get into this wing another way?" she asked,

keeping her voice down too. "Or only through the mudroom and the garage?"

"No, there's a hallway off the kitchen too."

"Oh, I didn't see it."

"Probably blinded by the gleam of my momma's furniture. Tell her that. She'll love it." He wore a grin in his voice that Joy couldn't see as he walked behind her. She reached a corner and only had one choice—right—so she went that way.

"Three bedrooms over here," he said. "Five in the other wing. Three-and-a-half bathrooms. All that indoor and outdoor living space."

"It's a big house," Joy said. "It's nice, Scott."

"My room was on the right there. Other two on the left." He squeezed past her and nodded to the first door down at the other end of the hall. "I think Lily and Chaz are staying for a couple of days. They'll be in that room on the end. That's the guest suite Momma set up years ago." He opened his door and added, "My room and Jeff's are for grandkids."

He entered the room and Joy followed him, blinking when he flipped on the light. "It has no windows."

"My momma erroneously thought if I didn't have a window, I wouldn't be able to sneak out."

Joy laughed with him, and it felt so good. Cleansing almost, as she couldn't remember the last time she'd laughed with Wendell. She'd gone out with someone else over the summer, and she'd laughed with him, but she'd known that relationship wouldn't last.

This thing she had going with Scott... It suddenly felt too big to be contained in such a small room, and Joy struggled to breathe. In front of her stood a bunk bed, both made up nicely with homemade quilts and fluffy pillows.

"Not your bed, I'm assuming."

"No," he said. "And I'm sure you've noticed how... untidy I am. My room was never this clean." He grinned at the spotless floor, the vacuumed rug peeking out from under the bunk bed, and the dust-free shelves.

"Oh, these have to be yours." She strode over to the shelf, where several trophies and medals gleamed in the overhead light.

"I played basketball in high school," he said. "One year of college."

She pulled down a team picture, clearly identifying Scott as one of the taller guys in the back row. None of them smiled, and the stoic expression didn't really fit with the man she knew. "Did you get injured?"

"No," he said. "I wasn't very good."

"Good enough to go to college," she said.

"I didn't get recruited or anything." He picked up a trophy, looked at it, and set it back down. "I've always loved being outdoors. I went into landscape architecture almost immediately, and my focus wasn't on the court."

Joy smiled at him and handed him the picture to replace. He did, and then he looked at her. "Did you keep your sons' rooms as they left them?"

"Heavens, no," she said. "I aired them out, stripped

everything, cleaned and cleaned and cleaned, and then put them back together into more useable space."

Scott grinned at her, hooked his arm around her, and reeled her right against his chest. "Yeah? Like what?"

"I made Walt's room into an office for Wendell the weekend after he went to college."

"Mm." Scott pressed her close and shut his eyes. Joy wrapped her arms around him too, and now they slow-danced in his old bedroom. "Why did Wendell need an office?"

"He ran a bookkeeping firm," Joy said. "And he worked from home sometimes, especially at tax season." Her chest started to storm, but she pushed past the bees buzzing there. "I was tired of him spreading his work all over the dining room table and leaving it for days or weeks, so I put together the office."

She swallowed, remembering how much she'd hoped and prayed that he'd like it. That he'd finally acknowledge how much she did around the house for him and the boys, that she had value in their family too.

"He only used it once," she said. "He claimed it was too hot in there, and he couldn't focus."

"I'm sorry," Scott whispered, seeming to pick up on all the emotional pieces Joy wasn't articulating out loud.

"I turned it into a sewing studio after trying to get him to use it for a few months."

"Do you do a lot of sewing?"

"Not as much anymore," she said. "Since the divorce, I

had to get a full-time job, and that, combined with the gardening, is mostly what fills my time now."

"Mm." Scott moved with her in a slow, easy way. "What about Hank's bedroom? What did you do with it?"

"Nothing for a bit," she admitted. "He and Wendell moved out within a couple of weeks of each other, and the house was just so...empty. I didn't change anything for a while."

"How long ago was this?"

"Almost four years," she said. "Since then, Hank finished college and got married. He lives in Dallas near Walt, Lexie, and Holly." Joy smiled to herself, because she loved her sons and granddaughter back in Texas, and she'd only gotten to see Walter, Lexie, and their baby girl, Holly, for about twenty minutes that morning.

Not long enough. Nowhere near long enough.

"I made his room a guest room," she said. "King bed, with one of those portable playpens. My sons come to visit every so often, but I usually go see them."

"So you still have the sewing studio."

"Yes," she said. "It's basically my cat's bedroom."

"Of course," he said amidst a chuckle. "What did you do with Toby for Christmas?"

"He's at my neighbor's house," Joy said. "They have three cats and weren't traveling this year. He loves it over there. He'll probably shun me for an equal amount of time that I was gone, but he's not being neglected, I can promise you that."

Shouts met her ears, and Joy stepped out of Scott's arms.

"My nieces are back," he whispered just before he leaned closer. "I give them three minutes to find us." He touched his lips to hers, and a fire ignited in Joy's belly and raged through her chest and throat.

She pulled away slightly, not truly wanting him to stop kissing her. "Then maybe you shouldn't kiss me like that."

"I have supersonic hearing," he said with a grin. "I won't let them catch us." He claimed her mouth again, and Joy let him be the one to set the pace, deepen the kiss, and then pull away. She just enjoyed herself, and when Scott swept away from her, laughing, and picked up a precious toddler, Joy couldn't stop falling, and falling, and falling.

"This is Wendy," he said, beaming at the girl. "She's three, and no one can understand a word she says except for Lily. Right, Wen?"

A string of gibberish came out of her mouth, and Scott laughed. "See what I mean?"

"Uncle Scott!" A wiry girl flew into the bedroom. "You've gotta come see this burn on my daddy's leg. It's *so huge.*"

"A burn?" Scott sounded concerned, and Joy certainly was.

"Is he all right?" she asked.

The girl looked at her, seemed to realize Joy was there, and nodded. "Yeah, but my momma is chewing him out good." She turned and left the room, gesturing for Scott and Joy to follow her.

So they did, using the hall that completed the circuit and spit them out adjacent to the hallway they'd come down from the front door. Out in the big family room, Lily's husband lay face-down on the sofa, the back of his leg exposed and bearing a bright red burn mark.

Lily definitely had the lecturing gene down pat, and she railed against her husband even as she cleaned around the burn, put ointment on it, and covered it with a clean gauze pad. The medical tape made angry sounds as she ripped it, but she placed it on the back of his calf lovingly despite the harshness of her tone.

"Now you have to meet Scott's girlfriend with a burn on your leg," she said.

Joy grinned at him as he got to his feet and tested his weight on his burnt leg, and Chaz smiled right back. "Aren't you exactly what Scott likes?"

She wasn't sure how to react to that, and she looked at Scott, who laughed. Lily, however, swatted her husband's chest and told him, "Go get cleaned up. You have to put the potatoes in the smokehouse, and then I'm putting you in time out."

Her husband smartly left the living room, limping as he went down the hall toward the other wing of the house, and Lily put her hands on her hips as she faced Joy. "All he means is that Scott likes blonde women. That's all, I swear."

Joy smiled, because she wasn't going to make a fuss over some comment, even if she didn't like it. "You must be Lily. I don't think my boyfriend introduced us properly."

Lily gave her brother a glare. "That he did not. I already had words with him about it."

Joy liked her so much more in that moment, and she laughed lightly. "I'm sure you did."

"You were busy with the chicken," he said. "And then buried in smoke. Not my fault."

Joy pressed back into his chest, not wanting him to go very far. His momma and Rowena still worked in the kitchen, and the scent of baking biscuits filled the air. Joy's stomach swooped and growled, for breakfast had been a long time ago now.

"Is there something I can do to help?" she asked as she stepped toward the kitchen.

"You can help me with your name and phone number," a man said.

Joy blinked as she focused on the near-twin of Scott's as he emerged from the hallway that led to the mudroom.

"Mark Daws Anderson," Franny said. "Outside. Right now." She shoved him in the chest, and he grunted as he fell back.

"Momma," Scott said from Joy's side.

"How dare you?" Lily raged at her younger brother. "You know she's here with him, and she's not as stupid as Melanie!" She threw Scott a sorrowful look. "Sorry, Scotty, but she obviously wasn't that smart if she ran off with *him*." She glared at her brother, who held his ground against the women in his family.

He held up both hands, his eyes locked on his mother's. Joy couldn't see Franny's face, as her back was to her, but she planted her fists on her hips, and Joy wouldn't want to cross the woman, day or night.

"You apologize to him right this instant," Franny said. "And then Joy. And then, if you're lucky, I won't put your food outside in the kennel with the dogs."

"Momma," Mark said.

"Mark, do not test me on this."

He sighed, his head dipping toward his chest slightly.

"Momma," Scott said. "It's fine. We're adults." He cleared his throat, gripped Joy's hand, and moved past Lily. "Howdy, Mark. This is Joy Bartlett, my girlfriend. Joy, baby, this is my younger brother, Mark."

Joy pasted a smile on her face. While Mark looked an awful lot like Scott, he put off a completely different air. He smelled like swagger and cheap cologne, and Joy wanted no part of him. Still, she could feign niceness, and based on Scott's example, she'd do just that. "It's so great to meet you," she said without extending her hand for him to shake. No part of her wanted to touch him, and thankfully, Franny refused to move so she didn't have to try to shake his hand.

"Nice to meet you too," he said flatly. He looked back to his mother. "Satisfied?"

"Not even a little," she said. "You owe him an apology for hitting on his girlfriend in front of everyone."

Mark's eyes, which weren't quite as vibrant as Scott's, blazed. "I'm sorry," he said through clenched teeth.

"No worries, brother," Scott said. "I know how hard it is to come off a break-up and then be around *so* many *blissfully* happy couples." He grinned at Mark, whose mouth didn't twitch up or down even a little. "And at the holidays too."

"Yeah, nothing happening in Seattle for Christmas?" Jeff

asked, his first contribution to the conversation. Joy had almost forgotten he and Rowena had been in the kitchen.

Mark flicked him an annoyed glance. "Not this year."

"Apologize to Joy for hitting on her," Franny said, and she finally stepped to the side, so Joy's view of Mark was unobstructed. She immediately wanted to tell him it was fine, she didn't get offended that easily, but her tongue wouldn't work.

The tension in the room could've spontaneously combusted, if the sliding glass door hadn't opened. Bill, Willow, and John walked inside talking, and Mark's muttered, "I'm sorry, Joy," barely registered in her ears.

She nodded once, and then everything froze again. "Oh, my disrespectful son has arrived," John bellowed so loudly that poor Willow winced away from him. "Come on, boy. Don't stand there lurking in the hallway. Come say hello to Lily's in-laws."

Joy couldn't help the genuine smile that played with her lips. She tried to keep them flat, but they wouldn't obey, and she had to turn away from Mark as he slunk between her and Lily to go meet Bill and Willow.

"Yeah, this one lives up in Seattle," John yelled. "Thinks he's better than the rest of us!"

Joy absolutely could not stop herself now, and thankfully she wasn't the only one who started laughing. Jeff's started in a loud burst, and Lily's flew from her mouth in a joyful string. Joy mercifully started after both of them, and Scott joined them all last.

"What's so funny?" a teenage girl asked as she came inside with a girl not much younger than her.

"Nothing," Rowena said. "Go wash up, so you can help me with these green beans. Did you get the four-wheelers put away right?"

"Yes," the girl said, obviously one of her daughters with the way she added a partial eyeroll to the statement. Like, *of course I did, Mom. Duh.*

"Yeah," Joy whispered as she turned into Scott's arms. "What's so funny, Scotty?"

He held onto her hips and touched his forehead to hers. "Merry Christmas, baby."

"Merry Christmas," she whispered back.

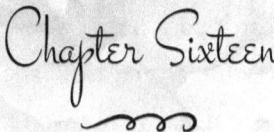

Chapter Sixteen

"This is a nice location," Bessie Clifton said as she turned her rental car into a shopping center that had two big-name retail shops in the building at the back of the parking lot. In front of it sat another building, this one square and housing two eateries. Rather, just the one—The Mad Mango—and the other one was for rent.

"What goes great with smoothies?" Wynona asked.

"Bread," Bessie answered with a smile. Bread went well with absolutely everything, as the extra weight around Bessie's very pear-shaped midsection would testify. Best of all with butter and jam, and she had such a hard time to keep from sampling the bread she baked with homemade raspberry preserves.

Those were her favorite—and she liked the fruit in smoothies too.

"Lots of cars here," she said.

"It's the day after Christmas," Wynona said.

"Yeah, and that means people might want something to eat while they return gifts or shop their after-Christmas sales." She smiled at her daughter as she pulled into a parking space labeled for The Mad Mango.

"Momma, you can't park here."

"We'll get a smoothie afterward," she said, unconcerned about it, though Bessie usually followed rules to a T. Besides, today, they were only driving by the commercial properties they'd found on their own. Bessie hadn't wanted to deal with a realtor quite yet, because she still had a lot of pieces to put in place before she could truly quit her stable job in Sweet Water Falls, move to Hilton Head, and open her own bakery.

She suddenly felt way too old to be doing such a thing. Didn't women her age have life figured out? They had husbands and families and extra money they could hide away for a rainy day. Bessie told herself she had a couple of those— her daughter certainly counted as family, and she'd always been exceptionally good at saving her pennies.

Right now, she had about twenty thousand dollars she could invest into a new business, and she yearned deep down for a bakery of her own. She was never happier than when her hands and arms had flour on them up to her elbow, and the dough she'd lovingly put together rose precisely right.

"Let's just go see first," she said. This wasn't the first place they'd driven by that day, but it would be the last. Grant had then promised them all a clam bake at his house, which would spill out onto the beach, and Bessie could admit she loved the white sand here in Hilton Head.

She loved that her friends lived here, and that their Supper Club could pick up and continue where it had thrived in Texas. She looped her hand through Wyn's arm as they went past the entrance to The Mad Mango and along the sidewalk in front of the building to the door of the place available for rent.

It wouldn't be open, but Bessie had cupped her hands around her eyes plenty of times in her life, precisely to peer into a window like the one in front of her. "It said it had been a bistro before," she said as she pressed her forehead to the glass. "Yeah, I can see the ordering counter."

She'd need one of those, of course. And maybe she could push it out toward the front of the store, because she didn't need as much room for tables and chairs. She'd been to Gourmet Goods here on the island, because none of her friends could stop talking about it. They served all kinds of pastries, as well as made special occasion cakes, and plenty of drink options too.

Bessie didn't want anything like that. She wasn't running a dessert and coffee shop. She wanted a bakery, where she could make honey whole wheat bread every day of the week, and then have a bread-of-the-day too.

Currently, she worked as the head baker at The Bread Boy in Sweet Water Falls. She'd learned a lot from being there, including the perfection of many of her own recipes, what time she needed to be mixing yeast, sugar, and water to have perfectly baked bread by eight a.m., and how much to charge to make a profit.

She loved her job there, but she craved the freedom to set

her own hours, try her own bread flavors, and run her own business. Bessie could almost taste the future on her tongue, and while she wasn't sure it would take place in this retail space, she had a very good feeling about making the move to Hilton Head.

"Can you see the kitchen?" Wynona asked, her own hands cupped around her eyes.

"No," Bessie said. "If we want to get inside, we'll have to call and ask for a walk-through." She and her daughter would be in town for four more days, and then they both had lives and jobs to return to. Sage was leaving at the same time to make the long drive back to Sweet Water Falls with her Newfoundland, but Joy was staying all the way through New Year's to spend more time with Scott.

The balloons that had been lifting Bessie's spirits got their strings cut, and she felt heavier than before as she leaned away from the window. "I'm going to add this one to the list." She still had the listing bookmarked online, but she took out her phone to tap in the name and number of the leasing agency, so she could make the call. "Maybe they'll let us come later today or tomorrow before we have to meet Lauren to look at bridesmaids dresses."

The last thing Bessie wanted to do was squeeze her body into a dress made for a five-foot-ten model, but she absolutely wanted Lauren to be happy. So she'd wear whatever horrible pastel color her friend picked out, and she'd smile the whole time, though the dress fabric wouldn't drape right over her hips.

"I could walk through it if you have to be at the bridal shop when they can do it," Wynona said.

"Yeah," Bessie said, but she didn't want her daughter to do this alone. Not because she didn't trust her, but because Bessie wanted to experience each space for herself. She'd be getting there very early in the morning, alone, and she liked to think she could connect with a physical space before she signed a lease.

"Okay, got the number," she said. "I'll call in the car, and then should we get lunch?"

"You need to get a smoothie," someone said, and Bessie spun to find a dark-haired man blocking her way back to the SUV. His perfectly sculpted eyebrows went up. "You parked in a smoothie space. Or didn't you see the sign?"

"We saw it," Bessie said, lifting her chin. "I was going to come get a smoothie." Why this guy cared, she wasn't sure. He didn't wear a name tag, nor an apron, and he looked like some post-Christmas shopper in his dark blue khakis and pale yellow polo. Seriously, who wore yellow the color of freshly churned butter?

Leave it to Bessie to bring everything back to a bread topping. She smiled to herself as the man in front of her frowned. In the space of a breath, she knew who he was. "I think we've met," she said.

"I meet a lot of people." He rolled his eyes and turned around. "I can have you towed if you don't actually come get a smoothie." He marched away from them, and Bessie looked wide-eyed at Wynona.

"I guess we better go get a smoothie," her daughter said.

"I kinda don't want to now," Bessie admitted when it had sounded delicious only a few minutes ago. She took the first step down the sidewalk anyway, thinking that the man who'd barked at them had been pretty delicious too.

"Who is he?" Wyn asked from behind. "You said you knew him."

"He's a friend of Grant's," she said. "And Harry's. He was at a barbecue I went to a long time ago." Two summers ago, in fact, and Bessie was blanking on his name. She half-expected to see the man getting in his car and leaving, but the parking lot didn't reveal him. She and Wyn went into The Mad Mango, which had a line gracing the entire length of the counter. Great.

They joined the line, and Bessie started studying the smoothie menu. She'd been to places like this before, and it sort of seemed like someone made some special dice with every fruit known to mankind, then threw seven of them, and called it a smoothie.

The concoctions here had fancy things like spinach and chia seeds in them, and Bessie didn't hate that. She made a nine-grain bread with chia seeds, and she actually really liked them. It wasn't until she'd ordered and moved to join the line to pay that she saw the gorgeous grump from outside.

The butter-yellow shirt should've given him away, but his menu had distracted her completely. He lifted those eyebrows as her turn to pay finally arrived and she stepped up to the register.

"So you won't be calling the towing company," she said, holding out her debit card.

He had the audacity to smile. "I suppose not today."

"How'd you know it was my car parked there?" she asked.

He swiped her card through the reader. "Lucky guess, I suppose."

Bessie didn't think so at all, but she didn't call him on his obvious stalker behavior. "I know you," she started, but he cut her off with, "You don't want that place next door anyway."

Her eyebrows went up as she took her card back from him. "I don't? Why's that?"

"The roof leaks," he said, ripping off her receipt and handing it to her to sign.

"I'm sure it's fine," she said.

"I think he's rented it," the man tried next.

Bessie scoffed out a half-laugh, signed her name, and thrust the receipt and pen back at the man. Just because he was gorgeous with all that thick, dark hair, those dreamy eyes, and that square jaw didn't mean she couldn't see what was happening here.

"I suppose *you've* rented it." She punctuated her statement with the raising of her eyebrows, only semi-asking him.

He smiled. "Maybe."

"Do you know Grant Turner?" she asked before he could put her off for a third time. "Harrison Tate?"

The man visibly swallowed and nodded. "Yeah," he said slowly. "They're two of my good friends. How do *you* know them?"

"Why wouldn't I know them?" She tucked her card back into her thread wallet and stowed it in her purse.

"Because that's a rental car," he said. "And I've not seen you in here before."

"You think every resident of this island comes into *this* smoothie shop?" Bessie couldn't believe the arrogance of this man. She was aware of Wyn's gaze volleying back to Mr. Handsome behind the register.

He indicated she should move along, and he took the next woman's ticket to ring her up. "Most do," he said.

"Oliver makes the best smoothies on the island," the woman said, as if Oliver needed her help to expand his ego. He gave her a grateful smile and took her credit card.

"Oliver," Bessie said. "That's right. That's your name."

He met her eye, and Bessie thought lightning might strike them both right then and there. Then the roof on this building really would be leaking, and there was no way she could rent the space next door.

"Oliver Blackhurst," he said slowly. "What's your name?"

"Bessie Clifton," she said, and she finally got control of her senses enough to indicate Wyn at her side. "And my daughter, Wynona. We're looking to open a bakery here on the island."

"That's wonderful," the woman said, but Oliver scoffed.

He reached for the ticket of the next person in line as the other woman went to join the lingering crowd still waiting for their smoothies, and he said, "We've got enough bakeries in Hilton Head, that's for sure."

Bessie's temper bubbled, and her fingers curled into fists. "Yeah," she said. "We passed at least four smoothie shops on the way here. So it's probably like that." Then she turned on her heel and marched out of the shop, Wyn in her wake.

It wasn't until she got outside, fumbling with the key fob to get the rental unlocked, that she realized that neither of them had gotten their smoothies.

Chapter Seventeen

O liver Blackhurst hated Christmas, and he hated the grump he'd become on one of the busiest shopping days of the year. He sighed as the strawberry blonde with pale eyes walked out of his store. He hadn't meant to take his irritation out on her, though she *had* parked in a clearly marked space, and it *had* sounded like she and her daughter might leave the premises without actually buying a smoothie.

"Twenty-four," one of his employees called, and he grabbed the two smoothies.

"Take the register for a minute," he told Cara, and then he hurried toward the exit. He'd just barreled through it when he collided with another body. Both smoothies smashed right into the woman's chest and torso, and Oliver sucked in a gasp and dropped everything in his hands.

He back-peddled quickly when he saw who he'd just

drenched in Beach Sunrise and Rainbow Over Troubled Water.

Bessie's daughter, Wynona.

"You have got to be kidding me." Bessie herself came charging toward him. She took in the scene—the two cups lying on their sides on the ground. Her daughter holding her arms out to the side like another smoothie attack might be coming. The way the tangerine slush dripped off her body in terribly long drops, combining with the deeper pink of the Rainbow already on the ground. The horribly shocked look on her face.

Oliver probably wore a similar one, and an apology had just started to form in his mouth when Bessie poked him in the chest. "You're refunding my money," she said, her blue eyes suddenly not as pale as they'd been inside. No, now they practically glowed with fire. "And you're making us new smoothies right away. No more waiting."

He fell back a step from the ferocious poke. "Yes, ma'am," he said, his mind simply parroting his years of business training. "I'll make them myself." He backed into the shop he hadn't truly exited all the way, and thankfully, a couple of employees came to clean up the mess. Or maybe not thankfully. The fact that they knew meant they'd seen him plow into a customer and smash smoothie all over her clothes.

"I'll pay for the cleaning," he said.

"Yes, that too," Bessie said. "I'll need your direct number. We're from out of town, you know, and we don't just have a plethora of clothes here." She didn't exactly keep her voice down, which Oliver didn't exactly blame her for. He hadn't been super nice to her outside in front of what had once been a Chinese buffet, nor had he been particularly cordial to her while ringing her up.

He had made every smoothie on his menu at least a hundred times each, so he put together a Beach Sunrise and a Rainbow Over Troubled Water in record time. He took them out to Bessie and Wynona, who both waited at a table in the seating area. "I'm so sorry," he said. "Did Cara take care of your refund?"

"Yes," Bessie said in a softer tone than before. Wynona had clearly been in the bathroom, as she wasn't dripping anymore. Her cornflower blue blouse simply held different hues than it should've.

He gave her the best smile he could as he said, "I'm sorry. Really. I was bringing the smoothies out to you when I realized you hadn't picked them up."

Bessie stood, her Beach Sunrise in her hand. "Thank you, Oliver."

He nodded and held out his hand. "Give me your phone, and I'll put my number in it. For the cleaning bill."

Bessie complied, her eyes wide and searching his in the time it took for her to place her phone in his hand. He found he couldn't look away from her either, and something stirred behind his lungs. He'd had a string of girlfriends over the past couple of years, and none had interested him half as much as the woman in front of him. A woman he hadn't even been that nice to, and who clearly wasn't interested in spending more time with him.

He cleared his throat and dropped his gaze to her phone, quickly typing in his name and personal phone number. "This is my cell," he said. "Just text me the amount, and how to pay you, and I'll do it." He handed her the phone back, and Bessie slid it into her purse with a nod.

"Thank you, Mister Blackhurst."

"Miss Clifton," he said. He watched the two of them leave, trying to pull the images from his memory of having met her before. She said they'd met, and all at once, Oliver remembered.

At Harrison's beachside house, before he'd gotten married and moved in with his wife down the street. Oliver rolled his neck as he groaned, "Of course."

Bessie wasn't from Hilton Head. She was part of the Texas Supper Club that Bea, Cass, and Lauren belonged to. Joy too, who was dating Scott Anderson—another friend of his—right now, and one more woman. As he turned back to the counter and cash register, the sixth woman's name popped into his head. Sage.

Doesn't matter, Oliver told himself as he nodded to Cara, and all of the roles got switched back to where they'd been before he'd decided to make a fool of himself and run smoothies out to the parking lot for customers.

It didn't matter that he thought Bessie was gorgeous, or that he wanted time and space to get to know her better. It didn't matter that his body had reacted in a way it hadn't in a while. She didn't live here—yet—and he wasn't dating. Ever again.

So it definitely didn't matter that regret lanced through

him every time he thought about the dry, sarcastic tone he'd used when telling her Hilton Head had enough bakeries. Or the lie he'd told about the space next door being rented already.

He'd considered renting it, because the same guy owned it, and The Mad Mango was bursting at the seams almost all the time now. He could barely keep the smoothie shop staffed, and he certainly shouldn't expand to a second location that was literally right next door.

He wanted to expand somewhere else, but he wasn't even sure it should be here on the island. *Maybe Carter's Cove*, he thought again for at least the fiftieth time. *Or maybe not at all.*

Oliver wasn't sure what he wanted to do with The Mad Mango, but he wouldn't be renting the space next door. He had no idea why he hadn't wanted Bessie to.

But now, he found he did, and he couldn't wait until she texted him with the cleaning bill. When she did, then he'd make everything up to her. He'd apologize the right way, and then he'd be able to sleep at night.

He didn't want to do all of that so he could ask her to dinner. *No.* He scoffed mentally. Definitely didn't want to do that.

"HEY-EY-EY, BROTHER." GRANT LAUNCHED HIMSELF out of his lounge chair and toward Oliver. He didn't grab onto him the way he normally would've, because Oliver carried Grant's to-go order in his hands. Two four-cup carriers, one in each hand, to be exact.

"Curtis," Grant said. "Come help a brother out." He relieved Oliver of one of the carriers, his smile huge.

"You're too chipper," Oliver complained, wishing his eyes didn't roam over the group who'd gathered at the outdoor pool at Lighthouse Point. "No beach today?"

"Meredith wanted the seafood chowder down here," Grant said with a grin as he handed the smoothies to Curtis, Bea's son. He took the other carrier, and Oliver now really had nothing to prevent him from scoping out the place for Bessie Clifton.

Bea chatted with her daughter, and they both paused to take one of the labeled smoothies from her son. Oliver finally found Bessie, Wynona, and Sage way down on the other end of the row, and he pulled in a breath that had some sound to it.

"What?" Grant asked, and Oliver cursed himself for being so obvious. Well, he really hadn't been, but Grant was more observational than any other male Oliver knew.

"Nothing," he said. "I have to get back to the shop."

"I owe you for bringing these."

"Yeah." Oliver didn't turn and walk away, and he stood poolside and watched as Curtis handed the last smoothie from his tray to Bessie. She tilted her head back to look at him, her blonde hair curling on the ends now that it was a bit damp.

Her eyes held laughter and life as she thanked the young

man, and then she went right back to her conversation with Sage.

"Who are you starin' at?" Grant asked.

"No one," Oliver said. "I thought I saw that woman I dated last Christmas." He gave a fake shudder and focused on one of his best friends. "When does Bea's family go home?"

"Day after tomorrow," he said. "Her friends will be here for another day after that, and then they'll be gone too." He grinned, because he was an extrovert who loved being around huge groups of people. New people, old friends, didn't matter. Grant had a story for all of them, and he liked hearing about their lives.

Oliver wasn't quite like that, and he tolerated the noise in the smoothie shop because he'd rather own his own business than work for someone else's. "Okay," he said. "Well, we should go golfing or something in the New Year."

"Yeah." Grant chuckled again. "See if you can get Scott to get us into the Country Club at Lion Point again. That course is *incredible.*"

"I'll talk to him," Oliver said. He lifted his hand to wave to Bea, and she grinned at him and held up her smoothie.

"Thank you, Oliver," she called down the row of chairs, and Oliver could smile at her. She was a nice woman, and she'd made Grant so stinking happy, he couldn't be upset by their recent relationship and marriage.

He wasn't. But Bea also served to remind him how very single he was, and how very hard he'd been trying to change his marital status in the past couple of years. He looked down the row again, and this time, his eyes caught on Bessie's.

Oliver spun on his heel and said, "I'll text you, Grant," over his shoulder as he left. The last thing he needed to do was embarrass himself further. The way the beautiful strawberry blonde Bessie addled his thoughts, he'd probably walk right into the deep end of the swimming pool.

He watched every step he took, and he'd just made it outside the side service entrance gate and reached for his sunglasses on top of his head when he heard a woman call his name. His pulse came to a complete stop and then raced forward, because that voice could literally belong to a dozen different women—none of whom he wanted to see.

Perhaps he could pretend he hadn't heard them. There were quite a few people at the pool today, with kids laughing and teens splashing. He'd taken two steps when she said, "Oliver, wait."

He had no choice then, for that voice belonged to Bessie, and she was practically on top of him. Oliver turned toward her and studied her as she took the last few steps to him. She wore a flush in her cheeks that only made her more attractive, as well as a billowy black coverup that left plenty of cleavage showing.

Yanking his eyes back to hers, he said, "Hey, Bessie." He nodded to the smoothie in her hand. "What did you get today?"

"This one is—" She stuck the straw in her mouth and took a suck on it. Oliver's whole body heated, and he had no idea why watching her drink a smoothie was somehow erotic. "I don't know what it is, but it tastes like peaches and strawberries and maybe some...lime."

"That's the Surfer Boy."

"It's better than the Beach Sunrise."

Oliver's eyebrows rose in a slow arch. "I think that's probably a matter of taste and perception."

Bessie grinned at him and stuck the straw back in her mouth. "I like this one better. It has more punch."

He put a smile on his face. "I'm glad you like it. Did you take Wynona's shirt to the cleaner? What do I owe you?"

"Oh, no, she just threw it away." She gestured behind her. "That's what I wanted to tell you."

Alarm pulled through Oliver. "Well...how much to replace it then?"

Bessie's eyes shone like sapphires, almost like she was teasing him. "You don't need to replace it."

He wasn't going to argue with her. "Okay," he said. "If you change your mind, you have my number." He could lie to himself and say he hadn't checked his phone ten times as often these past couple of days, hoping to see a text from her. Until she texted him, he didn't actually have her number.

And you don't want it, Oliver told himself sternly. He wasn't going to get himself a long-distance girlfriend. He couldn't even handle one who lived here on the island.

"Good to see you, Bessie," he said as cordially as he could. He didn't want any of his attraction to leak into the words, and he settled for a stiff nod as his parting farewell to her. Then he got the heck back to his vehicle before he could humiliate himself further.

Chapter Eighteen

S age Grady sucked in a breath and pointed, as if all the other women weren't already looking up. Of course they were, because they were getting a demonstration of how the roof retracted over this indoor hall—making it an outdoor paradise.

Trees and plants, bushes and flowers grew right out of the stones at their feet, as even when the roof was closed, the glass let in plenty of sunlight. The horticulturists and land-scapers here at Island Aisle kept the tropics perfectly mani-cured here in their most popular wedding hall, and Sage thought Lauren would get a miracle if she could book this place in a matter of a few months.

Places like this got reserved a year out, with new dates opening up and getting snatched by those on a waiting list. The whole room smelled like flowers and tangerines and another faint scent that also reminded Sage of something delicious. A memory just out of reach that made her smile.

"That's incredible," Cass said. "Look how it disappears completely." She spoke as the last of the roof halves vanished over the sides and the ferns that had somehow been planted up above waved in the breeze as it wafted down toward them.

"You have to book this place," Joy said.

"There's no way they're going to have something in March," Lauren said, and her voice carried a little bit of longing.

"You never know," Bea said, ever the optimist.

They weren't the only ones on the tour today, and a couple had come together, and then another bride and her aunt, and a mother-daughter team that reminded Sage of the time she and her daughter had spent before Tori had gotten married.

She smiled just thinking about her daughter, who lived in Santa Fe now with her husband Rod. They were due with their first baby by summertime, and Sage couldn't wait to take a road trip across the enormous state of Texas to see her and her first grandchild.

As the oldest in the group, Sage often felt like the other women were looking to her for some sort of wisdom or advice. She didn't speak up as often as Cass or Bea, and she did display more confidence than Bessie. Lauren and Joy had grown exceptionally close in the past couple of years, and Sage had maintained a level of friendship with all of them over the years of their Supper Club.

She had told Joy that she was going to leave Texas, find somewhere to rent here, and move to Hilton Head. With

Bea, Cass, and Lauren already here, it did feel inevitable that they'd all make the move.

Bessie and Wynona were looking at commercial properties for their bakery. Sage could easily move her salon to Hilton Head, as there were plenty of ladies here who'd require her coloring skills and experience. She had a tiny house on a less tiny farm, but she didn't live there. She only did hair in the house, which barely had running water.

She did love her chickens, her pair of pigs, the cats and goats on her little four-acre hobby farm, but it was in Texas. She could sell it pretty easily, hopefully, and she could load up her big black dog and make the drive to Hilton Head... and not go back to Texas.

She could do it any time she wanted.

The reason she hadn't yet was because of Joy. Sage hadn't known she was dating Scott until last week, and Joy acted like she'd just pack her bag, board the plane, and continue on her life and job in Sweet Water Falls.

She'd always been very good at compartmentalizing her feelings, her job, her time, and her relationships. But Sage had also seen the way Joy looked at Scott, and she'd heard her friend talk about him. They'd had an amazing Christmas Day feast at his parents' house, and Joy had never been more alive as she'd told story after story about his daddy who yelled everything to his black sheep younger brother who'd hit on her.

Not only that, but Sage had seen the way the man looked at Joy. He certainly wouldn't be happy with her moving on with her life back in Texas like they were nothing, but Sage hadn't inserted herself into their relationship. That was more Bea's or Lauren's style, maybe even Cass. Sage and Bessie were the watchful ones, though they both stepped in when they had to—usually to protect whoever was getting ganged up on.

"These are our Caprese skewers," the tour guide said. "And a miniature beef Wellington, and a crab cake. Our food options here are varied, and you can do appetizers like this for a select group or a full crowd, all the way up to a full, catered dinner." She spoke and smiled like she really enjoyed herself, and for all Sage knew, she did.

She knew she liked beef Wellington, so she took a puff pastry between her forefinger and thumb and popped it into her mouth. At times like these, she wanted to turn to the person next to her and see their reaction. Usually, she was with Jerry, her ex-husband. She knew exactly how he'd react to almost any bite of food, if someone rang the doorbell too loud, or if one of the cats jumped up onto the counter.

Her divorce had been final for only six months now, and while Sage missed having a constant companion, she'd felt freer than she had in a while. Free to find someone who was truly, madly, and deeply in love with her. Not just someone she'd been with for thirty years.

Everything about her life had become stale, and once she'd been able to work through some of the lonely nights, the grief at a life she'd once thought she'd had that had died, and the idea that life wasn't over though she'd turned fifty this past autumn, Sage had started to have hope for the future again.

Life was exciting again, right down to the perfectly spiced crab cake with some sort of creamy sauce that really kicked everything about it into a sophisticated class of food. "Wow," she said around the seafood. "That's incredible."

"We don't take bookings more than ninety days out," the woman said, handing the appetizer tray back to another worker dressed in all black. "If you're here just for the tour, you can stay in this room as long as you like. The outside gardens are also open, and the sun is shining brightly today."

She beamed with a smile like she'd personally pulled the sun out of the ocean and hitched it in the sky. "If you are planning or wanting to book with us, we do take names in advance of our ninety-day marker, and then we call to confirm the date and take a deposit to hold your spot."

She glanced around at all the women and the sole man in the room. He eyed the platter of beef Wellington, and Sage didn't blame him one bit. That beef had been immaculately cooked, with the exact right bite of mushroom under the puff.

Lauren stepped out of line where she stood between Bea and Joy. "Ninety days." Her dark eyes shone with excitement. "You guys, they're not even booking for March thirty-first right now."

"Well, that mother-daughter pair just got Nativity's attention," Cass hissed out of the corner of her mouth.

Lauren spun like she'd charge and tackle the bride-to-be to the ground. "What are the chances that they want it for March thirty-first?"

"What are the chances that they've given this tour three

times a day for the past however many years, and the waiting list for March thirty-first is already full?" Joy looked at all of them, her big, blue eyes broadcasting worry. "Not to be a downer, or anything."

"Let's just go see," Sage said. She stepped away from Bessie and linked her arm through Lauren's. "Come on. Chin up. All we can do is ask." She wasn't that much older than Lauren, but in times like these, Sage felt very matronly over her Supper Club friends.

Two more people who worked for Island Aisle had arrived in the grand hall, and Sage beelined for one of them. "Yes, hi," she said brightly. "Her wedding date is March thirty-first, and she really wants to book this hall."

"That's great," this new woman said. Her dark clothes matched her skin, with her shirt bearing the blue stitching for the wave logo of Island Aisle. "Let's see if it's available. Are you thinking a luncheon? Dinner? Just the ceremony?" She looked at Lauren for a beat and then focused on her handheld device, which reminded Sage of a label maker.

"I think a meal," Lauren said uncertainly as the others joined them.

"You definitely want a meal," Cass said.

"If you can afford it," Bea added, giving Cass a pointed look. That was a good point, because Cass sometimes forgot that the rest of them didn't have high-paying clients and a life insurance settlement that wasn't very old and had been very big.

"If she wants it, I can help," Cass said.

"No," Lauren said firmly. "I can pay for it. I just need to know the price."

"Lunch is generally cheaper," the woman said. "I'm RoniJean, by the way." She smiled a big smile at all of them, and they all responded with hi's and hello's and grins of their own. "Lunch usually means a ten-thirty ceremony, with lunch to follow. If you do that, we almost always book a dinner reservation too, if we have a couple who wants it. You technically have the facility from eight a.m. to three p.m., so the luncheon or dancing or whatever can go until then."

"Okay," Lauren said, her fingers wringing around one another.

"What's the option for dinner?" Sage asked. "Three p.m. until midnight?"

"We don't let our evening brides in until four," Roni-Jean said. "That gives us an hour to clean up and reset the room." She grinned like this was such great news. "And then it's four to eleven. We rent the grand hall in seven-hour increments."

She looked back at her device again, and Lauren turned to form a huddle with the six of them. She met Sage's eye first, clear questions in hers. Sage already knew what Lauren wanted. She was a sophisticated woman who had never been married. This was her "one and only" time, and she wanted the world.

Sage leaned closer to her and said, "Get what you want. Let us help you if you need it."

"I'd do dinner," Cass said, lifting her nose into the air.

"Of course you would," Joy said, giving her a smile. She

leaned into Cass and gave her a side hug. "Lauren, you want the dinner. Just see if they have the dinner."

"I have some good news," RoniJean said. "There's no one on March thirty-first right now, and there's no waiting list." She looked up, her brown eyes sparkling with laughter. "So you can choose lunch or dinner. Our lunch booking, which includes the hall, the use of all the dressing rooms you walked through, and a full, plated, sit-down meal is twelve thousand dollars. We have some premium food items, like scallops and seared salmon that can take the cost up a little bit."

She didn't even hitch over the price, nor did she apologize for classier food items costing more. Sage flicked a glance at Lauren, who hadn't moved besides to turn toward Roni-Jean. Bea, however, had eyes as big and as round as dinner plates, and Bessie's mouth had dropped open.

"Our dinner menu is a bit more robust," RoniJean continued, looking around at all six of them. "We typically have more protein options, and lots of fish and seafood options for our evening meals. We can include the tea lights, all the dressing rooms, and of course, this magnificent hall in daylight hours, through sunset, and into the evening." She looked up at the ceiling, and with the roof still open, Sage could see all the way into the atmosphere. "You haven't lived until you've seen the stars from this very spot."

"I'll bet," Joy said under her breath, earning her a sharp look from Cass.

Sage smiled and asked, "How much for the dinner slot?"

"Now, you can do appetizers, or a buffet, and the cost will go down."

"Slightly," Joy said right out loud this time.

RoniJean grinned her face off. "Yes, slightly. Our full cost for the full, plated dinner is seventeen thousand dollars. And I believe Minnie told you our capacity is two hundred?" She looked at Lauren, who nodded.

She sometimes went into numb mode when she got overwhelmed, and Sage whipped out her phone and took some notes. "What if she has a much smaller party?" she asked. "Say, fifty? Seventy-five? Significantly smaller than two hundred. Would the price be any different?"

"Yeah, that's a good question," Lauren said, throwing a look at Sage.

"We can do à la carte pricing, yes," RoniJean said. "These are all ballparks, but I can email you a complete list of our pricing. For smaller parties, it does sometimes make sense to choose your meal and pay per-plate. For bigger events, though, the flat rate is going to be the most cost-effective option."

"She wants the full pricing schedule," Cass said. "And she wants to book dinner on March thirty-first." She looked at Lauren, who just kept standing there, blinking. "Right, Lauren?"

Sage nudged her ever-so-slightly, and Lauren jerked to attention. "Yes," she said, immediately clearing her throat. "I want the dinner slot on March thirty-first."

"We have a non-refundable deposit of one thousand dollars," RoniJean said. "And then I'm happy to sit down with you and go over the food options right now, or you can make a follow-up appointment to go over everything with a catering specialist. Or you can just email us with what you pick from the choices in the pamphlet."

Lauren nodded and gave the woman her email address. Sage went outside with Bessie, Joy, and Bea while Cass stayed with Lauren to pay the thousand-dollar deposit. She drew in a deep breath and let it out slowly.

"This is going to be an amazing wedding," she said.

"She won't need anything else in her binder," Joy said. "This place has it all."

"And she won't have the budget," Bessie said.

Sage only smiled, because she didn't know Lauren's current financial situation. She'd lost her corporate job over the summer and started her own marketing firm, but she didn't send out bank statements or anything.

"Lauren might surprise you," Sage said, and that got all of them to look at her. "What?"

Bea grinned at her. "You're going to move here when Joy does, right?"

"I am not moving here," Joy said. She gritted her teeth and shook her head.

Bea didn't antagonize her any further by insisting she would. She simply smiled and asked, "When are you meeting Scott tonight?"

"He's picking me up here—"

"Hey, beautiful," he said, sliding right into the space between her and Bessie, startling them both. Sage had seen him step up onto the curb ten seconds ago, as had Bea. Clearly.

Joy released her breath and smiled. "Hey." She leaned into his side despite the fact that he wore the dirtiest pair of jeans Sage had ever seen and a long-sleeved black shirt with eight-inch pine needles sticking from it at various places.

"You're going to dinner right now?" Bessie asked. "It's three-thirty."

"Scott gets up really early for work," Joy said by way of explanation. "I just want to say good-bye to Lauren." She stretched up and kissed Scott quickly, then bustled off for the building again.

"We're going to go back to my place and drop off my dog," he said. "I'll shower quick, and then we'll go." He grinned around at everyone, landing on Bessie last. "And we're going to Charleston tonight. By the time we get there, it'll definitely be dinnertime."

"Would that have been so hard for her to tell me?" Bessie shook her head and let her gaze linger on Bea and then Sage.

"No, baby," Sage said. "She's just—" She didn't know how to finish that sentence in front of Scott, and she didn't want Joy to murder her in her sleep.

"She's what?" Scott asked, his smile never slipping, not even a millimeter.

"Joy is just amazing," Bea said, catching Sage's eye.

"She is," Sage said. "Although that isn't what I was going to say." She smiled to let Bea know she wasn't going to risk her life. "I was going to say that Joy likes to keep her plans to herself in the beginning. So we're afraid she hasn't...disclosed much to us about the...status of your relationship."

"She doesn't talk about you guys at all," Bessie said. "Like, why couldn't she have just said, 'we're going to dinner in Charleston, so it's actually not that early.'?"

"Here she comes," Bea hissed.

"I'm not trying to hide anything from her," Bessie said, actually raising her voice.

Sage shook her head, and while Bessie could get fired up, she also cooled in record time. So when Joy arrived and said, "Ready?" only a few seconds later, Bessie was calm, cool, and collected.

Scott looked at his girlfriend and then around the circle of women. "If you are," he said.

"Yep," she said. "Lauren knows what time I'll be home." She smiled at Bea and hugged her. "Bye, you guys." She embraced Bessie, and Sage sank into her hug when it was her turn.

"You two be good," she said as they walked away, and she ignored the semi-glare Joy threw over her shoulder.

The three of them watched Scott open the passenger door for Joy, then steady her with his hand on her hip as she climbed into the truck. "She's delusional if she thinks she's not moving here," Bessie said.

"I agree," Bea said. "But she doesn't want to hear it, Bessie." She gave her a warning look and turned toward the entrance. "How long does it take to pay a deposit? For crying out loud."

"Her blueprint has to be perfect," Sage said. "Give her some time, Bess."

Bessie nodded, her blue eyes blazing as she lifted her hand to her mouth and chewed on one of her nails. "Fine," she said. "Yeah...fine."

"You've been...tense the past few days," Bea said.

"I don't want to talk about it."

"We all know you're looking at places for your bakery." Sage watched her, and she knew instantly by the way Bessie didn't flinch that she wasn't nervous or tense about securing a property and opening at bakery here. So it had to be something else. What, Sage didn't know.

Her phone rang, and she lifted it from her purse. "Oh, it's Jerry," she said. "Excuse me." They weren't married anymore, but the marriage had ended on good enough terms for her to answer when he called. He wouldn't for just nothing, so she stepped away from her friends and swiped on the call.

"Hey," she said. "What's up?"

The squabbling of chickens came through the line, and Jerry said, "No! Get back from that! Stop it, you menaces."

Sage frowned and kept walking. "Are you at the farm?"

"Yes," he said.

"Why?" Sage asked. "I asked Cherry Forrester to come take care of everything, and I've been getting daily reports."

"Oh, Sally from next door called and said Harold was making a right ruckus. And he was—I could hear him on the phone and everything. So I came over to see if I could help him."

That donkey, Sage thought. "And?" she prompted when Jerry didn't go on.

"And he's stuck in the goat pen." He grunted and then yelped. He swore and added, "I just smashed my blasted thumb in this stupid gate."

Sage said nothing, because while she'd loved Jerry once-upon-a-time, she didn't have quite the patience for his pessimism as she'd once had. "He sometimes vaults the fence. Has to get a running start at it and everything."

Instead of answering her, Jerry started yelling at the donkey to come with him. Sage sighed and rolled her eyes. "You have it under control? Or do I need to call Jed and Cherry?"

"My shoes are covered in mud," Jerry said.

"I'm hanging up now," Sage said. "I'll text Cherry."

"I've got it," Jerry said in his completely irritated voice.

"Great, thank you," Sage said. She ended the call, and she texted Cherry anyway. *Hey, my ex is over at the farm freeing Harold from the goat pen. I know you've been today already, but could you check on him—the donkey, not my ex—in a bit?*

She sent the text and then added, *Well, maybe my ex too. I mean, if you find his body on the property, call the cops, okay?* She added a laughing smiley face and sent that message too.

Cherry sent a laughing emoji back and said she'd check on Harold.

"Ready, Sage," Lauren called, and Sage turned back to her friends. She'd been terribly lonely when she'd first separated from Jerry, and then through their divorce. But she'd realized it was because she'd withdrawn from her friends. It had been easy to do, what with Cass and Bea living here, Lauren working all the time, and Joy busy at the school and then in her garden.

But they hadn't let her disappear for very long, nor go very far. Now, as she rejoined them, she lifted her phone and said, "Harold is giving Jerry trouble." She grinned, and everyone else did too, and Sage felt so, so loved by this group of women she'd managed to find.

Her family.

"All right," she said. "Let's go get Wyn, and then we'll go to dinner too."

"At three-thirty?" Bea asked, plenty of teasing in her voice.

"Well, I have to get up early and hit the road," Sage said, sharing a secret smile with her.

"I don't get it," Cass said after a pause. "What did I miss?"

Bessie, Sage, and Bea burst out laughing, and Bea said, "I'll tell you in the car. Come on."

Chapter Nineteen

S cott reached for the handle of the best restaurant in Charleston. "They have the greatest mousse cups here," he said as he turned to look back at Joy. She wore a slinky black dress that would keep him up at night for the next month. Or two. Or twelve.

"Mimi's," she said, looking up at the sign above her as she went past him. "It smells great. Fantastic vibe."

The restaurant sat on the water, where the cheery lights from inside reflected on the gently moving waves. Scott smiled to himself as he followed her, because Mimi's absolutely had the best food, the best vibe, and the best dessert in this city. He hadn't been here in a long time, and he wasn't sure what he was doing here now.

He swallowed as he placed one hand on Joy's hip and held up two fingers on the other for the hostess. Because it was the holiday week between Christmas and New Year's, Scott had made a reservation, even though it was a Thursday evening. Joy would be here through the weekend, her flight back to Texas on Monday morning.

She had to return to her job at the elementary school in Sweet Water Falls on Tuesday morning, and she'd literally given him all of her vacation time. That fact wasn't lost on Scott, and he wanted to make the most of Joy's physical presence in his life.

"We have a reservation," he said. "Two for Anderson at six."

"Yes, we're ready for you," the woman there said, using a bright pink highlighter to scratch something off on the clipboard in front of her. He glanced down and saw his reservation there, and then the hostess grabbed two menus and said, "This way, please."

She led them into the restaurant, which had a lot of tables filled with diners. "Are you celebrating anything special today?" She peeked at them over her shoulder.

Joy walked in front of him, so she answered. "Just being together."

Scott sure did like that, but it made him wonder if the celebration would come to an end. He didn't want that, and he had to pull on his bravery briefs and talk to her about their relationship. He'd rather laugh, ask her about her sons, her grandchildren, and talk about the beach, dogs, alligators, and Southern food.

They settled at a table-for-two, and Scott pulled a menu in front of him while Joy did the same. He sighed out his nerves and checked to make sure Mimi's still had the surf and turf on the regular menu and not their evening specials.

They did, and his choice was made. He set down the menu right as the waitress appeared, and she had another woman with her. "Hey there," she said, tossing down those cardboard drink coasters. "I'm training Mabel tonight, is that okay?"

Scott didn't understand why they always asked. What was he supposed to say? No, I don't want you to train your new employees? He nodded and said, "Yeah, sure. Hey."

"Drinks tonight?" The waitress looked from Scott to Joy, her smile perfectly pinned in place.

"I'd love a margarita," Joy said with a smile.

"I'm driving," Scott said. "So just Diet Coke for me. With lemon, please. And I want a water."

"Do you want water too?" she asked Joy, who nodded.

"I'll give you a minute with the menu," she said, knocking twice on the table. "I recommend the oysters and the sliders for appetizers."

"I've had the sliders," Scott said. "They are fantastic." He smiled the women away, and then he focused on Joy.

"I don't like oysters," she said.

"They're not my favorite either." He reached across the table and took both of her hands in his. "Let me guess what you're going to order."

Her eyebrows shot toward her hairline. "This should be a fun game."

He laughed, glad when she smiled back at him with those soft, blue eyes. He could look at her forever and never get tired of the view, but he kept those thoughts to himself for now. "We haven't eaten out together too many times, but you've cooked dinner for yourself while I've been on a video call with you, and I think I know a lot of your favorites."

After releasing her hands, Scott picked up his menu and started scanning. His heartbeat hammered at him to *Get—this—ri-right*, and he seized onto the salad section. Joy adored salads, and she grew a lot of her own vegetables in Sweet Water Falls.

"Oh, this Mimi's Magnificent Salad Bowl looks interesting," he said.

Joy made a noise halfway between a scoff and a snort, and Scott looked across the table to her.

She pressed her lips together, smiled, and cocked her head at him. "What?" she asked. "I'm not going to tell you if you're right if you're just fishing. I need a final answer."

He grinned and went back to the menu. Burgers, no. Fish, maybe, but Joy had said she really only liked white fish, that everything else was too buttery, or greasy, or the texture wasn't right.

Chicken and steak, sandwiches... Scott put the menu down. "I have two guesses. If you're in a salad mood, it's the Mimi's Magnificent. If you want French fries—which I know you love—then you might choose a sandwich, in which case I'd get you the Crispy Cutlet, regular, with the fries and the Southern mac and cheese."

Joy's smile lit her whole face, and Scott felt himself falling for a couple of seconds. Then the restaurant righted itself, and before Joy could say if he was right—he already knew he was—he practically lunged across the table toward her and took her hands in his again.

"Tell me where we stand," he said, almost breathless.

Her smile faded slightly. "Scott?"

"You're leaving in three days," he said. "I hate it. I don't want you to go. I love having you on the island, and close to me, and me close to you, and I don't want this to go back to long-distance."

Joy blinked a couple of times, and Scott reined in his wagging tongue. He pulled his hands back, noting that Joy did hang onto his fingers for an extra beat before letting go.

"I have a job to return to," she said quietly.

Scott looked to the edge of the table, where the condiments and sugar packets sat. "I know."

"I have to talk to my sons."

He didn't know why that mattered, but he wasn't going to debate her on it. "I just—I need to know that it won't be three more months until I see you again." He pulled up the imaginary briefs and looked back to her, their eyes catching, hooking, and staying locked.

She wore a very troubled expression, and Scott wanted to erase it. He shouldn't have said anything, but he didn't want this to be their last conversation before she boarded an airplane and returned to her "regular life."

"You have to know I'm falling in love with you," he whispered. "I'll come visit next month. Maybe you can come for Valentine's Day. And then Lauren will be getting married, and you'll be here for that..." He trailed off, mostly because his throat had started to stick together with how much he'd said.

Where was their blasted water? He should've told the

waitress he didn't want the trainee tonight. He looked out into the restaurant, and there came the second woman. She arrived only a few seconds later, and she unloaded all the drinks on her tray. "Are you ready to order?" she asked.

Joy cleared her throat, drawing the woman's attention. "Yes," she said. "I'll have the Mimi's Magnificent Salad Bowl, and I definitely want those sliders for an appetizer." She flipped the menu over while waves of satisfaction rolled through him. He'd gotten her order right within seconds of looking at the menu. "Can I also get a cup of this baked potato soup? Extra bacon on top." She closed the menu and handed it back to the woman, who looked at Scott.

"Surf and turf, please," he said. "Medium-rare on that steak."

"Do you want the jumbo shrimp or the popcorn?"

"Popcorn," he said. "I also want the baked potato loaded, please. Extra bacon on top." He handed his menu to the waitress too, his smile back in place. It didn't fade as quickly as Joy's, who reached for her margarita and took a delicate sip with those lips Scott couldn't get enough of.

When she set down the glass, they were alone again. Scott unwrapped a straw and dunked it in his cola, then reached for a lemon wedge.

"I don't want to break-up," Joy said, and Scott dropped his citrus in his soda.

He didn't even try to fish it out. "I didn't know breaking up was even an option," he said.

Relief washed across Joy's face, and she slid to the end of

the booth, got up, and came to his side. He could've moved over to make room for her, but he did not.

She sat right next to him, and Scott put his hand on her thigh. He stared at his fingers, which sat along the hem of that super sexy dress. "Scott," she said quietly, her fingernails moving along the back of his neck. She had no idea what she did to him, and Scott could only swallow. "How about this?"

He looked up and into those eyes he loved so much. She wore a kind, amazing smile, and plenty of heat in her expression. "We'll talk every day, because we did throughout the fall."

"Okay," he managed to say.

"Videos and texts and calls."

"Mm hm."

"I'll come to Hilton Head in January," she said. "Then you come to Texas in February, and then I'll be back here for the wedding."

"The wedding is at the very end of March," he said.

"Maybe you'll have to come twice between my visit in January and the wedding." She leaned closer, and Scott let his eyes drift closed. She touched her lips to his, and an instant bonfire raged to life inside his chest.

He wanted to stay right where he was for a while, breathing in and out with her, their movement in perfect sync. But he broke the kiss after only a few seconds and said, "This doesn't solve our long-term problem."

Joy cuddled into his chest, her breath falling lightly across his collarbone. "I know."

"What does your blueprint look like?" he asked, going all-in with the hard conversations tonight. "Because I want us to build a life together. That's where *I'm* going with this." He did stir his cola now and take a sip of it. The cold and carbonation shocked his throat, and he nearly coughed.

"I can move my landscaping business to Sweet Water Falls," he said.

Joy jerked to an upright position. "Absolutely not."

Scott blinked at her sudden transformation. The mom-tone she'd used with him. The horror in her eyes. "Why not?" he asked.

"Because you have so many clients here." She shook her head. "I will *not* ask you to do that. No." She pressed one palm against his chest and leaned in like she might kiss him again. "It's so sweet of you, and I don't think you know that stuff like this makes me fall for you faster, but if you even *think* for one more second about leaving Hilton Head and relocating Anderson Landscaping to Texas..." She let the threat hang there, and honestly, Scott didn't want to know what came after it.

He let a couple of beats of silence go by, and then he said, "So what I'm hearing here is that you're falling in love with me too."

She scoffed, rolled her eyes, and swatted at his chest now. Joy returned to her side of the table, gave him a dry look, and reached for her drink again. Scott laughed, because he didn't want to think about her breaking up with him, or the work it would take to move a business to a different state and start over, or anything but Joy coming to live with him on Hilton Head Island.

Plus, laughing was way better than worrying, and Scott had turned to work and laughter in the past several years, and so far, they hadn't let him down. Joy was the more serious one of the two of them, though she did see things positively.

"Baked potato soup," the waitress said, sliding it onto the table in front of Joy. "And the sliders. Enjoy." She disappeared as quickly as she'd come, and Scott reached for one of the mini hamburgers while Joy stirred the bacon and cheese into her soup.

"So," she said. "Are you ready to hear about my ex-husband?"

Scott choked on his first bite of slider, which so wasn't sexy or appropriate, coughed, and when he could finally breathe normally again, he could only stare at Joy. "You've told me about your ex," he said. "Haven't you?"

Chapter Twenty

I t seemed like the night of terrible talks that needed to be done, so Joy figured she'd blurt out everything about Wendell, maybe cry a little into her soup, and then be able to enjoy the rest of her meal.

She knew she wouldn't be able to. Scott had literally just asked her for a complete blueprint, and she still had nothing. She didn't know what she wanted, other than to keep seeing him.

Her life felt torn completely in two, and Joy did not like it. She didn't know how to deal with the raging emotions on one side—the part of her that wanted to abandon her principal and the teachers who relied on her in Sweet Water Falls and stay in Hilton Head right now.

And she certainly didn't know what to do with the whispering voice in her head that reminded her of how much she had in Texas, how long she'd been there, how hard she'd worked to build *that* life. Of course she couldn't just walk away from it on a whim.

"I've told you some things," she said to the steaming deliciousness of baked potato soup with a lot of bacon. She'd needed it to get through Scott asking her where they went from here—such a great question Joy still didn't know how to answer.

With her plan, she'd basically put a Band-aid over a gunshot wound and started praying everything would turn out okay.

She took a bite of the soup, immediately getting the salt from the bacon, the soothing vibe from the cream and potatoes, and the richness from the cheese. "Mm." Feeling daring and reminding herself that this was *her* life to live. Her life to mess up. Her choice. The freedom she felt outweighed any humiliation she might experience.

"My ex was very controlling," she said. "Not in the traditional ways, either. Just...emotionally. If anything ever went wrong, it was my fault. *He'd* do something terrible, and if I dared to confront him about it or we just happened to get talking about it, *I* was the one who ended up apologizing."

She stirred her soup, her memories of Wendell too numerous to hold back all of them. "He got his feelings hurt very easily. He never did anything wrong. Ever. If he made a wrong turn somewhere, and I said something, he'd say something like, 'how do you know the route I'm planning on taking? I was planning to turn further down.' He had an answer like that for everything. He always knew better than me and pointed it out. He was always 'going to' do whatever I did for him next. That kind of thing."

"I—I have to be honest, Joy. I don't know what to say."

Joy looked up from the creamy orange depths of her soup.

"I'm sorry doesn't feel adequate," he continued. "That's awful? Because it is. No one should have to feel like that, especially with the partner who's supposed to love them and care for them."

"Wendell is a very sick man," Joy said as evenly as she could. "I'm not excusing him, because he was so small and petty in so many ways. But when he left, he said a lot of hurtful things, and stupid me, I actually believed him. I missed him." She didn't cry, but everything inside her felt shaky, from her lungs to her eyelashes.

"So I know you want an answer about us," she said. "But—"

"I did *not* mean to pressure you at all," Scott said, holding up both hands now that he'd finished his slider. "Not one bit, Joy. Honestly."

She offered him the best smile she could in the moment. "I know that, Scott. You're too sweet. You're not like Wendell at all, but I think it's only fair for me to tell you that I need time to really know a person. I'm...cautious, that's all."

Scott nodded, frowned, and then shook his head. "You are not cautious, Joy."

"With this, I am."

He grinned at her, a gesture she totally didn't understand. "I don't think you know yourself as well as I do."

"Excuse me?"

"Is there something wrong with the soup?" The waitress suddenly stood at the end of the table, and Joy looked over to her.

"No, not at all." She dipped her spoon in again and brought up a meaty bite with bacon and chunks of potato. "It's fantastic." She took the bite without blowing on it, which was a huge mistake. The waitress said she'd bring Scott another Diet Coke and left, and Joy did her best to chew and swallow without burning her entire tongue and mouth.

Now that she was alone with Scott again, she tucked her hair behind her ear and cocked her head at him. "I don't know myself?"

"I don't think a cautious woman would've sent me the text you sent me in September." He smiled and picked up a second slider. "That's all."

"Yeah, and how many times did you ask me out?" she asked. "How many texts came before that?"

Scott chuckled, the lines around his vibrant eyes so sexy. "All right," he said. "Fair point."

"When I'm ready to act, I do," she said. "It's getting to that point that takes me forever. So I hate to ask you to do this, but I'm going to ask you anyway. I don't want to break-up, but I have to finish the school year in Texas at the very least. It's five months, I know. That sounds like an eternity, but I'm going to—do you think we could just take it a day at a time? Then a week? Then a month, and we'll find ways to see each other in person more often than once every three months."

During her long ask, Scott had sobered. He watched her now, and Joy wondered what he saw when he looked at her. He kissed her like she lit a fire inside him, and as hard as that was for her to believe, she *felt* it every time he touched her.

"Absolutely," he said. "If I get impatient, only know it's because I want you, not because I think you're going too slow or doing something wrong." He cleared his throat and reached for his soda pop. "Okay?"

Tears did press into her eyes then, but Joy nodded without wiping them away. "Thank you," she whispered. She ate her soup, feeling better and better by the spoonful. When she finished, she got up and went to sit beside Scott again.

This time, he slid his arm around her and pulled her flush against his body. "Did I tell you how sexy you are in this dress?" he murmured in her ear.

She smiled at the tabletop, because he had, yes. "I'm going to finish my classes in the next five months too," she said. "I've decided. I'm going to apply to waive the student teaching, and maybe..." She didn't want to say too much, but he'd said things like, "I want you," and "I'm falling in love with you."

"Maybe when I move here, I can get a teaching job on the island."

Scott's expression danced with danger and delight, but he only nodded before he closed the distance between then and claimed her mouth. He kissed her for a lot longer than he had previously, and Joy didn't mind that at all.

JOY SAT AT THE DESK IN HER MAKESHIFT BEDROOM —Lauren's home office. She sighed as she uncapped the pretty purple pen her friend had gotten her for Christmas, and she smiled as she opened the yearly planner Lauren had included with the pen set.

Lauren had already gone through the book, and in her slanted, precise handwriting, she'd labeled New Year's Day in bright blue ink. That was Sunday, and in the box beside it— Monday—Lauren had written *Joy goes home* and included a frowny face.

As she flipped through the months, she found all the dates for Supper Club, either here or in Sweet Water Falls, all of the school vacations for her district in Texas, and all of the ladies' birthdays.

Joy moved back to March, where Lauren had drawn an enormous red heart around the thirty-first and written *Lauren marries the love of her life in Hilton Head and Joy will be the maid of honor.*

She gasped in a breath, then leapt to her feet. "Lauren!" she called as she rounded the desk. Just as she was about to leave the room, she lunged back to the desk to grab the planner. "Lauren!"

Lauren didn't answer, and Joy wondered if she'd left the house for a walk or to garden. She hurried out onto the back patio and didn't see her in the yard. Back in the house, Joy's heart hammered in the back of her throat as she rushed back into the office to get her phone.

"Did you call?" Lauren asked from the direction of her bedroom. She tied the knot on her robe, her hair up wrapped and knotted in a towel on top of her head.

Feeling panicky for some reason Joy couldn't name, she could only hold up the planner. Her face must've said it all, because Lauren smiled the way she would to a toddler who's just gotten in trouble and then been forgiven. "You found the notes."

"Maid of honor?" Joy asked, tears pressing into her eyes. "Lauren."

"Don't say no," Lauren said, plenty of panic in her own voice. "All it means is I get to blame you if the dress colors are terrible or I'm late because I cried off all my makeup the morning of the wedding." She smiled, but it wobbled on her mouth.

"I would never—" Joy pulled in a breath when hers was suddenly gone. "Say no." She flipped the pages of the planner sharply too. "Or let you be late to your own wedding. Not for the love of your life."

Lauren emitted a sob and drew Joy into a hug. "I know it's not easy for you, but you love me anyway."

Joy did love her, and it was easy. She didn't say that, though, and decided to simply hold her until she was put together the way she wanted to be. She hadn't said anything about the conversations she and Scott had had the previous evening, and now wasn't the time.

"Let's go get coffee," Joy said. "Unless you have something today."

Lauren stepped back and shook her head. "No, I was just out in the yard early today and needed to shower."

Joy looked down at the planner in her hands. "I slept late after an amazing dinner, and I got this out, because I thought I could find some dates where I could come back to see Scott." She lifted her gaze to meet Lauren's. "It's crazy, right?"

"Not at all," Lauren said softly.

"Can I stay here when I come?" Joy asked, her voice turning tinny as she started to lose the battle against her own emotions.

"Of course you can," Lauren said. "After March, you can live here...if you want."

Joy hadn't thought that far ahead, because she couldn't. It was too overwhelming to think of a month from now, or two, or three. She did like to have her whole future illuminated in front of her, and she was learning more and more that wasn't how things worked.

People got sick. They grew tired of their spouses. Sometimes, like Cass, they had to endure the death of a loved one. They found out a partner had been lying, that they weren't who they thought they were. Children moved on and built lives of their own.

Through it all, Joy only ever got one step at a time, and she had to take it with faith, hoping and believing that the ground wouldn't vanish beneath her feet.

"We're going to alternate who travels," Joy said. "I'm

taking January and March, so I can be here for the wedding, obviously."

"Obviously." Lauren smiled and retreated further down the hall. "Let me get dressed, and we'll go get coffee and just...be."

"That sounds nice," Joy said. She returned to the bedroom/office and replaced the planner on the desk. She hadn't picked dates or written anything in it yet—and she didn't need to. Right now, she was going to get coffee with her best friend, and then she and Lauren would go find Bessie, Wynona, Sage, and Cass, and when Scott got done with work, Joy would be ready to spend time with him and Ghost too.

One day at a time.

It had never been her motto before, but Joy found herself adopting it, ready to live it for the next five months until she could make a more permanent plan for her life.

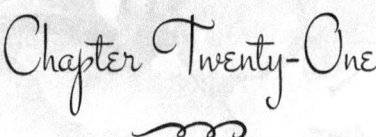

Chapter Twenty-One

Scott stepped out of the beach house and onto the back patio, where Harry stood in front of a smoking grill. "Here's where the party is," he said, grinning. "Look at this place. It looks amazing."

Harry twisted toward him from the grill, smiled, and went back to rotating the corn. "It came in nicely," he said.

"I'll say." Scott had seen the ultimate outdoor kitchen at the house down the street—where Harry had once lived. But when he'd married Cass over the summer, he'd moved in here with her and sold the home two or three down the road.

That house had everything a man needed to make a meal outdoors, and Cass's back patio hadn't even had a free-standing grill. It still didn't, as the one where Harry stood had been built into stone, with a flat countertop beside it which currently held a big, stainless steel bowl.

Harry reached for the basting brush and swiped, swiped, swiped the glaze over the corn before lowering the lid on the grill. "That just has to go for a few minutes, and then we'll take it inside."

"Are you doing steaks later?" Scott asked. He liked nothing more than steak, and Harry grilled a perfect medium-rare feast—at least every time Scott had found himself invited to the man's house.

"Yep," he said. "And chicken. Cass has all the ladies bringing salads, and I'm told there will be plenty of potatoes, so I'm happy." He bumped his fist against Scott's. "Ready for another year?"

Scott exhaled, not really sure how to answer. He'd never paid much attention to New Year's, because there was always another lawn to be mowed. Another retaining wall to put in, and client calls to deal with, and monthly bills to be paid. Thankfully, Jeff handled all the business bills and staffing issues, as well as the scheduling. Scott was the front-face of the business, charming clients and training personnel as he labored out in the South Carolina weather two hundred and fifty days each year.

"Ready," he confirmed. "You? What are you working on these days?" Harry had been involved in a huge build that had lasted years, and Scott hadn't kept up with his next job.

He too sighed and headed for the house. After sliding open the glass door and walking inside, he said, "I put in a bid for the new library on the island," he said. "Waiting to hear on that. Otherwise, I helped with the elevator renovation and install at the hospital, and I've been doing a few odd jobs here and there."

He didn't seem to be hurting for money, and from what

Scott knew, Cass had orchestrated the outdoor kitchen for Harrison as his Christmas present.

"The library should be a fun project," Scott said.

"If I can survive the City Council meetings." Harry spoke with a certain dryness in his tone, but Scott only chuckled.

"You sat on the Zoning Committee forever. I thought you actually liked it."

Harry grinned, shrugged one shoulder, and put the bowl of glaze in the sink. As he washed up, he asked, "How are things going with Joy?"

Scott didn't normally mind talking about his girlfriends. For some reason, he didn't want to spill the beans about him and Joy. "Great," he said with as much enthusiasm as he could. He thought he sounded pretty normal, but it was hard to tell. He had texted Harry on his honeymoon to get Joy's name and number, so he couldn't exactly hide his feelings from his friend.

"Gonna keep seeing her after she goes back to Texas?" Harry seemed to want to ask all the hard questions tonight.

"Yeah," Scott said as he nodded, his hands tucked neatly into his shorts pockets. "Yep, that's the plan."

"I don't envy you that," Harry said. "When Cass went back to Texas to list her house, I thought I might lose her forever."

"Yeah, that helps me worry less, thanks." Scott rolled his eyes and turned toward the front door as the bell rang. "I'll get it."

"Scott, I didn't mean—" But his voice got swallowed by

Grant's as the other man entered the house with a yelled, "Hey, it's New Year's Eve and the party has just arrived!"

How he had the energy sometimes, Scott would never know.

"Dad, you're so loud," Shelby said, and Scott went to relieve her of the big bowl she carried.

"Thanks," she said. "Bea has more in the car." She went that way to go help, and after Scott had put the bowl on the counter, he did too.

He returned to the kitchen carrying three bottles of wine to hear Harry say to Grant, "I already asked him, and he said they're going to keep dating."

"Talking about me?" Scott asked as he set down the first bottle. "Believe it or not, I'm not a teenager, and I can manage my own life."

"Where is Joy?" Grant asked, an apology nowhere on his lips.

"She's with Cass and Lauren," Harry answered for him. "They went to look at some flowers today. You know, for the wedding."

"I hear the venue is incredible," Scott said, because Joy had told him about it on three separate occasions. She'd said it was perfect for Lauren, but that if she ever got married again, she just wanted something simple. He'd wanted to know what that meant exactly, and she'd said, "You know, just something casual with family and really close friends."

That hadn't exactly given him a clear picture, but he wasn't anywhere near ready to ask her to marry him. He wasn't even sure he was in love with her yet. Scott knew himself, and he knew he tended to fall fast. He saw the good in people, which was why he liked to talk to complete strangers and come away feeling like he'd met a soulmate after a fifteen-minute conversation.

But the only woman who'd ever gotten close to his heart? Considering how well things with Melanie had ended, Scott had resisted any sort of relationship where he might even remotely fall in love—until Joy.

Something about her, standing right outside on that patio, fumbling with her swimming suit strap...and he'd started falling then.

She'd told him she had to go slow, and he'd told her he'd be as patient as possible. And he absolutely would.

"Have you been to Island Aisle?" Grant asked. "It *is* incredible. I keep trying to get a property over there, but no one will sell. The values are pricey, and no one wants to let one go."

"Hey, my cousin's son is looking for a job," Harry said. "I said you might have something."

Scott looked at Grant and then Harry. "Are you talking to me? Or him?"

"Both of you," Harry said. "He's seventeen, and a good kid. He's willing to work—wants to save for a car and then college."

"Sounds like your avenue," Grant said, smiling at Scott. "I only ever have need of a receptionist, and my wife can't be replaced."

"You've still got that other woman working for you too, right?" Harry asked. "She does all the filing and scheduling."

"Vanessa does all the filing and scheduling of services for the rentals," he said. "Yes. Bea handles all the client scheduling, emailing, stuff like that."

"She's your public face," Scott said.

"That she is." He glanced over to where she sat on the couch, Shelby crowded in close to her as they watched something on Bea's phone.

"Hey," Blake called, and then he added, "Take it in the kitchen, bud." His son appeared before he did, and he carried a big white box that had to have sheet cake in it.

"Tell me that's from your sister," Grant said.

"It's from my sister," Blake said as he followed the teenager into the kitchen. "And apparently, Julie thinks you won't have napkins or plates." He set a stack of each on the countertop. "I couldn't argue with her, so I just took them." He sighed like all sisters were like this, and Scott couldn't really argue.

"No women yet?" Blake glanced around. "Oh, there's Bea. Maybe I should text Lauren."

"Cass said they're on their way," Harry said. "We have all night, and I gotta be honest. I don't know if I'll make it to midnight." He yawned to punctuate the fact that New Year's Day was still hours and hours away.

"Want me to grab the corn?" Scott asked.

"Oh, shoot." Harry hustled over to a cupboard and got down a plate. "I forgot about it. Here." He disced the plate to Scott, who panicked but managed to catch it. He didn't want to be the one to tell Cass he'd broken one of her expensive plates because her husband had treated it like a Frisbee.

With the plate safe in his hands, he turned to leave the kitchen. "Now y'all can talk about me, and I won't have to hear you."

"Thank you for your consideration," Grant quipped, and Scott chuckled as he stepped outside. As he closed the sliding door, he heard Blake say, "Lauren told me that Joy—"

Part of him wanted to know what Joy told her girlfriends, and the other part absolutely never wanted to know. As he lifted the lid on the grill and removed the corn from it, he reminded himself that he trusted Joy. She was a good woman with a good soul, and she hadn't even wanted to tell her friends about them until very recently.

With the corn off the grill, he flipped the burners to off and set the plate on the built-in counter. He wandered to the edge of the patio, the wind along the beach here just like it always was: constant. If there was no wind on Hilton Head, it almost felt like a bad omen.

Not tonight, and Scott watched the water change colors as the sun continued to sink behind him. "It's going to be a good year," he told himself. He had Joy, and while they didn't live in the same state, they had a plan.

No, it wasn't his first choice of plans, but he also understood that Joy couldn't just quit and make a cross-country move without some sort of idea of what her life would look like. He hadn't asked her in-depth questions about her finances or if traveling back and forth or moving here would be hard for her.

He could pull some money out of the landscaping

company if she needed help, but he wouldn't offer it to her for a while yet. Not until he knew for certain she'd be moving here. "Lord," he whispered as a couple of gulls chased each other in mid-air. He wasn't particularly religious, but if there was one thing he wanted to pray about, it was Joy Bartlett moving to Hilton Head.

A dog barked, and that had him turning toward the house. Joy came out of it, the breeze instantly trying to capture her hair in its wicked fingers. "Hey, you," she said. "You're standing out here alone?"

"Just thinking," he said. "What's Beryl barking about?"

"I think he was trying to call Gypsy." Joy grinned as she went through the kitchen and past the oversized outdoor table. "Poor thing. I think he's lonely now that Sage and that huge dog are gone."

"Gypsy was a lot of fun," Scott said. "Ghost loved him." He took Joy's hand and curled her into his side, where he then put his arm around her. "How was the nursery?"

"Amazing," she said with a sigh.

Scott had the sudden idea that she could move here and run a nursery, because she loved gardening, flowers, shrubbery, and trees. He barely managed to keep the thought from flying out of his mouth, and he and Joy stood in each other's arms and listened to the New Year wind whisper secrets to them.

"I'm going to miss this beach," Joy said wistfully, and Scott didn't have anything to say that wouldn't drive a wedge between them, or make her feel worse for not being able to stay.

"What are you two doing out here?"

Joy glanced over her shoulder, but she didn't move out of his arms. Cass came up beside them. "There's something magical about this spot, isn't there?" she asked.

"It's almost like you can feel the earth here more strongly than anywhere else," Joy said.

"I think the ocean and the wind have loud voices that finally combine right here," Scott said, not entirely sure where the words had come from.

"I've stood here many times," Cass said, hugging herself. She drew in a deep breath through her nose and added, "It's the top of the hour, and we've got balloons to pop to tell us our activity for seven o'clock." She gave them a smile. "But I can make an excuse for you if you need one."

Joy looked up at Scott, and he leaned down and kissed her.

"Yeah, that's what I thought," Cass murmured, and then her footsteps receded. When they finally went inside, two games of Scrabble were in full swing, and the sun had set completely.

"No, that's not a word," Lauren said, standing up and leaning over the board, her phone extended. "Look at the dictionary. Not there."

"Fine," Bea said. "You're such a stickler." She removed her tiles while Scott grinned, because who played Scrabble on New Year's Eve? No one he'd ever been to a party with.

The plate of corn sat on the counter, along with various chips, crackers, and dip, and Harry said, "Our seven o'clock food came up as appetizers, and we're playing Scrabble. We'll pop new balloons at eight and get a new game and a new food."

Next to him, Cass started to lay out her tiles, and she seemed pretty pleased with herself as she said, "Twenty-four points for 'airway.'"

Harry whipped his attention back to the game while Blake said, "It's twelve."

"It's on a double-word space," Cass said, sliding one A out of the way. She beamed at the people in her game and picked up the pencil to jot down her score.

Scott didn't want to play games or pop balloons at the top of every hour. His perfect night would be laying on the couch with Joy in his arms, the way they'd done after they'd opened each other's Christmas presents. Something slow and soft and silent, where he could hold onto her for as long as possible.

But he couldn't do that tonight, so he ate a new dish every sixty minutes—finally getting his steak in the nine p.m. hour—and played a new game or participated in a different activity until they were all counting down the seconds to midnight.

On the TV, the ball dropped in New York City, and Scott could finally wrap Joy in his arms and kiss her, murmuring, "Happy. New. Year," between kisses.

If he could keep her, it would be his best year yet.

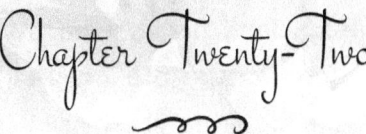

Chapter Twenty-Two

J oy couldn't stop kissing Scott, but she needed to stop kissing Scott. They broke the kiss together and breathed in together, and it felt very much like they should be planning the rest of their lives together.

"Call me when you get there," he whispered.

"The airport?" she whispered back. "Or Sweet Water Falls?"

"Both," he said, drawing back to his full height. "Then I'll know you made it to both places safely." He didn't wear an ounce of pain in his eyes—only happiness and desire. Joy felt so wanted and so necessary to him, and she could admit she hadn't felt that way in a relationship in a long, long time.

"Okay," she said, because she really had to leave now. She had to drive back to the airport and turn in her rental car, check her bag, and get through security. She should've left fifteen minutes ago when she first started kissing Scott good-bye. "I'll call you tonight."

Scott growled and hauled her close for another kiss. He didn't carry on too long, and this time, he opened the door to her SUV. "Call me tonight."

Joy got behind the wheel and waited for him to do the same. He'd parked behind her in Lauren's driveway, and once he'd backed out, she did too. She'd already had a tearful good-bye with Lauren, and as she turned right and Scott turned left, tears filled her eyes and ran down her face.

She made no attempt to stop them or wipe them away. "It's good you feel like this," she told herself. That meant she'd enjoyed herself in the past nine days, and she still wanted to spend more time with Scott. He wanted to see her again as soon as possible.

She'd sketched out a plan to come for the long weekend over the Martin Luther King, Junior holiday, as it would give her three days instead of two, and she wouldn't have to take a vacation day. She could fly out late on Friday and back late on Monday and have every minute possible with Scott.

Bea was hosting Supper Club this month, and she'd agreed to do it on that Saturday so Joy could attend in person. Bessie and Sage would video chat in from one of their houses, and Joy experienced some guilt about leaving them behind too. No matter which way she turned, she was letting someone down. Herself. Scott. Or her friends.

The weight of that accompanied her all the way back to Sweet Water Falls, where she finally pulled into her driveway after dark. The motion-sensor lights came on, and she eased into the garage.

She hated coming home after dark, to an empty house. For all she knew, someone could've been squatting here for the past week and a half, and she'd walk in after a long day of traveling to find someone making an omelet in her kitchen.

Such a thing didn't happen, but Joy still closed her garage door before she got out of the car and went inside. She had to go to work tomorrow, so she'd dragged her bag inside when she wanted to leave it and stumble to bed.

She set about unpacking, an old habit of hers, and she'd barely zipped her empty bag back together when the doorbell rang. Joy froze, her first inclination to ignore whoever had dropped by. Probably one of the neighbors who'd noticed the lights come on and wanted to make sure she was the one who'd triggered them.

The bell didn't ring again, and Joy left her bedroom, only glancing toward the front door as she turned the other way and went into the kitchen. She shrieked as she came face-to-face with another human being—one she wasn't expecting to see in her house.

"Sage!" She stumbled back a step, her adrenaline telling her to flee, but her brain reminding her that she and Sage were friends.

"You didn't answer your door," she said matter-of-factly. "I tracked your flight, and Bessie wanted you to have this bread. She says it's the best in the whole world."

Joy still had one hand pressed over her heart. "The whole world?"

"It's salted, cracked wheat, and I have to admit, it's a bit like crack, especially with butter and some of Cherry's homemade peach jam." She lifted the loaf of bread to the counter, a plastic bag swinging from her wrist. "And I happen to have some of all of the above."

She beamed at Joy. "How was leaving the island?"

Joy didn't want to talk about it, and her face must've said as much. "Fine," she said as Sage's smile slipped.

"We knew it would be really hard for you," Sage said. "Thus, why I'm here with bread, butter, and jam." She began unpacking the wares she'd brought. "Bessie wanted to come, but your flight was landing too late. She has to be to work in six hours."

"My alarm is going off not too far after that," Joy said, already yawning.

"Oh, I forgot." Sage bustled toward the front door. "Scott sent this."

"Scott—what?" Joy whipped her attention to Sage, but the woman had already unlocked and left through the front door. Joy followed her, keen to know what Scott had said to Sage, and when, and what he'd sent. And how.

On the porch, she hugged herself, wishing she'd thought to change before she'd come to make a cup of tea. Sage bent into the backseat of her car and seemed to be looking for something. When she finally emerged from it and slammed the door closed, Joy couldn't tell what she held in her hand.

As she drew closer, her mouth dropped a little more. Sage carried a light blue pastry bag, the kind that came from Gourmet Goods, on an island twelve hundred miles away.

Sage grinned from ear to ear as she mounted the steps

again. "I got it this morning, so it's fresh," she said. "He said he wished he could—well, you can read the card as well as I did." She handed the bag to Joy and brushed by her. "Come inside, Joy. I'll make some coffee."

"Tea," Joy said, staring at the blue bag in her hand. "I was going to make tea."

"That's fine too," Sage said. "I like tea."

Joy scrambled to follow her, and she toed the door closed as she opened the bag. Two chocolate croissants sat there, as did a small card, about half the size of the regular greeting variety.

She lingered by the door as she removed the card from the envelope, and she read the whole note—in her boyfriend's handwriting—in a matter of seconds. *I miss you already, and you're not even gone yet. You will be by the time you get these. I only wish I could stop by with your caramel coffee before work tomorrow morning. Can't wait to see you again, Scott.*

Joy looked up from the card, wonder and awe streaming through her. "How did he do this?" she wondered. "Sage," she called as she stuffed the card back into the bag and went into the kitchen at the back of the house. "Did you drive these home with you?"

"Nope." Sage set the kettle on the burner. "He had them shipped to my house. Came in a box with so much bubble wrap, I thought I was unearthing a bomb." She trilled out a laugh, but Joy had no idea what to think. He'd gone by Gourmet Goods to write this card and order these croissants while she'd been on the island with him. But when?

"Okay, you call him," Sage said. "I'll slice the bread and get the tea ready, then I'll bring it to you in the living room." She turned Joy around and gave her a little push to get her moving toward a softer seat.

Joy went, because she did want to talk to Scott, and she didn't mind being taken care of either. Sage was exceptionally good at that, and Joy decided she could let herself be pampered for just this one evening.

She sank onto her familiar couch, beyond glad to be home at the same time she wished she was back on that air mattress in Lauren's home office. *You sent me chocolate croissants?*

It was an hour later in Hilton Head, but Scott had obviously waited up to hear from her, because he responded in mere seconds with, *Oh, good. They got there, and Sage brought them to you tonight like she said she would.*

Joy glanced over to her friend, who worked merrily in the kitchen like she had nowhere else she'd rather be.

I miss you, Joy said. *But I made it home, and those croissants pretty much guarantee I'll have an amazing day tomorrow.*

I hope so, my Joy.

She could feel the depth of his emotion in those words, practically hear him say them in his deep voice, and taste his mouth against hers as if she were still standing in his arms in Lauren's driveway, kissing him.

Sage is making tea, and Bessie sent bread and butter.

You have good friends, he said. *And it's late here, so I won't keep you. I just didn't want you getting home to that dark house alone. I'll text you tomorrow.*

Joy didn't know why her chest felt like it might collapse at any moment. Because he didn't want to stay on and text anymore? Because he'd orchestrated Sage's visit, complete with her favorite breakfast croissant for tomorrow? Because he didn't seem to mind sharing her with her friends?

Or because he knew her well enough to know she hated coming home in the dark, alone?

He didn't text again, and Joy didn't want to keep him from getting the sleep he needed. She set her phone on the coffee table in front of her and leaned back into the couch, closing her eyes. She hadn't expected to fall asleep, but the next thing she knew, Sage said, "Joy, dear, I have tea if you still want it."

She blinked her eyes open, a wash of disappointment cutting through her when she saw her own walls, with photos of her boys and their families hanging there. Sage set a teacup next to Joy's phone and sank into the recliner with her own drink. It steamed, and at some point, she'd placed a platter of bread, butter, and jam on the table too.

"I didn't mean to fall asleep," Joy said.

"It's been ten minutes," Sage said with the wave of her hand. "I won't stay but a few more minutes." She watched as Joy leaned forward and picked up her tea. What she was looking for, Joy could only guess at.

"I can take care of myself, you know," she said after she'd taken a delicious sip of the herbal tea.

"Mm, I know." Sage didn't apologize for being there.

She'd always been a night owl, and Joy didn't want to know if nine-thirty was late at night for her or just the beginning of her evening. "But it sure is nice to have someone care enough about you to show up, don't you think?"

"Yes," Joy murmured. "Thank you, Sage."

"Bessie sent the bread and jam. Scott mailed the croissants." Sage tipped her cup back, and it looked tiny as she held it in both of her hands. "We all just wanted today to be...as easy as possible for you."

Joy nodded, her emotions rippling through her the way a flag did in a stiff, beach wind. She did have amazing friends, and the best boyfriend she'd ever had.

"So," Sage said. "What are you putting on your blueprint now that you've had your time in-person with Scott?"

"I don't know," Joy said with a sigh. She studied the depths of her teacup, but that didn't take long. "Right now, my baby blueprint has me finishing my teaching degree. It has me finishing the school year here. It has me telling my sons about me and Scott." She was pretty proud of herself for getting that far, actually.

"We have a visitation plan in place through the wedding. Then, it's only a couple of months until summer. We're taking it day-by-day."

"Smart," Sage said. She finished her tea and exhaled mightily as she got to her feet. Joy expected her to launch into a lecture after a sigh like that, but Sage only headed into the kitchen with her cup and saucer. "Okay, I better head out and let you get to bed."

She came back into the living room, and Joy didn't want

her to go. She quickly set down her cup and got to her feet. "You don't have to go."

"I have to color old Lydia's hair at nine o'clock," Sage said with a smile. "So I really do." She pulled Joy into a hug and held on tightly to her. It felt nice to have such strong arms hold her, and Joy hoped she could give the same support and love to someone the way Sage did for her.

Sage stepped back, her smile warm and genuine as she said, "You're a smart woman, Joy. But don't let your brain talk louder than your heart." She smoothed her hair down, tapped her right over her pulse with two light fingers, and left through the front door.

Both body parts had been talking to her a lot lately, and Joy never knew which one to listen to over the other. Maybe now that she was home, in a familiar place, with a routine, she could figure everything out.

As she walked her own teacup into the kitchen and placed it in the sink, she thought, *Maybe you don't need to have everything planned out before you take the first step.*

But that was her silly heart talking, and Joy had then experienced some of the worst heartache of her life after listening to the part of her that ignored rationality and focused only on emotion.

No, she'd go slow, and she'd figure things out step by step until she knew what to do—and then she'd take action.

After rewrapping the bread, Joy slid everything into the fridge and padded down the hall to her bedroom. She set an alarm for twenty minutes earlier than normal, because then she'd be able to chat with Scott before either of them had to go to work.

Then she fell asleep, dreams of her life with Scott playing out in her mind and giving her the one true love that she'd been longing for.

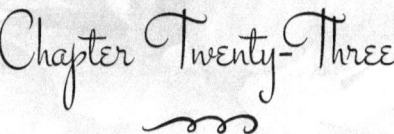

Chapter Twenty-Three

C ass turned back to the oven when the timer went off. She didn't love cooking, but Bea had put together the sweet and sour meatballs for that night's Supper Club, and all Cass had to do was bend and get them out.

She slid them, in all their bubbling, glazey sauce, onto the stovetop, bumped the button to turn off the timer, and turned back to Bea. "I'm just wondering if she'll really come."

"It's Supper Club," Bea said, finally looking up from the magazine she'd been leafing through since Cass had arrived twenty minutes ago. The rest of their friends should be here soon—well, Lauren and Joy anyway. Bessie and Sage would be calling in via video chat, and Bessie had texted to say they were at her house that night, making the same recipe.

It was Bessie's grandmother's recipe, one she'd made a Supper Club before. She'd then distributed the recipe to everyone, as they'd all fawned over the soft meatballs in a barbecue-vinegar sauce that really sounded weird but was the epitome of divine.

Even Cass liked them, and she didn't like red meat all that much.

"You finally tore your eyes from that thing." Cass glanced at the glossy pages of the wedding mag. "Anything good in there?"

"They only put the best things in here," Bea said.

"Anything for Courtney, I mean. We already know Lauren blew her budget on the venue."

"But it's going to be the most amazing wedding on the planet," Bea said with a smile. "And no, Courtney would never choose something from a magazine like this. She's more...down to earth is what I think Ted said."

Cass grinned. "Are they getting married in the brown barn or the red one?"

Bea looked like she'd just swallowed something sour. "Red," she said as she tucked her hair. She'd cut it a few years ago and maintained the pixie hairstyle, but it was getting a little long these days. "It's fine." She took a deep breath and put on her best mother-of-the-groom smile. "It's what she wants, and we all know the bride gets what she wants on her wedding day."

"Did you?" Cass asked. "The first time?"

"Heavens, no." Bea scoffed. "Norman and I got married so young, and my parents had no money. We got married in their backyard."

Cass smiled, because she'd heard this story. Seen the pictures too. But that was back when Bea had been happy in her marriage, before she'd found out Norman had been cheating on her with his secretary and wanted a divorce.

"I'm sure you did," Bea said. "Both times."

"Close enough," Cass said, because she didn't want to get into things with Bea. Not again. She didn't live a charmed life, no matter what any of her friends said. Just because she lived in a nice house didn't mean she didn't have challenges. "I'm thinking of going back to Texas this year," she said.

"What? When?"

"For West's...to visit West's grave." She didn't clear her throat, but she did move to the fridge and open it. Why, she had no idea, other than it gave her something to do, and she wouldn't have to look at Bea.

"It's in March," she said. "And Joy's doing Supper Club there. I don't have to be there on the exact date, though I'm sure she'd move it for me."

"I could go with you," Bea offered, exactly the way Cass had assumed she would. "But Lauren likely won't be able to. It'll be too close to her wedding for her to want to take a trip."

"I'm going to talk to her about it tonight," Cass said. "If she can't come, Bea..." She didn't know how to say Bea couldn't either. "My parents are there. I can have all the kids come. My sister."

"But I want to be there too." The barstool where Bea sat scraped the floor in the beach house she shared with Grant. Shelby had gone back to her mother's after the holidays, as had everyone else who'd come to visit, and Bea had admitted that she enjoyed the silence in the house. She enjoyed just her and Grant together in the evenings.

Cass knew exactly what she meant. She could sit on the couch with Harrison, neither of them saying a word, and it was pure perfection. He could even fall asleep, and Cass didn't mind. She just liked being with him.

Bea joined Cass in front of the fridge, which held a few bags of salad that would go with the meatballs, and one of her famous Texas sheet cakes. "You can't go alone."

"I actually can," Cass whispered. Whether she wanted to or not was another story.

"Harrison won't go?"

"It depends," she said. "The final meeting for the library build is this week, and he's in the top three."

Bea pulled in a breath and then swatted at Cass's bicep. "He is? Why didn't you tell me?"

Cass flinched away from her. "I just did." She grinned and closed the fridge. "I have to have something to say at Supper Club. Everyone always has such interesting news, and I'm...boring."

"You are not boring."

"No one wants to hear about Mister Myers' cat again." Cass quirked her eyebrows, satisfied when Bea didn't argue with her. "And that's my best story in the past three weeks."

"Like I'm any better," Bea said. "It's snooze-central over here."

"Whatever," Cass said. "You have fascinating stories about what people leave behind in their rentals. It makes me super self-conscious about when I travel."

"Good thing you haven't left the island in over a year," Bea shot back.

Cass laughed, and it felt good to do so. She was happy here—blissfully happy on the beach, with Beryl for company as she worked on her clients' portfolios. She'd gotten to meet a few people around the island with her interior design business, and Harry absolutely adored her. She didn't laugh much, though, and she really enjoyed the cleansing power of it.

"Ding dong," Lauren called, and both Cass and Bea turned toward the front door. Grant's beach house wasn't one of the big ones in Cass's neighborhood, and the whole first floor was open from front to back. Through an arched doorway sat their master suite, but Grant had actually swapped places with Cass tonight. Harry was grilling, and they'd hang out together tonight.

Lauren carried a huge garment bag, and Cass gave a little shriek. "Tell me that's the dress." She rushed toward Lauren, as she and Bea had gone wedding dress shopping with her the very moment they could after the holidays ended.

"No." Lauren beamed nonetheless. "And I can't show you guys what these are until everyone's on the call. Bessie will murder me from twelve hundred miles away."

"These?" Bea asked. "Plural?"

"They can't be bridesmaids dresses," Cass said, frowning. "You just chose a color last week, and we're getting our own. Right?"

"Yes, yes," Lauren said impatiently as she arrived in the kitchen. "Okay, I can't wait. I'll risk my life." She flopped the bulging bag onto the countertop and unzipped it. Layer of white upon white upon white spilled from the seam. "It's not just one dress. It's four."

"Four?" Cass peered at the fabric squooshing out of the bag. "Why do you have four dresses?"

"So the one I wanted they didn't have. It was on back order."

"No," Bea said with a gasp. "When did you find out?"

"Today," Lauren said. "So Maven—remember her? She was so great to help with everything—she called, and she's like, in tears, right? And she says to come in, because she has some great replacements for me. So I say I can't stay long, because I have our Supper Club, and she says I can take them and try them on for you guys tonight."

She started to pull the top dress out of the bag, but Bea covered her hand. "Honey, maybe we should do it in a room where there hasn't been barbecue sauce."

"And when the others can see too," Cass said, exchanging a glance with Bea.

"It's almost time, isn't it?" Lauren asked with a hint of impatience in her voice. "I was seriously rushing to get here."

The three of them looked at the clock right as the time ticked to the top of the hour. "My goodness," Bea said, spinning to get her laptop off the coffee table in the living room. "I wasn't even paying attention to the time."

"Joy's late," Cass said, eyeing the front door.

"Joy will be here," Lauren said.

"Will she?" Cass asked under her breath, having had this argument with Bea already. "I haven't seen her once, and she leaves tomorrow. How many minutes have you seen her since she touched down two days ago?"

Lauren frowned, as if she were really trying to add up all the minutes. Cass's point had been made, and she swept the gowns over her arm. "Let's put these over here for a few minutes."

"I want to try them on before I eat," Lauren said.

"That's fine," Bea said, putting her laptop up on the windowsill above the kitchen sink. "Wave, everyone." She waved to the machine, and Cass dropped the dresses on the sofa and hurried back into the kitchen to say hello to her friends in Sweet Water Falls.

"Bessie." She gasped. "Your hair is amazing."

Bessie fingered the long locks. "You think so? It feels a little unnatural still."

"It looks sensational," Bea said. "I would never ever guess those are extensions."

"Really flawless," Lauren agreed, her smile so big and wide.

"Where's Joy?" Bessie asked.

"She's coming," Bea and Lauren said again, and Cass heard the absence of her own voice. She wasn't sure why she didn't believe in Joy. The woman had literally never let anyone down, ever. She was loyal and true, honest and hard-working. She was also dating Scott long-distance, and Cass tried to remember what it had been like to be away from Harrison when she'd gone back to Texas to list her house for sale and finish the final clean-out.

"I have a good-news, bad-news scenario," Lauren said.

"Bad news is the dress I ordered is on backorder. So far that I can't get it for my wedding."

"Oh, no," Sage said while Bessie gasped and said, "No."

"Good news is I have four more to try on—live!—with you tonight!" Lauren bounced on the balls of her feet, this news obviously the best ever, and clapped her hands together. "So as soon as—"

"I'm here," Joy called, her statement punctuated by the slamming of the door. She walked briskly through the house to them, her cheeks harboring a bit of a blush. A lot of a blush, if Cass were being honest with herself. "I'm so sorry. I just lost track of time."

"That can happen when you're making out with your hot boyfriend," Cass said.

Lauren burst out laughing, but Bea chastised Cass and Bessie looked like she'd never kissed a man before.

Joy shot daggers at Cass but didn't say she *hadn't* been making out with her hot boyfriend. Which totally meant she had been. "What did I miss?" she asked instead.

"Lauren has four wedding dresses to try on tonight," Bea said. "So we'll do that first. Then I want to hear life updates, and then we'll eat."

"We can do life updates while Lauren is changing," Bessie said.

"Then she won't get to hear them," Cass argued back.

Bessie looked at Sage, who looked at Bessie. They clearly had something up their sleeves, and the tension in the room built and built. Funny how that could happen, even over a video call from so far away.

"I can't wait another second," Bessie finally said. She faced the camera again, her smile blinding in its brightness. "Wyn and I are going to move to Hilton Head right before Lauren's wedding. She's already talked to her boss on the ranch, and I'm going to do the same this next week."

Silence filled at least two houses in the world in that moment. Then Sage said, "And I'm coming with them. I can move my salon anytime, so I've decided to list the hobby farm for sale and make the move."

They smiled and smiled and smiled, and finally Bea said, "That's amazing! I'm thrilled you'll all be here!"

"Yeah," Cass said, her eyes locked on Joy. "That's amazing." Joy smiled, but there was no oomph behind it. She'd said nothing, and in fact, it looked like she might burst into tears at any moment. One of her biggest fears was being left behind, and Cass's heart broke as she realized that Joy would be the last of them left in Sweet Water Falls. She'd literally be left behind there once Bessie and Sage moved.

"Phenomenal," Lauren said, moving closer to Joy. She slipped her arm around her and drew her close. "Right, Joy?"

Cass stepped closer too, letting Joy lean back into her as she sagged a little. Bea linked her arm through hers on Joy's other side, and the three of them surrounded her, held her up, and hopefully told her how much they loved her—no matter where she lived.

"Joy," Bessie said.

"It's great," she yelled. "Really, just—so great. I can't wait to see what you do with the bakery."

Cass could only see her in the small video window on Bea's computer now, and while her voice sounded pretty normal, if she'd been Lauren, she'd have gone off camera and made up an excuse about someone being at the door.

"I think your phone is ringing," Lauren said. When only she moved, she added, "Joy?"

There was no phone ringing, but Joy spun away from the computer, her face crumbling as she did. "Yeah, I hear it."

Cass definitely heard the emotion in her voice then, and it sounded like her heart getting ripped out of her chest.

"Let's get you in a dress," Bea said brightly. She and Lauren bustled off, leaving Cass to face Sage and Bessie.

"Cass," Bessie said. "I knew it would upset her, but Wyn's in a transition with her job at the end of February anyway, and it turned out to be a good time to quit. She'll come here and help me with the house, packing, and then we'll just...come."

Cass nodded. "Of course," she said. "It's going to be amazing. Let me or Bea know if you need any help with houses or rentals or whatever." She smiled at the pair of them. "Joy's doing Supper Club in March, so maybe we can plan it to all be there then, and you guys can move after that?" She glanced over her shoulder, but Lauren and Bea had obviously taken the dresses into the master suite, and Joy wasn't anywhere to be found.

She faced the computer again. "I'm going to come visit West's grave in March, and I was hoping to do Supper Club there." She didn't need to say *because Joy will like that*. It was implied, and everyone heard it anyway. "I was going to ask her about the date tonight, so I can make plans."

"Sure," Bessie said. "We won't leave until after Supper Club in March."

That still gave Joy two whole months to live in Sweet Water Falls—alone—until the school year ended. She'd been nothing but clear about finishing the year there. She had classes to finish too, though those were online. She said she couldn't take on cleaning up her house to sell, packing, and moving during all of that.

But now she'd be alone, and Cass's worry for her doubled. She re-entered the room at the same time as Bea, and from across the room, Cass couldn't tell if she'd been crying or not, so Bessie and Sage likely wouldn't be able to either.

"This is the first dress," Bea said, and she gestured for Lauren to come out. She did, and by the stunning smile on her face, Cass knew she'd just found a second wedding dress that was "the one."

And people thought Cass lived a charmed life.

Chapter Twenty-Four

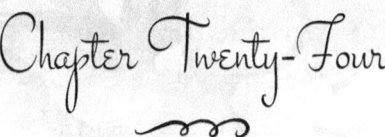

Scott smiled at the blinking Christmas lights on the pine tree in Joy's front yard. She obviously didn't have an HOA to send her a take-down notice within thirty days of the holiday, or those wouldn't be there.

They winked merrily in the darkening night, and Scott's rental car headlights cut across them as well. Lights flooded the front porch, steps, sidewalk and driveway, and he actually raised his hand to shield his eyes.

He'd worked until lunchtime in Hilton Head, then driven to the airport for his flight. Then he'd flown, eaten terrible airplane food, and picked up his rental car in Corpus Christi. As the clock sat near nine-thirty, he hoped Joy wouldn't be too tired to see him for at least an hour, and then he'd head to his hotel to check-in.

Texas sat behind Hilton Head by an hour, and he was the one living twenty-five hours today, and Joy had taken tomorrow off of her teaching job, so he couldn't sleep in then either. Not that he would anyway. Scott rose with the sun, no matter what time he actually went to bed.

Once he put the car in park, he reached over to the passenger seat for the two things he'd brought for Joy. One he'd carted all the way here from South Carolina, and the other he'd picked up on his way here. The winding roads to this small town on the Coastal Bend actually made him smile, and happiness paraded through him as he got out of the car.

Joy had been in Hilton Head when she'd gotten the news that Bessie and Sage—the last of her Supper Club friends—would be moving sooner than she'd expected. She'd stayed for the whole dinner, and when he'd picked her up later that night, she'd told him while she faced the window, one hand cradling her face as if her neck couldn't hold up her head all on its own.

Scott had tried to be more understanding. He'd tried to listen to her vent and worry and cry, and he hoped he'd helped a little bit. In his head, the solution was really very easy.

If Joy didn't want to be the last one left in Sweet Water Falls, she could list her house and move to Hilton Head, the same way Bessie and Sage were doing. The same way Bea, Cass, and Lauren already had done.

She felt duty-bound to her job here, and Scott once again found himself trying to understand. Jobs, to him, were just jobs. They could be quit at any time and re-gotten at any time too. No one he employed seemed to care much about when they quit, and he'd chosen to say nothing rather than tell Joy to quit.

Number one, it wasn't what she wanted to hear, and number two, it wasn't his job to dispense advice. He'd never been married, but he knew that much.

The moment his foot touched the first porch slat, the front door opened. His sexy, beautiful, amazing Joy stood there, and Scott managed to bring his other leg up before he came to a complete stop. "Wow."

She wore a pair of loose black pants that hung all the way to the floor, only her bare toes peeking out from beneath the hem. Since the swimming suit incident of last year, he hadn't seen her wear a lot of sleeveless tops, but she had on a tank top tonight that drove the breath right out of his lungs.

It too was black, and Scott's eyes skimmed all the dips and swells of her body—and that made his hot from head to toe.

"You made it." She smiled at him, her lips shiny and oh-so-kissable. Her voice prompted him to continue moving forward, and he practically thrust the roses and the pastries toward her. He felt like a complete loser of a boyfriend for literally bringing her flowers and candy for Valentine's Day, but her face lit up like the Christmas tree behind him.

Her eyes drank in the deep burgundy blooms before they came back to his, and she said, "You're my favorite person."

"You're mine." His throat sounded like he'd gargled with glass, but he kept himself from clearing it while Joy took the flowers.

"Come on in," she said, giving him a smile that said as soon as his hands weren't full, she wanted to kiss him.

He hadn't seen her in person in three weeks, and he couldn't wait to breathe in the soft, tropical scent of her hair, hold her hand, and taste those lips. The air conditioning blew inside her house, and that helped cool Scott a tiny bit as he followed her into the house.

The living room started immediately, with a dining set sitting behind the couch to mark the separation between the two rooms. "This place is great," he said.

"It does a good job," she said over her shoulder.

"You raised the boys here?"

"Yes," she said. "Wendell moved to Houston when he left." She spoke in an even tone, and Scott placed the blue pastry bag on the kitchen counter while Joy bent to get out a vase. "How was the flight?"

"The pilot bounced us on landing," he said. "But I'm here, so we obviously didn't die or anything."

Joy turned to him, set the vase on the counter, and Scott took the roses from here. "You can do this after."

She blinked at him, her long lashes covering those magnificent eyes for only a moment, then another. "After what?"

"After I kiss you." He took her into his arms effortlessly, and Joy melted into him instantly. Just what he wanted. He wanted this woman, and as he gazed longingly at her, she closed her eyes in a surrendering blink, and Scott knew then that he was in love with her.

Instead of saying it, he eliminated all the space between them and showed her the best way he knew how.

She kissed him back, and Scott absolutely could not live without this in his life. Not for another day. In the back of his mind, he knew he'd only be here for two days, and then part of another before his flight home.

Not only that, but Joy wouldn't be back in Hilton Head until the very end of March. Six weeks between this trip of his and the next one of hers, and Scott kept waiting for Joy to break their connection and duck her head.

She didn't, so he kissed her and kissed her, finally being the one to pull back enough to disconnect their lips. They breathed in together, and he fell even more with the coconut-peach scent of her shampoo, and the way she tucked herself right against his chest like God Himself had made her to fit there.

It seemed wrong that it had taken Scott so long to meet her. Forty-four years he'd lived alone, and he hadn't been all that upset about it. Until her. He absolutely felt like she'd been made to complement him in his life, and he gently wiped her hair back off the side of her face.

"I have missed you so much," he whispered, but they weren't the words he wanted to say. His hands tightened along her back, holding her right close to him. "Joy, I'm in love with you."

She didn't move, and Scott had a moment where he wondered if he'd spoken out loud or just thought the words in his head. Then he realized that Joy had gone utterly still, and that was her tell to let him know she had indeed heard him.

His muscles bunched as she tried to pull away from him, and he held her for another moment and then released her. Her eyes roved between his, hunting for the answers she needed. He smiled at her and leaned down to kiss the tip of her nose. "Don't say anything, okay?"

She didn't, and while Scott would've been over the moon to hear her tell him she loved him back, he knew Joy wasn't ready to say those words yet. He hadn't meant to pressure her, and he said, "I didn't mean to put you on the spot." He lifted his hands to her face and held her there. "I just—nothing's changed, okay?"

Something had definitely changed—*he'd* changed—because Joy's eyes misted over, and she let them fall closed. Scott gathered her back into the circle of his embrace and he pressed his lips to her temple. "I love seeing you. I love talking to you. I'm so glad I'm here."

"I'm glad you're here too," she whispered. Joy locked up from time to time, so talking meant she'd started to come out of her initial shock. "February in Texas is so amazing. We have the best strawberries right now, and I made some jam." She moved, and he let her step away from him to get the jar out of the fridge. "I made it, but I got the bread from Bessie, so it'll be good."

Scott rounded the small island and pulled out a barstool. "Are you going to make me some of your jam toast?"

"Yes." She didn't even ask him if he wanted any. They'd been texting about it since she'd been making jam after going to the strawberry fields and picking way too many berries. Her words, not his.

He grinned at her as she set two pieces of bread in the toaster, and when she faced him, she asked, "What?"

"Nothing." He kept smiling. "I just like being here with you."

Joy sighed and came to sit next to him. He took her hand in his and stroked his thumb over the back of it. "Are we going to make it?"

"I think so," he said.

"To summer?" She looked at him then, so much worry swimming in her eyes that Scott wanted to remove. He couldn't do that for her, and he knew better than to tell her not to worry. It was just in her nature, and getting her to stop now would be like trying to send the ocean waves backward.

"Well," he said. "I just told you I love you, so I think we'll make it in whatever we need to make it in."

"You don't even know what 'it' is, do you?" A tiny smile touched her lips and flitted away.

"If 'it' is me and you, then we're going to make it," he said firmly. "If it's you living here after Bessie and Sage move, I don't know. I sure hope so. You're a strong woman, and you've done harder things. If it's me and you having to live apart for a few more months, then yes, I think we're going to make it. If it's whether or not we're going to breakfast tomorrow, then again, yes, we're going to make it."

She leaned into him and nudged him with her shoulder. "Scott."

"Joy."

The toast popped up, but neither of them moved. Scott stood a moment later and went to butter and slather his own toast in jam. "What are the chances of me seeing your wedding dress?"

"It's a bridesmaid dress," Joy clarified.

"Yep, that one." He lifted his gaze to hers. "Maybe there's a misbehaving strap I'll need to help with."

Joy's smile bloomed then, stretching to cover her whole face. "I'll go put it on right now." She rose from the barstool and headed out of the kitchen and down the hall.

Scott had eaten both pieces of his toast and poured himself a glass of milk before Joy called, "Baby? Can you help me with the zipper?"

He definitely could, but he'd want to take it all the way down instead of closing it up. Still, he minded his manners as he met her in the hallway and pulled the zipper up to the middle of her back. The sleeves were wide and bunched over her shoulders, but with plenty of skin up her back, along her neck, and down the entire length of her arm, Scott had plenty to admire.

He leaned down and touched his lips to the curve of her body where her shoulder sloped into her neck. "Mm."

She turned in his arms and pushed gently against his chest. He fell back a step at a time until he returned to the kitchen. He stumbled back to the island and sat clumsily while she stood near the corner of the hallway. She put one hand on her hip, pushing the other out, and asked, "Well? What do you think?"

"I think if 'it' is me waiting until we're married to see you out of that dress, then no. We're not going to make it."

She smiled and shook her head, like he was a naughty boy whom she dearly loved anyway. She seemed to glide toward him, her feet not really on the ground, and that was when he realized her shoes.

"You got the clear ones," he said, his eyes traveling back up the length of her body to her face.

"Are they okay?" She looked down at her feet too.

"They're fantastic," he said, getting to his feet as she neared. The dress was the dark indigo of blueberry skin, and it hugged Joy's curves like a familiar lover. It shimmered and shone in her overhead lights, sometimes casting a rainbow along the surface of the fabric. "You are stunning in every way."

"I'm going to wear my hair up. Lauren's got pearls for all of us." She gathered her hair back, though it wasn't long enough for a ponytail. "I'm going to get pinned, and I'll have pearls in my hair too."

"Gorgeous," he said.

Joy put both hands on his chest and slid them up and around to the back of his neck. "Scott..." She didn't say anything else, but her face communicated everything he needed to know anyway.

"I said not to say anything," he said.

"I feel dumb."

"Why?" He grinned down at her. "Joy, I don't need you to say it back right now. *I* just needed to say it." He skimmed his hands over her shoulders. "This was me being selfish, okay?"

"You're not selfish," she said.

"I am, and I'm okay with it in this regard." He gave her what he hoped was a tender smile. "Now, I'm going to lay down on your couch while you change, and I hope you'll come lay with me until I fall asleep." He kissed her quickly and let her go, watching as she floated out of the room in her glamorous dress and shoes.

Then he kicked off his shoes and lay down on her couch. When she returned to him several minutes later, back in her loose pants and tank top, Scott wrapped her up in his arms and the two of them simply existed together while something played on her television.

It was the perfect day, because Joy had been in it, and he'd told her he loved her. Now, if he could figure out how to get her to Hilton Head faster, Scott would really have his future in the palm of his hand.

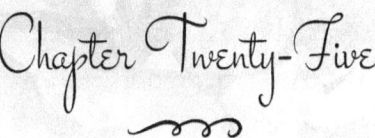

Chapter Twenty-Five

Lauren lifted her coffee mug to her lips and took a sip, the hot liquid soothing the dryness in her mouth and down her throat. She sighed, and that simple sip of coffee allowed the tension to seep out of her shoulders.

It was her wedding day, and her brother had come from California. He'd brought his wife and children, and Lauren had survived the dinner last night.

She took another sip of coffee, mentally telling herself to be fair. She hadn't just *survived* the dinner—she'd enjoyed it. Jess and Rena had brought both of their daughters, and there had been hugging and smiling when they'd met at a steak and seafood joint where Lauren loved their artichoke dip. She'd barely eaten more than a few chips, and her stomach still didn't feel entirely settled.

The wedding wouldn't be until later that day, and when she'd told her mother she was getting married and when, the tickets for her, her step-father, and her half-sister had been booked for that morning.

They only had a hotel for tonight, and they'd return to Minnesota tomorrow. Lauren had wanted to tell her mom not to come at all, but she hadn't acted on the selfish impulse. She'd issued the invitation, and she had to let her mother make her own choices.

Deep down, Lauren knew her mom didn't make her own decisions. Her husband, Rowland, made them for her, and she went along. She'd left Lauren behind years ago, and she hadn't even seen her in years.

All of the tension and worry bunched up in her muscles again, and Lauren took a sip of her coffee to try to relieve it. Some of the tightness dissipated, but not all of it.

"Babe?"

She turned away from the window where she stood to face Blake. He strode toward her in his sexy slacks and polo, his smile bright. Everything would be okay now, because Blake was here.

He took her straight into his chest, and she pressed her cheek to his chest so she could listen to his heartbeat. It boomed steady and strong, further anchoring her. "We're getting married today," she said.

"Finally." His voice rumbled in his chest, barely tiptoeing across her eardrums.

She smiled, because she knew and felt how badly Blake wanted to be married.

"Did you decide what to do with the house?" he asked

without moving. She appreciated how stalwart he was, and that she could rely on him so completely.

"No," she said. "I keep thinking Bessie or Sage or Joy will want it."

"You're not just going to give it to one of them?"

"No," Lauren said again, now stepping out of his arms and sagging into his side. "But Bessie has an offer on her house. It took longer than she wanted, but she's coming here." She hadn't been as involved in the happenings with her friends as she'd been running her business and planning this wedding.

"Sage will too," Blake said. "She'll leave the farm and let it sell while she comes here."

"I think so too." Lauren turned toward the kitchen. "Do you want coffee?" When she reached the coffee pot, she faced him again. "Where's Tommy? I thought we were all going to breakfast."

Now that she'd had some caffeine, her brain felt more functional. She looked toward the front door, but Tommy didn't walk through it.

"He's on the phone with his mother," Blake said. "Out in the car." He came nearer, and Lauren poured him a cup of coffee he probably wouldn't drink. He stirred it anyway, the silence between them comfortable but a bit somber.

"I thought last night went really well," he said, almost under his breath.

"I did too," Lauren agreed. She looked up at him, their eyes engaging and locking. "Thank you for being there.

Thank you for being so kind and easy for Jess and Rena to connect with."

"I didn't do anything," he said with a smile. "I think the wedding is going to go just fine."

"Yeah, I'll just have several strangers there, watching."

Blake slid his arm around her waist. "But you'll have so many others who love you," he said. "My family, your friends, your clients...me and Tommy. Who cares if there's a few people there who you haven't seen in a while?"

Lauren let the people who loved her walk through her mind, seeing each of them smile at her and feeling their arms wrap around her until she was encased with layer upon layer of love. "You're right," she said.

She drew in a deep breath. "Let's go to breakfast." After that, she'd come back here and get ready to go to Island Aisle and prepare for the single thing she'd been looking forward to for years and years now.

Finally.

"YOU'RE PERFECT," BEA SAID LATER THAT DAY. Cass still fussed over a clip on the left side of her head, but Lauren stood perfectly still as she looked at herself in the mirror. Her dark hair had been curled by Sage and then pinned in an elaborate up-do that looked like a crown.

Cass had strategically placed sparkly butterfly clips in various places that made her feel like the queen of the fairies.

Coupled with her shimmery wedding dress, Lauren looked absolutely the way she wanted to.

"Thank you," she murmured to Bea, who pressed her cheek to Lauren's.

"Done," Cass said, and Lauren turned away from the mirror. She embraced Cass, unable to lift her arms too high because of the ruched, fluffy sleeves that had the pearlescent fabric bunched into flowers. Cass had also attached butterflies there, but these were not clear or pearly, but bright pink, blue, and purple.

Lauren wore a bright pink bra and panty set that no one but Joy and Bea knew about, as they'd been with her when she'd purchased them. Everyone would be able to see her matching shoes and fingernails, and as Lauren moved to hug Bessie, moisture threatened to ruin the masterful makeup job that she and Joy had painted on her face.

She held back the tears and whispered, "Thank you, Bessie. I love you."

"I love you too," Bessie said, the statement so simple and pure that it rang one-hundred percent true in Lauren's heart.

Bca wiped her eyes as Lauren stepped back from Bessie and then into Bea's embrace. "You are a goddess, and he is so lucky," Bea whispered.

"Thank you," Lauren whispered. She stepped over to Sage, who wore the widest, most beautiful smile on her face. She'd done her hair up too, along with everyone else's, and they'd all picked their own dresses.

Lauren hadn't given them any color restrictions. In the beginning, she'd thought she wanted all the traditional things a wedding would bring. But the moment she'd decided to get married in Island Aisle open garden, her vision had changed.

She wanted her friends to be there and be totally comfortable. Cass wore a bright green dress that fit her figure precisely, because Cass had the best fashion sense in the world. She wore a belt around her trim waist that boasted every color in the rainbow and fastened with a buckle in the shape of a bright white butterfly.

Bessie wore a purple gown that stretched tightly across her bust but flared everywhere else. It rivaled Lauren's dress with all the skirt layers, but Lauren had a train on her wedding gown. The same clear clips that crowned Lauren's head had been clipped into some of the layers of fabric on Bessie's dress.

Bea wore a pink dress that complimented her blonde-haired, blue-eyed looks. Her pixie cut had been doctored up with a pale pink headband adorned with a simple, single butterfly.

Sage wore a black dress with a single strap over her left shoulder. It bore an enormous ruffle that nearly touched her earlobe, and as Lauren stepped back, she fixed the fabric of the sleeve, so it sat right again.

"Thank you, Sage," she said. "You've made me beautiful."

"God made you beautiful," Sage said, and once again, Lauren felt the truthfulness of her words. Her fingers fiddled with the blue butterfly that rose inside the glorious black fabric of Sage's sleeve. She didn't wear an earring on that side, but on the right side, she wore a single earring—a silver butterfly.

Lauren finally turned to Joy, both of them tearing up instantly. Joy's mouth pinched as she fought her emotions, and Lauren's eyes grew hot. Her chest sank and then expanded, sank and expanded, and she wanted so much happiness for Joy.

"I love you," she said as she stepped into her best friend. Joy wore a dark blue dress that reminded Lauren of an inky midnight sky that had been drenched in a layer of gasoline. Rainbows shimmered across the surface of it, and she'd found some rainbow butterfly patches online and she'd used fabric glue to adhere them to the dress.

"You deserve every happiness in the world," Joy whispered in her ear. "I love you. Don't worry about me, okay?"

Lauren nodded against Joy's shoulder, but she didn't know how to stop worrying about Joy. She'd arrived four days ago, and she'd insisted she was there for Lauren. She'd stuck to her side, helped with every last detail, though Lauren knew she wanted to spend as much time with Scott as she could.

As she moved back, someone opened the door. A woman dressed in all black stood there, and she beamed into the room. "Are you ladies ready? We've just gotten the groom into position."

Lauren sniffled and reached to wipe her eyes. "Am I okay?" she asked her friends, the five of whom stood in a semi-circle facing her.

Her makeup had been painted on in pink sweeps over her eyelids and out toward her temples, like butterfly wings. The blue eyeliner had seemed like a lot at first, but Lauren loved it now. She'd plastered her eyelashes with thick black mascara, and then Joy had tipped the very ends of her lashes with snowy white costume makeup.

Her lips had been painted a pale pink which complimented her eye makeup perfectly, and her earrings were actually homemade cocoons done in sterling silver and painted to be playful. Lauren had seized onto the butterfly theme, because she felt like she'd been given new life with Blake and Tommy.

"You're ready," Bea said.

"It's perfect," Cass said.

Joy, Bessie, and Sage didn't say anything, but Joy smiled as she nodded, and Bessie moved to pick up Lauren's train so she could turn. She did, and then her friends fell into line beside her.

Bea stood on her left, with Joy on her right. Cass flanked Bea, while Sage linked arms with Joy. Bessie handed her the bouquet, which was a bunch of flowers with plastic picks that made it look like a kaleidoscope of butterflies were hovering over the blooms. She loved her bouquet almost as much as her dress, and she took the first step toward the rest of her life.

Ready.

Finally.

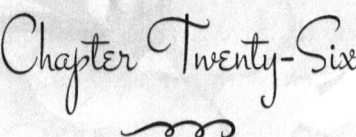

Chapter Twenty-Six

J oy stepped in sync with her five best friends, Lauren leading them out of the room and down the hall. She had broken from tradition by not choosing colors and refusing to stay separate from her husband-to-be on the wedding day. She'd introduced color into the wedding, and it played well with the venue.

Lauren had requested two aisles for the wedding, and the six of them would be walking down the main aisle, where a father might usually escort his daughter to her waiting groom.

But Island Aisle had created another aisle for Lauren that ran in a spoke only several chairs away.

Lauren took a deep breath at the corner, and she looked to Joy. Joy's smile hadn't gone anywhere in the past few days, because this was the most important thing to Lauren. Therefore, Joy would do whatever she had to do to make sure she got her perfect wedding.

"Ready," she said to Lauren, not asking her a question. She looked to Bea and Cass, who looked radiant and joyful. Sage and Bessie likewise seemed to beam joy from their very pores. Bessie's house had an offer on it that she'd accepted. Sage had decided to leave her hobby farm on the market while she moved here with her sister, and Joy nearly broke into a sob at the thought of returning to Texas all alone.

That wasn't the actual case, because Bessie and Sage hadn't been able to make the move before the wedding. But they'd be gone in a matter of two weeks, and Joy would definitely be alone then.

She was so tired of thinking about the future. The indecision raged inside her, and Joy had to tamp it down as Lauren moved forward. They had to bobble their position to get aligned in the hallway, and Joy stayed right at Lauren's right side.

Blake and Tommy waited several paces down the hallway, both of them wearing nearly identical smiles. They both wore midnight-black tuxedos, complete with pristine bow ties, their hair swept and gelled to the side, and their hands clasped in front of them.

"You're stunning," Blake said as Lauren reached the door she'd walk through. It reminded Joy of Scott, and the things he'd told her the night he'd said he loved her. That weekend had been one of the best of her life, while simultaneously being the worst.

She hated being apart from him. As she watched Blake gaze at Lauren with such longing, love, and adoration, Joy didn't want to go home.

Home wasn't in Texas anymore.

She needed to be here.

Her stomach cramped, and her lungs felt like they'd just lost all their drive to inhale and exhale. She couldn't take a step, but the double-doors in front of her had started to open.

Her weakness lifted, and Joy's cheerful smile refashioned itself on her face. So many people had come to celebrate with Lauren, and though she didn't have a close relationship with her family, they'd come.

Joy knew that made Lauren uncomfortable and nervous, but she didn't flick her gaze around to find them. Lauren looked straight down the aisle toward the altar and the pastor there, and Joy did the same thing.

She escorted Lauren to the altar, step-by-step, in sync with Tommy and Blake, and when everyone had arrived, their Supper Club finally broke up.

Lauren hadn't wanted anyone standing at the altar with her, and Cass peeled off to Harrison's side, while Bea eased into the spot next to Grant. Sage and Bessie took their seats on the left side of the altar, where Wynona and Sage's sister waited.

Joy took the end spot on the aisle next to Scott and waited for the cue to sit. It came, and she smoothed her skirt under her and took her seat.

Scott's arm came around her, and Joy leaned into him as Lauren hugged Tommy, who went to sit with his mother right behind Joy. That left Lauren and Blake at the altar, facing each other, so much glee and excitement lifting into the air.

Joy tilted her head toward Scott, and he leaned down so she could murmur in his ear. "I can't do this."

He lowered his head even more. "Hon?"

Joy simply shook her head, because she couldn't explain right now. The pastor started talking about matrimony and marriage, vows and covenants and promises. Joy wanted to be present for all of it, and what she'd meant was that she couldn't keep up the long-distance relationship with Scott.

She felt trapped, without a solution to the obstacles keeping her in Texas. *Two more months*, she thought, and that alleviated some of the anxiety streaming through her. Enough that she could focus on her best friend, listen to the beautiful vows Lauren and Blake spoke to each other, and she finally let her tears fall as the pastor announced them "husband and wife."

Blake grinned like a loon and pressed his curved lips to Lauren's. They laughed together as the crowd started to clap. Joy got to her feet, her hands coming together over and over and over as water ran down her face. She didn't care, because this was such a beautiful moment, and she was so honored to be here to experience it.

Lauren turned, gently kicking her train behind her, and Blake lifted their joined hands. Beside her, Scott whistled through his teeth, and a fresh breeze blew down from the open roof above.

Joy didn't want a wedding like this, but she was so glad

Lauren had gotten the exact ceremony and event she'd wanted.

She stepped forward, and Joy engulfed her in a hug. Bea, Cass, Sage, and Bessie came around Lauren, kernelling her in the middle of all of them, and together, the six of them wept together. Joy had watched two of her other friends get married here on Hilton Head too, but they hadn't been as emotional as this one for some reason.

Perhaps because this was Lauren's first marriage, and she'd wanted it for so long. Perhaps because they'd lost some of their closeness, but this wedding had reunited them in a way they hadn't even realized they needed.

All Joy knew was that she needed to be with these women, and they were all going to be here—not in Texas. Now she just had to figure out how to make it happen. Soon.

JOY WOKE IN A CALM, PEACEFUL PLACE, THE blankets around her fluffy and soft and purely white as the driven snow.

Lauren's bed.

She'd come back here to change out of her party clothes, leave her wedding dress and other items, shower, change, and take her pre-packed bag to leave on her honeymoon. She and Blake had spent their first night as a married couple at a five-star hotel in Charleston, and they were flying to Halifax today.

Joy had been staying with Lauren in the office, but last night, she'd strayed to Lauren's bed. Lauren had told her over and over that she could move into the house any time she wanted, and Joy rolled onto her side and looked toward the big windows set into the wall in front of her. A sliding glass door actually led out of this room and into the backyard, and Joy watched as a bird flitted across her view.

"Why can't you move here?" she asked herself. Really asked this time, instead of insisting that the blueprint she'd been clinging to all this time was the right one. Maybe it wasn't. Maybe she needed to knock down a wall and rearrange the layout of the house.

Joy let time tick by as she watched nature move by outside, and she just let herself breathe in and out in whatever rhythm her lungs wanted. She felt calmer this morning than yesterday at the wedding, and because her flight back to Texas wasn't until later that afternoon, she expected Scott to arrive at any time.

They hadn't really made plans for today, because Joy didn't want to call attention to the fact that they'd be parting ways again.

When the doorbell rang, Joy reached for her phone. She texted Scott quickly that he could come in, and she'd be out in a few minutes. She sat up and stretched, listening for the sound of Scott entering the house. She barely heard it, but he texted to say he'd brought "her favorite," and Lauren's cats both went to the door to be let out.

Joy opened the bedroom door and both Oscar and

Chloe streaked out of the room and down the hall. "I just need to get dressed," she called.

"Take your time," Scott said back.

Joy got dressed and cleaned up, slipped into a pair of puffy socks that made her feel like she'd be spending a cozy day with her boyfriend, and went into the kitchen. She expected to find a blue pastry bag or box from Gourmet Goods, but Scott had spread a whole feast on the island in Lauren's kitchen.

"Wow." Joy grinned and stepped into Scott's arms. "What's all this?" She saw crispy hashbrowns, plenty of bacon and sausage, and even individual bottles of milk and orange juice.

"I asked Row and the girls to help me prepare you a special post-wedding breakfast," he said. His voice wrapped her in warmth, and Joy absolutely didn't know how to walk away from him this time. "I made the bacon, and Sandy did the sausage, because I know you like both breakfast meats."

Joy half-sobbed and half-laughed. She'd told him that she didn't understand why she always had to pick one breakfast meat when she ordered a meal at a restaurant. Why couldn't she have both?

He'd brought her both.

"The eggs are dry scrambled," he said. "Row did those, and she added some sort of fancy cream so they're still fluffy."

Joy began to cry then. "You're amazing," she said, though she stepped out of his arms. "Eggs cooked the way I've ordered one time? You remember that?"

Scott gaze coasted over to her, almost wary. "Of course I remember that. I helped shred the potatoes, because you like them grated, not sliced."

"Scott." Joy paced away from him, upset that she was upset about this special breakfast. It said so much, and Joy spun toward him. "I can't do this."

His mouth snapped closed as his eyes raged with indecision. "You said that yesterday," he said. "I need to know what 'this' is."

"I can't walk away from you again," she blurted out. Her eyes turned into full moons on her face. She couldn't believe she'd just said that. Or that Scott's worry melted from his face and into a joyful smile.

"Great," he said. "Then don't. Stay here." He came toward her and gathered her close. "This house is here. It's ready. Stay." He pressed his lips to her temple, then swept them down her cheek to her lips. "Please stay."

Joy kissed him, desperate to do what he wanted. What *she* wanted.

She simply didn't know how to do it. She'd never canceled an airplane ticket before. She'd have to extend her rental car. Call her principal. She'd only brought a few changes of clothes.

She couldn't just stay—not right now. She simply had to find another way to get to Hilton Head—to Scott, to her friends—sooner.

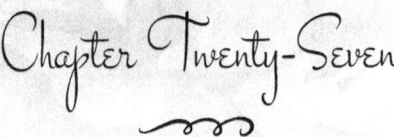

Chapter Twenty-Seven

S cott sensed Joy was kissing him as a distraction from the conversation she didn't want to have. He kept going anyway, because he missed her already, and she didn't leave until this afternoon.

He finally broke their kiss and moved his head so his mouth lingered near her ear, and his cheek pressed against hers. "I know you're not going to stay," he whispered, so she'd have an out. So she wouldn't have to tell him she was still going to leave.

Joy was the type of woman who did what had to be done. Just because she didn't want to leave didn't mean she'd stay. He breathed in with the words *it's just two more months* running through his head.

These past six weeks had been some of the longest of his life—ten times worse than the three months between when Joy had first texted him back in September until she'd come to Hilton Head Island for Christmas. Back then, they'd been flirting and getting to know one another. Now, he knew he loved her, and he was ready to move forward with plans to build a life together with her.

She still hadn't told him she loved him, and a slip of impatience moved through Scott. He stepped away from her and said, "Row wanted you to text her and tell her how much you loved the pancakes."

Joy wiped her eyes and moved over to the island. "I don't see any pancakes," she said.

His heart felt too big for his chest, almost like someone had attached it to a bicycle pump and blown it up until it occupied every spare space behind his ribcage. It labored to beat properly, because he just wanted Joy to be happy.

Being here only made her sad. When he went to Texas, it upset her. The longing for the next two months to be gone already struck him with a white hot pain through his stomach, but he managed to say, "I put them in the oven to keep them warm."

He went around the island to open the oven, only to discover he hadn't turned it on. "That probably would've worked better if I'd remembered to push the button." He bent and pulled out the foil-covered tray of buttermilk pancakes Rowena had made for Joy.

"I'll get everything heated up," he said, and Joy didn't stop him. She helped him by putting a pan on the stove and putting the sausage on one side and the hashbrowns on the other. She put a lid over that while he got the oven heating and the pancakes back inside. Then he put the syrup Row and the girls had sent into the microwave, and he pulled plates out of Lauren's cupboards.

"Harry and Cass are having a party next week," he said. "He got the bid on the library."

"I heard," Joy said, her voice bright. "Cass texted us."

"Mm, of course." He glanced over to her. "Do you want me to forward you my flight info?"

Joy kept her focus on the food, though it was already cooked, and she'd put the burner on low. She couldn't seem to look at him, and Scott hated that. He waited, because he knew she'd heard him.

She finally raised her head and looked at him, and he found her so strong and so sexy. She might want to avoid something for a time, but she always pulled herself together and did what she had to do.

"Yeah," she said. "I feel bad it's so soon, and then we don't have anything until the summer."

"We'll just have to plan something in May," he said.

Joy nodded, but her smile didn't grace those kissable lips. Their food was ready, and Scott let Joy go through everything and take what she wanted first. He took her individual bottles of orange juice and milk to the table, and then said, "Oh, coffee."

"I'm already buzzed this morning," she said, giving him a playful look. "That kiss really got my juices flowing." She grinned now, and Scott couldn't stop himself from returning such a smile.

He dished himself some food and sat down at the table-for-two with her. He didn't want to bring up the topic of her moving here again, but Bessie's house had sat on the market for a couple of months before it had sold, and well, Joy's summer vacation was only a couple of months away.

"How are things in your yard?" he asked. She'd sent him plenty of pictures as her world had bloomed and sprouted and grown. She really had a lovely yard there, and Scott couldn't wait to see it again.

"Amazing." She squirted ketchup all over her hashbrowns, and then salted them liberally. He didn't tease her about it this time, because he'd learned that Joy liked her food really salty. He didn't like it when people teased him about innocent things he liked, so he saw no point in mocking Joy for her saltshaker habit.

"How's Johnathan doing?"

"So much better." Joy smiled, and he'd much prefer her to keep doing that than wiping her eyes and using him as a distraction. She didn't talk about very many of her students, but Jonathan had moved from Russia, and she'd been working with him on his English for a couple of months now. She said he was a sweet boy, eager to learn, and she'd loved him instantly.

"And your classes?"

"Finals in a couple of weeks," she said, her smile slipping. "I'm going to pass, and they've been sending me email after email about graduation."

Scott nearly dropped his fork. "I'm sorry, did I miss an email or a text or a video call?" He blinked at her, sure she hadn't just dropped that the University of Texas was going to let her skip her student teaching. She'd been waiting for over a month now, and he knew he hadn't missed a message.

Joy emitted a squeal, and then said, "They approved my request to waive the student teaching, and I'll be done in a few weeks. Like, done-done."

"This is the greatest news ever!" He stood and then immediately dropped to his knees in front of her. "I'm so happy for you, sweetheart."

She took his face in her hands and gazed at him. "I know what you're doing."

"What am I doing?"

"You're priming me with all these easy, happy questions so you can then ask me what my summer plans are."

"You're only half-right," he said. "I don't want to know what your summer plans are. I want to know what your beach blueprint looks like here in Hilton Head. No more Texas. I want to know when you're going to list your house for sale, and when I can fly in to help you pack everything you own and drive your big moving truck here to South Carolina."

With every word he said, her eyes got wider, and her face grew whiter. "I want to know when you'd like to get married, and I'd like to know if you feel as strongly about me as I do about you."

Scott told himself to stop talking, because Joy looked like he'd started hovering above the ground and might have a seizure at any moment. Foolishness raced through him, and while Scott had known he'd fallen faster and deeper than Joy, he'd been fairly confident she'd catch up to him at some point.

His knees ached, as he wasn't in his thirties anymore, and he couldn't kneel on a hard floor for long. He backed up, got to his feet, and went into the kitchen to get something to drink. He hadn't made or brought coffee, and he pulled open Lauren's fridge. She'd been planning to be on her honeymoon for the next week, and when she returned, she'd be moving into Blake's house. So she didn't have much food and even less to drink

Scott closed the fridge and pulled open a cupboard a little too hard. A slicing pain moved through his wrist, but he ignored it as he caught sight of bowls and not glasses. He found what he needed behind the next door, and he pulled down a glass cup to fill with water from the sink.

The water came out lukewarm and didn't get colder very fast, so Scott filled the glass and took a couple of gulps he immediately wanted to spit back out. Joy hadn't said anything, and Scott hadn't heard her chair move or her feet against the tile as she walked.

She just suddenly appeared at his side, and while his natural inclination was to lift his arm and draw her into his side the way he had countless times before, he didn't. This time, he didn't.

She leaned her head against his bicep and linked her arm through his, and Scott enjoyed the shiver that went down to his fingertips. He loved the scent of this woman, and the way she had no problem claiming him as hers.

She just hadn't said it, and Scott hadn't realized how much he needed her to say it. To say something.

"I'm so stupid," he said.

"You're not."

Lauren didn't have a window above her kitchen sink, and Scott had nowhere to look but at Joy. "Tell me what I am then."

"You're my favorite person in the whole world," she said without missing a beat.

"When you say you can't walk away again, I'm not sure what I'm supposed to take from that," he said, deciding to lay it all out for her. "When I say *stay*, Joy, I mean *stay*. I mean I don't want you to walk away either, but we both know you will. So I'm not sure what I'm supposed to think. I'm not sure what you want me to do or say."

"I know," she said. "I don't know either, Scott. I'm so sorry."

Scott didn't mean to sigh like she frustrated him, but in some ways, she did. He'd been trying to be as patient as possible with her, and with himself, and with the situation. He'd known she didn't live here last summer, and he should've been smarter with his heart.

"I didn't mean to ruin breakfast," he said.

"You didn't."

Scott couldn't stand there with her delicate hand resting on his forearm, so he shifted, and she moved away an inch or two. "Let's eat." He went past her and back to the table, leaving his glass of tepid water behind.

He sat down, surprised once again to find Joy only a

half-step behind him. Before he could scoot in and continue eating his bacon and pancakes, she slid onto his lap and ran her fingernails up the back of his head and through his hair. "Scott, forgive me," she whispered, her eyes drifting closed as she leaned her forehead against his. "I'm not trying to be difficult. I'm not trying to irritate you."

Her mapley breath drifted across his face and down his chin, and Scott only wanted to breathe her in over and over again. When she sat on his lap, he couldn't resist planting his hands on her hips and holding her intimately.

"I can't stay mad at you, anyway," he said as his own eyes closed. "And I'm not mad. I'm...I don't know what I am. Frustrated that it's only April first, I guess."

Joy touched her nose to his. "I'm going to start working on the details when I get back to Sweet Water Falls."

His ribs constricted as if someone had wound a roll of plastic wrap around them and kept tightening the layers. "What kind of details?" he asked. "I need the details on the details."

"I'm going to go see my sons the day before you come," she said. "I'm going to talk to them about leaving Texas."

Scott's eyes popped open, and Joy put some distance between them so they could look at one another. He couldn't seem to get a lock on her gaze, as it bounced all over the place just over the top of his head.

"I'm going to get my house listed for sale," she said. "That's a big detail. I'm going to talk to Lauren about living here and find out how much the rent will be. I'm going to apply for any teaching or teacher's helpers' positions here on the island and maybe even down in Beaufort or Carter's Cove."

"Joy," Scott said.

"Those kinds of details," she said. "Are those the details you wanted?" She finally zeroed in on him, something almost defiant resting in her slate gray eyes.

"Yes," he said, sure he hadn't heard her correctly. "But Joy, you have to understand..."

"Understand what?"

"When you say you're going to list your house for sale, and tell your sons you're moving here, and look for jobs here...you're really telling me you love me." His eyebrows went up, the pair of them adding a question mark to what he'd said. "Is that what you're telling me?"

Joy's lips twitched, a smile curling the ends of them for a moment before she straightened them. "I don't know, Scott."

"You don't know?" He chuckled and shook his head. "Why are you moving here then?"

"Maybe it's for my Supper Club friends," she said haughtily. She slid from his lap and returned to her chair. "I'm going to text Row and tell her that everything is absolutely delicious." She flicked him a look, like she needed his permission, and focused on her phone.

Scott finished his sausage while she did that, a certain satisfaction and giddiness growing inside him though she still hadn't said those three little words he'd said to her a couple of months ago.

But he suspected she loved him and just needed to have

some of the final details worked out before she said the words, and he could give her another week or two to get things into the shape she wanted them in.

Another week or two, he told himself, and then he'd have a hard decision to make if Joy still couldn't tell him what he needed to hear.

Chapter Twenty-Eight

~∞~

After her bagel run, Joy pulled into her son's driveway, relieved Hank's truck sat there already. She could enjoy everyone at once, tell her news once, and cry on the drive home. It took six hours to drive from Sweet Water Falls to the Dallas-Fort Worth area, and Joy had spent yesterday behind the wheel and last night at Walter's. She'd eaten dinner with him and his wife, Lexie, and their little girl, Holly.

Joy adored her granddaughter, and her sons, and everything Texas, and her throat felt like someone had rubbed it with the roughest sandpaper at the hardware store. Everything burned lately, and Joy just wanted the fire to be turned off.

She felt the pressure from her job, as they were in the thick of what Joy called the "Changing Season." Teachers moved schools, retired, or announced that they weren't coming back. Hourly workers were renewed for next year or not, and Joy had a meeting with her principal on Monday to declare her status for the following school year.

Once she told him, the whole school would know something had disrupted her life. Scott Anderson had done exactly that, but in the best way possible. At least that was what Joy hoped to communicate to everyone in the next few days. Her sons, her daughters-in-law, her friends and co-workers. She had no idea what her neighbors would think, and Joy dismissed them. She'd held her head high when Wendell left, and everyone should be happy she didn't have to live the rest of her life alone.

"Gammy's here," she called as she opened Walter's front door. She carried a big bucket of bagels and a plastic bag filled with tubs of cream cheese.

"Momma," Hank said, jumping to his feet. Her younger son had a head full of bushy brown hair and a beard to match.

She dropped breakfast on the couch and let her tall, strong son take her into a hug. They both laughed, and Joy simply couldn't contain her pure happiness. Hank had always been a bit of a momma's boy, though he had gotten married to the first woman he'd seriously dated.

"Oh, it's so good to see you," she said as he released her. His wife, Morgan, had risen to her feet too, and she wore a pink glow to her cheeks as she smiled at Joy. "Hello, dear." Joy hugged her too. "Thanks for coming over for breakfast."

"Of course," Morgan said. "It's good to see you. You haven't been to Dallas for a while."

"I sure haven't," Joy agreed. She'd grown up in a small

town closer to Austin, and she didn't like the huge metropolis that had become the Dallas-Fort Worth area, but her sons and their wives had jobs here, and they all seemed to like it.

Thankfully, no tears had wetted her eyes, and Joy followed Hank as he grabbed the bagels and cream cheese and took them into the kitchen at the back of the house. "Where's Walt?" she asked when she found that room empty too.

"Right here, Momma," Walt said from behind her. He emerged from the hallway with his one-year-old daughter on his hip. "Look, I told you Gammy was here." He smiled at Holly, who'd clearly been crying.

"Oh, my precious." Joy took the little girl quickly and wiped her wispy hair off her face. "What was your daddy doing to you, mm?" She pressed a kiss to Holly's forehead, and the baby girl curled into Joy's chest.

Her heart felt like folding into a tight box, because she wouldn't get to see her sons as much as she did now. *Why not?* she asked herself. Of course she could. It would take the same amount of time to get here from South Carolina as it did now, and they'd always welcomed her with open arms, a prepped guest room, and plenty of smiles.

No, it was an excuse Joy had been using, and she shoved against it as hard as she could. No more excuses.

Walt's wife, Lexie, entered the kitchen too. "Who wants coffee?" she asked. "Thanks for going to get the bagels, Joy."

"They're my favorite," she said. She took Holly over to

her highchair and buckled her into it. "Do you want strawberry cream cheese, baby?"

Holly looked at her with her big brown eyes and nodded solemnly. Joy gave her a big smile and another kiss before she went to get a bagel for her granddaughter. Activity filled the kitchen, and by the time Joy fed Holly and then returned for her own bagel and coffee, her son had poured her a mug.

"Thank you, Hank." He took good care of her, and she noticed him doing the same to Morgan. He was the last one to arrive at the table, and Joy looked at her boys and their good wives. She expected tears, but they didn't come. Only a grin.

"Okay," she said. "I'm sure you're wondering why I'm here." She took a bite of her raisin oat bagel with veggie cream cheese.

"I'm not," Walt said. "You went to Hilton Head for Christmas, so it makes sense you're here for Spring Break." His gaze traveled to Hank across from him, and then to Lexie, who seemed a bit concerned.

Alarm rang through Joy. "I'm not here for Spring Break."

"You're not?" Walt asked.

She shook her head and reached for a napkin. Bagels didn't go well with unspoken confessions, and Joy needed to get talking. "It's next week, and my boyfriend is coming to Sweet Water Falls."

Hank's mouth dropped open, and Walt choked on his sip of coffee. "I'm sorry," he said. "Your...boyfriend?" He exchanged another glance with his wife. "Well, that's...just great."

"Don't sound so enthused," Joy said with a sniff.

"No, Momma, it's not that," Walt said. "It's just that's what Lexie said you'd tell us today, and I was sure that wasn't it."

"Why were you sure that I wouldn't have a boyfriend?" Joy watched him as he looked at everyone at the table except for her. When his gaze did meet hers, it was filled with fire and determination, and Joy saw herself so much in her son.

"Because, Momma," he said. "You and Daddy..." He cleared his throat. "Hank?"

"He was a jerk," Hank said, his eyebrows drawing down. "You were beat up by him, Momma. To be honest, I didn't think you'd date again, and I'm a little surprised to hear about a boyfriend too."

"Yeah, the jaw-dropping told me that," Joy said. She shrank into herself, wondering what her sons had seen of her and Wendell's relationship, what they'd thought of it. "I... Your dad—" She wasn't married to Wendell anymore, and she didn't have to defend him or his image anymore. His sons were adults, and they had lives and opinions of their own.

"Daddy was mean," Walt filled in. "Especially to you." He covered Joy's hand with his. "I—we—didn't know how to help you."

Her insides shook and Joy did the same with her head. "It wasn't your job to help me."

"Momma," Walt said, a kind smile on his face. "I tried to

talk to Daddy about it once, and he shut me down pretty fast. Told me to mind my own business, in that tone he used on you all the time." He tossed a side glance to his wife. "I felt so stupid. He has a special way of making a person feel two inches tall, and I know you bore the brunt of that for decades."

Joy didn't know what to say, and she looked over to Hank. "Did you talk to your father about this too?"

"No."

That was a relief, because Wendell probably would've destroyed Hank, who'd always been more sensitive than his older brother. Walt had started balding last year, and he shaved his head completely now, but he still filled a room with his presence, and he'd always been Wendell's favorite.

"I told Daddy that if he wasn't going to treat you better, he should leave," Walt said. He cleared his throat. "He moved out the next week."

Joy pulled in a breath. "Walt."

Her son's dark brown eyes only got darker. "You deserve better," he said. "You have from the beginning, Momma. I couldn't stand to see the way he treated you."

Joy looked helplessly at Lexie, who gave her a sympathetic smile and then pulled off another piece of bagel for Holly.

"So this guy better treat you like a queen," Walt said. "When do we get to meet him?"

"Yeah," Hank said. "We should make sure he's going to take care of you."

That caused her to smile. "I can take care of myself," she

said. "Scott is fantastic. Very sweet and adoring…and, he lives in South Carolina. I'm going to move there this summer."

"He—what?" Walt's mouth fell open this time, and Hank stared at Joy, his eyelids having gone into a frenzy as he blinked quickly.

"South Carolina?" he asked.

"All of my friends live there now," she said, her voice starting to rush as if she had to get this explanation out before her sons cut her off and wouldn't listen. She took a breath to slow herself. No, her sons would listen to her. Scott listened to her.

It was only Wendell who hadn't, who she'd had to have a precise explanation for for everything from why the grocery bill was twenty dollars more than anticipated or why she wanted to help Hank with his tuxedo for prom. As if a mother needed a reason to help her child.

"My Supper Club friends," she said. "You remember Bea and Bessie and Lauren? Sage and Cass? They've all moved to Hilton Head Island now." Her voice broke on the last word, and both Lexie and Morgan reached for her.

She shook her head and waved them away. "I'm okay." She sniffed, for the nose always knew when the eyes wanted to cry, and it wanted to run when they did. "But they're my family now," she said. "I met this man—Scott—last summer. He's really great, and he loves me, and I—I love him, and I want to be with him."

Walt's gaze lightened when she said she loved him, and as Joy had finally admitted it out loud, she too felt like someone had removed a heavy load from her back and shoulders. "You love him?"

"Yes," Joy said. "We've been dating long-distance for several months now, and he's coming for Spring Break next week."

"Perfect," Walt said. "We'll come meet him then." He looked over to Hank. "Can you check your schedule and maybe we can go on Friday?" He met his wife's eyes. "Do you want to come? We could—"

"No," Joy said, her mind blurring facts and details. "You can't come next week. I'm going to call him and tell him not to come."

"What?" Hank asked. "Momma, you're not making sense."

"I know," Joy said, ideas and details colliding in her mind. With all eyes on her, Joy shifted and squirmed in her seat. With another deep breath, she started to lay down the bricks of her blueprint. "He was going to come here, but I think I should go there."

"Why?" Lexie asked.

"I haven't told him I love him," Joy said. "I've been—it's been a very hard decision for me to leave my job, my house, and Texas in general. To leave my boys here."

Hank gave her a smile meant to tease or reassure, she wasn't sure which. "Momma, we're not boys."

"You'll always be my little boys," she said with a fond smile for both of her sons. "But you're right. I spent a lot of years under your father's thumb, and I'm ready to move on. I'm ready to discover what life can really be like when I'm fully living it. When I'm not afraid to say something someone doesn't agree with, and when I'm free to be myself."

"You never cared if I agreed with you," Walt said dryly. "Remember when you wouldn't let me take Mindie Gregson to the prom because her dress had no straps?"

"That is not true," Joy said with a hint of bite in her tone. She met her son's eyes, and several silent conversations happened.

"Daddy," he said, falling back against his chair. "Momma, you made that seem like it was you."

"I'm sure your wife will do the same for you someday," she said quietly.

"Momma."

"Please," Joy said. "I don't want to relive the hell that was my life with your father." She kept her eyes on her uneaten bagel, wondering when this conversation would be enough.

"So you're going to Hilton Head for Spring Break," Morgan said. "And what? Tell this Scott man that you're in love with him?"

Joy looked up, a sudden spark in her brain. "Yes," she said. "That's exactly what I'm going to do."

"Does he love you, Joy?" Lexie asked.

She nodded, the warmth of his deep, rumbly voice filling her from head to toe. "He's told me a few times now. I was too afraid to say it back to him."

No one said anything, and Holly hollered for another bite of bagel, which Joy gave to her.

"That's my news," she said. "I'm in love with Scott Anderson. I'm quitting my job at the elementary school, and I'm listing the house for sale."

"I want it," Hank said.

"Hank," Joy and Morgan said at the same time.

"I can work from home, love." He took Morgan's hand in his. "I don't want to raise our baby in the city."

This time, Joy's mouth dropped open. She shrieked as her brain put the dots together, and she slid back and stood so she could hug her son and his wife. "Another grandbaby," she said, laughing. "Oh, I'm so excited."

"Congratulations," Lexie said with a warm smile. "When are you due?"

"September," Morgan said, one hand moving to rest protectively on her stomach. She smiled around at everyone, the gesture fading when she met her husband's eyes. "We have to talk about the house in Sweet Water Falls."

"Yes, ma'am," he said, but Joy knew that look in her son's eyes. It had allowed him to graduate in three years instead of four. Hank knew how to work hard and earn what he wanted, and if he wanted the house in Sweet Water Falls, Joy knew he'd get it. "Momma, can we talk about it before you sell it to someone else, please?"

"Yes," she said as she retook her seat. "And next time Scott comes to Texas, I'll have him fly here, and y'all can meet him."

"Can Hank and I walk you down the aisle together?" Walt asked.

Joy tipped her head back and laughed, but no one joined in with her. "What?" Hank asked.

"Five minutes ago, you both were puffed up, demanding to meet him and make sure he wasn't going to hurt me. Now, he's asking to walk me down the aisle." She gave her oldest son a pointed look, though she wasn't anywhere near upset.

"The question stands," Walt said.

"Yes," Joy said. "If I haven't ruined things with Scott yet, and he still asks me to marry him, you can both walk me down the aisle."

"Ruined things?" Lexie said.

Joy switched her attention to her. "Yeah, I—it's been strained between us with the distance." She got to her feet. "I have to go call him right now, then book some tickets to Hilton Head. I'm going to go broke flying there, but it has to be done."

She bustled out of the room and into the living room to get her phone out of her purse. She didn't have all the details worked out for this impromptu trip, but she knew she had to go to Scott and tell him how she felt about him. About this cleansing trip to see her sons, and that all of the things he'd said a week ago that he wanted—she wanted them too.

She wanted to be his wife.

She wanted to build a life with him on Hilton Head.

She wanted him to know she loved him, that her feelings ran as hot as his, and as deep.

And she could only do that in person, in Hilton Head.

Now, if he'd just pick up the phone...

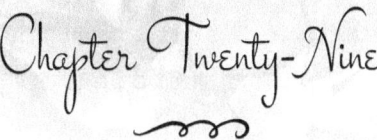

Chapter Twenty-Nine

S cott scrubbed up to his elbows as the soap dripped off his body in a dirty brown. He rinsed and then squirted more soap into his palms and got sudsing up again. He'd been working on the shrubbery, covering flower beds with weed preventing plastic, and then shoveling rocks at one of the biggest shopping centers on the island. All week long.

His shoulders and back ached, and he couldn't wait to get to his massage appointment later that day. He normally didn't work on the weekend, but he'd needed to finish this project, and Jeff had arranged a special meeting with the director of the Historical Society here on the island, as they wanted to completely re-landscape around the Civil War Memorial, and Scott wanted that project as much as anything he'd done in his career.

It would allow him to use his landscape architecture degree, which was something he didn't get to do very often.

Out in the main part of the office where Jeff kept track

of everything, he didn't find his brother or anyone else. He might have been in the big room around the corner where they had staff meetings from time to time.

Scott sighed as he opened the fridge and pulled out a bottle of cold water. He drank half of it as the liquid burned his throat with its icy touch, and then the phone in his back pocket vibrated.

He pulled it out, smiling when he saw he'd missed a call from Joy. She'd left a message instead of texting him, which was a bit odd. He tapped to get the voicemail dialed, and he waited while the line rang. Her voice filled his ears, but Scott's smile slipped.

"Scott," she said, and he couldn't tell if she was happy or not. "I don't think you should come to Sweet Water Falls next weekend. Please cancel your ticket, and I'll see you soon."

She hung up, and Scott stared at his phone as it started to list his options for him. Perhaps he hadn't heard right, and he tapped to listen to the message again.

Please cancel your ticket.

"What?"

She was in Dallas this weekend, and he wondered what her sons had said about her relationship with him. He tapped to delete the message, and then he dialed her back.

Thankfully, she picked up on the second ring. "Scott, hey," she said.

"I can't come next week?" he demanded, his voice too harsh. But he didn't know how to soften it.

"No," she said. "I've—"

"Are you breaking up with me? Over a voicemail message?"

A beat came through the line. "No."

Scott's brain misfired too. "I'm so confused."

"There you are," Jeff said, gesturing to him from the doorway. "He's here. Come on." He wore urgency in his voice and on his face, and Scott started that way.

"Listen," he said. "I have a big meeting right now. We'll talk later, okay?"

"Okay," Joy said.

He hadn't expected her to argue with him, but it kind of bothered him that she didn't. That she didn't blurt out that of course he should keep his airplane tickets for six days from now.

"Good luck with Tim," she said, and then she ended the call. Scott shoved his phone in his back pocket as he strode through the doorway into the conference room. Tim Frost was there, peering at a blueprint Scott had done for another project that would be similar to the museum.

"Here he is," Jeff said with plenty of enthusiasm in his voice. Probably too much.

Tim looked up, and Scott stuck out his hand. "Mister Frost," he said.

"Doctor," the man said, and Scott wanted to roll his eyes. If he hadn't just gotten Joy's message, Scott wouldn't be annoyed by this correction at all.

So he smiled and said, "Doctor Frost, welcome to Anderson Landscaping." He'd have to deal with his sore muscles, bruised ego, and Joy later.

Scott punished himself that week, his airplane ticket canceled, and daily trips to Harrison's to soak in his hot tub. He completed his second massage of the week, paid for the treatment, and got behind the wheel of his truck.

He took a moment to push all the breath out of his lungs, ready for the weekend. Tomorrow was Friday, and Jeff had given him a family home to get the yard in tiptop shape after a few months of neglect. They'd apparently gone to Europe for the winter and decided not to come back to the island, but they needed their yard taken care of.

He anticipated a lot of raking of pine needles, mowing of course, trimming, debris clean-up, and Jeff had said they had a rock wall that had a lot of weeds in it. Scott would spray those tomorrow and then pull them out more easily next week when he went.

Joy's spring break started tomorrow after work, and he'd planned to fly in at night to spend the week with her there. She'd called after his meeting, but she'd only said she had so much to do to get ready to move to Hilton Head that she needed her Spring Break to do that.

He couldn't be mad about her prepping to sell her house so she could move here, but he couldn't help being disappointed. He told her every day he missed her and wanted to see her, and she said the same.

Those three little words hadn't come up yet, but he said,

"You don't have a deadline for this woman, Scott. Be patient."

He didn't want to be patient, however. He wanted her to call him and give him permission to book the next ticket to Texas. Part of him wondered what she'd do if he showed up anyway. Would that push her further from him or show her how dedicated he was? He wished he could climb inside her mind and see what she was thinking.

Joy didn't have as many shields up as she'd had before, but he couldn't help feeling like she was running from him and planning to move closer at the same time. It didn't sit well in his gut, and Scott reached for his phone and tapped to dial Rowena.

"Scotty," she said by way of hello. "What's up?" He sighed, and Row's breath hitched. "Do not tell me you're pining over Joy."

He was, so he didn't say anything.

"Scott," she said.

"Can I go to her?" he asked.

"No," Row said. "I've only met Joy a couple of times, honey, but I know her well enough from those meetings and what you've told me. She won't like that."

"Did Jeff tell you she's planning to move here?"

"He did."

"She has to be serious about me, right?"

"Scott," Row said firmly. "Listen to me. That woman is in love with you. She has a plan to tell you, I guarantee it."

He looked out the side window, regretting this call. He didn't want to be the worried, droopy boyfriend. He didn't want to put pressure on Joy. He didn't want to air his woes and his insecurities to his brother's wife.

"I'm on my way to get Ghost," he said. "Thanks for taking him during my massage."

"He's the best dog ever," Row said. "I might just keep him."

Scott couldn't imagine how lonely he'd be then, and Row wouldn't really keep his dog. He said, "Be there soon," and ended the call. He made the drive to her house, gave her a hug that she wouldn't let him out of, and then decided to just hold on.

"She's going to surprise you," Row said as she stepped back. She tucked her dark hair behind her ear and gave him a look only a woman could. One that said she knew more than him, but only because she had two X-chromosomes. Scott had never professed to understand women, so he only nodded.

"Was it like this with you and Jeff?" he asked.

"Oh, that man." Row waved her hand while her smile grew and grew. "Begged me for three months to marry him." She turned and picked up Ghost's leash. "I didn't even use this."

"He never needs it." Scott took the leash and met Row's eyes again. "I just want to see her. I know it's pathetic, but—"

"It's not pathetic." Row's smile softened. "It's sweet how much you miss her. She doesn't think you're pathetic."

"I feel pathetic."

Row touched his chest, right over his heart. "That's because you love her, and loving someone is not pathetic."

Scott nodded, his emotions playing tricks on him as they rocketed up and then spiraled back down. He couldn't remember the last time he'd cried, but probably when his forearm had been sliced open by a shovel on the job. Seventeen stitches later, he'd healed.

"Love is an amazing thing," Row continued. "It makes you stronger, not weaker."

"I'm not sure I've ever been in love," Scott admitted.

"It's not something to apologize for," Row said. "I know you don't want to hear it, but be patient with Joy. She came from a hard relationship, and you're so amazing, and you fell for her so fast, and she just needs some time to acclimate to that."

Scott's eyebrows bunched down. "I don't know what that means."

"It means she probably doesn't feel lovable," Row said. "So she's confused as to why you love her."

"That's ridiculous."

"Only to you." Row patted his chest and turned as the sound of the garage door lifting met their ears. "That'll be Jeff. Go on. I don't want you distracting him tonight. He promised me a hot date at Houser's, and we have to leave in a half-hour." She herded him toward the front door and Scott had just stepped out onto the porch when he heard his brother's voice.

"No, he's just leaving," Row said. "Bye, Scott!"

"Thanks, Row," he said over his shoulder, the last part of

her name almost getting cut off as she slammed the door. Ghost looked up at him, and Scott grinned down at the dog. "Let's go get some dinner, bud."

He loaded up his dog and went home. He didn't drive through anywhere, because the Mediterranean place didn't have a window. They did deliver, and he called to put in his order for hummus and pita chips and a sausage and olive pizza, dropped his phone on the counter, and collapsed onto the couch. Ghost jumped up beside him as he picked up the remote, and Scott hesitated.

He didn't like a house full of silence. He always had something playing on his phone, the television, or the radio. Something he could listen to or ignore if he wanted to. He glanced over to the kitchen and dining room, grateful to be back in his own house but wondering why it felt so foreign at the same time.

This place felt lifeless, like a bachelor and his dog lived here, but only in the evenings. He closed his eyes and let his fantasies roam. He saw Joy in this house, and the scent of her roses out front lining the walk. He'd sweep her into his arms when he got home from work, the way Jeff did to Row, and they'd have date nights planned to keep their relationship interesting and vibrant.

He sighed, flipped on the TV, and the imaginations in his mind disappeared. He didn't want to let them grow too many roots, because he'd learned from experience that things he let grow in his mind and heart were very hard to get out once they'd gotten roots. *Just like weeds*, he thought. They had to be ripped out, and in the past, they'd took big patches of his heart with them.

The doorbell rang, bringing him back to consciousness. He hadn't realized he'd dozed, and he grunted as he pushed himself to his feet. "Coming," he called as he rounded the couch and headed for the door. His stomach growled, and Scott couldn't wait to devour his pizza and listen for Joy's call.

He pulled open the door, the words he'd been about to say dying in his throat.

"Hey, baby," Joy said with a shy smile, and Scott blinked, because right now, his eyes couldn't be trusted.

Chapter Thirty

J oy really liked Scott in his dirty jeans and T-shirt. He exuded charm even while standing there mute, and he reminded her of a rugged cowboy—minus the hat. He worked hard for a living, and he loved it. He was honest and kind and so handsome it almost hurt to look at him. His hair stood up a little in the back, and that only made her grin wider.

"Did I wake you up?"

"I thought you were my dinner," he said.

She stepped up and into the house, because Scott hadn't backed out of the doorway to invite her in yet. She'd only been here briefly before, but the address had been stored in her phone, and she'd made the drive from the airport in record time.

His hand slid along her waist, and tingles flew down both of her legs. "We can probably arrange that," she whispered.

"Oh, hey," someone said from behind her, and Joy eased past Scott and into the house so he could receive his dinner order. She'd surprised him all right, just like her daughters-in-law said she would. She couldn't help smiling and smiling and smiling, because she wanted Scott to be happy. She wanted him to know how she felt about him. She wanted to be with him.

"Come on in," he said as he closed the door. "I can share."

"I ate a little on the plane," she said.

"Okay, but that's gross." He went into the kitchen, Joy right behind him, and set his pizza box with the Styrofoam container on top of it on the counter. When their eyes met, Joy rushed toward him.

His breath whooshed out of his mouth, but he caught her. "Whoa, okay." He chuckled, and while Joy had gotten an uneasy vibe from him when he'd opened the door and seen her, that had disappeared.

"Scott," she said, looking up at him. She had so much to say, and she didn't know where to start. Could she just open her mouth and let it all vomit out? She tipped up to meet his lips with hers, and he kissed her a bit stiffly for a moment, but then easily melted into his usual adoring touch.

He deepened the kiss, growling in the back of his throat, and pressed her against the fridge. Joy's pulse raced with excitement as she tried to keep up, and she threaded her fingers through his hair as his hands ran up and down her back.

"You're here," he said, a gasp following. After he'd taken

a breath, he moved his mouth along her jaw to her ear. Joy loved being with him, and she once again couldn't stop the smile as it spread across her face.

She couldn't stop the feelings of love as they filled her from head to toe, left to right. "I love you," she whispered, but her voice was nowhere near loud enough. "I'm so in love with you."

Scott pulled away, his eyes searching hers. She slid her hands down the sides of his face. "You're my favorite person in the world. I love you, Scott Anderson."

Sunbeams broke free from his face, those pretty blue eyes crinkling at the edges, and pure happiness pouring from him. "Yeah, you're in love with me."

"Yeah, I really am."

He kissed her again, but it was a sloppy, smiling kiss, and they both ended up laughing. With those words out of the way, Joy stepped back and opened his Styrofoam container. "Oh, hummus."

Scott eased up behind and to the side of her, his hand sliding along her waist. "I thought you would be too busy getting your exit strategy in place to see me."

Joy picked up a pita chip and swiped it through the hummus, which had a beautiful red oil along the sides. "I hate not being with you," she said. "I went to see my sons last weekend, and I was telling them about you and that I wanted to move to Hilton Head—and they are so cute. They want to meet you to make sure you're going to treat me right."

ELANA JOHNSON

She popped the chip and hummus into her mouth and smiled with her eyes in his direction.

"Your sons know what you've been through," he said. "I'd love to meet them so they feel good about us."

"Good," Joy said after she'd swallowed her first bite. "Because Walt and Hank will be here tomorrow."

Scott's eyebrows shot up. "Oh, wow." He glanced around his house. "I better get someone to come clean this up. And by *someone*, I mean *me*." He laughed, and Joy never wanted to live another day without that laugh in her life.

"I love that laugh," she said with a grin. "I realized while I was sitting at the table with my family that I could admit I was in love with you. So I told them I was in love with you, and a plan sort of formed from there."

Scott slid the hummus from the pizza box and opened it. "What plan? I feel like I missed out on some important pieces."

"My sons were willing to come down to Sweet Water Falls to meet you, but I wanted to show them Hilton Head. Neither of them have been here, and they're bringing their wives and my granddaughter. Oh!" She leaned into him, so much chemistry sparking between them. "Morgan is pregnant and due in September, so that will be fun."

"That's great," he said. "A nice fall trip to see the new baby." He lifted one eyebrow, almost asking her a question.

"Yes," she said. "We'll have to make sure we don't schedule the wedding that month."

"Oh, you think there's going to be a wedding this year?"

"I think a wedding in October or November would be

350

nice," Joy continued as if he hadn't spoken. "I know it's not much time, especially because I'm not wearing a ring yet, but I think it would actually be perfect."

Scott lifted a piece of pizza from the box and took a big bite.

"You did ask me when I wanted to get married, didn't you?"

He nodded enthusiastically, chewed faster, and swallowed. "That I did," he said quickly.

"So I'm thinking October or November, because of Morgan's due date," she said matter-of-factly. "We don't have to get engaged right away, obviously."

"Obviously," he said. "Since I don't know what kind of ring you want, and I want you to get what you want."

Joy picked up another chip and pulled it through the hummus. "I put the house up for sale. That's why I wanted to come here, so we didn't have to be out of it for showings this week."

Scott tossed his pizza back in the box, and drew her closer to him. She giggled as she lifted her hummus'ed chip above his shoulder. "I'm going to get dip all over this shirt."

"I don't care," his voice rumbled, and then he kissed her. Joy tossed the chip as far as she could, as she didn't really want to smear hummus all over his shoulder or the back of his head. "I love you so much, Joy. You're the first woman I've ever been in love with, and I'm just so...happy."

"Me too," she said. "Happy, I mean." They swayed together, and Joy rested her head against his shoulder. "I didn't know I could be happy with a man." She kept her voice low, because she'd never said these things out loud.

"I didn't know if I could leave my house and boys behind, but I've learned it's more important to me to be with you than to keep a house or have to fly to see my kids instead of driving."

"I didn't mean to throw a wrench into your whole life."

"You did too." She smiled and straightened. "And I'm so glad you did. I've been dying a slow death in Texas, and I didn't even know it until I met you."

He ducked his head, shaking it slightly. "My Joy," he whispered.

"My sweet daughters-in-law took off a few days of work this week, and they helped me get my house cleaned up and cleaned out. It went up for sale today."

Scott leaned closer and buried his face against the soft skin of her neck. "Where are you staying tonight?"

"I'm moving into Lauren's house this weekend. That's partly why the boys are coming. I need their muscles."

He straightened then, his eyes growing wider by the moment. "You're moving in? Did you drive here?"

"No," she said, enjoying the closeness between them. She picked up the hummus and the pizza box. "Let's sit." Instead of taking the food to his dining room table, she veered over to the couches in the living room. "Oh, Ghost."

She practically threw the boxes down so she could give the dog a good scrub. His tail wagged and wagged, but he didn't move from the couch. Scott chuckled and pushed

Ghost further down the sofa to make room for the two of them.

"He's so cute."

"He'll love you forever if you feed him." Scott grinned at her as he sat and took another piece of pizza from the box. "So...I need more details. You didn't drive here with any of your stuff. But you're moving into Lauren's house this weekend. I'm meeting your sons. When are you leaving?"

"I'm not," Joy said. "I met with my principal on Monday, remember?"

Scott's pizza drooped in his hand as he stared at her. "Yeah, you said he took you leaving at the end of the year well."

Joy laughed lightly and shook her head. "Do you really not mind if I have a piece?"

He handed her his slice of pizza and reached for another. "Joy, I need the details."

"So I'm not the only one who needs a blueprint."

Scott chortled and finally took a bite of his pizza. "My request stands," he said around his mouthful.

"I met with Doctor Wadley, and I told him I wouldn't be back next year, and in fact, I needed to put in my two weeks' notice that very day."

Scott stared at her, almost unblinking as he took another bite of his dinner. Joy wasn't sure why his reaction to her presence and her statements was so adorable. He was so hot, and so understanding, and so forgiving.

"So I worked a couple more days," she said. "Then my daughters-in-law helped me clean out my little room, because I took the rest of my vacation days for this week, and then next week is Spring Break. So I'm...done." An initial blip of sadness flowed through her like a jolt of electricity. It hurt for a moment, a burn lingered, and then it dissipated.

"Joy, you're done?" He looked somewhat panicked. "I didn't mean for you to do that. We were flying in and out. It was okay. I could've waited. I—"

"Scott, baby." She placed a finger over his mouth, and he fell silent. "You didn't make me do anything. I'm here, because I want to be here. I quit, because I'm done. I cannot watch you drive away from me in Sweet Water Falls again. I can't walk away from you, not even one more time. I just can't."

Several moments beat between them where she said nothing, and Scott seemed to be trying to find the right thing to say or do. His eyes fell closed in a slow blink, then opened again to reveal those beautiful blue eyes. "You're my favorite person in the whole world."

"And you're mine," Joy said. Their first kiss was a make-up kiss, full of feelings and understanding. The second was their passionate kiss.

This time, when Scott touched his lips to hers, Joy catalogued the kiss as one between two people who loved each other deeply.

———

"THAT'S HIM," JOY SAID, POINTING. "HE'S WEARING that flat-billed hat. See him?"

"I see him." Scott's hand tightened in hers. "And Hank's right behind him?"

"Yep." Joy waved her arm, and her sons detoured toward her. Walter turned toward his wife and took the little girl from her. They cut through the crowd, the four of them, and Scott's smile started to look more natural.

"I suddenly understand how you felt coming to my parents' house for Christmas dinner."

They stood near the baggage claim in the Charleston airport, and Joy giggled and said, "It's going to be amazing."

Her sons arrived a moment later, both of them lifting her off her feet as they both hugged her at the same time. "Hey, Momma," Walt said, and the three of them laughed.

They set her down, and Joy immediately fell back to Scott's side. She looked up at him, beaming, and said, "Guys, this is Scott Anderson. Scott, this is my oldest son, Walt." She indicated him. "His wife Lexie, and their darling daughter, Holly."

Joy took the little girl, who lit up at the sight of her. "Yes, hello, baby. It's Gammy." She laughed at the baby. "And my youngest son, Hank, and his wife, Morgan."

"It's so great to meet you," Scott said, his long arm reaching out to shake the hands of her sons. He kissed the cheeks of her daughters-in-law, and chatter broke out about how the flight was, if they had everything they needed or if they'd checked bags, and where they wanted to go for lunch.

As Joy left the airport, she couldn't believe this was her life. She'd been living inside the gaslit version of her life, and it had eaten her up and killed her. Bea's move to Hilton

355

ELANA JOHNSON

Head had awakened something inside her to this fact that part of her was dead, and she'd been trying to get it reawakened for all this time.

Scott fit right into her family, as she'd suspected he would. He was the perfect companion for her too, and she stepped out of the airport and into the South Carolina sunshine, a completely different person—and ready to start building her new life according to her blueprint.

Chapter Thirty-One

Sage shoved the last pillow into the back of the already overstuffed back of her SUV. She wiped her brow, because the end of April in Sweet Water Falls wasn't exactly cool. In a month, it would be the middle of summer.

She closed the back of her SUV and turned toward the field across the street. The last of the poppies and bluebells had wilted, and Sage thanked God above that she'd been in Texas for one last bloom. She loved the wildflowers in Texas, and she told herself there would be things she'd love about Hilton Head Island too.

She didn't have a man drawing her there. Bessie didn't either, but they'd determined they didn't want to do Supper Club via video anymore. Sage felt like an almost silent member of her Supper Club, but as more of her best friends had started to make the trek to the East Coast, Sage had realized she didn't want to lose this piece of her life.

She'd lost so much already. So many things in her life had

morphed and changed over the past couple of years, and her ladies in the Supper Club were an anchor for her. An anchor she needed in her life.

"Well," Thelma said, and Sage turned toward her sister. "That's everything."

Sage moved to stand next to her sister, who'd been born a decade after her. When their mother had died of cancer when Thelma was only ten, Sage had left college to return home to care for her and their brother. She'd made sure they got fed and to school on time, that they did their homework and treated their teachers right.

Once they'd graduated and gone on to college themselves, Sage had gone back to college too. She'd earned a business management degree and done styling and aesthetics on the side. She really loved color the most, and she'd taken and continued to enroll in any color theory class or workshop she could.

Some of her clients had said they'd fly to South Carolina to have her keep dying their hair, and that was a huge compliment for Sage. Whether they actually would or not, Sage didn't know. She knew she was going to move to Hilton Head Island with her sister.

Thelma had never been married, and she had three cats that should make the twelve-hundred-mile drive with Gypsy really interesting. He already sat in the backseat, his big tongue panting out of his mouth. Sage loved him so much, and she smiled at her big, black dog as she looked back to the condo she'd moved into after her divorce had been finalized.

She'd already left behind her family home where she'd

raised her daughter and spent twenty-five years with her husband. Nora went to college in the Denver area, and Sage really felt like she didn't have much tying her to this place she'd loved living.

The hobby farm hadn't sold, but Jed and Cherry Forrester said they'd take the animals over to Cowboy Ranch until it did.

"Ready," Sage said, and she moved to open the driver's door. Thelma went around to the passenger side, and Sage navigated them out of the condo's parking lot. She knew the way to Hilton Head, and she picked up her phone and handed it to Thelma. "Will you text Ty and find out if we got that rental?"

She sure hoped they did, because if not, Ty Parker only had three days to get them one. With Sage and Thelma driving, they'd need to keep checking to be able to sign a lease, or perhaps Ty could meet them at a rental with the paperwork they needed.

She'd met him through Bea, Cass, and Lauren, and apparently Tyler Barker was the best real estate agent on the island. He'd said that it was a good time to get a rental, because the summer season hadn't officially started yet.

"We can get a vacation rental if he doesn't have a residential one," Thelma said.

"I'm sure," Sage murmured, because she didn't want to argue with her sister. Not over finances. Thelma had been working in the private finance sector for twenty years, and she had plenty of money. Sage wasn't hurting, but she had to watch her pennies a little more closely than staying in a vacation rental long-term would allow.

She could ask Cass to stay with her, and her friend wouldn't even bat an eyelash. In fact, if Sage couldn't find a suitable apartment for herself and Thelma, and she didn't ask Cass, Cass would be upset.

Sage usually didn't mind relying on her friends, and she didn't have the mental strength to worry about the women already on the island right now. Everyone was there except for her, as Joy had surprised them all and quit her job over Spring Break and flown to the island without packing more than a single suitcase.

Her house had sold a few days ago, and Sage had gone by to get a couple of things Joy wanted before her youngest son and his pregnant wife moved in. She and Scott would be back next week to pack up the house, and Sage had heard Joy's boys would come to help too. Cherry and Jed Forrester had said they'd bring their cowboys too, so the job could get done quickly.

Sage had used Cherry's offer of her cowboy power to help her pack up, and she'd paid a professional driver to bring the moving truck. She and Thelma had put all of their most necessary items in the back of her SUV, and they'd brought their pets.

"He says he'll know in a couple of hours," Thelma said. She placed the phone back in the cupholder. "But even if this one doesn't go through, he's already reached out to an owner in that building that Harrison finished last year."

"Oh, that would be nice," Sage said. "We can afford that?"

"If Ty's reaching out to them, I'm sure we can," Thelma said. She'd always been more carefree than Sage, and Sage had worked hard so that Thelma *could* be that way. So she didn't say anything, because she didn't trust her voice not to pitch up in a way that said she disbelieved her sister.

Behind her, Gypsy panted. Thelma opened her ereader and started reading. Sage drove. And drove. And drove.

———

THREE DAYS LATER, SAGE WAS STILL DRIVING WHEN they crossed the bridge and arrived on Hilton Head Island, though she and Thelma had alternated throughout the trip. "Can you put the address in?" Sage asked.

Thelma turned toward her from where she'd been staring out the passenger window. They'd talked and talked over the past three days, and they'd both fallen silent a few hours ago. Only Gypsy still seemed to be enjoying himself, because the cats had been meowing for at least the past half-hour.

Her sister didn't say anything as she reached for Sage's phone and pulled up the address. They hadn't gotten the first apartment, but Ty had gotten them into the complex Harry had built last year.

"Bea texted," Thelma said. She tapped a couple more times and set the phone so Sage could see it.

"What did she say?"

"That she'll be a few minutes late."

"A few minutes late for what?" Sage cut a look over to her sister.

"I don't know. That's what she said."

Sage kept driving, and several minutes later, she pulled into another parking lot with big, beautiful apartment buildings in it. "These are nice," she said, trying to keep her voice lighthearted and casual.

"It looks great," Thelma said. "Sage, you worry too much." She reached over and squeezed Sage's forearm. "I'm going to be happy to be here with you, no matter where we live."

Sage smiled, but it felt tight on her face. She did want her sister to be happy. She wanted to be happy, and she'd just uprooted herself and moved across the country as she searched for that.

"Let's see...oh, there's Ty." She turned left and pulled up to the curb alongside a handsome, blond-haired man wearing a full suit from head to toe. Sage had only met the man one other time, and he'd been dressed to the nines then too.

She parked though the curb boasted bright red paint and got out of the car. She stretched her arms high above her head and groaned at the pinch in her back. She'd left the driver's door open, and Gypsy whined.

"Hey, Ty," she said. "Let me get Gypsy out." She opened the back door and grabbed the leash from the floor. She clipped it to Gypsy's collar and said, "Stay by me. Stay. By.

Me." Only then did she back out of the doorway and let the giant dog down.

He was nothing but a big, black marshmallow, and he did stay right by Sage. She led him up onto the sidewalk to the narrow strip of grass that then ran parallel to the apartment building behind it.

"You're on the first floor, as requested," Ty said as Sage held the leash so her dog could take care of his business. He grinned at her, and Sage thought he had a nice smile. She wasn't sure of his age, but he had plenty of lines on his forehead and around his eyes. He had straight, white teeth, and she could admit she found him attractive. She wasn't going to do anything about it, but she could admit it.

She took the two lanyards he extended toward her, each bearing a white keycard and a silver key. "These are?"

"Cards for the clubhouse," he said. "Great workout room, swimming pool, hot tub, and big party area with a ping pong table and pool table. And those are keys to your apartment." He turned toward the building behind him. "You're around the back side, which is nice, because you can see the ocean on that side. This is building E, and you're in twelve, down near the end."

He smiled at her once again, and pure gratitude streamed through her. "Thank you, Ty," she said. "You're a miracle worker to get us this apartment."

"Yes, thank you," Thelma said as she stepped up onto the sidewalk. She took the leash from Sage and moved closer to Gypsy. "The cats are going nuts."

"We've got the keys," Sage said, handing her one of the

lanyards. "Take them and go check it out." She glanced back to Ty. "I'm sure we have to sign some things."

"I can help you get into the apartment," he said. "We'll sign there."

Sage nodded, ready to be done with this trip. She'd driven it before, but this time had felt doubly hard—probably because she knew she wasn't going back to Sweet Water Falls.

She collected one of the cat carriers from the back seat that held two of Thelma's cats and handed it to Ty. "I'll get this other one," she said.

Once they had the cats, Ty indicated she should go first down the sidewalk that ran between two perfectly rocked beds. Palms rose from them, with a few other bushes. Whoever did the landscaping here worked at it meticulously, and she followed Thelma to another parallel sidewalk that concealed the first floor of the building. She could now see that the sidewalk continued through the building to the other side of it, and they went on.

"Twelve is to the left," Ty said. Step after step they went, until Thelma stood outside of unit twelve. Thelma fitted her key into the lock, twisted, and opened the door.

Sage heard something scrape, and then her sister entered the apartment with Gypsy in front of her. She stepped into the apartment next, and Sage paused to take in the apartment she'd call home until she figured out a more permanent solution. *If* she even wanted something besides this. She hadn't minded the condo in Texas, because they had amenities and activities, and she'd never felt lonely or alone.

With Thelma living with her, she thought she wouldn't be lonely or feel alone, especially with three cats and a dog.

"Surprise," a round of voices said, and Sage blinked as a smile formed on her face. And all of her friends—every single one of whom stood in the apartment.

Bea, Cass, Lauren, Joy, and Bessie. Bea held up a bottle of wine, her face radiant. Cass indicated a cheesecake with plenty of dark blue fruit and syrup on it, some of which ran down the side. Sage's mouth watered at the same time her eyes teared up.

Lauren held up two brown paper bags that had panda bears printed on them—Sage's favorite Chinese food from a restaurant she and Lauren had found last summer.

Joy wore an enormous grin, and Sage couldn't wait to get her hands on her hair to fix up the blonde. Joy had been too busy to do it in recent months, and Sage loved working on her hair. She held up a puffy, white pillow that better be made of feathers, and Bessie lifted a set of dog and cat bowls that she'd surely fill with food and water as soon as they finished hugging.

Cass looked down the row of them and said, "Ready, guys?" Only a moment later, they all chorused, "Welcome home, Sage and Thelma."

Sage started to laugh even though tears filled her eyes enough to allow the moisture to spill over. She wiped at her face, handed the cats to Thelma, and rushed into the arms of her friends. They enveloped her and held her up, the same way they'd been doing since their Supper Club had formed years ago.

Sometimes she knew how much she helped her friends, but sometimes she had no idea. She hadn't known she wanted her friends here for this moment, but she absolutely did. She didn't want this move to happen in isolation, and she said, "You guys have no idea how much I needed this."

"Oh, I think they knew," Thelma said, and their group widened to include her sister too. Sage loved them all the more for that, and she was suddenly re-invigorated for her new life here in Hilton Head.

"All right." Ty's crisp voice broke into their huddle. "I just have a few forms for you to sign, Sage."

She stepped back and wiped her eyes. "Yes, of course." Then she turned to face him and sign her name on the papers that would start this next chapter of her life.

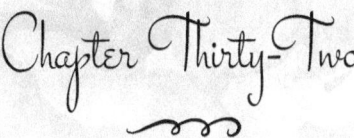

Chapter Thirty-Two

"I think that's all for here." Scott stretched up to grab the rope tied to the handle of the door. It sounded like he was pulling down the whole building, the rollers on the track at this storage unit so dang noisy. He gave it one good last shove, and then used his boot to get it all the way to the ground.

Stooping, he looped one arm of the lock Joy had bought through the hole just as she said, "Wait, I have one more box."

Scott turned to see what he'd missed, and Joy held a white box. Not a moving box. "I thought that was for Hank and Morgan."

"No, I got the stuff out of it I wanted for them."

He re-lifted the door just enough to take the box and duck back inside. He set it on top of the nearest stack, noting that there was still plenty of room to walk around, as well as get more items should Joy or Lauren need them.

The heat inside the unit drove him right back out, and Scott wiped the sweat off his forehead before he closed the door again. He fitted the lock through the holes and snapped the end back into itself. As he straightened, he told himself the job was now half-done.

"All right," he said while smothering a sigh. "Back to your place?"

"Yep," she said, taking his hand into hers. "But Harry said Oliver is bringing smoothies, so it should go fast with the extra help—and smoothies."

Fast sounded good to him. A smoothie sounded amazing too, and he opened the passenger door of his truck to help Joy in. He hadn't put a diamond on her finger yet, though they'd visited a couple of jewelry stores here on the island.

Scott had a better idea of what cut she'd like, what setting, and how he might pop the question. It wasn't that he thought she might say no; it was that he wanted to gift wrap the world, hold it in his hands, get down on both knees, and give it to her.

And he hadn't figured out how to do that yet.

"It's such a beautiful day," Joy said with a soft sigh that spoke of her contentment.

Scott looked out his side window, his eyes soaking up the bluest of blue skies, the green palms clawing up into it, and a golden glow surrounding all of it. "It sure is," he said. May in Hilton Head was one of his favorite months. Things had been regrowing for several weeks now, and Scott had nearly all of his clients' yards and exteriors looking amazing. He knew his routine now that summer was here, and Jeff had started a wait-list for new clients.

They'd been talking about hiring more people, but they'd reached a pinch point where it would be tight for a few months before the income from new clients paid for more equipment, more overhead, and more of everything.

Scott hadn't signed off on it yet, because growth was scary. Pinching hurt, and he wanted more time to sit down with Jeff—a solid businessman in his own right—and talk through things a little more. He'd mentioned it to Joy a couple of times too, and she'd said expansion sounded like a good option for him.

She'd volunteered to come help run the office so Jeff could go edge, clip hedges, and mow lawns, but Jeff didn't want to do that. He loved running the office, and he didn't mind helping out in a pinch, but he didn't love getting his hands dirty the way Scott did.

"Are you really okay to go to the beach after we get every-thing moved into the house?" Joy looked over to him, and Scott swung his head toward her too.

"Yeah, sure." He reached over and slipped his fingers between hers. "I took the whole day off to help you get things moved around." She'd finally put a date on the schedule to go back to Sweet Water Falls to pack up her house and get her belongings moved to Hilton Head. Her sons had come to help, Scott had gone with her, and even her neighbors had shown up.

Now that they'd returned to the island, she'd wanted her own bed in the house she was renting from Lauren, and they'd spent the past couple of days moving things out of the house that belonged to her and into storage, filling another unit with Joy's unnecessary-for-now items, and the last leg of the move—getting her bed and furniture set up in the house now that there was room.

At the house, her sons waited on the front porch, glasses of sweet tea in their hands that made Scott's mouth twice as dry as it had previously been. They were good men, coming to help their mother over and over in the past month since Joy had decided it was go-time on her blueprint.

Scott got out of the truck and waited for Joy to join him. They approached the house together as her youngest came down the steps. He held two more glasses of tea and handed one to Joy and then Scott as he said, "How'd it go?"

"Just fine," Joy said. "There's lots of room over there."

"Good," Hank said. "Then you can move more of that stuff out of the office."

"I might need it," Joy said.

"Momma." He grinned and shook his head. "When's the last time you sewed something?"

"You never know," she said with a hint of forced casualness in her tone that said she wasn't going to sew anything anytime soon. Scott had known she'd once been a sewist, but the amount of material in her house in Texas had surprised him—and she'd moved it all here.

"The yard will keep you busy enough," Hank said, shooting a look over to Scott. "Unless he's going to take care of it."

"I like doing yard work," Joy said, also looking at him.

"I can't take you on as a client right now anyway," he said. "Jeff'll have to put you on the waitlist."

Joy's eyes widened and she planted one hand on her hip. "You would *waitlist* me?"

Scott laughed and turned to go with Walt as he went past to start getting the last of the items out of the truck. "We're full, baby," he said over his shoulder.

She muttered something Scott didn't catch, but Hank's laughter filling the yard certainly met his ears. He grabbed one end of the mattress while Walt took the other, and together, they hauled the bed into the house.

When they came back outside, Harrison and Oliver had arrived with cup holder upon cup holder of smoothies—far more than the four of them there—and within two minutes, Joy's friends started to arrive too.

With more manpower, they had the moving truck empty and everything inside Joy's house within twenty minutes. The women gabbed as they unpacked her kitchen items and moved about the house putting towels in the linen closet and breaking down the boxes as they got emptied.

Scott needed an ice bath to shock his muscles back to a quiet state, but he settled for a Summer Serenade smoothie and stepping onto the back patio. The sun had risen enough to start filling the space back here with sunlight and more heat, but he didn't mind either.

Joy had done an incredible job of keeping up the yard, and she'd gotten a job at the library while she went through the application process for the elementary schools here.

She'd had to take a test to be able to teach in the state, and she hadn't heard on that yet.

"Things are really coming together," Grant said as he stepped to Scott's side.

"Yeah," he said. "They are."

Harrison also came outside, and he whistled at the beauty of the yard. "This is a great place," he said. "Are you gonna move in here when you two get married?"

The sliding glass door opened one more time, and Blake joined them. Both of Joy's sons followed him, and finally, so did Oliver.

"Thanks for the smoothies," Scott said. "What do I owe you for them?"

Oliver exchanged a glance with Grant. "Nothing," he said. "Grant and I worked it out."

Scott looked between the two of them, sensing something he didn't know about. "What does that mean?"

"It means—" Grant said, but Oliver said, "Nothing. It means you owe me nothing."

Tension rode on the air for a moment, and then Blake said, "Lauren does love this house."

"You two won't have kids," Harrison said. "Right? So it's big enough for the two of you."

"It's better than my place," Scott admitted. "I don't know. I haven't talked to Joy about it."

"That's because she's not wearin' a ring," Walt said dryly, and all eyes turned to him. "Better get that done soon, Scott."

"Yeah?" Scott liked Joy's kids a whole lot, with Walt

being the older, take-charge brother who'd been more stand-offish than Hank, who was more like a big golden retriever. He could look scary charging you, but it was just because he wanted to get as close to you as he could, as fast as he could. Then he could lick you and love you, and you could give him a rub.

"Yeah," he and Hank and at least one other man on the patio said.

"I mean, what are you waiting for?" Grant added.

"Great question," Scott mused.

"Sounds like there's something," Harrison said gently.

"I just—I've never asked a woman to marry me," Scott said. "I don't know how this goes." He refused to look at any of them. "I have no plan, and if there's one thing Joy likes more than anything, it's what something will look like before she takes action." Maybe some of that had rubbed off on him.

Walt chuckled. "My momma is like that."

"She just wants you to ask her," Blake said. "What ideas do you have?"

"I don't even have the ring yet," Scott said, unable to keep his eyes from flicking toward Blake.

"So we solve that this afternoon," Grant said, like buying the perfect diamond ring for the woman he loved was so stinking simple. Maybe for him, it had been. Scott's stomach felt like it had been tied in knots over this.

"Then, brother, you just ask her." Oliver spoke with a gentle lilt, and Scott knew he wasn't trying to make light of this.

"Yeah," Scott said almost absently. "I'll get it done."

"She told us to mark off the second half of October and the beginning of November," Walt said. "So we did, and if you don't ask her soon, she won't have much time to plan."

"Lauren made things work in only three months," Blake offered helpfully.

Scott only nodded, because he was aware of how many months stood between May and October. It was only the first weekend of May, besides, and even if he didn't propose for another month, Joy would still have over four months to plan for a mid-October wedding date.

"I'm going to ask her soon," he promised just as the sliding door opened again.

"Guys," Lauren said. "Pizza's here."

"Praise the Lord," Walt said as he immediately turned to re-enter the house. "I thought all I might get today was blended up fruit." He went back inside while a couple of others laughed.

"What's wrong with blended up fruit?" Oliver asked, and that caused a loud round of laughter to spill from Scott's mouth.

"Nothing, brother," he said as he clapped Oliver on the shoulder. "Nothing at all."

Chapter Thirty-Three

J oy's eyes met Lauren's for a microsecond before Lauren turned her back on her, her attention solely on her phone. A vibration trembled through Joy's chest, but she didn't say anything. She'd gotten off work at the library that afternoon, and she'd come over to Lauren's to help her prep for Supper Club that evening.

Bessie had already arrived, and she currently bent to get a perfectly browned and baked loaf of bread out of the oven. She gazed at it with such adoration that Joy wondered if she'd ever loved anything as much as Bessie loved baking.

"Looks amazing, Bess," she said. "I love the smell of freshly baked bread."

"There's nothing like it, is there?" Bessie brushed the top of the bread with melted butter in quick, professional strokes of a pastry brush. Then she dropped big chunks of sea salt over it, and Joy's mouth watered for this salted honey

ELANA JOHNSON

whole wheat bread. If that was all she ate for Supper Club tonight, she'd exist in utter bliss.

"Who are you texting?" Bessie asked, and Lauren spun to face them. Guilt etched across her face, which also bloomed a healthy pink.

"No one." She shoved her phone into her back pocket and looked at the kitchen. She seemed to have forgotten what she was doing, but after a couple of seconds, she picked up the wooden spoon and started stirring the onions in the pan again.

She'd planned a Memorial Day barbecue menu, though the holiday wasn't until next weekend. Joy would never say no to a good hamburger or hot dog, especially with freshly baked bread and a perfectly ripe watermelon. She'd recently learned at a nursery class how to pick such a thing, and she'd had no idea that watermelons came in male and female varieties, nor that the sunspot should be yellow and not white.

She'd told Lauren she'd pick and bring the perfect melon, and she had. She popped another piece into her mouth, something she needed to say making it hard for her to swallow. She managed, then cleared her throat.

"Lauren," she said as Lauren pulled her phone from her pocket again. "I want to buy the house."

Lauren dropped her phone into the pan of caramelizing onions, swore, and quickly fished it out. When she faced Joy, there was obviously something wrong. Very wrong. She stared at Joy as if she'd never seen her before, then shot a look over to Bessie.

Joy followed her gaze too, wondering what in the world

was going on. Bessie wore a serious expression, but she seemed mildly confused by Lauren's behavior too. They both looked back to Lauren, and Joy pushed out a hip. "Okay," she said. "What's going on?"

"You can't buy the house," she blurted out.

Joy blinked, not expecting that. Lauren had told her several times in the past five weeks since Joy had been renting that she'd sell her the house if she wanted it. When her brain finally caught up to the conversation, she asked, "Why not?"

"Oh, the burgers." Lauren rushed past Joy and out the back door, where the charcoal grill was spewing forth puffs of smoke. She lifted the lid, waved the spatula around like that would do anything, and started removing the meat.

"She won't sell me the house?" Joy edged closer to Bessie. "She's acting weird, right?"

"Very," Bessie agreed. "Could she be...pregnant?"

Their gazes locked, and Joy's mind raced. Lauren was forty-three years old, and while that was a bit on the older side to get pregnant, it wouldn't be impossible. "Could be," she murmured. "Then why is she looking at her stupid phone every two seconds?"

Among all the chaos of the smoke and fire, Lauren paused to do exactly that.

"Maybe she just found out and she's just told Blake."

"Then we shouldn't be here tonight," Joy said, a measure of impatience moving through her. She started for the patio too, with Bessie saying, "Joy," behind her. She carried on anyway, and she stepped outside to help Lauren with the grill.

She capped it again, sealing the smoke inside so the cheese could burn off. "Lauren," she practically barked. Her friend almost dropped her phone again, bobbling it but managing to save it. "What's going on?"

Joy picked up the plate with the slightly over-charred burgers. "Are you pregnant?" Bessie came to her side, and the two of them peered at Lauren.

Another flush moved through her face. "What? No."

"Who are you texting then?" Joy nodded to the phone, which had a dark screen. She'd raised two boys; she knew deceit when she saw it.

Lauren's dark eyes blazed. "None of your business." She took the plate from Joy and marched inside. More voices filtered out to them, and that signaled the arrival of at least one other Supper Club member.

Sure enough, when Joy stepped inside, she found Cass and Bea had both arrived. Sage entered with a long tray of burger toppings next, and they all chattered as the island got covered with condiments, buns, and side dishes.

"All right," Lauren said once everything was laid out. "I just threw the hot dogs on a few minutes ago, so I'll just grab those, and we'll be good to go." She dashed outside to do that, and Sage picked up a plate.

She started fixing herself a hamburger, and Joy decided she didn't want to try to get any news out of Lauren. So she practically lunged to be the next in line, and she looked over to Sage as she smeared yellow mustard over her bottom hamburger bun.

"Did you get the salon space, Sage?"

"No." She smiled as she said it, though, so it couldn't be all bad news. "I decided I don't want to pay for booth space. I interviewed at the Mionic Salon instead."

"Wait, we're doing news?" Bea asked. "Sage has news." She made it sound like the crowd was so big that they couldn't all hear Sage talking in the kitchen as she put lettuce and tomato on her hamburger.

"It's not big news," Sage said. "I decided not to rent booth space. I don't want to be an independent stylist here. I want to work at a salon, so I interviewed at Mionic yesterday."

"Oh, that's great," Cass said.

"Yeah," Bessie echoed as others offered their congratulations and support too, Joy included. "My news is that Wyn and I got approved for our business funding. We're going to get our supplies and appliances ordered this week."

She wore a look of pure giddiness on her face, and Joy's heart exploded with happiness. "Bess, that's great." She leaned into her and hugged her from the side.

"When will you open?" Bea asked.

"We're aiming by the Fourth of July," Bessie said. "It's just a matter of when things can be delivered. We have the permits and the recipes. I know how to run this business." And she did, Joy knew. She'd talked to Bessie plenty in the past several weeks, because they were both working odd jobs right now until they could do what they really wanted to do.

When no one else said anything, Joy figured she could go next. As she squirted mayo onto her bun, she said, "My diploma came, so there's that. And I passed the test here in South Carolina to be able to teach."

"You did?" Bea practically shrieked. "Joy, that's so amazing!"

Cass wore an enormous smile, and Lauren, now at the back of the line, asked, "When will you apply for a job here?"

"I started the application process today, in fact," Joy said, almost annoyed that Lauren had been the one to ask, and Joy had to answer her. "I have to do fingerprinting and stuff for a background check. Then I guess I'll be able to apply for jobs."

Even if she didn't get hired as a classroom teacher, Joy still wanted to work in the schools. She didn't dislike the job at the library, but it wasn't full-time work, and it didn't pay her enough for her to do it long-term. Perhaps combined with another part-time job in an elementary school, and she could do both.

"You'll get something so fast, Joy," Sage said, and Joy appreciated the vote of confidence.

"Not much for me," Cass said. "Except Harrison and I are going to take a trip to Jerusalem this fall."

Joy's chest caved in as every eye landed on her, especially Cass's. "I mean, I'm not going to go when you get married," she said.

"*If* I get married," Joy said. Scott still hadn't asked, and Joy honestly didn't know what he was waiting for.

"Of course you're going to get married," Bea said. "In October or November, just like you're planning."

Joy finished with her burger and scooped up a spoonful

of watermelon. Then she lifted her left hand for all to see. "Well, I don't know about that. There aren't any diamonds here."

To feed her great irritation with the woman, Lauren had gone back to texting. During Joy's complaint about not being engaged. She wanted to knock the phone from her friend's hand, but she refrained. Barely.

Bea said she and Grant had bought another rental property, and Lauren said she'd signed two more clients before they all sat down to eat. Joy tried to sit as far from Lauren as possible, but it was hard with a round table, and she ended up directly across from her.

Their eyes met, and Lauren smiled like she hadn't been acting weird all day. Joy cocked her eyebrows, said nothing, and took a bite of her burger.

The doorbell rang, and the conversation slowed to a trickle. But Lauren didn't move. "You're not going to get it?" Cass asked.

Joy found that odd as well, but she kept her thoughts to herself.

"It's Supper Club," Lauren said. "I'm not expecting anyone." She said the last sentence really loud, and Joy frowned. Bessie and Sage looked equally as perplexed, and Bea got to her feet when the doorbell pealed again.

"I'll get it then," she said.

Lauren jumped up too. "It's fine," she said, blocking Bea from going to the front door. "I'm sure it's nothing." The two of them faced off, and Joy glanced around the table to the other women before she looked back to Lauren and Bea.

Lauren returned to the table, and put her phone face-up on it. "It's fine."

Bea looked like she wasn't sure if she should stay or go, and she hadn't moved when a voice said, "Just go in." A male voice that sounded very much like Blake...

"She didn't say I could go in," another man said. Joy stopped chewing at Scott's tone.

"It's *my* house," Blake argued back. "*I* say you can go in."

"Can someone open the door already?" Harrison grumbled. "This isn't easy to hold."

"Lauren?" Cass asked.

Joy wanted to ask the same thing, but scraping and footsteps filled the air, and she'd finally located the source of it—Lauren's phone. Her doorbell cam.

Whispers and arguing from the front hallway had them all looking that way, and Lauren hissed, "Bea, sit down." She did just as Scott lurched into sight, almost like he'd been pushed.

He glared over his shoulder, which testified that he had indeed been pushed out of the hallway, and he swept his hand through his gorgeous hair, looked toward them, and found Joy easily. Shock coursed through her, because she'd texted with him an hour ago, and they'd planned to meet up after this.

Scott regained his composure, his trademark smile coming easily to his face. He moved forward, those blue eyes calling to her the way the waves of the ocean did. "Joy," he said. "My Joy."

She smiled too, because she loved it when he called her his. Sage and Bessie got to their feet and moved around to the other side of the table, so all five of them faced Joy and Scott had an unobstructed path to her.

He took it too, moving right close to her and dropping to his knees in a fluid, swift movement. "I fall more in love with you every time I see you."

"Aw," a couple of the women sighed, but Joy couldn't look away from Scott. Was this really happening? Was he going to propose at Supper Club?

Another thought struck her while Scott swallowed. Had Lauren known? Had she helped him plan this? Joy's eyes blitzed across the table to find out, but Scott said, "I planned this whole speech, and then I erased it all. You know how I feel about you, because I tell you all the time. I want you in my life forever, and I love you so much I can't stand waiting until the fall to marry you. I will, because I will do anything you want me to do."

He tugged something free from his pocket and held up a sparkly, shiny diamond ring. "My Joy, will you make me the happiest man on the planet by agreeing to marry me?"

Tears spilled down her face. "Yes," she said, her voice strangled and high-pitched. "Of course I'll marry you."

Scott slid the ring on her finger while Joy wiped her face with her right hand. Sniffles from her Supper Club filled the air, and then whooping and whistles when Scott touched his mouth to hers and kissed her.

She started to laugh, and she ducked her head and buried her face against his chest as the applause continued. Scott got to his feet, and he pulled Joy to hers too. "There's one more thing, baby."

He nodded to the men who'd come around the corner from the hallway at some point, and Harrison lifted the round end of a gigantic cake. Grant held the other end—the jagged teeth of a key. The cake easily spanned three feet, and Blake held up a serving spatula. All three of them grinned like fools, and Scott wore the gesture in his voice as he said, "This is for you."

"A key cake?" Joy asked, finally tearing her eyes from all the white frosting. The key had been outlined in blue, and she wondered if the decorator had thought it was for some sort of warped baby shower.

"It's a present for our engagement."

"For Supper Club," Blake said, and the three of them moved to put the cake on the table.

"But there's something in it you need to find," Scott said as Lauren quickly scraped chairs out of the way and then ducked to the side so Grant and Harrison could put the cake down. They did, dropping it almost, with a thunderous *thunk!*

Joy's hand went to her pulse, which had picked up speed. She had no idea what to do with this much cake. Even if she ate it for breakfast, lunch, and dinner for the next month, she'd still have leftovers.

"All right," Scott said. "I think we've interrupted you enough." He slipped away from her right when Joy wanted him to stay.

"You're leaving?" she asked.

He turned back to her, such kindness in those eyes. "Yeah, baby," he said. "Lauren said if I could propose in less than ten minutes, she'd allow it." He pulled her close and kissed her properly—if only for a moment. "I'll see you afterward, okay?"

He rejoined his friends, and the four of them faced the Supper Club. "We can talk about the gift when I pick you up." With that, he led the way out of the house, and since the doorbell camera was still activated on Lauren's phone, they all heard him say, "I think that was only eight minutes, so she can't be upset, right?" from the front porch.

"No way," Blake said. "You were in the timeframe, bro."

"Do you think she'll be able to find the key?" Harrison's voice could barely be heard, as the men hadn't lingered on the porch to chat.

Silence fell over the house then, and Lauren tapped to close the doorbell app. She straightened the chairs, and the six of them looked at the almost-baby-shower cake. Joy looked at her friends, only one question in her mind.

"Key?" she asked. "A key to what?"

Sage picked up the serving spatula. "Only one way to find out." She cut right down the middle of the cake as all of them leaned over it. Joy half-expected something to burst out of the dessert, but nothing did.

Nothing happened at all.

"Joy," Bessie said, picking up her knife. "How clean does this need to be?"

Joy had no idea, and in fact, she felt like someone had hit

her with the three-foot-long cake. She picked up her fork. "Let's do this."

They attacked the cake, each taking a big section of it and going at it with utensils. It only took about thirty seconds for Bea to say, "I found it! Here it is!" She held up a silver key that looked like it had been buried in the center of a cake pop. Frosting dripped from her hand, and Joy's laughter burst from her.

"You didn't even use a fork?" Lauren asked, her voice dripping with disgust. "Bea, what is wrong with you?" She took the key and rushed over to the kitchen sink to rinse it.

"I found something," Bessie said, and her shredded cake looked like someone with some civility had gone through it. She held up a plastic bag with plenty of cake crumbs clinging to it.

Bea put one finger in her mouth and said, "It's good cake."

That made Sage and Cass laugh, and Joy's smile started to form too. She was slowly coming back to her senses, and she took the plastic bag that had been baked into the cake and opened the zipped top.

It held a single piece of paper, and she'd just unfolded it when Lauren returned to the table with the cleaned key. Joy couldn't read fast enough, and the words she did read made no sense.

"What is it?" Cass asked.

Joy handed it to her and sank into her chair, numb.

Cass gasped. "He didn't."

"What?" Sage asked. "What is it?"

"He bought us a house," Joy said, the words barely belonging to her voice. She looked across the table to Lauren, who'd also sat down. "You sold him your house."

"It's for the two of you," she said, her eyes filling with tears.

"You've been texting him all night."

Lauren nodded, and Joy felt like a fool for being irritated with her. She got up and moved around the table to hug her best friend. "He loves you so much," Lauren whispered. "I do too."

"Thank you, Lauren," she said back. Part of her wanted to stay here, but she absolutely had to be with Scott right now too. She pulled away and searched Lauren's face.

"Go," Lauren said. "I told him to wait outside for a few minutes."

"Can I?" Joy asked, glancing around to everyone in their Supper Club. "Just a few minutes."

"Go and don't come back," Bea said. She now held the baked-in paper. "He bought you a house, Joy. Go!"

Joy didn't wait for permission from the others. She hurried after Scott, and she hit the front door running. Outside, she dashed down the steps, sure he'd be gone by now.

He stood next to his truck, one hand in his pocket and the other holding his phone.

"Scott." She jogged toward him, and he shoved his phone away in time to catch her in his arms as she arrived there. They laughed together as he swung her around, and

Joy felt like she'd fallen into the perfect ending of the best romance movie ever made.

He set her on her feet, and she gasped for air. "You bought the house."

"I bought *us* the house," he said.

"You just want that backyard," she teased.

"Only if you come with it." He smiled that adoring, filled-with-love smile down at her. "I love you so much, Joy. I'd live on rocks to be with you. You know that, right?"

"Yeah," she whispered. "I know that."

He swept his lips along her jaw, and Joy knew what he was waiting for. "I love you, Scott," she said. "Maybe we can move the wedding up so it happens before the baby's born."

"I would marry you tomorrow," he said.

Joy needed to be told such things, and she took his face in her hands, smiling with everything she had. "You're my favorite person. I love you."

"You're my favorite person too." Then he sealed such a wonderful statement with a kiss that told her he loved her more than words could say.

Keep reading for a sneak peek of **THE TROPICAL TICKET,** the next book in this romance and friendship fiction series. It features Bessie Clifton and her journey toward opening her own bread bakery...and falling in love with someone she least expects to.

I hope you enjoyed Joy, Scott, Cass, Harrison, Lauren, Blake, Bea, Grant, and everyone else in *The Seaside Strategy*! **Please leave a review for the book if you did.**

Scan the QR code below to preorder THE TROPICAL TICKET, the next book in the series.

Sneak Peek! The Tropical Ticket Chapter One:

~~~

Bessie Clifton shook her head as one of her best friends held the blow dryer over it. She scrubbed her fingers along her scalp, because she'd been sitting with the bleach and dye on it for what felt like a long time now, and she needed relief.

Behind her, Sage laughed, the sound barely registering over the blowing of the dryer. Bessie had been getting her hair cut and colored by Sage for several years now, since they'd met and started attending Supper Club together.

That life felt like it belonged to someone else. Certainly not Bessie, who'd been married and raising a teenager when she'd first gone to the initial meeting for a Supper Club in Sweet Water Falls, a small town along the Coastal Bend of Texas.

She was currently divorced and lived with her adult daughter on Hilton Head Island, in South Carolina, and the only thing that even remotely resembled the life she'd had a decade ago was the Supper Club.

Not even the women who belonged to and attended the Club. Just the fact that the Supper Club still existed. And to Bessie, that was significant, because for a year or so there, she'd thought they'd disband and go their separate ways.

A new kind of relief filled her when she thought about how they'd saved their Supper Club. Her and Sage. Because they'd realized that if they didn't make the move to Hilton Head, the monthly dinners would have to end.

Bessie usually held her tongue and didn't make close friendships with very many people. Those she did tended to be very close—like her Supper Club ladies—but she wasn't very confrontational. She knew a lot of people on the surface, and she recognized people who came into the bread shop where she worked.

People had come and gone in her lifetime. Friends for a season. There, then gone. She knew that once common interests were lost or too many miles separated two people that it became harder to stay friends. Harder to stay in touch. Easier to focus on those closer, or those who shared new common interests.

And, as she'd watched her friends lose husbands, go through divorces, become empty nesters and widows and reinvent themselves, she hadn't wanted to lose her connection to them. She hadn't wanted to watch Bea, Cass, Lauren, or Joy walk out of her life, never to be heard from again.

Or, if she did hear from them, it was a lame social media

message after a few years, stating how they'd "lost touch," and wanted to catch up.

No, that wasn't good enough for Bessie, and it hadn't been good enough for Sage either. They'd gotten together, and they'd made plans to move to Hilton Head too, each with a loved one, so they could keep and continue their relationships.

Bessie lived with her adult daughter, and Wynona made dinner almost every night. Bessie didn't much care to spend time in the kitchen if it wasn't to bake something golden and delicious, and Wyn could put together something simple in a matter of minutes. Sage lived with her sister, Thelma, and the two of them got into so much trouble together, even now that Sage was in her early fifties.

Sage switched off the hair dryer and asked, "Well? How do you like it?" Her hair bore the same color as freshly churned earth, but it looked a little washed out to Bessie today. Sage insisted that she never dyed it, but Bessie wasn't always sure she believed her.

Bessie reached up, shaking her hands loose of the drape she wore buttoned tightly around her neck, and ran her fingers through her hair. "It's really blonde," she said.

"The dark smudge offsets it," Sage said, fingering a lock of hair. "I think that turned out great. It might be my new favorite thing to do." She smiled at Bessie in the mirror, and she really was the best colorist Bessie had ever met.

"I love it too." She grinned back at her friend. "Thank you, Sage."

"You're gonna be the talk of the island, what with your

sexy new 'do and your new bread bakery opening up." She switched on the blow dryer again and blew it over Bessie's shoulders and down her back to dislodge any errant hairs. Then she silenced it, holstered it in the compartment at her station, and unsnapped the drape.

Bessie sighed as she got to her feet, the chemically smell of the salon one of her very favorite things. It meant she was taking time for herself, doing something that made her feel good, and spending time with a friend. She stepped into Sage's arms and hugged her. "You'll be at the grand opening on Saturday, right?"

"I'm not even going to answer that," Sage said. All of her friends had promised and re-promised to be there. Bessie wasn't sure why she was asking. Probably because her guts writhed at the thought of truly doing what she'd been dreaming of doing for the past four years: Opening her own bakery.

Not just any bakery. She wasn't making double-fudge brownies or eclairs, raspberry pistachio tarts or birthday cakes. All Bessie wanted to make was bread. Loaves of bread in all shapes and sizes. Rolls and croissants for parties, family functions, and the holidays.

She and Wynona had been back and forth about the name of their joint-venture bread bakery since the moment they'd started discussing it. They'd narrowed it down to two —Flour Power or Bread & Butter—and Bessie still hadn't told her friends what the name of the shop would be.

"See you Saturday," Bessie said after she'd checked out and booked her next appointment, and she left the high-end salon that seemed to be made of glass, metal, and light in a strip mall near the beach. She loved the beaches here in Hilton Head, and she visited them far more often than she had in Sweet Water Falls.

When she pulled up to the shop, she smiled fondly at her daughter's sedan parked out front. She took a moment to imagine a line of eager bread lovers extending out the double-glass doors. They currently hid behind a painter's cloth that covered the name of the bakery.

Wynona had bought into the business as the business-woman working behind Bessie's beautiful bread. She'd come up with the idea to reveal the name of the shop at the grand opening, and she'd put out all of the press releases to the local papers, online forums, and social media groups. She'd passed out flyers and visited with other small businesses and managers of local interest around the island, including the various Country Clubs, the public library, and other non-competitive businesses who might be able to simply put a stack of flyers about their grand opening on the checkout counter.

Bessie had stopped keeping track after the library, the restaurants, the historical lighthouse, the quilting and yarn shops, and the bigger outdoor malls had agreed to shelve their event flyers. Even the owner of Gourmet Goods—a direct competitor for croissants—had gushed over the fact that there'd be a new bread bakery in town, and grumpy Oliver Blackhurst had also agreed to put some on the counters of The Mad Mango. Bessie had sent Wyn to do all of that community outreach and education alone.

She ducked under the drape and into the shop to find Wyn sitting at one of the front tables. She'd wanted to go in the French direction, as so many people equated good bread with France. But she didn't want to be kitschy or outdated too fast. She didn't want people to assume she only made baguettes or that they wouldn't find their favorite regional bread in her store. Because they would. They absolutely would, as Bessie had homemade bagels on her menu every day of the week, along with a German pretzel recipe that wowed every person who'd ever tried it.

She'd recently perfected arepas from Venezuela. She usually made hers straight up to be savored with coffee, but she'd been known to stuff them with meat and cheese too. She adored pitas from the Middle East—if someone had never tried a homemade pita, the way she scored it into a grid and then baked it... They hadn't lived yet—in Bessie's opinion.

Her mouth watered every time she thought of her Egyptian bread recipes, as well as the naan she'd been working on for a while too.

"Hey, sissy," she said to her daughter. They could've decorated the shop in any number of styles, from French or European to Moroccan or Middle Eastern. In the end, they'd gone with classic, beautiful tables with a muted metal frame and pure wood tops made from planks—almost mirroring some of the seasoned wood planks Bessie had been cooking on for years.

The tables held two or four and had chairs that matched in frame and wood. They'd bought restaurant-standard napkin holders and equipped each table with a container of plastic knives for butter and jam spreading.

At her old job at the Bread Boy in Texas, a friend had made jams and brought them into the shop. Wyn had been working on a partnership with a local farm to provide and feature their jams instead, and Bessie only bought the best butter from an Amish community in Pennsylvania she'd gotten to know through her connections in Texas.

The quality of a loaf of bread came partly from the ingredients, so Bessie paid close attention to those. The rest came as the dough got worked with the hands of a master, and Bessie went by her daughter and into the kitchen. "When is the final staff meeting?" she called.

"Two hours," Wyn answered.

Bessie whipped an apron from the hook by the back door that led into the narrow parking lot behind the shop. Her new bakery sat second-down in a row of little shops, and she loved the location. Only a couple of blocks from the beach, she shared the row with a kite shop, a bistro that only served dinner on weekdays and lunch and dinner on week-ends, and a wig shop down on the other end.

It sat about six blocks from the place she'd looked at beside The Mad Mango a few months ago, and only one and a half miles from the house she and Wyn were renting together. She'd wanted to be close to her commercial space and feel like it was in a safe spot, because she'd arrive early in the morning and probably work for hours in the strip shop alone, before any other employee showed up, including her daughter.

Two hours was enough to get something going that would be ready by the end of the final staff meeting. They'd hired eight people to help them run the shop, and that included one custodian, an assistant baker, and six people to man the cash register from the hours of six-thirty a.m. to three p.m.

Bessie's adrenaline kicked in, and by the time the meeting started, she had a batch of quick-yeast dinner rolls ready to go into the oven. She slid the tray with all the dough balls pressed together into the waiting oven, set a timer in her phone, and went to join her daughter in the front of the shop.

Everyone else had arrived, and someone had brought coffee. Bessie took the last remaining cup—the one with her name on it—and sat down at the table with Wyn and all of her papers.

She leaned over and said something to a man named Winslow, who would be their custodian in the shop. He'd come in close to noon and work for several hours, staying after the storefront closed to get the trashcans emptied, the floors and counters cleaned and ready for the next day, and perform any maintenance on her ovens and mixers that might arise.

"How's Darla?" she asked.

His face lit up. "She's doing so much better," he said. "Claire is thrilled with the progress, and she's eating more." Their Pomeranian had just had puppies, and the fourth one had been born late. His wife had thought they might lose it, especially when the little pup wouldn't eat.

"I'm seriously considering taking one of them," she said.

"She's only sold two, so we have a couple more," he said.

"All right, everyone," Wyn said. "Let's get started. I've got a game plan for the grand opening in a couple of days, and I want to go through it and make sure there are no questions." She stood in the middle of the grouping of tables but moved over to where Bessie sat and collected a thin stack of papers.

Bessie knew the game plan already, and she pulled Wyn's yellow lined notepad closer and started making a list of the breads she needed to make tomorrow for the following day's grand opening.

Four hours of a grand opening. A name reveal. One ribbon-cutting ceremony. A tiny, short speech. Coupons. Samples. An email list. Special orders. And any sales they could rustle up.

Bessie had decided to start with what most people loved —sourdough, whole wheat, classic French white, croissants, dinner rolls, and her signature salted honey whole wheat.

She couldn't wait to come in at three a.m. tomorrow morning and start baking.

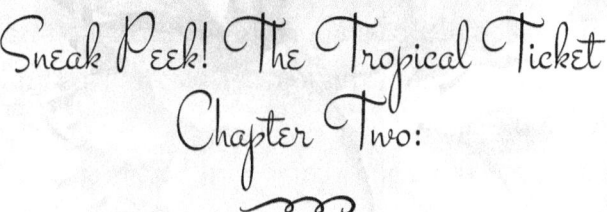

Sneak Peek! The Tropical Ticket Chapter Two:

B essie stood next to Wynona, both of them wearing nearly identical outfits. They'd wanted to come across as casual but professional, and they'd chosen black slacks or jeans, along with a pretty blouse they felt comfortable in, with their baking apron tied around their waist.

The sun had already heated the entire island, despite the event being at nine o'clock in the morning. Bessie couldn't believe how many people had showed up for the grand opening and the name reveal of the shop, and more people kept gathering. The clock ticked to time, and Bessie glanced over to her. "Should we begin?"

Bessie did a quick check—Bea and Grant had arrived, as had Cass and Harrison. Lauren and Blake had been here since seven, helping Bessie put the bread into the display cases and onto the shelves, as well as printing and cutting the one-time-use coupons.

Joy and Scott had taken all the trash out this morning,

and they'd helped Bessie clean the kitchen after she'd made several more loaves of bread this morning. No bread bakery worth its salt didn't smell like something golden and delicious had just come out of the oven, so while Bessie had done the bulk of her baking yesterday, she couldn't have this grand opening without the scent of yeast, milk, and butter hanging in the air.

Sage stood front and center with her sister, and Bessie didn't recognize a lot of the other faces. Tyler Barker, who'd helped her find this place, stood off to her left, and she nodded to him. He smiled like he attended all of his clients' functions, and perhaps he did. She didn't know him well enough to know.

"Mom?"

She nodded, and Wynona put her movie star smile on her face. Bessie's stomach swooped, and when she blinked, the whole world went black, despite the brightness of the sun. Her vision cleared quickly, and her eyes landed on a dark-haired man that shouldn't have accelerated her pulse quite the way he did.

Oliver Blackhurst had been dipped in all the best gene pools, and Bessie sure did like the sweep of his thick, dark hair across his forehead. The way his nearly black eyes zeroed in on her, and that slight, arrogant curl of his lips as he smiled.

Oh, the man was dangerous to her health, as her stomach dropped to her knees and her heartbeat accelerated. Again.

She gave her head a small shake, and Oliver cocked his

right eyebrow. She hadn't realized she hadn't looked away from him before moving, as she hadn't meant to communicate with him. She'd been telling herself *no*. A very solid, very loud, *No*.

She wasn't interested in Oliver Blackhurst. Not only was he one of the grumpiest men she'd met on this island, but she didn't have room in her life for a boyfriend. Especially not one as hot as the surface of the sun.

"Welcome everyone," Wynona said, and Bessie tore her attention from the gorgeous Mister Blackhurst. Why was he here anyway? "My mother and I have had a dream of opening a bread bakery for a few years now." She glowed as she looked over to Bessie, her smile genuine and pure and oh-so-good.

"We're excited to have found this perfect shop, on this perfect island in South Carolina, and we're first going to reveal the perfect name." She look up and to her left, where she lifted her hand and gripped the drop cloth still covering the sign.

"Without further ado, I give you...Flour Power!" She tugged on the cloth and it came down just as she'd rehearsed. The gorgeous logo Bessie had commissioned from Lauren, which was a bright pink daisy with a perfectly golden-yellow center—in the shape of a loaf of bread.

Applause broke out and filled the air surrounding the new shop, then the whole parking lot. The dropping of the cloth was the cue for their employees inside the shop, and they spilled out onto the sidewalk. Bessie and Wynona parted and both gestured to the held-open doors, and Sage and Thelma were the first to surge inside.

"Hello," Bessie said to the woman who followed them. "Thank you for coming. Good to see you. Thank you. Hello." She greeted everyone who streamed past her, and soon enough, the crowd had filled the shop and more remained on the sidewalk in front of the shop.

Thankfully, Wyn's game plan had anticipated this, and before Bessie could say "Hello," again, one of her employees, Rachel, handed her a silver tray full of samples. Wyn got one too, and then the three of them started walking around the crowd still mingling outside.

Just her luck, Oliver stood on her side, and she couldn't avoid him. "Bessie," he said. "This is fantastic." He seemed perfectly pleasant today, but he couldn't very well act like Oscar the Grouch in public. Many of these people were probably his customers too.

"Thank you," she said. "This is my salted honey whole wheat, but Wynona has the French white, and Rachel has the sourdough."

He didn't look away from her as he said, "I'd like this." He reached for a sample, which already had a toothpick speared through it.

"There's butter and jam on the tables," she said, wondering if he'd started to melt out here too. That was the reason her skin felt seared, and not because Oliver still hadn't looked away from her.

She forced herself to turn toward someone else, but

Oliver said, "Wait." Bessie turned back to him, her eyebrows lifting into a silent, *Well?*

"There's a small business...thing here on the island. For locals who own small businesses." He reached up and pulled at his collar, then quickly dropped his hand. He stuffed the bite-size sample of bread into his mouth, those handsome eyes widening. "Bessie, this is fantastic."

"And you didn't even have it with butter," she said with a smile. "There's nothing better than bread with butter, you know."

"Oh, I can think of a few things," he said, and Bessie felt sure her eyes had started to see red, for Oliver was blushing. *Blushing.* He cleared his throat. "The Island Collective meets every month, and I think you'd benefit from attending." He held out a card.

Bessie wanted to toss the sample tray and take the card, then devour the words on it. Instead, she blinked at it and then Oliver. He smiled, and wow, he shouldn't be allowed to do that in public.

"We meet this coming week, and we'll be talking about the upcoming Heritage Festival."

"The Heritage Festival?"

"It's a huge celebration in October," he said. "We have booths for each of our businesses, and the city gives those of us who are in the Island Collective better placement, special consideration, and the first chance at sponsorships."

Bessie was a long way from sponsoring anything but paying her own rent, but she took the card from his fingers. "Thank you, Oliver."

He nodded, kept that glorious smile on his face, and said, "Now, I need to go buy a whole loaf of this salted whole wheat bread." He dodged through the crowd and managed to get inside the shop, all while Bessie stood there and watched.

WEDNESDAY MORNING, BESSIE HUNG HER APRON on the hook by the back door. "Hillie, I'm headed to a meeting, okay?"

"No problem, Miss Bessie," she said, her hands working the dough on the board in front of her without looking. She'd grown up out in rural South Carolina, and she'd been baking since the age of five. Bessie had loved listening to her talk about her mammy and grammy, and the interview had been more storytelling than questioning.

Bessie had also hired her at the end of that, and she'd been happy she had. They'd been baking together for about three weeks now, as Wyn interviewed and hired the rest of the staff, as the tables and chairs and napkins holders had come in.

She went out the back door and over to her SUV, her hands feeling too hot and everything else suddenly too cold. The overheated interior of the vehicle made breathing difficult, and Bessie got the engine started and the air conditioning vents blowing right on her face.

By the time she arrived at the community center where the Island Connection meeting was set to take place, she felt like throwing up. Bessie didn't normally eat breakfast, except for a couple of bites of croissant and the coffee Wyn brought her when the shop opened. She hadn't eaten more than that now, but maybe she should've.

She looked toward the entrance, but she couldn't make herself get out of the car. A couple of women who were dressed like they might be on their way to the meeting went by and inside, and Bessie took a deep breath.

"You can do it, girl," she told herself. She hadn't seen Oliver yet, and she didn't want him to find her sitting in her car, too scared to go inside. She told herself she'd left work early for this meeting. She told herself she wanted this opportunity. She told herself it would be good for her to meet other locals who also owned small businesses.

None of those got her out of the car, and Bessie found herself kneading the steering wheel though she then wouldn't be setting it to rise the way she did her flawless dinner rolls.

"Come on, Bessie," she moaned the words as she leaned her head back against the rest. Her eyes drifted closed, and a twinge of exhaustion stole through her. She'd been getting up in the middle of the night for years, so she wasn't really tired yet.

The grand opening had gone so well, and they'd had a steady stream of customers in the four days since. Word seemed to be spreading, as Wyn had been having their cashiers ask how people had heard about Flour Power when they came in to buy.

She and Hillie had sold through all of their inventory

every day so far, and Bessie told herself these things as motivators to get herself inside the community center. It still didn't work, and she told herself she didn't want to leave the air-conditioned interior of her car and step out into the near-July heat and humidity.

The fact that the community center also had air conditioning didn't weigh on her decision, because she couldn't let it.

A sharp knock met her ears, and Bessie yelped as she shot forward. She jerked her attention to the side window as her adrenaline spiraled up into her brain and down into her toes. She tingled, and not in a good way.

Oliver stood there, and he backed up as he lifted both hands in surrender. Amusement rode in his expression, and Bessie pressed the on-off button and practically pushed the door open into his body.

He chuckled and said, "I'm sorry. I didn't realize you were taking a nap."

"I wasn't taking a nap." Bessie turned back to the car and pulled out her purse. It was really more the size of a small carryon, and the only reason she could carry it around was because she had some pretty impressive arm and shoulder muscles from all the kneading.

She slammed her door, and they fell into step beside one another as she started toward the community center. "You're late, you know."

"You were sitting in your car, apparently asleep." He didn't even look over to her as he said it. When they reached the door, he opened it and lifted his eyebrows to usher her through it. A blast of the blessed AC hit her in the face, and she went into it willingly.

She didn't know which way to go after that, and Oliver put his hand on the small of her back and said, "To the right. Down that skinny hallway there."

"You call hallways narrow, not skinny," she hissed at him as she started that way. Now she had to deal with her irritation with Oliver Blackhurst as well as the queasy feelings of walking into a meeting with complete strangers.

"Next doorway," he said from behind her, and Bessie didn't break stride as she made the turn and entered the room. Unfortunately, they were late, and that meant a whole room of local business owners turning to take them in.

Men and women, and several of them broke out into smiles. "Ollie," a woman said, and that nearly made Bessie roll her eyes. The room was small, but Bessie hadn't anticipated it being so full.

Only two chairs remained, and she edged over to one, only to have Oliver's perfectly cologned body drop into the one beside her, trapping her on the row between his sexy Versace scent and a woman wearing more foodstuff on her clothes than Bessie ever wanted to see outside of a kitchen.

She gave the woman a tight smile and tried to inch a little closer to her. That was a mistake, as the scent of stale oven cleaner met her nose.

"All right," the woman up front said. "So as I was saying." She shot a look toward the corner where Oliver and Bessie sat, but it didn't feel like her eyes roamed anywhere near Oliver. "We'll need to be in pairs for this year's Heritage

Festival, and you'll be working closely with that person to advertise the Festival, come up with marketing ideas, and this year, you'll be able to cross-promote each other's businesses in a whole new way."

She acted like these things were so amazing, but Bessie had no idea what she was talking about. Oliver had said that they'd be talking about the Heritage Festival, and Bessie did want to be involved in that. She simply thought it would be an introductory meeting. She cut a glance at her phone and saw that they'd only been eight minutes late.

The whole intro to an entire Heritage Festival couldn't have happened that fast, could it?

She didn't dare look over to Oliver, as he'd been through this before. Maybe she could ask him a question or two if she got partnered with someone who acted like she should already know everything about this island and its traditions.

The woman up front talked for a few more minutes, and then she said, "We'd like to welcome any new members." She zeroed in on Bessie again, and she managed to put a smile on her face before she added, "You guys missed the sign-ups, so Oliver, would you be willing to introduce the woman you brought and be her partner for the Festival this year?"

Bessie gaped at the woman, then switched her attention to Oliver. "We missed that much?" She faced the front again, barely able to bear the load of all the eyes in the room which had landed on her. "We were eight minutes late."

"*Thirty*-eight," the woman said, and Bessie's heartbeat flailed behind the bars of her ribs.

She turned more fully to Oliver. "Thirty-eight minutes late?"

He actually lifted his arm to the back of her chair like he might fold her into his side. He smiled at her and then up to the woman standing in front of everyone. "I totally forgot we switched the time for our summer meetings," he said easily. "I apologize, Amy." He looked at Bessie, who blinked at him like he'd gone crazy.

His smile slipped a little, and he shifted on his chair though he still broadcasted the picture of ease. "This is Bessie Clifton," he said. "She just opened the best bread bakery on the island—Flour Power." He leaned closer to her, and Bessie's first inclination was to do the same to him.

But she had no idea what game he was playing, being snarky and throwing banter her way as they walked in— thirty-eight minutes late—and then turning into Mister Nice Guy Oozing Charm for this meeting. So she didn't move a single inch.

"And sure, I'd love to partner with Bessie for the Heritage Festival this year."

They're partners?! This is going to be so much fun...

Preorder THE BEACH BLUEPRINT now! Scan the QR code to preorder now.

Books in the Hilton Head Romance series

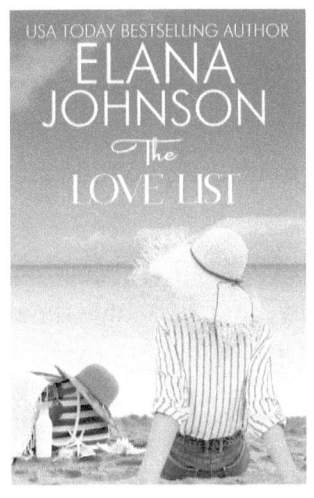

The Love List (Hilton Head Romance, Book 1): Bea turns to her lists when things get confusing and her love list morphs once again... Can she add *fall in love at age 45* to the list and check it off?

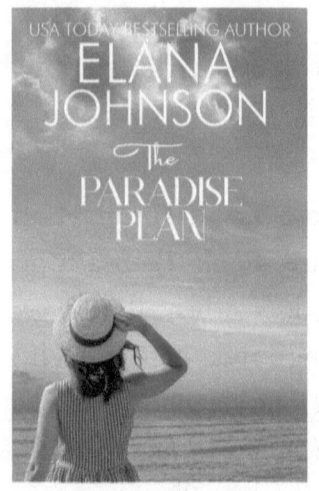

The Paradise Plan (Hilton Head Romance, Book 2):
When Harrison keeps showing up unannounced at her construction site, sometimes with her favorite pastries, Cass starts to wonder if she should add him to her daily routine... If she does, will her perfectly laid out plans fall short of paradise? Or could she find her new life *and* a new love, all without any plans at all?

The Seaside Strategy (Hilton Head Romance, Book 3): Lauren doesn't want to work for Blake, especially not in strategic investments. She's had enough of the high-profile, corporate life. **Can she strategically insert herself into Blake's life without compromising her seaside strategy and finally get what she really** wants...love and a lasting relationship?

The Beach Blueprint (Hilton Head Romance, Book 4): Joy Bartlett needs a blueprint before she takes a single step in any direction. She loves seeing what she's getting into before committing, and moving 1200 miles from Texas to South Carolina just because half of her Supper Club has doesn't mean she's going to start packing boxes. Can she figure out how to arrange all of the pieces in her life in a way that makes sense? Or will she find herself cut off from everyone who's ever been important to her?

The Tropical Ticket (Hilton Head Romance, Book 5): Bessie Clifton adores baking. With her daughter Wynona by her side, she's turned her passion for the perfect loaf of bread into a dream for a bakery. They move to Hilton Head Island and work to get their shop open with the help of Bessie's five best friends.

It's not just a relocation.

It's a reinvention.

Will Bessie's journey to self-discovery lead her to the love she's always craved?

Cross Cowboy, Book 1: He's been accused of being far too blunt. Like that time he accused her of stealing her company from her best friend... Can Travis and Shayla overcome their differences and find a happily-ever-after together?

Grumpy Cowboy

Grumpy Cowboy, Book 2: He can find the negative in any situation. Like that time he got upset with the woman who brought him a free chocolate-and-caramel-covered apple because it had melted in his truck... Can William and Gretchen start over and make a healthy relationship after it's started to wilt?

Surly Cowboy

Surly Cowboy, Book 3: He's got a reputation to uphold and he's not all that amused the way regular people are. Like that time he stood there straight-faced and silent while everyone else in the audience cheered and clapped for that educational demo... Can Lee and Rosalie let bygones be bygones and make a family filled with joy?

Salty Cowboy

Salty Cowboy, Book 4: The last Cooper sibling is looking for love...she just wishes it wouldn't be in her hometown, or with the saltiest cowboy on the planet. But something about Jed Forrester has Cherry all a-flutter, and he'll be darned if he's going to let her get away. But Jed may have met his match when it comes to his quick tongue and salty attitude...

Books in the Hope Eternal Ranch Romance series

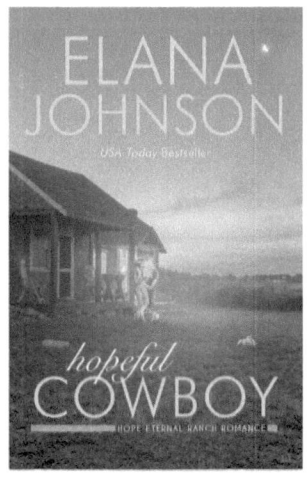

Hopeful Cowboy, Book 1: Can Ginger and Nate find their happily-ever-after, keep up their duties on the ranch, and build a family? Or will the risk be too great for them both?

Overprotective Cowboy, Book 2: Can Ted and Emma face their pasts so they can truly be ready to step into the future together? Or will everything between them fall apart once the truth comes out?

Rugged Cowboy, Book 3: He's a cowboy mechanic with two kids and an ex-wife on the run. She connects better to horses than humans. Can Dallas and Jess find their way to each other at Hope Eternal Ranch?

Christmas Cowboy, Book 4: He needs to start a new story for his life. She's dealing with a lot of family issues. This Christmas, can Slate and Jill find solace in each other at Hope Eternal Ranch?

Wishful Cowboy, Book 5: He needs somewhere to belong. She has a heart as wide as the Texas sky. Can Luke and Hannah find their one true love in each other?

Risky Cowboy, Book 6: She's tired of making cheese and ice cream on her family's dairy farm, but when the cowboy hired to replace her turns out to be an ex-boyfriend, Clarissa suddenly isn't so sure about leaving town... Will Spencer risk it all to convince Clarissa to stay and give him a second chance?

Books in the Hawthorne Harbor Romance series

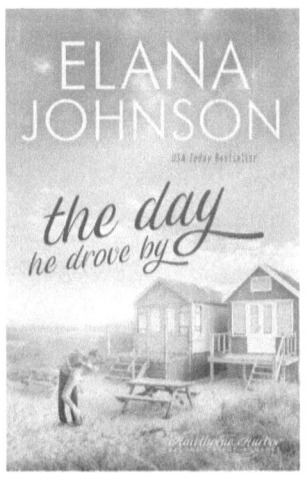

The Day He Drove By (Hawthorne Harbor Second Chance Romance, Book 1): A widowed florist, her ten-year-old daughter, and the paramedic who delivered the girl a decade earlier...

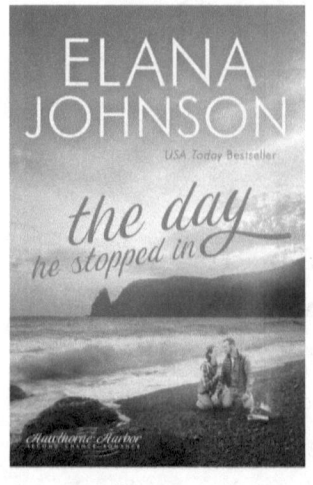

The Day He Stopped In (Hawthorne Harbor Second Chance Romance, Book 2): Janey Germaine is tired of entertaining tourists in Olympic National Park all day and trying to keep her twelve-year-old son occupied at night. When longtime friend and the Chief of Police, Adam Herrin, offers to take the boy on a ride-along one fall evening, Janey starts to see him in a different light. Do they have the courage to take their relationship out of the friend zone?

The Day He Said Hello (Hawthorne Harbor Second Chance Romance, Book 3): Bennett Patterson is content with his boring firefighting job and his big great dane...until he comes face-to-face with his high school girlfriend, Jennie Zimmerman, who swore she'd never return to Hawthorne Harbor. Can they rekindle their old flame? Or will their opposite personalities keep them apart?

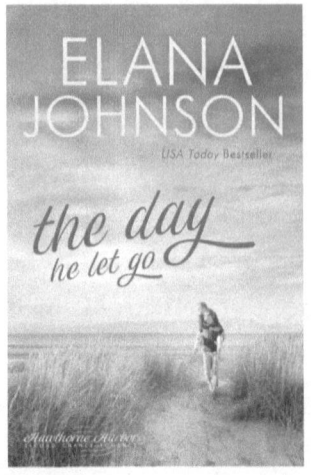

The Day He Let Go (Hawthorne Harbor Second Chance Romance, Book 4): Trent Baker is ready for another relationship, and he's hopeful he can find someone who wants him and to be a mother to his son. Lauren Michaels runs her own general contract company, and she's never thought she has a maternal bone in her body. But when she gets a second chance with the handsome K9 cop who blew her off when she first came to town, she can't say no... Can Trent and Lauren make their differences into strengths and build a family?

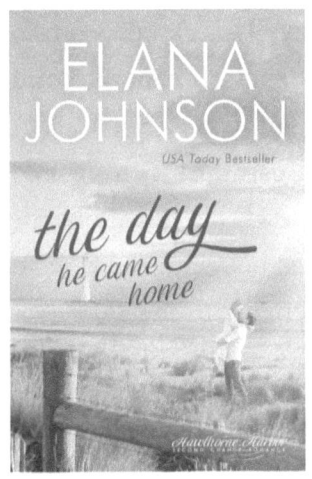

The Day He Came Home (Hawthorne Harbor Second Chance Romance, Book 5): A wounded Marine returns to Hawthorne Harbor years after the woman he was married to for exactly one week before she got an annulment...and then a baby nine months later. Can Hunter and Alice make a family out of past heartache?

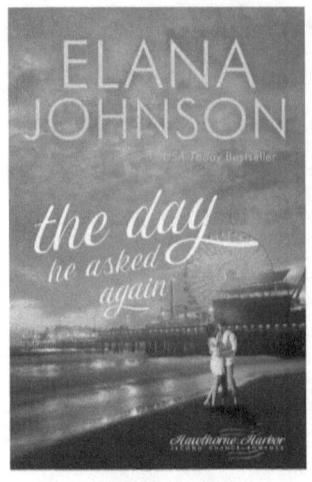

The Day He Asked Again (Hawthorne Harbor Second Chance Romance, Book 6): A Coast Guard captain would rather spend his time on the sea...unless he's with the woman he's been crushing on for months. Can Brooklynn and Dave make their second chance stick?

About Elana

Elana Johnson is the USA Today bestselling and Kindle All-Star author of dozens of clean and wholesome contemporary romance novels. She lives in Utah, where she mothers two fur babies, works with her husband full-time, and eats a lot of veggies while writing. Find her on her website at feelgoodfictionbooks.com.

www.ingramcontent.com/pod-product-compliance
Lightning Source LLC
Chambersburg PA
CBHW020005120726
47903CB00004B/1148